JEN L. CROW was born in Edinburgh and has lived in Scotland all her life. She currently lives south of Edinburgh with her husband, Chris, and their Border Collie, Midge. Jen went to university in Dundee, gaining a Bachelor of Design from Duncan of Jordanstone College of Art and Design, followed by a post-graduate qualification in education. Her first novel, written as Jen Mouat, was *The Bookshop of New Beginnings*, which was published by HQ Digital. Jen's a yoga enthusiast, hillwalker and reader of murder mysteries and urban fantasy novels. She enjoys drawing, swimming and visiting book festivals with her best friend.

The Silent Twin

JEN L. CROW

ONE PLACE. MANY STORIES

HQ
An imprint of HarperCollins*Publishers* Ltd
1 London Bridge Street
London SE1 9GF

www.harpercollins.co.uk

HarperCollins*Publishers*
Macken House, 39/40 Mayor Street Upper,
Dublin 1 D01 C9W8
This edition 2026

1
First published in Great Britain by HQ,
an imprint of HarperCollins*Publishers* Ltd 2026

Copyright © Jen L. Crow 2026

Jen L. Crow asserts the moral right to be identified as the author of this work.
A catalogue record for this book is available from the British Library.

ISBN: 9780008783662

This novel is entirely a work of fiction. The names, characters and incidents
portrayed in it are the work of the author's imagination. Any resemblance to
actual persons, living or dead, events or localities is entirely coincidental.

All rights reserved. No part of this publication may be reproduced, stored
in a retrieval system, or transmitted, in any form or by any means,
electronic, mechanical, photocopying, recording or otherwise,
without the prior written permission of the publishers.

Without limiting the exclusive rights of any author, contributor or the publisher of this
publication, any unauthorized use of this publication to train generative
artificial intelligence (AI) technologies is expressly prohibited.
HarperCollins also exercise their rights under Article
4(3) of the Digital Single Market Directive 2019/790 and expressly reserve this
publication from the text and data mining exception.

Printed and bound in the UK using 100% Renewable
Electricity by CPI Group (UK) Ltd

*For Granny Hendry, who planted the seed of story in me.
And for anyone who's ever felt silenced.*

Extract from website:
www.HavenArtEscapes.co.uk

Nestled in a hidden hillside on a remote Scottish island, Haven is a glorious retreat with a difference, offering all the peace and creative inspiration you could need. It's a space to heal, recharge and reconnect. Here you will meet like-minded people, walk in nature, partake in life-drawing lessons, yoga classes and mindfulness, and dedicate the time you need to art. Equipped with throwing wheel and kiln, an airy studio and plenty of cosy nooks in which to curl up, Haven welcomes arty folk of all kinds. Come, be inspired, soothed, rejuvenated ...

Come home.

Proprietors: Naomi McKinnon and Gina Allardyce. Contact by e-form below. Rates on request.

Prologue

On one hand, it's easy to see how the crash could have happened, but to those who know the woman behind the wheel it seems impossible.

A filthy night, rain bouncing, one of those dense island fogs that fall like the folds of a cloak, deepening the inky dark, creating shadows in the night. The island roads are single-track, with bends like mountain switchbacks; the accident site an inconveniently placed bridge, at the wheel an inexperienced driver …

A perfect storm.

Quite literally – these autumn squalls are the worst: gold-masked, the ghost of summer's warmth in the seas, a prelude of winter's bite in the winds that race and chase across the lonely moors.

It is mid-October. Where the bridge sits in a dip occluded by trees, the road is carpeted with fallen leaves mashed slick beneath scores of wheels. Easy to lose control, clip the corner going too fast, plummet down the bank to a river swollen with rainfall.

The woman behind the wheel hasn't driven in years. It's the talk of the island when news of the accident spreads by word-of-mouth wildfire next morning. She hasn't driven in years because she hasn't *left home* in years. She hasn't left home because she can't.

Everyone round these parts knows it, even if they don't name it.

Police Officer Ben Carmichael arrives on the scene after a local farmer calls it in. He pulls up, blues striping the smudgy dark of the forest that lines the remote stretch of road, exhausted from a rough week of policing. Clambering down through clinging bracken to the river's edge where the car tips half in, half out of the water, Ben stops short when he recognises the pale face through the splintered window.

Naomi McKinnon: painter, recluse, owner of the arty commune up on the hill – the place at the epicentre of island gossip this past week.

Why, he wonders, would she choose a grim night like this to venture out in her car for the first time in half a decade?

Especially *tonight*: when half the island turned out for the Allardyce boy, and her place was with her family.

His heart sinks as he realises he will be making another trip up the hill to Haven. Hasn't that family been through enough?

The place is a strange set-up: artists milling about more like family than paying guests. But Ben likes the atmosphere, the sense of fellowship, the cosiness of their home.

His heart pounds as he reaches through the window to check her pulse, dodging spears of glass and trying not to dislodge the car and send it skiting into the river, taking both him and the unconscious woman with it.

She is alive, but barely. He climbs back up the bank to the road where the farmer has returned with his tractor ready to drag the car to safety. Ben gets on the radio to check that medical help is on the way.

She's going to need it.

Chapter 1

Eve

'Don't panic, sweet girl—'

My mother's voice is frail with fatigue around the familiar endearment. There's an edge of fear too, flooding me with alarm. Of course I answer at 4 a.m., stupid with sleep; I'm always on call for her.

'*Finn?*' I say, startled awake, tuned to the frequency of panic despite my mother's instruction. '*Holly?*'

How can she expect me not to panic at a middle-of-the-night call that begins like that ... when I am so accustomed to worrying on account of my family ... and so *good* at it.

'No, no. The twins are fine ...' Naomi sounds wired as well as knackered – like she's not yet been to bed. 'It's Jay.'

I sink back with a guilty surge of relief. Jay – my brother's schoolfriend, Gina's wayward nephew – does not worry me overmuch.

It's dark in my room – as dark as the city gets with its acid everglow – and I hear the muted hum of vehicles flowing along the main arteries. It's that blurred space between Friday night revelry and Saturday morning business-as-usual. City nights, so different from the island ones I grew up with: the soft stretch of dark, silence broken by moaning wind and crashing waves, the splatter of rain on the windows. I reach for the lamp, flood the room with light.

'What's wrong with Jay?' I tug a hand through tangled bed-hair and push aside a nostalgic tug of home. I've made this city home, left behind great patterned skies, sweeping beaches and wild spaces. Carved out a bright-lights life – like I dreamed from the heathered slopes above Haven, waves booming in our secret cove below.

A life of words; freedom I could never find on the island for all its vastness. *This* is what I wanted – cobbles, soot-stained buildings, spaces abuzz with knowledge and ideas; the pleasure of losing myself in a crowd, between shelves, between pages …

So far from my mother and siblings, I worry constantly. And if my life here is not all I imagined … well, whose is?

A sea-eyed boy with a gentle smile swims into my thoughts but I push him away too: Struan Fraser – my childhood friend, and teenage partner in crime. And more recently, a whisper of possibility, the promise of *more*. It's a possibility I can't allow myself to think about, because to consider it would be to contemplate a life tied to the island.

My heart races as I wait for particulars from Mum. *Not Finn or Holly* I remind myself – my siblings are safe. My brother rarely causes me worry, but Holly frequently gives me the fear. She's too like Mum with capricious twists and turns of mind and mood. Finn has breezed through his teenage years, but not so Holly. The bullying began when she first started secondary school; over time she's retreated into her shell, losing herself.

Mum sighs raggedly. 'Jay's missing.'

He moved in with them in March after a bust-up with his dad – I don't know the details. Gina, Mum's partner in life and business, didn't hesitate to take in her brother's boy despite being omitted from his life for so long. Jay's been in bother before without Mum feeling the need to wake me in the middle of the night – so why now? Something feels different, something in my mother's voice is … *off*.

It shouldn't surprise me, Mum perceiving a crisis where there isn't one – she's never been one for coping.

'When you say *missing* …' I can imagine Jay being brought home in the back of a police car, injuring himself in some daredevil exploit. All summer he ignored any curfew, religiously broke Gina's rules. He's seventeen, like the twins, but wild: a charmer, a flirt, a truckload of trouble.

Gina and her brother were never close, and Jay's childhood was spent trailing his dad around the world in planes and yachts and fancy cars. Barely a postcard or email for his aunt. Christian made no secret of the fact that he *didn't approve* of his sister … though whether because Gina married a woman or because she chose to plough her share of Allardyce money into Haven, I've never been sure.

Christian returned to renovate the family estate a year ago, with his glamorous bride and wayward son. Shades of olden-day gentry clung to them, with their crisp shirts and tweed, their fleet of Range Rovers and Champagne-soaked gatherings.

Inexplicably, for they couldn't be more different, Jay and my brother became friends.

Jay's run away before. Turned up high on hallucinogens, living rough on his father's estate in a den he built in the woods. Gave everyone a scare, sold it as a lark. 'You must admit, Mum. Jay's got form—'

'I know, but this feels … *different*.' There it is again, the twist of inexplicable unease that sets my heart thrumming. *Like she's not telling me something.*

'How long has he been gone?'

'He went for a run just after eight, but he didn't come home. He's not answering his phone.'

'Probably a party.' Jay is the degenerate moth drawn to every frivolous flame. 'Didn't Finn go running with him?' When I was home at Easter, the boys were inseparable. Less so this summer.

'No ... Finn hurt his knee – don't worry, he's fine. He was in his room, lost track of time. I was with the artists. When Finn went to check on Jay, he wasn't there. His car is here. Finn went looking. He checked the route they always take – daft, he's made his knee worse – but there was no sign. We called the police, but they're not *doing* anything.'

'It's too soon. Jay's probably just gone off somewhere—'

'*Where?*' My mother's voice frays. She doesn't deal well with upset and a sleepless night won't help. I picture her at the table in the lamplit kitchen, head in her hands, fair hair strewn. Finn's dog, Cashew, spanned across her feet.

I close my eyes, and I am there, safe within Haven's stone walls. A skirl of mist beyond the windows, the air a jumble of spices and essential oils, the room cluttered with unread mail, books on art and ancient civilisations vying for attention in teetering piles. Discarded throw blankets, cushions slipping from the sofa ...

Home comforts is a concept made for Haven. The guest wing is always fully booked when I snoop on their website to check how the business is doing. Returning is like slipping beneath one of those cosy blankets. When I'm there I can't seem to find the impetus to leave.

But when I'm *here*, I don't want to go back.

I push aside another wave of longing and focus on Jay. 'He'll be partying, Mum. Boozing on a beach or mucking about in town.'

'*Yes.*' She sounds doubtful.

I start braiding my hair, the rhythm of my fingers soothing. 'What's Gina saying?' She dotes on her nephew as much as she despairs of him.

'She's at an archaeology conference in Stirling. I haven't called her yet. I didn't want to worry her—'

'*Mum*—'

'I know, Eve; I *know*, darling. I'll ring her soon. She'll want to jump on a ferry straight away and she can't do that until morning anyway—'

'She needs to know ... Look, I'm sure Jay will turn up. Try not to worry.' I speak firmly, using the no-nonsense voice I reserve for her – for reining in flights of fancy and irrational fears.

Guilt thickens Mum's silence: she's wondering how this happened on her watch. 'You're probably right. Maybe I'm worrying for nothing, but Finn's concerned too and there's a storm on the way—'

On the island, there's always a storm either on its way, in progress, or blowing itself out.

'Do you want me to come?' I calculate how quickly I can get there. I can take time off from The Bookish Beat, skip class on Monday – it's too far for one night. With a storm brewing, there'll be a narrow window while ferries run. We are frequently cut off for spells during autumn and winter. Spring too, sometimes.

'No, it's fine. Like you say, he's probably just gallivanting.'

I finish my braid, sort through my thoughts. Mum has always suffered with anxiety – the hurricane that rampages through her blows us all off course sometimes. The agoraphobia started after we moved to the island. It confines her to a small patch of land around Haven, but she says she has everything she needs right there ...

I picture her again in the smoky darkness. Perhaps the twins have stayed up, nursing tea by the warmth of the Aga. I must speak to my brother in order to gauge how worried I should be – Finn's a more reliable barometer than Mum. I'll give him a call. 'Why don't you try to sleep, Mum. Ring me later if Jay hasn't surfaced. I can rearrange things, swap shifts at the bookshop. I can come; it's no problem.'

'*Thanks*, sweet girl. So sorry to have woken you.' Relief floods her tone, and I feel the familiar weight of my burden settle.

I'm the one they turn to ... and I wouldn't have it any other way.

Chapter 2

Last Summer

The ferry port sparkles and bustles. Tourists swarm the quayside beneath a blowy sky. Cars crawl into waiting bays, windows open, music blasting. People chat, admire the view as they wait.

Holly half closes her eyes, lets the colours bleed, sounds too: a melee of voices, laughter, clanging metal, grinding gears, radios. There's a hint of sweetness in the air that takes the edge off the salt and seaweed stink: gorse on the hills, honeysuckle in the hedgerows. The scenery is rugged-pretty, with heathered hills and towering cliffs. Miles of grey-green ocean ripple before her like bolts of unrolled silk.

As long as Holly can remember she's been drawn to the sea, staring at it for hours from the clifftop at Haven – too close to the edge for everyone's comfort, though the height has never bothered her.

The ferry cuts through teal waves, trailing a knife-edge of frosted wake into the harbour. A belch of diesel chokes the air, tarnishing the sweetness. Holly watches the disembarkation. Family saloons, stowed out with suitcases, pillows, paddleboards; summer folk, fickle and fleeting. Gooseflesh prickles, and she hugs herself, regretting her T-shirt. It's July, but still it's the Western Isles. The boys are in T-shirts too, but hale and hearty, tanned in the healthy, wind-whipped way of lads who spend their days outside, mostly in cold water.

Jay slings a friendly arm around Holly's shoulders, the other around her brother, connecting them in a chain of camaraderie. He's grinning, crackling with energy. He smells of grass and lemons. Holly stiffens lest she slip up, slides an arm about him, strokes the muscles that bracket his spine.

These feelings are new, exciting … *scary*. She's on guard lest anyone notices – rejection would be unthinkable.

'Here comes the golden girl,' Jay says cuttingly, laughter lighting his burned-toffee eyes. He is rarely serious, or rarely shows it. Holly is extremely serious, but despite their differences, attraction unfurls, subtle as smoke. Mutual, she hopes …

At night she lies awake, fevered in her bedsheets, thinking of him.

Jay loves to tease her, like another brother. But she sees more in his smiles, hears something beyond brotherly in his voice.

Finn fits between them in temperament: neither so extroverted as Jay, nor as insular as Holly. They form a comfortable triangle, scalene but strong. Holly hasn't confided her feelings to Finn – she's living a trope, falling for her brother's best friend.

Weeks of summer stretch out. Jay and Finn will mess about in the sea. Holly will drift in their wake with her sketchbook. She might attend one of Ryan Campbell's infamous parties, if Jay and Finn will take her—

Her friend Layla has been dragged on a family holiday. The alternative to trailing around after the boys would be to lurk in the artists' studio, gatecrashing her mother's social life. The guests tend to outstay their intentions, seduced by the trifecta of landscape, cosy accommodation and the landlady's effervescent energy. Holly is intrigued by the artists, curious about the life journeys that bring them here. She wonders if she should be hanging out with a bunch of various-aged women, drinking gin and gossiping about art, failed relationships and feminism? Or seek a life journey of her own …

With Jay as her road map.

'Don't take the piss,' she chides. Only *she* is allowed to complain of her sister's prodigal status. 'Mum is super excited about Eve coming. We all are,' she adds loyally, waving to Eve as she steps off the boat.

Despite the show of devotion, Holly has to work to muster enthusiasm for her sister's arrival. She loves her dearly, but Eve is curious about the twins' lives in ways Naomi isn't. Holly prefers her sister in short bursts.

Jay laughs again. 'Oh, I know. She's bought up half the Prosecco on the island but won't let anyone touch a drop. Mind, she could have *cleaned*—'

Finn snorts, which Holly considers disloyal. House-proud Naomi isn't. Domestic duties are Gina's domain, when she's home, supplemented by seasonal workers they employ to keep Haven habitable. The artists' quarters are always immaculate, their home less so. 'I doubt Eve's going to notice a bit of mess,' she says. Holly sometimes wishes her mother would pay attention to something other than her painting and her guests … her home and children, for example.

The way *Eve* notices is nice … as comforting as it is annoying. Like when Holly's moods dip and the world gets on top of her. And the voices of the bullies ring in her ears.

Freak …

Finn snorts again. 'Oh, she'll notice …'

Mum might be treating Eve's homecoming as an event, but she's not the only one in a tizz. The twins' English teacher has been haunting Haven and insisted on coming to meet the ferry. Struan Fraser, Eve's childhood friend, shifts from foot to foot on the quay, until Kirsty McLennan, Eve's best mate, gives him a dunt with her elbow. '*Chill out*, Fraser.'

Holly hasn't adjusted to calling Struan *Mr Fraser*. He's still the boy with the lazy smile who taught her and Finn how to steer a boat and cast a line, toss a frisbee so it soars. He and Eve are bonded by books and the sea, and the untimely loss of Struan's father in a fishing accident. He's half in love with Eve, as far as Holly can tell.

Eve's been away a long time – degrees stacking on top of each other. Sometimes Holly wonders what she's running from. Maybe Mum, maybe the weight of expectation for her to settle – like Kirsty with her farmer boy. Along the quay, Kirsty shoogles her baby in her arms, waving as Eve comes towards them staggering beneath the weight of her enormous bag. Struan gallantly dashes forward.

Finn groans as Struan and Eve hug for far longer than necessary.

'Who do they think they're fooling?' Jay says, with a wink at Holly that warms her.

After getting his teaching qualification, no one was surprised when Struan moved back to work at the island's high school. His mother is here, his boat, his grandfather's cottage, which he's been renovating since he was a teenager …

Eve isn't like Struan and Kirsty, with the soil of the land seeped into their bones, its history wrapping their hearts. Eve's dreams seem too big for the island to hold.

Since they arrived twelve years ago, the twins have embedded themselves here, while Eve has always been ready to drift off on a stiff breeze. Holly likes the island. Mind, without her phone – her gateway to other worlds – she would go mad through a dark island winter. Miles of nothing, the same faces all the time.

Maybe that's why she likes the artists – a break in the monotony. Exotic birds among grey gulls.

'Wow,' says Jay. 'They're *still* hugging. They aiming for some record or something?'

'Shut *up*,' Finn moans. 'It's horrible.'

Kirsty shoots them a look of reproach. 'They'd make a cute couple. Frankly it's about *time*.'

'Adorable,' retorts Finn. 'Is someone going to break this up or are we going to just watch like creeps?'

Kirsty steps into the breach. Thrusting baby Mac at a startled Jay, who holds the child awkwardly aloft, she goes over to the couple clapping her hands like she's breaking up a fight. 'All right, stop monopolising her, Fraser.'

Struan breaks away from Eve with a sheepish grin. Eve embraces Kirsty and squeals with joy.

Their friendship is a thing of beauty. Holly wonders what it would be like to have Eve as a friend instead of relentlessly, ruthlessly, her big sister.

It comes of their upbringing, she supposes: Eve's inability to let go of the reins. Like Holly's leaning towards solitude, Finn's old-fashioned manners. They are products of their past: the heady, uncertain, sociable whirl of their lives before they came here, growing up in a house-share in Glasgow filled with transient artists, ever-increasing circles of found family.

Holly loves Mum – she's creative, energetic, manic, kind, a lifelong collector of waifs and strays. But she's not always been the mother they need.

That's where Eve's stepped in.

Eve and Kirsty stroll back, Struan following with Eve's bag. The ferry reloads in preparation to return satiated holidaymakers while a fresh crop, indicators blinking, peel off seeking hotels, campsites and cottages scattered across the island.

Eve holds her arms out, and Finn and Holly tumble into her embrace. Despite her overbearing ways, Eve's hugs feel like home, like *safety*.

They don't look alike. Holly and Finn are stretched silver birch saplings – Finn growing muscle now to match his height. In looks it is dark, diminutive Eve who is the changeling. In other respects, Holly feels the odd one out. Her mother and siblings are sociable, noisy, secure.

When she's with them, Holly feels invisible.

Jay makes her visible. She slants a look at him, glowing in the sunshine.

'I've missed you,' Eve says. She looks Holly up and down. 'You've lost weight. Are you eating?'

'She's eating fine,' Finn interjects, and Holly flashes him a grateful look.

'And *you've* got taller again.'

Finn chuckles. 'Aye, I must stop doing that. I know how it annoys you.'

Eve shoves him playfully, turns to Jay. There's a coolness in her tone when she greets him. Jay says a quiet hello, uncharacteristically subdued. 'I hear you've moved in,' says Eve.

Finn sighs. 'Eve. Be nice.'

Eve is fierce, eyebrows drawn. 'I'm always nice. How are you, Jay?' She's made no secret of the fact that she thinks him a bad influence. Which is fair enough.

'Good,' Jay says.

It amuses Holly to see him discomfited. She's in danger of idolising him, hanging on every word like the girls at school do with popular lads like Jay and Ryan Campbell – Finn too, who has no idea how many lassies are crushing on him since he's only got eyes for Isla Maxwell.

Eve links Kirsty's arm. She's wearing her leather jacket, wavy brown hair skimming her shoulders. 'Come on, I want to hear everything about this little one …' She tweaks one of Mac's tiny feet as they start back to the cars.

Jay throws his arms around the twins' shoulders again in a burst of bravado, but Holly can tell he's rattled. He's used to people falling at his feet.

Kirsty says, 'Och, he's grand. I hope you're coming in my car with me and Mackie. I want to get all the gossip before your mother gets her claws into you. She's planned quite the homecoming—'

Eve's lips twist. 'I see she didn't come to meet me …'

'You know she can't,' interposes Finn, ever loyal.

'I know she *won't*. Not the same.'

She's still sore about graduation. They travelled to Edinburgh – Gina, Kirsty, Struan, the twins, even Jay. Everyone but Naomi. Eve pretended not to mind. For Holly, it confirmed the severity of her mother's condition – if *that* wasn't sufficient motivation to conquer her fears, what could be?

'She's planning a barbecue,' Kirsty continues, beginning the convoluted process of strapping the baby into his car seat. 'It's going to be epic.' She finishes securing Mac and smirks at Finn. 'Think you can keep up, McKinnon?'

Finn laughs. He's not had his licence long, but he loves driving. 'Aye, no bother.' He's in Mum's battered blue Volvo, and Kirsty in one of her boyfriend's ancient farm vehicles. Holly sighs; the roads are too tight and narrow for their games. It's why she hasn't passed her test yet: the island roads scare her.

Finn and Jay pile into the front, leaving the back seat to Holly and Struan. She was hoping to share the back with Jay.

'Awkward,' she mutters, side-eyeing her teacher. She doesn't mind him and Eve being friends, but it's embarrassing having to hang out with him. She pushes aside memories of teenage Struan fashioning a rope swing over the gully in the woods, showing her how to gut fish, which plants were edible in the hedgerows by Haven. And, later, watching over her in school when the bullies bit.

She jams in her earbuds, scrolls her phone, pulls up one of her favourite influencers. Reminding herself that there is life beyond this tiny rock and its small-life inhabitants.

As they pull out of the terminal, Jay twists in his seat and winks again. Another vibration, another shift between them, and her belly twists. This summer might be the first step on her journey … but where the road will take her, Holly cannot know.

Chapter 3

Now

Finn

Fog settles over the island like a blanket, hampering the search efforts. Jay still isn't home, passing the magic twenty-four-hour marker and tipping us into fear. I can't handle the way other people's emotions layer over my own – particularly Gina's. And Mum and Holly, vibrating with panic. The aether of Haven is strained, ready to spark; the whole island speculates over Jay's disappearance.

I go with Kirsty and Holly on Sunday to meet Eve from the boat, glad to escape the oppressive atmosphere of home. With the weather worsening, it's dark as night at 3 p.m. and the folk huddled on the quayside are ghosts in the gloom.

The predicted storm is shaping up to be all it promised and more. Last night, we sat in the kitchen, listening to the wind lamenting among the chimneys. Holly was upstairs, and no amount of coaxing would bring her down. No amount of *we're-in-this-together* ...

Mum was freaking out, drinking tea laced with whisky,

shooting off on wild tangents. Gina was outwardly calm, asking over and over where I thought Jay could be until I ran out of options to offer.

Drizzle and spatters of spindrift sting my cheeks as I watch for the ferry. My life is disintegrating around me, melting into the puddles at my feet. I've lived in a nightmare, these past forty-eight hours …

I just want to know, Gina said this morning. *If something's happened to him it can't be as bad as my imagination.*

Saturday morning, Mum called Gina at her conference. By noon she was ringing Eve again and by nightfall, Jay was officially a missing person, and the police were taking interest. They sent an officer to Haven to take details and this morning a social media appeal was shared with a smiling photo of Jay taken last year on his dad's yacht: *Anyone with knowledge of Jay Allardyce's whereabouts is asked to come forward … becoming increasingly concerned for his safety.*

In the picture, Jay looks untroubled: tanned and lean and grinning into the lens. They've checked CCTV from the ferry ports, and it doesn't show Jay leaving the island that way. Patrol cars are out looking, but so far, nothing.

I shiver as I shift from foot to foot on the quay beneath a wicked sky, fear sinking into my bones.

Everything is changed from the last time I stood here waiting for Eve – that cracking summer's day. My memory of it is vivid: the air sweet, our skins gold as ripe plums. Eve was happy, Mum calmed by the prospect of an extended visit from the daughter who always keeps her on an even keel.

Now everything is twisted, dark. Not just the weather … *us.* The biggest change is in Holly. She's not the carefree girl who mucked about with me and Jay, dreaming of summer romance and doing a bad job of hiding it.

A girl who *talked.*

It's been six weeks and two days since Holly spoke a word.

Eve doesn't know about her silence yet, and I'm dreading telling her. Holly used to love social media, posting prolifically on all her favourite sites, but that's gone too. At the same time she lost her voice, she deleted all her accounts.

And yet, she's still so often glued to her phone—

I *know* Eve will have noticed Holly's online defection – she confessed to me last summer how she stalks our sister on social media to try to understand her better, to get inside her head.

Now Eve doesn't even have that.

Holly drifts away from me in the mist, the toes of her plimsolls pushing over the edge of the quay as she stares into the dark swirl. I reach to grab her, tug her back from the precipice. 'Holly. *For fuck's sake!*'

She's blank, and so far away I can't reach her.

I try to pretend it was a misstep, that she wandered too close to the edge, that she *wasn't* thinking about how it might feel to slip beneath the cold weight of water. I keep my gaze trained on her. She's wan and knackered, and I know I don't look much better. We've barely slept.

'Just be careful, aye.' I shove my hands in the pockets of my hoodie, dark with rain. I didn't think to bring a coat. Beside me, Kirsty paces and checks her phone, impatient that Eve hasn't replied. Reception can be patchy across the island, and the storm won't be helping. This will be the last crossing of the day …

Kirsty's curls are snarled from the wind, her energy high. She came to Haven as soon as she heard. There wasn't much she could do but driving to the ferry to meet Eve was an easy win. Kirsty's always been there for us, part of the family. We pretend not to know that she keeps tabs on us for Eve.

Behind us the mountains glower and sulk through a curtain of mist. A sinister, looming presence. There are plenty of wild spots on this island, places you could go to get away from it all. Search parties have been out all day crawling across the moors, into the hills. The artists mobilised, went out to help under the orders of a scary ex-army captain turned ceramicist named Fran.

I spot my sister on the deck of the approaching ferry, turtled in folds of red Gore-Tex. The waves are rough, the ferry rising and dipping, spewing foam as it slides into the sanctuary of the harbour.

'Look!' Kirsty points out the ferry through the murk. Her voice is pitchy with relief – Eve is here to save the day.

If only …

I slide another glance to Holly as the boat creeps closer. Mum and I have kept quiet about her silence – both, I assume, for the same reasons: we were hoping Holly would spontaneously start talking again, like last time. No need to worry Eve until we had to. I wonder if Kirsty has mentioned the silence to Eve, or if Struan has.

Since Kirsty had Mac she hasn't been quite so involved with us; hopefully she's put Holly's silence down to teenage moodiness. I don't know *what's* going on with Eve and Struan. Mr Fraser has been grumpier than usual at school, and Eve hasn't been home in ages. Who knows if they're even still friends …

It bothers me that Struan knows stuff about me, that he might share his knowledge with Eve. He's probably not allowed to – some teacher code – but I can't rely on his discretion. A few months ago, I'd not have cared. There would have been nothing to tell.

But now …

'*Thank God*,' Kirsty says fervently. 'I was beginning to think the ferry had been cancelled for the storm. Imagine what your sister would have done then.'

'Stolen a boat and rowed across?'

Kirsty laughs, and the sound is like glass against my skin. It feels wrong to be joking, laughing. Mind, I was only *just* joking. Nothing could keep Eve from us if she decides she's needed. She thinks we're incapable without her.

From the corner of my eye, I see Holly step to the edge again. She tips forward, closes her eyes. Swell laps up the green-slimed wall to meet her. 'Nah,' Kirsty says, oblivious, spearing me with a friendly elbow to my ribs. 'She'd have covered herself in goose fat and swum.'

Kirsty hasn't cottoned on to the seriousness of this yet; she still thinks Jay will show up any minute with a good story to tell.

I watch my twin teeter. Not a word in forty-four days ... *Not since the party, the photograph.*

'*Holly*!' I yell as she tips forward again. I grab for her and pull her back as her shoe slips on the wet stone. She stumbles against me, lets me save her. I'm not sure if her sigh is of relief or disappointment, and that scares me more than anything.

Holly scowls, pushes me off. Kirsty shoots us an anxious glance, picking up on our weird vibe.

Eve will be here in moments, determined to get to the bottom of things. She thinks she can sniff out a secret, can fix any problem. Usually, she's right, and usually that's a comfort to me.

If Eve were home, she'd have done something about Holly's silence sooner. She wouldn't have rested until she'd uncovered the reason. Everything that happened at that party would be dragged out in the open, talked about—

She can't fix Holly now; can't fix *this*.

I should have supported her better, forced her to confront what happened and get help. I should have said something to Eve or Mum after Ryan Campbell's party.

I should never, *ever* have let it come to this.

Guilt writhes inside me. It's too late now; we can't go back, and the weight of that is too much.

It takes ages for the ferry passengers to disembark. I close my eyes, let the rain slide down my face like tears. I haven't cried yet. Crying would expose me in a way I'm not ready for. Last night I watched Gina weep in my mother's arms, and I felt numb.

Things are getting serious – the police with their questions, the volunteer search parties swarming across the moors, coastguard mobilising as long as the weather allows.

After she'd dried her tears, Gina phoned everyone she could think of on the island to ask if they'd seen Jay. The artists played to their strengths – making tea, co-ordinating searches, sharing the social media appeals with copies of that old holiday snap of Jay grinning against a Mediterranean sky.

I'd wanted to go with the searchers this morning, but my busted knee and a rare burst of parental authority from my mother stopped me.

Kirsty puts a hand on my arm. She's grave now, all traces of laughter gone. 'It's going to be okay. We're gonna find him, Finn.'

I blink rain from my eyelashes. I wish I could believe her.

The ramp is down and cars crawl onto the island. Eve is caught in a meandering group of autumn tourists, craning her neck to peer past the anoraks and rucksacks. I shift my weight, wincing at the pain that spears my knee. Eve carries a holdall in one hand, her leather laptop case in the other.

I bite my lip; I should have prepared her for seeing Holly, for her silence. It's going to come as such a shock …

We learned everything we could about the condition last time Holly stopped talking, around the time the bullying started. But this is different. Most people who are selectively mute don't stop talking altogether; they speak in familiar places, with people they're comfortable with.

Not Holly. Her silence is absolute.

Even with us …

Even at Haven.

'Wait here,' I mutter to Kirsty, and fast-limp along the quayside, pushing between the shoulders of the hikers and birdwatchers, cursing my knee, the carelessness that led to the injury: tripping over my trainers like an idiot, falling downstairs.

'Eve!' I halt, helpless in front of her, rain slicing between us.

Eve drops her bags, pulls me into her arms. I bury my face in her shoulder for a moment, clinging to her comfort like holding on to the last scraps of my childhood.

She has to stretch on tiptoe to hug me. 'Finn,' she murmurs. 'You okay?'

'Yes,' I lie, muffled by her jacket.

'Jay's going to be fine,' she insists, in unconscious imitation of Kirsty. Everyone keeps saying that, as if they can make it so. 'You know what he's like. Probably sleeping it off somewhere, laying low.'

'Aye ... That's what the police said, at first.'

They're not saying it now – they're not saying anything. Just looking grim and kicking into action. Asking questions and searching everywhere – even the outbuildings at Haven, as if we might be hiding Jay ourselves. They found something: a spot in one of the crumbling buildings they thought was interesting – flattened ground, remains of fire – sparking brief hope in Gina, though why Jay would be hiding in our rotting barn is beyond me.

I glance to where Kirsty and Holly are waiting. Kirsty's looking at her phone, Holly peering over the edge again. I grind my teeth and will her to step back. 'Listen,' I say urgently. 'I need to tell you something, about Holls—'

Eve's gaze sharpens. 'What about her?'

'She's stopped speaking ... again.'

'Because of Jay?'

I shake my head. 'It's been six weeks or so.'

I don't mention the party. Sooner or later, she'll have to know—

'And you didn't *tell* me?' I can see that Eve's raging, trying to hold it in because she feels sorry for me.

'You weren't here. You haven't been home since summer.' I don't mean it to sound like an accusation, but that's how it lands.

I see her tense. It's a low blow, and a fair point. 'You could have called, you never mentioned it! You should have told me, Finn.'

I lower my gaze. 'I know. I didn't want to bother you ...'

Eve presses her lips together, gives me the look I deserve. 'We can deal with this. She stopped talking before and we got through it. She got better.'

I envy her confidence. It's tempting to tell Eve everything, let her sort it out – sift through the pieces, arrange and rearrange until the patterns fit. It's Eve's superpower, seeing logic where none seems to exist.

But there must be a limit to Eve's powers – and this might be it.

'Don't look like that, Finn. It's all right. We'll figure this out.' Eve squeezes my arm. I want to let her take charge, and be the kid protected by my big sister again.

But I am the protector now.

I pick up Eve's holdall and trail her along the quay, trying not to hobble on my bad knee. My sister is dressed for the weather in her rain jacket, jeans tucked into boots, hair pushed beneath a slouched beanie.

Rain falls in icy torrents, blinding me, making me shudder. 'Finn,' Eve calls crisply over her shoulder, as I try to keep up. 'Are you limping?'

'Um, no. I'm fine—'

'Mum said you'd hurt your knee. What happened?'

'Fell down the stairs.' I'm embarrassed to admit it. 'I'm fine, honest.'

Eve snatches her bag back from me and shoots me a dubious look. Fair enough, it was a stupid way to injure myself. 'You should be resting,' she says sternly. I see her eyes linger on the bruise on the back of my hand too, lips pursed.

I look beyond her: Holly is poised on the quay, framed by an ever-darkening sky. Waves are rearing against the harbour wall, gathering strength.

'I'm *okay*,' I say, hoping to convince Eve to let it drop.

We resume walking, slower now. 'Mum said you were out for ages searching for Jay – on your injured knee?' I nod. 'Oh, *Finn* ...'

Despite myself I want to lean against her, let her coddle me.

We reach the others, and Eve gives Kirsty a hard hug before turning to Holly. She looks as if she wants to gather Holly in her arms, fold her like tissue paper that might disintegrate in the rain.

But there's a remoteness about Holly now that repels even Eve. Usually she can reach her in a heartbeat. And for all that Holly moans about her, it's Eve she wants in a crisis.

I catch Eve's eye, see the questions simmering, shock at how far I've let things go.

Holly walks towards the car. Eve and Kirsty divide Eve's belongings between them and follow, chatting quietly. I trail behind them, letting out a huge sigh of relief. I wasn't aware of the significance of the moment until it came – wondering what would happen when Holly saw Eve, if it might loosen Holly's tongue.

What will she say if she finally starts to talk?

For weeks I've willed Holly to speak. Now I pray for silence. Holly reaches the car and leans against the door. She tilts her face to the sea, silver-blonde hair blowing across her eyes. The violence of the weather suits her.

Her gaze slides to me and I feel our old connection pulse, despite everything.

We are flies, trapped in the same web.

Chapter 4

Finn

On the drive home, Eve takes charge like I knew she would, tries to draw Holly out, but she stays glued to her phone. Eve bombards me with questions. She speculates about search parties, bothies, boats … frowning intently like she does when she's raring to solve a puzzle.

She berates me – gently – when I tell her I've lost my phone, frown deepening when I shrug and say I've no idea where I lost it – the truth, as it happens.

I omit how panic strikes each time I wonder *where* and *how*. Because I know *when* I lost it, and it's not ideal.

They're questions I've been asked already. By Gina, and the police officer with the silver-studded beard and kind eyes, the dad of one of my schoolmates. *Do I have any idea where Jay might have gone? Does he have other friends we might have overlooked? What was his state of mind?*

She slates Jay for his selfishness, and her words pierce me, since he's not here to take the hit.

She's so determined, sure that if she asks the right questions she can pull an answer out of the air, make Jay somehow materialise, succeed where others have failed. Again, I wish to be that trusting child, blinded by the light of her confidence.

I tell her I've no better idea than anyone where Jay might be, and look away from her displeasure. Kirsty takes pity on me. 'Everyone's turned out to help search,' she tells Eve, peering into the murk through a rain-soaked windscreen.

'Of course,' says Eve stoutly. 'Island folk look after their own.'

It's true. Even those who don't like Jay's father, who click their tongues with disapproval and call Jay a chip off the old block – *not* a compliment. He's tarred with his father's brush and playboy landowners don't go down well around these parts. But he's an island lad when the chips are down.

No one knows where Jay's dad is. Gina thinks he's maybe gone off on the yacht somewhere with Cassie, the trophy wife. It's typical of him not to bother telling anyone he was going. Selfish. Since neither Jay nor Gina keep in contact with Christian Allardyce, it's impossible to say how long he's been gone. He's not answering his phone and has no idea his son is missing.

I close my eyes against my exhaustion, the pain thoughts of Jay bring. We haven't known each other long, but we've been growing close.

He was pale beneath the bruises the night he came to Haven seeking his aunt's refuge, the shadow of what had happened between him and his dad hanging over him. I was glad he'd come to stay. I liked having someone to talk to and play video games with late at night, to swim and run and surf, to joke around and sneak a beer in the woods. Someone who's not my mother, my damaged twin, my pushy big sister. Nor a stranger wandering into our lives from the guest wing. I'm used to the artists by now, but I wish Mum kept better boundaries – or kept the connecting doors between our wings locked. A bit of privacy, a space for just family.

Rain batters the windows as we drive through fog so thick the world turns white. It must be disorientating for Kirsty at the wheel, but she knows these roads like the back of her hand.

Beside her, Eve sighs, and I sense her impatience at us for being so inept as to lose Jay, for needing her to come and sort out our mess as usual.

Even though she *loves* to be needed.

Holly is silent beside me. I watch her hunch over her phone again, thumbs tapping furiously. I don't know who she's messaging.

Kirsty and Eve make small talk, mostly about how Mac's grown, about Gav and the farm. And Struan Fraser, Kirsty asking if Eve has plans to see him while she's back. Eve is noncommittal – one leg hugged close to her body, chin resting on the ridge of her kneecap. 'He came by,' Kirsty says. 'He's been searching with everyone else.'

Eve says nothing. The road winds up towards the Capenish headland, leading nowhere but Haven and the cliffs. We're nearly home.

The radio crackles in and out. A weather report confirms what we know – high winds and heavy rain predicted to sweep the island for days, with only brief lulls. An amber weather warning. Nothing new, but Eve frowns. 'Christ, if he's out in this …'

A news segment follows, and we listen in silence to the story of the missing boy as if he's a stranger – *last seen in the largely unpopulated Capenish area of the island … not thought to have left the island but anyone travelling by ferry on Friday night or Saturday asked to come forward if they remember seeing anyone meeting his description.*

Eve swivels to look at me. She asks the same questions different ways, determined to get something from me. The woman should be a detective. She asks about the older crowd Jay was seen with in town last summer. I press my hands between my knees. I wonder if she heard the rumours that circled him.

Older lads, bad crowd. A dangerous game that brought in cash.

I assume not; if she'd got wind of that, I'd know all about it.

We reach the turning for Haven. The forest presses on either side: dark spaces between close-knit trees, a carpet of moss, shadow paths slipping between the trunks, spiked branches deterring entry like joined hands. Layer upon layer of trees mustering. Everything is ragged, damp, miserable.

Kirsty leans over the wheel, white-knuckled as more fog rolls off the hills, long skeins that blanket the road. The wipers squawk back and forth, and wind slices into the car.

My anxiety rises with the wind, with every mile closer to home. We're on our track, bumping through potholes. Eve leans between the seats. 'If there was something going on with Jay that you're not telling us, you need to speak up, Finn. I know you're loyal, but the most important thing is finding him.'

Kirsty shoots us a glance, but doesn't intervene. I catch her eye in the rear mirror. If Eve hasn't heard the rumours, I'm pretty certain *Kirsty* has – an island girl like her.

'I don't know what you mean,' I say, chest tightening with the lie.

Eve must have seen the changes last summer: Holly's world shrinking as she grew infatuated with Jay, and me trying to keep up with him. He was a lot – the parties, reckless driving, a coterie of girls hanging about him, his manic energy. He was always on the go, restless, seeking …

I was more inclined to take risks when I was with him, to defy expectations. For a while I liked that. Eve tried to suggest he was a bad influence, but I wouldn't hear it. I stuck to Mum and Gina's version – that I would influence *him* for good.

I failed.

We turn a corner. If not for the fog, we'd be able to see the house: the old stone façade hunkered in the landscape, the glimmering glass of the guest wing. Instead, there are only shifting shadows in the secretive gloom.

I feel Holly's gaze and when I turn, I flinch from what I see – *terror*. Pupils dilated, consuming her irises. I shake my head, scared of Eve seeing her like this. I've seen that expression before … when she opened her eyes at the side of the road after being carried up from the beach the night of the party. And again, in recent days.

Mud gives way to gravel as we pull up outside the house. I see the shapes of vehicles through the mist that chokes the driveway. *Too many.*

'There are more cars than before,' I say. Holly presses her face to the window.

Kirsty parks, turns off the engine, swivels to look at me. Her expression is serious. 'Finn … Eve's right. Everything Jay was into is going to come out. Now that he's missing, he's fair game. *Nothing* is private. You have to tell the truth, even if it might get him into trouble.'

She's *definitely* heard the rumours.

I swallow hard, choose defiance as a defence. 'Why is everyone so quick to judge him, say he's trouble?'

'*Troubled*,' Kirsty mutters. 'Not the same.'

My eyes travel over the cars – two police cruisers and a van. *Too many.*

The door to Haven opens, light spilling onto the gravel.

'If there's something you didn't mention to the police already,' Kirsty continues. 'Then you must. There *can't* be secrets. That's what I'm saying—'

I spot my mother running out onto the drive, scramble to release my seatbelt. Eve does likewise.

Mum halts in front of our car, blinded by the glare of Kirsty's headlights, one hand pressed to her mouth in anguish. One look at her face, and my heart sinks like a stone.

It's over.

Chapter 5

Eve

I can't stop thinking about my last homecoming and comparing – the carefree car journey from the ferry with Kirsty singing and Mac's baby talk in the background, my mother on the steps to greet me, hair loose on the breeze, shoulders dusted with summer freckles. Cries of 'my girl!' and hugs all round. Gina dancing as she presided over the barbecue on the deck. Prosecco popping, Finn, Jay and Holly mucking about on the lawn.

And Struan, smiling, our shoulders touching as we stood on the deck and gazed out over the tangle of grass and gorse to the sea.

It felt like a precipice, a moment of change, but I didn't seize it, and it slipped away. Five weeks later, he tried to kiss me on the beach at Liath Bay, and I didn't know what to do. I let that moment pass too.

Our friendship felt too precious to lose, Struan too rooted to the island with his cottage, his boat, his grieving mother, the memories of his dead father. And I was too independent, too convinced I needed to build a life elsewhere.

Now I walk through a veil of rain and mist on leaden feet. My mother falls into my arms, shuddering with sobs. Finn joins us. He's grown tall, but he's still my little brother and my need to protect him is as strong as ever. I include him in our embrace, as Mum cries on my shoulder.

The moment I saw her I knew. All the hope I'd harboured on the journey collapsed like a deflated lung.

I haven't come here to find Jay alive and well, sheepish and sorry for himself. I haven't returned for a weekend of good food, wine, conversation. Any dream of hiking up hillsides ablaze with autumn fire, glasses of Pinot Noir and a book by the wood burner, dinner roasting slowly, Gina and Mum singing badly to old-school ballads – crumbles to dust.

Jay is not just missing.

He's *dead*.

My mother's face said it all, and her words confirm it as we bundle into the long hall of Haven, Kirsty shepherding Holly behind us. 'He was found on a ledge halfway down the cliff, across the road from here—' Her voice is thin.

I navigate the jumble of boots and coats. Jay lies dead, not a mile from our door. Finn barely holds it together. He goes white, teeth digging into his lower lip. Mum takes his face between her hands. 'I'm sorry, baby.'

She assumes that after Gina he will feel Jay's loss most keenly. She overlooks Holly, who I suspect was in love with Jay. I glance around for my sister – grey as parchment, eyes like holes burned in cloth.

She worries me – the stark planes of her face, her translucent skin and haunted eyes.

Her silence.

It's been six weeks, according to Finn. What happened six weeks ago to steal her voice? That's when school went back, so perhaps Struan knows. But if he does, he won't say; he keeps professional boundaries where the twins are concerned.

Mum walks ahead of us towards the kitchen. I hear voices, feel the warmth from the Aga. Gina must be gathered with some of the artists. I don't find the prospect of the kitchen filled with people comforting. Especially if they are strangers, guests who imagine themselves friends. Mum has always blurred those lines.

Voices emerge as Mum opens the door: '... *must have been out all night. Slipped and fell, I suppose ... didn't make it. Such a cold night, poor lad. Horrible to think of him lying there alone—*'

There's a flurry of movement behind me, as Holly shoves past Kirsty and out the front door.

Mum throws up her hands. 'It's freezing out there. Where does she think she's going?'

'I'll go.' Finn hurries past me.

Mum mutters in frustration, before turning to me. 'Come along, Eve.'

Things are bad, I think, as I let her take my hand and lead me. It's not just Jay; there's tension flexing between my siblings: Finn looking like the weight of the world is on him, Holly turned to stone.

I'm angry no one told me she'd stopped talking, but there's no point being mad. I need to figure out what's going on with her if I'm to help, but now isn't the time.

Maybe Jay dumped her, and she couldn't get over it. Or she's being bullied again – it was a wee group of mighty personalities last time. Ryan Campbell and his band of bitches. Popular kids. Finn helped stop it, fighting her battles for her, and now he's part of that same crowd ...

I need to get my brother alone to ask for more information – Holly's silence feels solvable in a way Jay's death is not.

In the kitchen, Gina is bewildered in grief. She rises to hug me, and I hold her tight, murmur words that can't help. 'I'm sorry, Gina. I'm here. Whatever you need ...'

Gina pulls back and looks at me. 'Maybe they've made a mistake,' she croaks, with flimsy and heartbreaking hope.

'Oh, Gina ...' I look from her to my mother. 'What happened?'

'They don't know.' Mum wrings her hands, looking away. 'It

seems like he fell from the cliff path on his run. I'm always telling the boys to be careful on that path.'

Finn

Holly is a blur heading for the track at the bottom of the garden that leads to the woods and eventually the cliff. I need to stop her, but she's fast as a fox, darting over tussocks of grass. With my knee, I'm struggling to keep up. I catch a gleam of silver hair like a banner, the yellow flash of her Converse, and she's gone.

Holly loves the cliff. She's never been afraid of heights like me. She can stand on the edge, looking down at the crashing waves in our cove, across the sea to the clusters of islands that emerge from the water like primeval beasts unfurling their bones, all ridged spines and pointed elbows.

My head spins if I step close to the edge. I love the seclusion of our beach, though, where no one but us goes. It's an effort picking my way down the vertiginous path to the sand, but I do it, head whirling, not risking looking at the cliff towering above or down to the vortex of sea sucked against the rocks. I focus on the narrow path, the pristine glimpse of sand, the shades of the sea – turquoise, emerald, slate, depending on the island's mood.

It's worth it, for our secret beach, our patch of paradise.

Thinking of the cove reminds me of summer: a July heatwave, long days of baking sun and frigid seas. We had a good time, the three of us. Jay adores summer – he's a hedonist at heart.

Was a hedonist.

Past tense jars, doesn't feel real.

I stumble towards the woods after Holly, hoping to catch her before she slips between the trees. My knee spikes with pain and cold bites.

I recall lying in the basin of the cove, heat radiating off the rock face above. The shock of the water when I dived in. Jay leaping in the waves, throwing a rugby ball the length of the beach. Burying me and laughing his head off as he filmed me emerging from the deep, roaring and shaking off sand …

Him and Holly sneaking off to steal kisses when they thought no one was looking.

I know the ledge – a lip of rock that juts out from the cliff, an overhang concealing it from the road. Dangerous to climb up or down that way – not that I would try. Holly's done it from underneath: free climbing to the ledge, sitting there smug and exhilarated. My heart was in my mouth watching her. We've never told Eve about that …

Both cove and cliff are tarnished now. The thought of Jay lying on that lonely ledge, rocks stained with salt air and bird shit. Just wind and waves for company—

Was he alive when he fell? Did he lie in the dark waiting for death? It doesn't bear thinking about. I hope it was quick, in the end.

I sniff, feel the heat of tears that don't come.

I catch Holly by the fence line as she's climbing the stile. I pull her back. Immediately she starts angry-crying, falling into my arms and slapping at my chest.

'Holly, *shh*.' She thrashes against me like a panicked bird. 'It's okay, Holls. It's okay.'

She looks up at me, wild-eyed. There's a distance between us now; something in her expression that freaks me out. Tears tumble down her cheeks. I hush her again and wrap her in a bear hug. My thoughts race along with my heart as I try to work out what to do, what to say. Tears nudge at me again, letting me know that grief is waiting …

I take a deep breath, but words don't come. The ledge, I think. *That fucking ledge.* I'm close to losing it.

But Holly needs me. I need my wits. We stand for a moment, the chill piercing, fog lowering. I'm trying to psych myself up to go back to the house and face everyone. She breaks away, sniffing. 'We're going to get through this,' I say, and look for some sign that she agrees. *I can't do this alone.* When she gives nothing, I throw up my hands in frustration. 'Holls, please.'

We look at each other, lost in this unrecognisable, post-death landscape. Neither of us really understands the nature of my plea. It might be: *Holly say something …*

Or: *Holly, don't do anything stupid …*

Things are bad enough – I don't trust her on the cliff, like I didn't trust her on the quayside earlier. She's a danger to herself. To us both.

Or even: *Holly, keep your mouth shut.*

I hate that she's in pain, but I need her silence now.

I shake my head, thoughts slipping and sliding. One rises above the others, pulsing with my heart. *The ledge. The ledge. The ledge.*

Nothing to be done about it now. 'Just … stay strong,' I say. It's not enough, but it's all I have. I tug at her sleeve. 'We need to go back.' Everyone is waiting for us at Haven: Mum, Gina, Eve … The police.

Resignation covers Holly's face, and she spares the cliff a final glance before letting me lead her home. There's nothing here for us now.

Chapter 6

Last Summer

The light is bright, burnishing the insides of Holly's eyelids as she lies in a bikini on the sand. The cove is a bowl of liquid sunlight, trapped by the high sides of the cliffs. The sand is soft, pale, sea frosted with diamonds. Holly opens her eyes and squints at the stoic silhouette of the cliff, tufts of marram grass waving on a breeze that, down here, she can't feel.

It's a perfect day. They've had a run of them and everyone's making the most of it – summers here are hit or miss, but so far this one is epic. Mum has been persuaded to venture down the path. It's the farthest she'll travel from Haven, only with Gina by her side and never for long.

Holly regrets opening her eyes when the boys and Cashew careen over her, throwing a scatter of sand in her face as they clear her in flying leaps. The sand stings her eyes, coats her tongue. She splutters and sits up, gazing after them as they cavort down the beach. She smiles, leaning on her elbows, pointing her toes in the sand. Cash weaves between the boys' legs, ears flapping as he joins their conversation with excited yips. Holly pretends to watch the dog, but really she's staring at Jay, at the chains of golden muscle that rope his ribs.

The boys are tight. Despite Holly's hopes, despite the attraction she thought was unfurling, she's finding it hard to infiltrate their tribe of two, turn them into a three.

Or better still, *a different two*.

She's biding her time. She turns her head to look down the beach. Gina and Naomi are strolling the water's edge, stooping for shells: Mum in denim cut-offs, her hair in messy braids, looking like a girl – like Holly – and Gina in garish board shorts and a white shirt, gold anklet gleaming. Her hair is a scarlet riot, tied up at her nape. They're laughing, lost in each other. Mum is pushing the limits of her comfort zone out here, but with Gina by her side she seems almost at ease.

Holly watches them, envious. She turns her head, gaze travelling past the boys, loudly splashing in the waves now, to the far side of the cove, where Eve and Struan are picking their way across the rocks.

Everyone's a pair except her.

She rifles through her bag for sunglasses and puts them on. From behind her shield, she stares at Jay again. He's lithe and glowing, body defined and sleek, with water droplets glinting on the fine hairs of his arms. Head thrown back: teeth gleaming, bronze hair tousled – he's wet from when Finn dooked him in the sea.

She's been watching Jay for weeks. When she's not watching him, she's drawing him, which is worse because it leaves a trace. She keeps her sketchbook close, hiding it when it's not on her person. She's not ready for her secret to be exposed.

Was she imagining things – on the quayside that day with his arm around her shoulders, in the car when he winked at her? She'd hoped something was brewing, but so far, nothing's changed to take them from friends to the longed for, nebulous *more* …

Surrounded by people, Holly's summer has been solitary, but that's okay: she's an observer, not a participant. The current crop of artists doesn't interest her – she's befriended guests before, but this lot are boring. She draws and trails after the boys: watching, thinking, dreaming of Jay noticing her, imagining the conversations they'll have, the taste of his kiss.

She stays on the beach while the boys surf or swim, spins herself on the tyre swing on the oak in the dell. She waits. The boys are confident, secure in their skins, taking up space. Holly wonders what that must be like – *to know you belong*.

When she's not sketching, she's on her phone: scrolling, curating, commenting … Instagram is her anchor, her umbilical cord to the world. She makes TikToks in her bedroom, or out on the bluff. She distorts herself with filters because the face she presents to the world must always be perfect.

She misses Layla, who is still on holiday. Misses her siblings, though they're right here.

Misses *herself* – the girl she was before high school, before Campbell and his cronies decided she was strange and worthy of abuse.

Ryan Campbell's hot now by anyone's standards, but Holly still hates him … and, perversely, craves his attention too.

She lies back with a sigh. Closing her eyes, she lets the heat and light hypnotise her. She's not sleeping exactly, just relaxed; thoughts of Jay come loose and unspool. She is startled by a touch, a brush of sun-warmed skin on hers. She has no idea how much time has passed when she opens her eyes, turns to see Jay looming over her, blocking the light, his hand pressed over her mouth to quiet her surprise.

Her eyes fly wide. She doesn't know what to do. She nips at his palm with her teeth, making him grin.

He lowers himself to the sand. There's no sign of her mother or Gina – they've probably gone back to Haven to see to the artists and start dinner. They like to eat together, a jumble of guests and family on the deck when weather allows. A loose, relaxed vibe, with wine and conversation flowing.

Eve, Struan and Finn bob in the sea, treading water, chatting happily. An occasional burst of laughter drifts back. Cash plays with a tennis ball at the tideline, burying it in wet sand.

Her stomach clenches; she's alone with Jay. *Finally*.

He smiles lazily, hooks an arm behind his head. His bent arm displays a slope of golden muscle. He's dusted with a fine layer of sand that Holly fights the urge to brush off.

'Hey,' he says softly. She blinks and stares at his lips. 'You're burning.' He trails a hand across her collarbone, runs his fingertips down her upper arm.

She holds her breath. It's not true – she's slathered in sunblock – which means it's an excuse to touch her.

'Shall we take a walk?' Jay asks, innocently, and she wonders if she's imagining the tension mounting, the weight of the question. The heat in her belly, the flame in his eyes.

She doesn't think so.

She scrambles up, brushes herself down, too aware of her body: the flat plane of her stomach, fish-pale and vulnerable; long limbs and jutting hip bones, the mermaid-scale bikini-bottoms skimming her pubic bone. She picks up her abandoned hoodie and drapes it over her shoulders, scoops her hair out and meets Jay's eye. He's staring, unabashed. Strangely, the hoodie makes her feel more bare.

He holds out a hand and their fingers brush, sparks flinting. She glances over her shoulder to make sure no one sees them go.

She follows him into the shade of the cliff, skin tingling, mind whirring. In a few sandy footsteps they cover a vast distance, crossing some line as they take themselves beyond sight of the others. There's a scatter of boulders that look like they've been dropped by a giant hand. Jay leans against a rock, concealing them from view. He's breathing fast, a wicked light in his eyes.

Looking at him now is like opening an old book expecting to read a familiar tale, only to find the words have arranged themselves into a new narrative.

He slides his hand inside her hoodie, wraps his fingers around her hip. When she leans into his touch, he flips them so her back is to the rock, presses against her, hands gripping more tightly. She's burning up, loving the heat of him, the feel of his body, the scrape of rock on her back, the thrum of every nerve.

His mouth covers hers. She tastes alcohol, from a sneaky beer at lunchtime. His breath is warm, quickening at her touch. The kiss is deep, soft, hungry.

She breaks it, trails a path of butterfly caresses down his neck that make him inhale sharply. He tightens his grip on her, and a soft groan tears from his throat as she kisses lower, skimming her lips over his sandy chest. He pulls her to him and his lips land again, more sweet than bitter now, desperate. When he kisses her, all the parts of her slot into place and she is whole. She knows she should feel whole without him, without *this*; but her body betrays her better sensibilities. *He is what she wants.*

The summer explodes with possibility.

Chapter 7

Now

Eve

I recognise the police officer in our kitchen – I used to babysit his kids. The room is warm and smells of home: herbs and cotton candles, potting compost, coffee; but I take little comfort in it. Ben Carmichael sits at the table: broad, bearded and sombre. He's kind, one of the friendlier officers on the island, his deep, booming laugh well known about these parts.

He's just broken the worst news to Gina, so there's no hint of that laugh now.

Gina is surrounded by tissues, untouched drinks and well-meaning women. My mother slides into the seat beside her. Ben nods at me, clears his throat. 'Eve, good to see you. Not in these circumstances, of course.'

I nod back, eye the guests grouped about my mother and Gina. They must be close confidantes, to have been allowed to stay at such a time. There's a pink-haired girl about my age with a vine tattoo snaking her forearm, an elderly lady with long, grey hair and a dress suited to a different era, and a red-faced, fiftyish woman in expensive hiking gear. My gaze skims over them, fixes on Ben. 'Tell me everything,' I say.

I shiver when he describes discovering Jay's body balanced on that ledge, spotted by the coastguard on its last sweep before the weather closed in and the search was called off for the day. Ben had to pick his way down through the gorse-filled gully even to get sight of the body, and there was no way for him to reach the boy on the ledge.

I shudder again. 'What do you think happened?'

'Your brother says he went out for a run, so I assume he slipped and fell. The cliff path is on their running route—' Ben looks around, registering the absence of the twins.

I know that ledge: Holly's climbed up to it, taken Instagram selfies from the edge of the world, but she doesn't know I know about that – for once, I spared her the lecture. I think about our beach, the golden hours of summer frittered away beneath that cliff …

'I've warned the boys about running that path,' my mother frets again, nudging closer to Gina's side. Gina sniffs and covers Mum's hand with her own. I remember all the times I've spent with Gee in this kitchen – the tower of strength she's been to us since she came into our lives and hearts. Winter afternoons dancing to jazz while Gina taught me to blend this spice with that, and chop onions fine as tissue paper.

I love her. She loves us.

Family.

Despite everything, Jay is – *was* – family too.

I'm used to seeing Gina polished and perfect, her make-up sharp and red hair shining, outfits always on point. Now she's puffy-eyed, wearing joggers. The sight of her undone pulls my pain to the surface, and I bite my lip to keep from coming apart too.

I'm not sure how she comes back from this. She'd only just rediscovered her nephew.

'I'm sorry for your loss,' Ben tells me gravely, and it doesn't feel like *my* loss: it's Gina's and Finn's, and maybe Holly's and my mother's. But in a way, it's everyone's – the island's. That's what happens in a place this size, everyone has a claim on everyone, and the death of a teenager will be particularly hard to bear.

Ben's police radio crackles with a burst of static, a string of shapeless words. He lowers the volume. Gina bombards him with questions he can't answer, but he does his best. He tells us the body and ledge will be examined – though it seems obvious what has occurred. When he tells us about the post-mortem – *standard procedure* – my mother goes still, and Gina covers her face.

The artists cluck in sympathy, closing ranks. There's no space near Gina or my mother, so I'm seated at the far end of the table, by Ben. Kirsty hovers, leaning against a sideboard laden with tiny pots of hand-grown herbs. I try not to resent the artists, but I'd like to tell them to piss off back to the guest wing where they belong. My mother turns strangers into friends so fast it can be hard to keep up.

I'm certain she doesn't charge them enough for their stays. I've told her more than once she's not running a charity, but in a way I think she is: her artists tend to be female, damaged in any of the myriad ways the world *can* damage women, and they come to be healed.

I worry about how easily Mum lets strangers slide into the twins' lives, as if they belong, but Mum only laughs if I complain, tells me how lucky the twins are to meet a variety of people. Holly can be nervous of strangers, but she likes to skulk in the artists' studio watching, listening. Finn talks to anyone: charm personified.

Eyes roving, I search the cluttered corners of the kitchen, feeling the absence of the twins. The absence of Struan too, if I'm honest. Haven without him is strange. *I should let him know I'm home.*

'I can't believe it,' Gina says bleakly, lifting her head. The artist in hiking gear pats her arm, and the girl with the pink hair gets up and asks if anyone wants more tea. No one answers but she makes it anyway.

Jay should be here, nicking a beer from the fridge, kicking off dirty boots on the rug. He should be playing his music too loud, working his magic with that legendary grin …

Not lying out there: cold on the cliff.

There's a glimmer of hope in Gina's voice. 'Maybe it's not him? Do you know *for certain* it's Jay?'

Ben's expression softens. He wants to humour her, but it isn't kind to prolong her pain. He shakes his head. 'I can't formally identify him – that will fall to you, Gina, as next of kin as Jay's father hasn't been located – but the boy on the ledge matches Jay's description.'

I look at him. He is more than police, he is *island* police, part of our extended family. 'You know him,' I say. 'You *know* if it's Jay.'

He swallows, squares his shoulders in his bulky stab vest, his face heavy with sadness. 'Aye, I know him … It's Jay.'

Gina dissolves into a fresh storm of weeping, and Mum smothers her in an embrace. 'Come on, Gee, let's go upstairs and get some rest.'

Gina only cries harder. The artists murmur in sympathy again.

Pink-hair and Kirsty make tea. Kirsty's at home in our kitchen, and the artist seems comfortable with the place too. She reaches into the cupboard for Mum's artisan pottery mugs.

A flurry of rain beats the window, and I glance up. Where *are* the twins? The pink-haired girl asks me if Holly's okay as she places a mug by my elbow, and I shrug, murmur my thanks, wiping tears I wasn't aware were falling.

Pink-hair hovers. Hiking-gear looks up, a worried expression on her face. 'I wonder if we ought to go and look for her …' she says.

I frown. It's not her place to care about my siblings.

Pink-hair bites her lip, seeming to understand the intrusion. I see her catch the eye of Hiking-gear and nod towards the door, but the older woman ignores her.

Ben blows on his tea. I wonder if he's sat in similar kitchens delivering similar news. Road deaths, the demise of someone's relative. He'll be used to peering into life's dark and murky corners – though not like police on the mainland. Here there's seldom anything more dramatic to deal with than a car going off the road or a brawl at one of the island's three pubs.

I sip my tea, as Gina unravels in my mother's embrace.

Hiking-gear reaches to clasp Gina's forearm, Pink-hair and the old woman exchange glances, both wiping away tears. The sympathy of strangers swells to surround me, but I can't connect to them. I want my siblings.

'I'll need a statement off you, Ms McKinnon,' Ben says. 'Finn too—'

'Can't that wait?' My mother pales further. 'We've all had a terrible shock.' She looks at me. 'Eve, where *is* Finn? Where are the twins? They shouldn't be out in this. I don't know *where my children are*.'

I put down my mug, ready to go and find them before she falls apart. Kirsty meets my eye and I know she'll come and help, but the door flings open before any of us can move. My siblings sweep in on a surge of petrichor, a gust of cold that swirls about us. They stand before us, heads bowed, dripping on the flagstones.

My mother rounds on Finn. 'Where have you *been*?'

'We were just … talking.' A lie unless Holly is at least communicating with Finn. I *hope* she is, but his expression suggests not – he looks awkward in his untruth.

The twins shiver, puddles forming around their feet. 'I'll get towels,' says Kirsty and heads for the stairs.

Mum turns away, buries her face in Gina's shoulder. Holly slides past us, goes to the window seat where she curls herself into the nook, skinny limbs folded. The oldest of the artists goes to sit with her, and gently pats her back. I'm surprised that Holly doesn't shrug her off; she even leans into her.

My brother turns to the police officer. 'Is it true? You've found Jay?' The catch in his voice nearly breaks me.

'Aye, lad. We have. It looks like he fell while he was out running. That's what you said, isn't it? That he was on a run?'

Finn frowns. He looks young. 'I … I think so.'

Ben's face crumples. I wonder if he sees his own boy standing there, hurting. Or if he sees his son in place of the dead boy every time he closes his eyes and pictures that grisly discovery on the ledge. If he thinks about what might have been.

There but for a sliver of good fortune.

And for us, a sliver of bad. Life turns on the twitch of such a moment: a slip, a stumble.

Kirsty returns, hands Finn a towel, Holly another. When Holly doesn't react, the older artist takes the towel from Kirsty and starts to dry Holly's hair.

'I don't know what comes next,' Gina says, talking half to herself. 'I don't know what we do.' No one has an answer. I think about a funeral, the arrangements that Gina will have to make since Jay's dad can't be located. How strong my mother will have to be to support Gina through this. I doubt her capacity to manage it.

Hiking-gear reaches across the table to squeeze Gina's arm again. 'Don't worry about all that now, dear. Time enough for that.' She looks up and catches my eye. 'I'm Fran, by the way. I've heard much about you. This is Leah—' she indicates the strangely garbed, grey-haired lady towelling Holly's hair '—and Cate. Whatever you need, we're here for you all.' The pink-haired girl flashes me a small smile, but again looks uncomfortable amid our turbulent grief.

Finn scowls at Fran, and before I can respond, snaps, 'Why don't you all just *fuck off*.'

Everyone stares at him: my gentle giant of a brother, a sweetheart with those old-fashioned manners that endear him to people. I've never seen him like this. Holly starts to hum in the strained silence. Leah hugs her to quiet her, but she keeps on.

'Well,' says Fran. 'How rude. I realise you've had a shock, young man, but there's no need for such language. We're all just trying to help. Cate's been doing *all* the cooking of late, and I personally led the search party into the hills yesterday. Co-ordinated and planned the routes. Without me, half the searchers would still be wandering around aimlessly up there—'

'Fran …' Cate says softly. She's on her feet, glancing at the door as if she wants to be anywhere else.

'We don't need your *fucking help*!' Finn snaps, his voice cracking. 'What's the point in a search party that didn't find him? He was already dead. Jay's *dead*.'

His chin drops and I go to him, wrap my arm around him, lest anyone hurt him further.

'*Finn*,' Mum protests, but she can't quite muster a rebuke.

'He's right, we should go.' Cate jerks her head at Leah who rises at once, then looks expectantly at Fran.

'Indeed!' Fran's lips purse in outrage. 'I won't stay here to be insulted.'

'Oh, Fran …' my mother protests, but doesn't stop them when they troop as one towards the door, Cate shooting a look of apology over her shoulder.

I am shocked when Holly unwinds herself from the window seat and scurries after them.

Ben excuses himself to the cliff. He tells us there's a pathologist from the mainland who will examine Jay in situ. Then, the recovery operation will begin, though it will be hampered by the weather. The storm is due to peak around midnight, so they must work quickly. He reiterates that he needs to speak to Finn and take a statement, and I ask him to wait until tomorrow.

My brother is in no fit state. After the artists leave, Finn sits heavily, lays his head down on his arms and cries.

I sit beside him, my hand on his back. Gina gives in to Mum's persuasion and goes upstairs to rest. I hope she takes one of Mum's sleeping pills and finds a few hours of chemical peace.

The evening wears on, with nothing for us to do but sit here.

Outside, the light fades from the sky as storm clouds roll in. Kirsty pulls the curtains across the windows, says, 'I hope there are no more accidents out on the cliff … that path will be treacherous in the fog.'

I wonder if it was foggy on Friday too, if that's why Jay plunged off the edge of a path he knew like the back of his hand after months of running it.

I picture the circus out there: the floodlights and hi-vis jackets, pulleys and ropes, and shouted commands. Jay dead at the midst of it all. I shiver. Haven is cosy, but the warmth no longer comforts me.

Kirsty says goodbye – she wants to be back at the farm before the worst of the weather hits – and I am left alone in the kitchen with my brother. Cashew creeps over to lie at our feet and I think of Holly, seeking comfort with strangers.

Does she speak when she's with them? That would seem too great a betrayal.

Finn scrubs a hand across his face, takes a steadying breath. 'Sorry, Evie,' he whispers.

I don't know what he's apologising for – swearing at the guests or showing his pain – but I nod. 'Does Holly often spend time with them? It's strange that she'd choose to be with strangers at a time like this?'

Finn shrugs. 'She likes all the artists, but she's closest to those three. Personally, I think Fran's a pain. She's always interfering.' He pulls a face. 'But I shouldn't have shouted at her like that.'

'No.'

Finn stands, rolls his shoulders. 'I'd better apologise. I'll just let Cash out first—'

When Finn has gone to the artists' quarters to make amends, I tidy up the kitchen, pile cups into the dishwasher. None of us have eaten, but I don't have an appetite. I make a bit of toast because I know I should have something and I eat standing up, eyeing my phone and considering texting Struan.

Kirsty's words uttered more than once – over lattes in our favourite coffee shop, or wine in her farmhouse kitchen, over phone lines spanning the distance from here to the mainland – rise up in my mind. *Don't string him along, Eve. If you can't love him, let someone else.*

But I don't *know*; that's the problem. My mind shies away from the familiar ache of this conundrum.

Finn doesn't return – probably gone to bed. I wish him oblivion, hope he can sleep and forget for a while. I take my bags up to my room, find the bed bare. It takes me a while to find sheets and wrestle them onto the mattress. The room resonates with summer vibes – memories waiting to trip me: shells I collected in the cove arranged along the windowsill, in a scatter of sand, my gold flip-flops kicked off beneath the dressing table. I suck in a breath, let memories assault me. I have a shower, change into pyjamas, get into bed listening to the wind creep beneath the eaves, thinking about that night at Liath Bay, the end of summer … when Struan leaned to kiss me. And my reaction … to freeze, pull away, make light of it.

To flee.

Rain hisses on the gravel outside, and the sea booms far below as the waves rise. The weather is wild and suits my mood. I burrow beneath my duvet.

Chapter 8

Finn

I persuade Holly to leave the artists' quarters where I find her at Cate's feet with her sketchbook on her knee, phone in one hand, and a glass of buttery wine in the other. Cate is braiding Holly's hair in a convoluted twist, chatting quietly, and Leah is leaning in, laughing, admiring her handiwork and tucking a missed strand of Holly's hair behind her ear.

I offer my apologies to Fran. She sniffs a bit, but she's a couple of gins in, and she likes me, so she forgives easily. After what's happened, she'd be heartless not to. She's not so bad I guess, though she's nosy, and she likes a drink.

Holly should be with family tonight – she's been through so much, with what happened at that party, and now losing Jay. I've nothing against the artists. I think it's good she's found friends, though I wonder what's in it for them – a silent, ghost girl can't be much company. Holly's of an age to be a little sister to Cate, a daughter to Fran, a grandchild to Leah. I don't know their stories, but perhaps in her they see family members long-lost or non-existent. Or perhaps they have hero complexes like Eve, and think they can save her from herself.

Perhaps my sister seeks the company of strangers because she just can't stand to be around *me* now.

Holly puts down her glass, shoots the artists an apologetic look, follows me with less fight than I expect. We climb the stairs to the attic, where my room and Jay's are side by side beneath the eaves. She baulks at going into his room, so I go.

I switch on the fairy lights strung haphazardly over his bed, and prise up the floorboard I know to be loose, find the box he kept there. There's not much, enough for a single joint, which we pass back and forth, smoking in silence, blue smoke spiralling above our heads as we sit with backs pressed against my bed, gazing up at the skylight puddled with rain.

We smoke Jay's weed together without talking. It feels like a memorial of sorts. A goodbye, to Jay and ourselves – we are changed, now. As individuals and as siblings. Our bond is stretched, strained.

At least that's how *I* feel – I'm not sure about Holly. Even when we're alone she won't talk.

We've never needed words to understand each other. Mum never tires of telling how it took Holly years longer than me to speak. She didn't need to when she had me to talk for her. She spoke to *me* before she spoke to anyone – our twin language that served us well. I wish I could remember those made-up words; perhaps she'd communicate with me that way still …

I relax as the drug slips into my blood. I tip my head back and exhale a stream of smoke. I wonder what tomorrow will bring. I'll have to give a statement to the police, and Mr Fraser is opening the school for a while though it's half term – Holly showed me her phone, the message he put out on Facebook saying he wants the kids to have somewhere to go, to come together and remember Jay.

I don't want to go – my pain's not for sharing – but I know I will. Isla will be there. I'm not sure how I feel about seeing her.

Holly takes the joint from me in long fingers. She takes a draw, holds the smoke in her lungs so long it must burn, then releases a sweet stream. 'It's going to be okay,' I tell her, my voice low and emphatic, though who I am trying to convince, I couldn't say.

Holly hands me back the joint and her fingers move fast, making clumsy gestures. It takes me a while to realise what she's doing – signing. I learned sign language before, when she stopped talking, and I taught it to her. It reminded me of our twin language, and the secrecy appealed to me. We were only twelve, then, and I didn't have the fear of her silence that I do now. I didn't associate it with my mother's moods and mania, the grip of anxiety that keeps her Haven-bound. I didn't think of my sister as someone who had something wrong with her. And my sister didn't look at me then like she's looking at me now: like we're not on the same side anymore.

You don't know that, Holly signs, a deep crease between her brows.
I do. I promise. I'll make it okay.

I mean it, though I have no idea how I'll keep my promise.

Holly gives me a blank look I easily translate: she doesn't believe me.

Whether she doubts me or not, my conviction doesn't waver. I will *always* have her back.

At some point, while we sit there smoking the last of Jay's weed, our breath slowing as we relax, I hear the squeak of a floorboard in the hall, and I know it's Eve, checking on us.

Not checking *up*. Not spying – not exactly.

Just checking. Reassuring herself. *Being Eve.*

Holly sometimes misconstrues Eve's concern, but I understand my sister's need. She feels responsible for Holly like I do. She feels responsible for us both.

I wait, breathing another cloud of ghostly smoke into the gloom, knowing it's too late to try to hide what we're doing, and wait for Eve to make herself known, but she doesn't. I tip my head back against the wall with a dull thump, and hear another creak as she moves away.

Chapter 9

Eve

I fall asleep to a lullaby of storm, a maelstrom of thoughts spinning into dreams. I wake to a milk-pale dawn, fingers of sunlight pushing through pink-edged clouds. The storm has blown out. Strangely, I slept well, but still my brain buzzes with fatigue as I drag myself downstairs to the coffee pot. On the way I slip into Finn's room, and Holly's, to reassure myself that both are safe and sleeping: Finn lumped beneath the duvet, Holly graceful, with her head pillowed on her arm. Both breathing soft and even.

In the kitchen I stare out of the window as I wait for the coffee machine to do its thing, curling my bare toes on the stone floor. The sea in the distance is green, gentle, but it's an illusion, the swell softened by distance. Out there, the waves could still be deadly. When the machine grumbles to let me know it's done, I take my mug, whistle Cash from his basket, shove my feet into a pair of boots, and step out onto the cold deck.

I can see my breath in the air. I blow on my coffee and take a sip. I don't know what the day will hold but I assume it will be long and draining. I will need my wits, and caffeine. A swathe of pines has come down in the forest at the edge of the property.

There's an ugly gash where the wind swept through, toppling tree after tree. It will leave a scar, but the forest will heal, absorbing needles and branches, reclaiming fallen trunks into its landscape. All the same, the destruction saddens me.

I sit on the ornate bench Gina had shipped from the mainland for Mum's fortieth a couple of years ago. I think about my siblings and what I learned last night, lurking outside Finn's door. His words: *the last of his stash, he'd want us to remember him this way.* No reply from Holly, which answers a question – even with Finn, she doesn't talk.

Jay brought drugs into our house.

It shouldn't surprise me. I wonder if it was just the weed, or more, and if there's a connection to his accident. Maybe he was out of it that night and toppled off the cliff path with judgement impaired, reactions slowed …

Uneasy, I rise and step down from the deck, walk through the long grass with the dew soaking the hems of my plaid pyjamas. I skirt the fence line, past the overgrown track that cuts up across the hill, crosses to the cliff path and weaves back through the woods. If not for the pyjamas, and an intimidating sprawl of briars and bracken, I'd be tempted to head down to the cliff and see what's going on for myself.

I assume all traces of tragedy have been cleared away.

All traces of a boy who had hardly begun to live. A boy who, regardless of what I thought of him, was important to my brother, was Gina's *family*. A boy who deserved better than this callous fate.

As soon as Jay moved in, he and Finn bonded like brothers, and Holly was infatuated with him. Maybe they saw something in him that I missed. Something buried deep beneath the layers of recklessness and rebellion.

I can only assume so.

The police car pulls onto the track as I am walking back to the house. Ben Carmichael slides the window down and leans out as he slows. 'Morning.'

'Good morning.'

He glances at my attire. 'You need a lift up to the house?' To his credit he doesn't ask why I'm out for a hike in jammies.

I shake my head. 'I'm getting some air. Have you got news?' I'm not sure what news there can be, but presumably he's here for a reason.

Ben hesitates. I suspect he's debating whether to tell me or wait for Gina. I tip the scales in my favour. 'Shall I make you a coffee? You've had a rough few days too, I imagine.'

'Aye … not as rough as yours. Coffee would be great. Thanks.'

'There's a pot on the go. Head up to the house and you can fill me in on what's going on at the cliff.' I appoint myself unofficial spokesperson for the family – Gina's in no fit state, and no one trusts my mother in a calamity.

Ben accepts the easy bribe and slides the car into gear. He drives up the track and I follow, dodging puddles. Back in the kitchen, Ben leans against the counter while I pour coffees from the warming pot. 'Grand!' he says. 'Thanks, Eve.'

'So,' I prompt, barely letting him take a sip. 'If you're here for Finn's statement, you're too early. I'm letting him sleep as long as possible.'

Ben nods. 'I do need that statement, but no rush. There's one thing in particular I wanted to check with him. In the meantime, I can catch you up on the operation at the cliff, and you can let Gina know.'

I nod, take a sip of my coffee without taking my eyes from the officer.

'We wrapped up early last night for the weather. The doctor examined Jay where he fell, and we've been able to remove him to the mainland. Gina will be able to go across and see him. Or … we can identify him from dental records and photographs if she prefers, but some people like to see their loved ones for a final time. They find it … *comforting*.' He clears his throat and takes a swallow of coffee, wincing at the heat, smacking his lips as the burn fades.

'I think Gina will want to see him,' I say. 'I'll check with her later and let you know. I don't think she'll be up to it today, but perhaps tomorrow?'

Ben nods. 'Aye, that'd do fine. It won't be me in charge, though. There's a detective appointed from the mainland to investigate.' He downs another scalding mouthful. 'Terrible business all this. I feel for your brother. My boy's right cut up about Jay too … He's going down to the school today with the rest. Struan Fraser is letting the kids gather there, nice idea that.'

'Yes, I think Finn will go. Maybe not Holly though.' Something nags at me at the mention of a detective … an investigation. *Surely there's no need …*

'That's right … your sister is home-schooled, isn't she?'

I choke on my coffee. 'I'm sorry … *what*?'

His face falls. 'Oh, I thought that's what my laddie said. She's not been going to school. She's a … quiet girl, eh?'

'She's selectively mute,' I say, stern.

'Right … sorry.'

I soften. 'No, *I'm sorry*. It's been a rough couple of days, like you said … I didn't realise Holly had stopped going to school.' It makes sense, with not speaking – school would be excruciating for her.

I wonder how long she's been out. I don't for a minute believe she's actually being home-schooled. Reading teen romance novels on the floor of the studio while my mother paints; possibly completing some assignments sent home with Finn – I can but hope – but that'll be the extent of it. No way is my mother *home-schooling* her any more than she home-schooled me before we came to the island – she taught me to read, and I taught myself everything else. High school was a wake-up call for me, but not in the way it was for Holly.

Ben sets down his cup, remorseful. 'They're good kids, Eve. It was a shame, everything that happened with Finn too, but still, he's a good kid.'

My heart sinks. Another unwelcome revelation. 'What do you mean?'

'I seem to be putting my foot in it this morning …'

'Tell me,' I say, weary to the core and wondering what's next. Finn's always been a model student – good grades, good athlete, polite, well-liked by his teachers …

'Well,' says Ben. 'There was the fight … I don't know about it in an official capacity, just what my son said. Kids talk, you know. Tell you nothing at all about what goes on at school until there's some drama. I was surprised to hear that your Finn had got himself excluded. Doesn't seem the type.'

I resist the urge to jump up from my chair. I actually don't have the energy. '*Excluded*?'

Ben climbs to his feet, uncomfortable. 'Aye … well, thanks for the coffee, Eve. I'll pop back this afternoon to speak to Finn.'

I walk him to the door. 'What was it you wanted to ask Finn; it sounded urgent?'

He pauses. 'Oh, aye. I wanted to ask him if he was *sure* about Jay heading out on a run on Friday.'

I frown. 'I think so. They always ran together, but Finn slipped on the stairs earlier that day and hurt his knee.'

Ben nods, perturbed. 'But is he *sure* Jay was going running when he headed out?'

'Why do you ask?'

He rubs at his beard. 'Just … Finn said that Jay was wearing orange trainers when he set out, that he saw him from his bedroom window, setting his smartwatch to record a run. We realised when we got him up from the ledge that this can't have been the case …'

'Why not?' A pulse pounds in my right temple.

'He wasn't dressed for it. Unless, of course, he liked to run in thon baggy jeans the laddies wear now … and biker boots.'

Chapter 10

Eve

Once Ben is gone, I head back to the deck, wrapped in a long, soft scarf of my mother's, as big as a blanket, another cup of coffee warming my fingers. I don't want more; my blood is already fizzing. But Ben has given me plenty to think about and I think best with a cup in my hand.

I mull over the revelations of Finn's exclusion and Holly's school refusal as I watch the wind pick up and the swell darken out to sea.

A detective from the mainland, an investigation we're all part of …

I think of Christian Allardyce, likely sunning himself on his yacht, oblivious. He might not be much of a father, but he's still Jay's dad. He's only ever shown interest in family when it's suited him, foisting Jay on Gina a couple times a year when he needed a free babysitter and shunning her the rest of the time, keeping her nephew from knowing her.

Since the argument in the spring, Jay's hardly seen his dad and it seemed like he and Gina were bonding, building something. I'm devastated for her, as I am for Finn.

It doesn't feel real.

I wonder if Christian learned Jay was doing drugs and that's what they fought about. Gina would never have let Jay bring drugs into our home, surely.

My brother comes yawning across the deck. He rakes a hand through his hair, eyes me warily. 'Morning.'

'Don't *morning* me,' I say. He sighs and slumps on the bench, looks covetously at my coffee. I hand it to him. 'I've had too much already.'

He takes a sip. 'Go on, lay into me. I can tell you want to.'

His tone is flippant. I side-eye him sharply. 'I have questions, and in the circumstances, I'd say they're reasonable.'

He sighs, as only a teenager can. 'What questions?'

'It's hard to know where to start – the fact that Holly stopped going to school or that you got yourself excluded. Or that no one told me *either* of those things.'

Finn looks at me, wide-eyed. 'I thought you were going to have a go about last night … I heard you on the stairs.'

'Yes, well, I was, but these are more pressing matters.'

Finn winces. 'We were going to tell you.'

'Of course you were.' My voice drips sarcasm, and he winces again.

'Be reasonable, Eve.'

'*Reasonable*?' My temper flares, and I tamp it down with effort, remembering him coming apart last night, crying for his friend. 'Just … tell me what happened.'

'Holly wasn't speaking so school was miserable for her.' He flicks messy hair out of his eyes, stares out to sea. I can tell there's more to this story. Plenty he's not saying. There has to be – Holly's seemed better, these past few years. Finn says, 'I got excluded for fighting. It wasn't a big deal.'

'Not a big deal? Finn … you've never even had a detention!'

He smirks. 'So you'd like to think …'

I ignore that. 'It must have been bad if you got suspended for it?'

'I don't want to talk about it.' He turns to the sea again, his eyes matching the sullen waves.

'*Too bad.*'

He swallows, and I relent. 'I'm worried about you. You can talk to me. You used to …'

He shakes his head. 'Please, Eve.' He sounds desperate – the part of him that wants to spill his secrets like he once did warring with this new, secretive side.

'There's so much I don't understand – what happened to Holly to turn her mute again and stop her going to school, how you got into a fight bad enough to be excluded for … oh, and the fact that you both do drugs now and I'm just supposed to be okay with it. I'm guessing that was Jay's doing – you changed after he moved in …'

I'm losing control, words firing like arrows with no target in mind. I don't mean to speak ill of Jay, and I stop abruptly, knowing I've overstepped.

Finn's face is thunderous. 'His dad was violent, Eve. Did you know that? Jay was at rock bottom when he moved in with us. You were always so convinced he was a bad influence … It wasn't fair.'

'No,' I agree. 'It probably wasn't. I'm sorry; that was uncalled for.'

He presses his lips together. Fighting with himself again, like he wants to speak but can't get the words out. Our conversation tips on a hinge point. Perhaps the next time he opens his mouth he'll speak his truth …

But before either of us can say anything, there's a thump from the kitchen behind us, then Mum's voice, panicky and impatient. 'Eve! The Aga isn't working, and I don't know what to do. Please fix it.'

Finn

We eat a silent breakfast – me, Eve and Mum. Gina stays in bed and Holly hasn't appeared either – she'll be in the artists' wing, again. I shouldn't grudge her what comfort she can find. A new anxiety nags at me. I want to keep her close … but she seems determined to pull away.

The tension of my argument with Eve hangs about, acrid as a snuffed candle. I want to say something to make amends, but fear saying too much. I've always trusted Eve, and my secrecy hurts us both.

Eve got the Aga going and Mum cooked bacon, sliced a loaf and left us to help ourselves. Mum's not eating, just drinking black coffee and biting her nails, sighing every few seconds and flicking her gaze over me like she needs to keep constantly checking I'm okay. I eat because she's gone to the trouble of cooking, which she almost never does.

There's so much I wanted to tell Eve on the deck, explanations I wish I could give. I hate lying to her. Eve is good at giving advice – if you've got a problem, she listens.

She throws herself at it like it's her own to solve, like it's *life or death*.

This time I can't confide. I can't tell her why I got excluded without the story of the party coming out, the photograph, the cave.

That's Holly's tale to tell.

Gina drifts in, creased and confused from sleep, dressing gown trailing behind her and scarlet hair in a bun atop her head. Mum leaps up to hug her. Gina smiles sadly, then stoops to kiss us both.

I watch her pad around the table to the coffee pot. Every time I see her, it makes this so much worse – Jay's death standing out in sharp relief. 'I hoped it was a bad dream,' Gina says. 'But when I woke up it was still true.'

She's not crying this morning, but somehow her hollow-eyed stare is worse.

A moment later, Holly comes in. Her hair is still in the braids Cate did last night, a halo of golden fuzz where she's slept on them. She's wearing my grey hoodie, and it drowns her, hanging over her fingers.

She makes a cup of herbal tea, curls up in the window nook

with Cashew in her lap, frowning at her phone. 'Good morning to you too,' chides Eve softly, and I shoot her a reproachful look.

Eve returns it with interest, and takes the last bite of her toast. 'Ben Carmichael was here this morning,' she says, licking her fingers.

'What did he want?' The stab of hope in Gina's voice would break me if there was anything left to shatter.

Eve holds my gaze, contemplative. 'He wanted to talk to Finn.'

I frown at my plate, toy with a stray piece of bacon. Mum leans forward, fidgety. 'He needs to take a statement; he said so last night.'

I feel Eve's eyes on me; Holly's gaze whispers over the back of my neck.

'He wanted to ask Finn if he was sure about Jay going for a run,' Eve says with a shrug as though it's not important.

But it is.

Gina startles, sets down her cup. 'Where else would he have been going?'

'I don't know, but apparently he wasn't dressed for running.'

Gina looks at me. 'Finn …'

'I … I thought he was wearing his orange trainers. I saw them when I looked …' I pause, swallow hard, gathering my thoughts. 'When I looked out the window, he was leaving. He was looking at his watch, so I thought he was setting it for a run. He always did that.'

Eve's frowning at me again, head on one side. Mum's looking at me too.

'It was a filthy night,' Mum offers. 'I don't know where else he'd be going if not running … not that I understand what possesses those boys to run in the dark and all weathers.' A smile flickers, fades fast as if she's remembering that Jay will never run again.

'I don't know,' says Eve, 'but Ben Carmichael says he was wearing jeans and boots, and he definitely didn't look like someone who was going running. Maybe he was meeting someone?'

'*Who?*' My voice is louder than I intend.

'Yes, who?' Gina echoes after a beat. 'Jay was always with Finn and Holls …' Her words trail off and I wonder if she's remembering the times when he wasn't … when he came home stupid late, sneaking in with no explanation, occasionally worse for wear, how he avoided her questioning if she caught him, ignored her or shouted at her or threatened to leave …

Eve shrugs again. 'I don't know; I'm just repeating what Ben told me. He also said you've to call him and arrange a time to go over to the mainland and see Jay.' Her tone softens as she looks at Gina, and a lump clogs my throat when I think about the ordeal facing her.

Gina nods. 'I have to get hold of Christian. I don't want to make decisions without him. Perhaps I'll try another email—' She slides off her chair and goes to the sideboard to grab her laptop.

'I suppose you're going over to the school today,' Eve says to me. 'Are you taking Holly?'

I look at my twin who shakes her head frantically.

'I think you should, Holls,' Eve says.

Holly stares at her without blinking, so disconcerting that Eve looks away. 'It's nice of Struan to do this … The kids need somewhere to go … I assume you'll be driving, Finn?'

'Sure,' I say distractedly.

'Remember the car,' Mum says softly. Our gazes collide and my palms start to sweat. I press them together beneath the table.

'What's wrong with the car?' Eve frowns, probably expecting Mum to say she's overlooked the tax reminder again, or forgotten to get an MOT.

'It's the brakes,' Mum says lightly. 'That's what you said, Finn, when you drove it back from school the other day, isn't it?'

I hesitate, and hope Eve doesn't notice. 'Yeah.'

Although I'd rather not think about the car at all, I am wondering how I'm going to get to school with it out of commission when Mum pipes up again, 'Actually, Finn, Struan Fraser called earlier and said he'd come pick you up, if you want. I accepted on your behalf.'

'Struan's coming here?' Eve sits up straighter.

Holls unwinds herself and comes over to the table, nudging my arm. She shoves her phone towards me, showing me her cracked screen. My heart thumps with trepidation as I lean in. *What am I about to see?* I relax a little when I see it's a WhatsApp message from Isla.

Then my heart takes off like a racehorse again – *a message from Isla.*

She always has this effect on me, even now when I think we're probably over.

Finn, Holly told me you lost your phone. Now it makes sense why you haven't been in touch all weekend. I just want to say how sorry I am about Jay. It's terrible. You must be devastated. Will I see you at the school later?

I push the phone away. I feel Eve's curiosity burning me, but of all the things I don't want to talk to Eve about, Isla is up there. The conflict of wanting her and knowing I can't have her is a pain like no other.

My thoughts fill with Jay's orange trainers and how I got it so wrong …

I stand abruptly. 'I'm going to get dressed.' Everyone but Gina watches me leave the room. She's tapping away two-fingered on her laptop, sending another desperate message to her brother. He might be a shit brother and crap dad, but for Gina's sake, I wish he'd show up.

I should expect Eve to follow me and wait for me while I shower, but I still give a shout of surprise when I find her outside the bathroom.

'Fuck!' I slap a hand to my heart, take a few exaggerated breaths. 'You're a creep, Eve, you know that?'

'I want to apologise.'

I eye her warily and head for my room. She follows. 'Can I get dressed, please?' I say, heading her off at the door.

'I just need a minute—'

'*Sure*,' I say. 'Come in, make yourself at home.'

She ignores my sarcasm, and sits on my unmade bed, wrinkling her nose – I try to remember when my sheets were last washed. I open a drawer, pull out a T-shirt and pull it on over my towel. I already put on clean boxers in the bathroom, so I chuck the towel and struggle into sweatpants, hopping on one foot and losing my balance.

Eve smirks. 'Graceful.'

'Shut up, aren't you supposed to be grovelling?'

'I said apologise, not grovel. My timing sucked this morning … I still think we need to talk, but I agree that now is not the time.'

I nod. 'Yeah … okay. About the smoking—'

'I'm not going to say anything to Mum if that's what you're worried about. Though, frankly, she lived like an art student most of her twenties; I doubt she's a stranger to a joint or two.'

I *know* she's not, and nor is Gina, but I decide this is not the time to tell Eve so. 'You're a legend, Eve. Mum's got enough on her plate at the moment without worrying about us.'

'Yeah, Gina's going to need her …'

I nod, decide to offer Eve a crumb … admittedly, more for my benefit than hers. I don't want to hold on to more secrets than I have to, carry more weight than I must. I want my sister on my side. 'Mum's been a bit … odd lately.'

Eve leans forward, cupping her chin in one hand. 'Odd *how*?'

I shrug. 'Her anxiety is worse than usual.'

Eve raises an eyebrow. 'A mute daughter and her son getting excluded from school might make anyone anxious.' I stare at her with silent reproach. 'Sorry,' she says. 'I know I said I'd ease up.'

'But you just can't help yourself.'

Her lips twitch in acceptance.

I sit on the bed beside her, feeling the weight of the last few weeks. Holly's silence and increasing seclusion, all the shit at school, Mum jumping at shadows, refusing to leave the house even. Freaking out when any of us go *anywhere*. 'Sometimes I think she'd like it if we were *all* agoraphobic. Then she could keep us here under one roof ... keep us safe.'

Eve touches my arm. 'I know it's not easy for you, looking after them both when I'm at uni and Gina's on the mainland for work.'

'Yeah.' I'd never say so, rarely even let myself think it: Eve gets to escape, and I hold the fort here; that's the way it is.

'She needs help. It infuriates me that Gina just *enables* her. She doesn't even try to persuade Mum to see a doctor.'

'We don't know that,' I point out. 'Maybe she does.'

'She lets her be *helpless*,' Eve continues as if I hadn't spoken. 'And now this ... Once we get through this, we need to act, *make* her get help.'

I stare at my sister. I'm not sure how we can make Mum do anything. It's been ten years since she left Haven; there's no reason for her to change. 'Sometimes I wonder what will happen when Holly and I finish school. If we were to leave the island too, what then?'

For once it's Eve who avoids the question. She brushes her hands on her jeans. 'I'll try to have a chat with her later. You go to school, see your friends ...' She's almost out the door when she stops, turns, swipes my wet towel from the floor – she knows it'll stay there if left to me – and meets my eye gravely. 'You know, the police will be back later to take your statement. A detective from the mainland, Ben said. You'd better be clear about what *exactly* you saw that night, Finn.'

Chapter 11

Finn

The school comes into view before I'm ready. The thought of others' grief, a cloud of mourning hanging over the place, makes me want to hide in my room or take a long walk with Cash. But I have to face this.

Without my phone, I have no idea what's going on. There will be messages flying across the island like firing synapses. Kids will come together to share their hurt, memories of a fallen classmate. They won't mean to, but they'll dramatise it, try to make it about them.

If things were different, and it was anyone but Jay who'd died, I'd probably be the same. We'd talk about how awful it was, how unbelievable …

But Jay is my friend; his loss more than a passing sadness, a dazzle of shock soon worn off.

Mr Fraser picked me up at the end of the track – I didn't tell Eve he was there, and she didn't notice when I left. There's something going on there, I'm certain: she flinches every time his name is mentioned.

There are cars in the car park when we pull in. Mr Fraser goes to talk to a couple of teachers rounded up to come and support us. Kids mill about in front of the school as if waiting for instruction.

I'm the main attraction already, eyes on me, whispers starting up. People come to talk to me, check in, offer words of support, more for their benefit than mine.

Hands in pockets, I head into school. There's the beginning of a shrine by the fence lining the main path into school. Flowers wrapped in cellophane, colours cheap, rustle in the wind; a couple of fluffy teddy bears are tucked into the gaps in the fence, like they've been strung up by the neck. I look away, fighting my emotions.

Jay would hate this – if it were for someone else, he'd say it was tacky; he'd call out the folk that barely knew the poor guy who died, but wrote these heartfelt messages punctuated with love hearts and kisses. Clichés that don't mean anything, right out of a sympathy card or Instagram quote.

Except that they do, in the moment, mean something. They mean a lot and it surprises me.

I have no doubt that for the girls sobbing on the front steps, locked in tight huddles, or those who penned the platitudes, and coloured love hearts in pink pen, the pain is real.

It's not true grief – it's not about Jay. It's our first brush with death, the over-feeling of youth, the shock that someone so alive and vital can be gone with no warning.

The swift, fiery anger that something like this can happen, and fear that it could happen to *anyone*.

I mill around the cafeteria, impressed at the turnout. Most of our year has come, which maybe Jay would be touched by – once he was done being pissed off about being dead. My hands tremble, and I bury them in my pockets. My thoughts are grim, my mood inimical.

I look around at the crying clusters of students, teachers consoling them, a group of kids kneeling on the floor painting signs on big sheets: *#RIP Jay* and *Gone, never forgotten*.

Recreating the social media posts that are reaching far and wide – all over the country not just the island. Jay's death made the Scottish news this morning.

Someone has blown up a colour photograph of him and taped it to a cardboard placard. It bobs above the heads of the crowd, smiling maniacally. I turn away. I'm not crying – *should* I be crying? Are people watching and wondering why I'm not? My skin prickles with the heat of a hundred eyes.

I make myself chat with a few mates, accept the fist bumps and shoulder slaps, the mutters of '*Shit, man!*' and '*Finn ... mate, what the fuck?*'

Everyone's shocked, gutted, and I have no words to reassure them.

I don't realise I'm looking for her until I spot her, and my lurching heart lets me know: Isla Maxwell.

Her mane of red hair blazes across the cafeteria. She's looking for me too, stretching on tiptoes to see above the heads of her friends.

For a moment I consider ducking out of sight. I want to see her, talk to her – badly.

But she'll have questions. So many questions I can't answer.

We only got together properly at the end of summer – Ryan's big bash was our first real date – but Isla's commiserations are the only words that matter, her comfort all I crave.

We can't be together now.

She was there Friday, in the library; she saw what happened. I'm not ready to talk about that. *I can't* talk about it. I'm surprised Struan Fraser didn't say something in the car. I spent most of the journey on edge, expecting it. He was there too—

Isla spots me before I've made up my mind to hide. Our eyes meet across the room, and she says something to one of her friends and steps out of their huddle.

She walks towards me. She's wearing jeans and a green and white baseball tee. Her hair hangs in a fiery ponytail that skims the small of her back. She's perfect.

She throws her arms around me. I let her – God help me, I do. She smells of rain and flowers and, faintly, the sea.

'God, Finn, I am *so* sorry. I can't believe it.' Isla pulls back to look at me, navy eyes swimming with misery. 'I've been calling and texting you all weekend.'

'Yeah.' I rub my chin. 'I lost my phone. Sorry.'

'I even texted your sister, asked her to get a message to you—'

'Yeah,' I say again. 'Sorry.'

Perhaps it's the grief that's damaging us, ripping apart everything I hold dear. Like a scavenger, eating away at anything still whole and fresh and hopeful.

And perhaps it's the secrets, my lies catching up to me. Coming between us.

Isla shakes her head. 'It doesn't matter. I can't imagine what you've been through these past few days. What *happened* though? Everyone's saying something different.'

I tell her the barest facts. Isla's eyes fill with tears. 'We weren't close, but it's awful. I'm crying for you as much as for him.'

I hug her again, focus on the feel of her in my arms, the brush of her skin on mine, the orangey scent of her shampoo. My senses anchor me, keep me from drifting away.

Isla steps clear of the embrace and looks at me, curious. I want to hide from her scrutiny, but I can't. 'About Friday, Finn, in the library—'

There it is.

'Don't. Please.' My voice shakes.

'But …' She bites her lip again, leaving a white dent in the rosy flesh. 'Did you and Jay talk? Did you make up?'

I take a breath that feels like too-cold air in my lungs, the stabbing of a stitch. Slowly, I shake my head.

Isla slips an arm around my waist, rests her head on my chest. My heart thrums beneath her cheek and I cherish our closeness because I know it won't last. 'That sucks,' she says. 'But … you can't hold on to that. Just because you had an argument doesn't change anything. You and Jay were best friends; nothing can take that away.'

It was more than an argument, but I appreciate the sentiment. 'I'm sorry ... about Friday, the library. I should have kept it together.'

'You're not to blame, Finn. It was *him*. I don't know what got into him.'

I can't let this conversation continue. Who knows where it might lead? 'Don't, Isla, please ...'

'Okay ... We won't talk about it.' She looks at me, the inquisitive tilt of her head making my heart hammer again. 'I just wondered though ... that message I sent you Friday night – what did you think? When you replied on Saturday, you said it was nonsense, but ...' She shakes her head. 'Was I overthinking things?'

I nod, trying to form words – agree *too* wholeheartedly and I risk sparking further interest. But I need her to think she jumped to the wrong conclusion with her theory.

I am spared having to reply as a figure fills the doorway, their shadow leering over us.

Ryan Campbell.

He stands silhouetted against the light streaming through the refectory windows. He's flanked by mates as he saunters in, sucking the air out of the room. I can't breathe. Menace seems to drip from him. Even now I still hate him.

We were friends, until I smashed his face in. My skin prickles; a growl starts in my throat. Isla wraps her fingers around my arm. 'Don't ...'

Ryan looks at me, a sneer twisting his lips, amusement in his eyes – even today. He doesn't say anything, but a flush of rage sweeps me.

We were here the last time it kicked off, almost this very spot ... Nothing has changed between us – I still want to hurt him. He started all this, and he's just standing there with that look on his face.

Ryan would love for me to make another scene. It would amuse him, to see me lose it – so messy, so public. He'd love to recover his pride, land a good hit, but it would suit his purpose if I started it.

My head is full of noise. Old anger surges, catches me in its grip. I remember with satisfaction the thud of bone beneath my knuckles, the spill of blood, the shrieks of onlookers like outraged crows.

The sense of *justice*.

I take a step, involuntary, fists tight. Isla's hand slips uselessly from my arm.

'Go on,' Ryan says, getting in my face. 'I dare you—'

I swallow hard, ready to burst with violence. But Struan is there instantly, as if he has been watching me. 'Everything okay, boys?'

His voice is low. No one wants this gesture of support and solidarity to degenerate into a spectacle thanks to another stramash between Ryan Campbell and Finn McKinnon, least of all Struan. He stood up for me last time, pleaded a lifetime of good behaviour to get my sentence reduced when they could have kicked me out.

'Fine, sir,' says Ryan, with a smirk. 'I was just telling Finn how sorry I am to hear about Jay. Terrible, sir, isn't it?'

Struan eyes him coolly. Ryan's tone toes a disrespectful line. 'Well, you've told him now. Given the history between you two, perhaps it would be best if you left it at that. Finn, with me.'

It's not a school day. I could point that out, deny his authority. But it suits me to go, escape from Ryan *and* Isla. Ryan's a prick for his part in the destruction of my sister, and Isla's too smart, too likely to figure everything out …

Throwing a half-apologetic glance at my girl, I wonder if it's the last time I'll think of her that way. I follow Struan Fraser out of the room to face the lecture I've got coming.

It's the least I deserve.

Chapter 12

Last Summer

It's late, with only the final traces of light as the sun bleeds into the undersides of the clouds. The air is ripe with summer sweetness – too sweet, like fruit gone bad. It's the end of the season, the last hurrah before school starts, the short days and seclusion of an island winter looming.

They all feel it. Although the party is as boisterous as always, there's melancholy too, a sense of closing circles and lasts: final year of school, final party of the summer.

It makes everybody reckless, the sense of dwindling freedom.

Maybe Finn doesn't feel it then as they set out in Naomi's old car – maybe he's too focused on Isla and their sense of promise. But Holly does – she's felt Jay ebb and flow like a tide all summer. He's a wave, crashing over her then retreating. She knows what it will take to rekindle his interest, but she's not ready for that and Jay's not noted for his patience.

He's always off out somewhere, sleeping late, brooding when awake. He's got something on his mind, but Holly knows he's also punishing her for not giving him what he wants.

Half the school has turned out to the house on the bluff, with its showy architecture and designer decor. Ryan's parents have a weekend bolthole in Glasgow. Ryan has taken advantage with a series of theatrical parties, each more outrageous than the last. They've shaped the story of the summer. Each a waymarker, a defining moment. Reputations made and lost.

Instagram feeds and Snapchats go crazy the morning after – drunken sunsets, selfies and not-so-secret hook-ups. Messages fly phone to phone, posts and snaps are shared, liked, commented on as the latest party is unpicked, gossiped about – always some drama, some eejit who disgraced themselves to exclaim over – whilst anticipation for the next builds.

Finn drives. He's not fussed about drinking and Jay is. They don't want to rely on Gina, a willing guest, or – worse – island taxis. Jay is in the passenger seat, fiddling with the radio, cursing the lack of Bluetooth in the car as he tries to find tunes for a suitably memorable soundtrack. In the back are Holly, her pal Layla, and Isla. The girls are excited, chattering away.

Finn catches Isla's eye in the rear-view mirror. He blushes, and she holds his gaze, steady and promising. He darts his eyes back to the road, cursing and jerking the wheel. She shines so bright, hair glowing, as the sun streaking through the dirty windows sets it aflame.

Jay smirks, makes a grab for the wheel. 'Head in the game, mate.'

It was a surprise to Finn to hear that Holly wanted to come to this party; usually social stuff isn't her thing. She hasn't come to any of Ryan's parties before. Maybe Layla persuaded her, or Jay. Finn sees how Holly is with Jay, but he's seen her fade recently … darting doubtful looks at Jay. Jay spares her little notice; perhaps his interest is waning as Finn suspected it would.

Probably for the best; Jay's charming but he's not known for fidelity, and Holly's never had a boyfriend. Finn doesn't want to do the big-brother thing and warn him off.

Finn has been to all Ryan's parties but since the first, he's stayed sober. They're not exactly friends; he's just someone Finn knows, talks to in a voice that isn't his own. Someone he humours, tries not to get on the wrong side of …

Having his licence is an excuse for Finn not to get embroiled in the mayhem. He once made the mistake of drinking with Ryan and that lot. It got messy, though Finn managed to extricate himself when the lines of powder were tipped out.

Still, it took him the weekend to get over his hangover, longer to get back in his mother's good books after he crawled home close to dawn. He was ashamed when he saw the photos of that night – allied with Ryan and the rest of them, loud and unruly, throwing their weight around. Entitled, like the rules don't apply to them.

Everything he hates about that crowd. Since then, he's distanced himself.

Finn has his wits about him as he arrives at the summer's-end party, one arm slung about Isla's shoulders. He's not here to be the main attraction in the pictures tomorrow, the brunt of the gossip. He's here to make memories with Isla.

A pulse of reckless energy thrums through the house on the bluff, spilling out into the garden, trailing down the sandy steps to the beach. The place is bouncing. Layla steers Holly away, and the girls' laughter floats back as they run off. Finn's last glimpse of his sister: she's disappearing into the crowd, tossing her curtain of shimmering hair. She's wearing a dress he hasn't seen before: short, oyster silk. It seems to flow across her bones like water.

She's a creature of twilight and sea tonight. Apprehension and a surge of protectiveness creeps over Finn as he watches her slip into the melee.

Jay hangs out with Finn and Isla for a while. He reaches the pinnacle of happy-drunk. He's loquacious, a riot. But he tires of being third wheel and soon wanders off. Finn's memories of the night blur, despite being sober. He and Isla drift into the throng and dance. Then, hot and tired, they head down the garden and sit on the swing. It's dark by then, no longer warm enough for the beach, so most folk are sticking to the house and gardens. Those who ventured down to the sands initially, think twice. Finn assumes the tide is on the turn. He hears the sea, the rhythmic babble and whoosh of waves stroking the shore.

Isla's in his lap, legs wrapped around him. Her hair drapes his chest as she bends to kiss him. She tastes of beer and honey lip balm. The kiss is deep and slow and hot, the press of her body and the feel of her spine as he strokes his hands up and down her back make it hard to concentrate. His thoughts fly free.

From a distance, he hears Layla's voice, but it takes a moment to process that she's talking to him. Layla rolls her eyes, hands on hips. 'Sorry to *interrupt*. Any idea where your idiot sister has got to?'

Finn flushes. 'I thought she was with you.'

'Not for ages. She was being ridiculous – making eyes at Ryan Campbell of all people.'

Isla shifts in Finn's lap, looking at Layla, worry creasing her face. She's big on people sticking together at parties, cautioned them on the way here about the dangers of drink spiking. They'd laughed at her – things like that don't happen here. Maybe on the mainland …

'*Campbell*,' Finn says. 'She hates him.'

'Well, she wasn't immune to his charms earlier,' Layla snorts. 'Maybe she wanted to make Jay jealous, show him what he was missing. He's been blowing hot and cold—' She stops herself. 'If she's gone with him just to prove a point …'

Finn sits up straighter. 'Gone where?'

'The caves. He acts like he *owns* that beach. I mean I know his family owns half the island …'

Isla untangles herself from Finn. Her hair is wild. She looks gorgeous, but Finn tries to focus on his foolhardy sister, who is entirely – possibly *literally* – out of her depth. 'The tide's on its way; they can't still be down there.' He knows the caves: a network of passages and chambers carved into the cliffside, the entrance accessible from the shining bay spread out below Ryan's grand house.

Layla shrugs. 'That's what he said. He asked her if she wanted to see the caves and she giggled – *giggled* – and went. Like it's not a terrible idea to go off alone with a guy like that. Jay saw them flirting and didn't look happy about it. She's not even drunk, so she's got no excuse …'

Finn knows Ryan has a cavalier attitude towards sex. He can't stand the thought of Holly being the latest in a string of meaningless shags. He doesn't understand why she'd even *consider* getting with Ryan, after he led the bullies against her all those years ago. He and Ryan have forged a sort-of truce since – though it's the main reason they'll never be proper friends – but Holly has always hated him.

Surely she wouldn't go for Ryan, even to make Jay jealous. If so, she's playing a dangerous game.

Layla glances at her phone. 'We argued about it, then she flounced off. I need to go; my brother's picking me up. Tell her to call me when she's come to her senses.'

When Layla's gone, Finn turns to Isla. 'We need to go and look for her.'

Isla's already tying back her hair. 'Absolutely.'

They hurry across the garden and check the house, in case she's come back up. Isla tugs on Finn's hand. 'Let's try the beach.'

The stars put on a sparkling display. The beach is shadowy, but from the road they can tell that the tide is coming in fast, streaking the sand. 'Shit,' Finn says, when he sees how far up the beach the sea has progressed. 'They can't still be down there—'

Sea swirls against the base of the rocks. The cave opening is narrow, little more than a crack in the cliff. Finn remembers the fear that swarmed over him when Ryan dared him to go inside. Once through the gap, the caves open up; it's a labyrinth down there, at high tide almost completely submerged.

'Look!' Isla crouches at the top of the steps, where a pair of shoes are half hidden in a drift of beach grass. 'They're Holly's, aren't they?'

Finn frowns as he examines the kicked-off pair of yellow Converse. The shoes confirm that she went this way. He draws in a sharp breath – what if they've had an accident … have been trapped by the rising tide?

Before he and Isla can descend to the beach – the thought of going into those caves in the dark, with the sea sweeping in, terrifies him, but of course it's what he'll do – a figure appears on the steps, struggling with a bundle in his arms.

The bundle morphs into human form – a trailing arm, a head tipped back, throat exposed. They're nearing the top of the wood-framed staircase before Finn realises it isn't *Ryan* with Holly in his arms, silver hair spilling in spirals over his arms, it's Jay.

He staggers up the final few steps, knees buckling beneath the weight. Finn and Isla help to balance his burden, assisting him to set Holly gently on the ground.

Finn crouches by his sister, looks questioningly at Jay on his knees, sides heaving as he recovers his breath. Holly is unconscious – dead drunk it seems. Her dress is torn in a deep slit from hem to hip, stained with salt water.

'The bastard left her there,' Jay spits, when he can speak. 'He knew the tide was coming in and he *left* her.'

@QueenBee

Shocking statistics out today – see below. Sexual violence on the rise – 45% increase in reported assaults in a decade. Is this a national outrage, or are we finally getting better at reporting? Rape and attempted rape up 60% yet conviction rates remain poor. Not enough being done – which of my queens agree? #stillnotsafe #dobetter #womensupportingwomen

Chapter 13

Now

Eve

The house is quiet when Finn leaves. I don't see him go, and miss seeing Struan – possibly for the best. Gina pops another pill and goes back to bed. I don't think that's a great idea, but I can't bring myself to challenge her. Gina is ton-of-bricks practical, a force to reckon with; seeing her thrown off-kilter like this is unsettling.

Mum drifts off to her studio. I hear music and glance in. She's at her easel, working on an abstruse seascape in sinister shades of green and grey, layering paint with a palette knife. Her painting reminds me of the storm last night, and the hundreds of them that sweep our island each year. There's violence in her work, but I like it. It evokes some sense of freedom – a storm that cleanses as surely as it destroys.

I leave her to it, distract myself with housework. I stick to the family areas, but I'll need to turn my attention to the artists' wing soon. We'll have guests leaving in droves, and I want my mother to have a business to her name when this is over.

What am I thinking: it'll *never* be over. Grief endures. For Gina particularly, and my brother. But life goes on. Sometime – *soon* – I'll need to head back to Edinburgh, to my job, my studies, my flat.

With that thought in my head, I pause hoovering to make a call to my boss at the bookshop, beg for another week, at least until after the funeral. With a post-mortem looming, who knows when that might be. Given wider worries about my family, my place is here. I compose an email to my tutor, let her know what's going on.

I'm feeling maudlin when I finish the ground floor. I head into the kitchen, teary and annoyed with myself – I'm here to support, not succumb. I busy myself: unloading the dishwasher, watering plants, stacking the mail. I wonder what's happening at the school …

Kirsty calls as I'm plumping cushions on the kitchen sofa. I snatch up my phone, eager for distraction. 'Evie, how's things?'

'Not great.'

'Shall I come over? I want to talk to you. Gav and Mum have Mac covered – I could stay …'

'Sure. Maybe you can help me understand what the hell has happened here.'

Kirsty pauses. 'Huh?'

'Never mind. See you soon.'

We end the call. I pop into the studio to see if Mum wants a cup of tea. There are several artists with her. Conversation flows around the studio. I'm happy for Mum that she's got company, comfort. I leave her to it, look for Holly. I find Fran in the artists' sitting room, tidying up. She tells me Holly went for a walk with Cate and Leah. She looks a bit put out not to have been invited.

It's an opportunity to find out more about one of the women who has my sister's ear and heart. I offer to make tea, and we drink it in the sun room. 'I'm sorry if it feels like we're in the way,' Fran says. 'Cate thinks we should be keeping a low profile. But your mum has done so much for us, for *me*. I just want to pay her back, in any way I can. What happened to Jay is horrendous.

And poor Holly! I never had kids, but if I did, I'd want a daughter like her. She's so sweet.'

I sip my tea and listen, letting my silence do the work. Fran, it transpires, likes to chat.

'Your mother and Gina do good work here. I've tried every therapy going, but I didn't believe I could heal until I came to Haven. I've made real connections with Cate and Leah and with your mum.'

'What happened to you?' I ask, aware that I'm pushing boundaries I would normally give a wide berth. I've always known that there's more to Haven than the art, but I've never dug in with any of the guests like this. I've always shied away from others' pain.

I expect Fran to tell me to mind my own business, but she leans forward, steepling her hands. 'Firstly, there are plenty of lovely men in the army, but there are predators too. I encountered the latter. I had an unfortunate incident with a group of drunk squaddies who didn't appreciate an educated lesbian in their midst. They decided I needed to be taught a lesson.'

I stare at her. She's so matter-of-fact, but I can see the pain shimmering beneath the surface of her composure.

'I buried it for so long. It was only when I hit midlife that I realised I need to unravel my feelings, process what happened to me. Like I say, I tried therapy but Haven hits different. Your mother is an amazing woman.'

I feel guilty that I haven't seen that side of Mum more, haven't appreciated her better.

Fran locks eyes with me. Her gaze is intense. 'I'm worried about your sister, Eve. Something happened to make her lose her voice. Something bad. I think someone hurt her, and that's why she's drawn to us. Many of us have been hurt by men, and I think Holly needs to be seen, understood.'

Her words chill me, and I quickly finish my tea and excuse myself. It occurs to me to check Holly's room for some sort of clue as to her state of mind – Fran's suggestion has me worried. I don't do it. I can't invade her privacy like that.

When Kirsty arrives with an overnight bag, she finds me on the sofa with Cashew, reading, a cold cup of tea by my elbow. We hug. 'I'll make a fresh pot.'

Kirsty waves me away. 'I'll do it. Do you want to tell me what's going on? What did you mean …?'

It's a relief to pour my worries out. We get through two cups while I explain my concerns. Kirsty grimaces when I mention Finn's suspension and I stare at her. 'You *knew*?'

'I knew he'd been in trouble.'

'Jesus, it's a fucking conspiracy.'

'Don't be melodramatic. It's not like that. You're never here; you can't expect—' She trails off, wincing again at her blunt-force honesty.

'I suppose you also knew that Holls hasn't been going to school and Mum's mental health is worse than ever.'

Kirsty frowns. 'I told you, I haven't been round much. Sorry, Eve.'

'Not your fault,' I grumble, annoyed with myself. 'Now, what did you want to talk to me about?'

'It's not about your mum or the twins … it's Jay.'

I put my cup down. 'Go on.'

'Don't shoot the messenger … I was talking to Gav about Jay being missing – this was before we knew he was dead. Gav told me something that I think you need to know … Jay was … *selling drugs*.'

'*Dealing*?'

Kirsty nods.

'I *knew* he was dodgy.'

'Congratulations,' she deadpans.

I pull a face. 'Shit. That was …'

'Wildly insensitive, yes. Look, I don't want this to be something you interrogate Finn with, okay?'

There's no chance to argue or agree – I'm not sure *which* I'm more inclined to – as the sound of tyres on gravel interrupts our conversation before I can explore her revelations. 'Eve …' Kirsty pursues, but I'm at the window. Struan's car is in our driveway, parked behind a police cruiser.

It isn't the reunion I imagined. Struan stands across the kitchen from me, but with Kirsty shooting me warning looks, Ben Carmichael's sombre presence, and Holly, Cate and Leah piling in from their walk, the moment is stolen from us.

Like otherwise I'd jump him, right here in the kitchen – *get a grip, Eve!*

I'm entranced by the flecks of gold in his eyes, the way his tawny hair falls across his forehead, the curve of lips that make me remember that kiss …

I *shouldn't* be thinking like this. We're friends.

Ben clears his throat. 'Eve, could you get Gina, please. There's something I need to tell her.'

'She's sleeping,' I say. 'Mum—'

'I'll get them.' Finn moves quickly, not meeting my eye. Holly skulks in the shadows, eyeing Ben warily.

Ben's seriousness infects us, and no one says anything until Finn returns with Mum and Gina in tow – Gina unsteady on her feet, eyes clouded. 'Perhaps this is a moment for family,' Kirsty mumbles. Cate and Leah nod and head for the artists' door. Struan whistles for the dog and Kirsty follows him out. I feel their absence keenly. My heart races – what is Ben about to tell us?

Maybe the police have found out about the drugs and want to break it to Gina that Jay was up to no good.

'Out with it.' Mum sounds robust, but I hear the edge the others will miss. Her frailty. I glance over, concerned. Her energy tips towards manic.

Ben takes a breath. 'There's no easy way to say this, Ms Allardyce …'

Gina looks frightened and Mum slips an arm around her. Holly creeps closer to Finn.

'The initial findings are back from the pathologist. Jay has bruises that were received *before he died*.'

We stare at him. Finn takes Holly's hand. Mum covers her mouth. 'I don't understand,' says Gina. 'What does that mean?'

'He'd been in a fight. He was hit in the face. And …' Ben looks away. 'There are other injuries that the pathologist is … concerned about …'

'He fell off a cliff.' Mum sounds clipped, crisp. 'Of course there are injuries.'

Gina stares at her.

I take a sharp breath. '*Mum—*'

'Sorry, but …'

Something about the way Ben won't look at us sends chills down my spine.

He says, 'These injuries are inconsistent with the fall and throw up questions about how he died.'

Chapter 14

Eve

Mum and I sit on the deck in the shadowed evening. It grows cold as the light fades, and we wait for the detective to arrive: DI Imogen Isherwood. Ben has driven to the ferry to collect her. The sky is grey and ominous, the sea smooth. For now, the weather is dry. It feels like the calm before another storm.

Mum is on edge. She hasn't brushed her hair, and her plait is unravelling. She huddles in her oversized cardigan, darts glances across the garden to the forest with its tumbled trunks and brooding energy.

'I don't understand why we need this detective,' she frets. 'Ben can figure this out. He knows us.'

'Ben told you: he's going to be our family liaison officer. The Isherwood woman is in charge of the investigation.'

Mum's hands tremble in her lap. 'I don't want strangers,' she says, petulant.

'You don't have a choice. Don't you want to know what happened to Jay?'

My mind goes a million miles an hour trying to work through plausible theories. Jay's injuries change things, though they don't necessarily mean that his death wasn't an accident. Combined with what Kirsty told me about Jay dealing drugs, things have taken a slightly sinister turn.

Finn has clammed up, avoiding me. He's helping Kirsty with dinner, while Struan chops logs for the guests' fireplaces – it's going to be a cold night.

'Until the detective gets here, there's nothing we can do but wait.' I sound calmer than I feel.

'Of course I want to know what happened,' Mum says vaguely, studying the horizon again. Curled on the bench, with a hole in the knee of her leggings, her hair in that straggling plait, she looks young and unnerved. She's uncomfortable, would prefer to retreat inside, batten down the hatches.

'There's nothing out here, Mum,' I say softly, following her gaze. 'Nothing can hurt us.'

Mum swallows. 'When they were searching for Jay, the police found what looked like a makeshift camp in the barn.'

I can't hide my incredulity. 'You think someone is hiding in our barn?'

'No, of course not … oh, *I don't know*.'

Not for the first time I wonder what happened to Mum to damage her so – something suffered before I was even born? As long as I can remember she's been frangible: startling at shadows, hiding from the world.

Whatever it was started her quest. She put Aunt Maisie's inheritance money to good use and set up Haven, not to make her fortune, but to provide a refuge.

I reach to squeeze Mum's hand – she looks brittle, skin bleached in the pale light, eyes distant. It's impossible to judge her harshly and I feel myself weaken. 'Mum, did you and Gina know about the drugs? That Jay was dealing.'

She stares. '*No!*'

'Gav says so, and there's not much goes on that he doesn't know about. Kirsty's been sitting on this for days – she didn't want to worry me. There must have been signs—'

'I didn't notice anything.'

'Like you didn't notice Holly …' The words are out my mouth before I can stop them. Mum looks hurt. 'Sorry, I didn't mean that.'

'I'm biding my time, Eve, letting her find her voice. Just because it's not your way doesn't make it wrong—'

She reaches out to tuck a strand of hair behind my ear, the gesture loving, fingertips rough on my skin from the turps she uses to clean her brushes. 'You and Holls are different, Evie. You deal with things differently.'

I hold her gaze. 'She doesn't deal with things at all.' *Just like you*.

'She needs time.' Mum drops her hand.

'What if something happened to her, Mum? There must have been a catalyst, something that stopped her speaking.'

Mum unfolds slender legs and stretches, casts an anxious glance over her shoulder at the forest, trees beginning to shudder as the breeze stirs them. 'Let's go inside, Eve. I don't like it out here.'

I'm cynical again: another conversation diverted. This is how she gets round Gina and the twins – invoking sympathy, playing wounded.

Harsh.

But true.

The kitchen smells of gravy and juniper berries. Kirsty's stew is bubbling on the Aga, filling the room with a sense of comfort that goes beyond food. If I close my eyes to the sober faces, it could be any family gathering, friends and loved ones pressing close as I unbend into the ease of home.

Struan catches my eye with a nervous smile. I return it, not sure what it means. Gina is at the table, hair tucked behind her ears and heavy-framed reading glasses on her nose. Mum perches in a chair beside her. Gina's frowning at her laptop. 'Christian, where *are* you? I'm trying some of Cassie's friends,' she tells Eve. 'On Facebook.'

Finn limps across the kitchen trying to disguise his hobble. His knee must be hurting him.

My eyes roam speculatively over my brother. Kirsty is certain he's not involved in the drugs – she told me so as we grabbed a private word in the pantry earlier, Kirsty searching through Gina's impressive stores and me leaning on the doorjamb trying to marshal my chaotic thoughts, inhaling the co-mingled scents that swirl into one distinctive fragrance: *Haven*.

'He's a good kid, Eve.'

'Good kids do stupid things.' *Like getting in fights and getting suspended.*

'Not Finn, not drugs.'

I watch him lower himself onto the sofa. He and Holly were smoking weed last night, and I don't believe that if Jay was dealing then Finn *didn't* know. Kirsty is watching my brother too – her mother is a nurse and has taught her well. 'Right,' she says. 'Let's have a look at that knee.'

'It's fine.' Finn barely hides his grimace.

Kirsty digs in our freezer for ice. 'When did you last run?'

'Friday.' He catches my eye, flushes. He didn't tell me that. 'Before Jay got home from school. I didn't do it running, I fell on the stairs.'

'Why did you run without Jay—?' I begin, but Kirsty cuts me off.

'Let me see.' He rolls up the leg of his joggers and she inspects his swollen knee. 'You should have taken better care of this,' she scolds.

'We had other things on our minds. Cate brought me frozen peas … She heard me fall. I had the peas on it, while I was watching TV, but then Jay didn't come home, and we got worried.'

She wraps his knee with bandages liberated from our first-aid box, makes him sit with his leg on a cushion. 'Ibuprofen,' she insists. 'For the swelling.'

Obediently, Finn swallows the pills. A gleam of late sun

candy-stripes the kitchen: a break in the rain that started up again as soon as Mum and I came inside. Struan retrieves Cashew's lead. 'I'll take him for a proper walk before dinner. Want to come, Eve?'

I do. I want the familiar comfort of Struan, our old ease. But since that night on Liath Bay, things feel *different*. I'm not sure what he'll say if we're alone together … I'm not sure what *I'll* say. I've been keeping him at such distance these past months, unsure what I want.

'No!' my mother cries, clutching Struan like a woman possessed. He startles. 'You mustn't go out there; it's not safe.'

'*Mum—*' I say, mortified.

Struan gently detaches her hands. 'It's all right, Ms McKinnon, honestly. There's nothing out there …'

She calms at his touch. 'You know to call me Naomi. Still, stick to the grounds …'

'Cash needs a decent walk,' Struan says. 'And I'll have Eve to protect me. No one messes with her.' He flashes me a grin that melts me.

Not just friends.

Mum laughs, but looks anxious. I'm about to collect my boots, when I hear the sound now synonymous with bad news: tyres on gravel, a police car pulling up.

Ben is striding across the grass with a younger male officer with overly styled hair. A statuesque woman in her thirties, wearing a well-cut suit, follows. She looks around, gaze hawk-sharp. She's wearing heels that dig into the grass, but it doesn't deter her.

'I think I'd better stay,' I say, as she reaches the door and raps sharply on it.

@QueenBee

IDK who needs to read this, but … for any of my queens still suffering in silence, I hear you. I feel you. There's support out there – links below. I'm living proof that there's life after sexual violence. If you're ready to reach out, I'm here for you #survivors #womensupportingwomen #thrivedontjustsurvive

Chapter 15

Finn

The kitchen is crowded with not one, but three police officers. The air is charged. Ben introduces DI Isherwood. DC Campbell, I know – I'd recognise Ryan's brother anywhere. I sink deeper in my seat.

'DC Campbell is going to search Jay's room,' Isherwood announces. 'While I talk to Finn.'

Eve pipes up: 'Could you check the outbuildings? Just to make sure there's nothing suspicious.' She slants a look at Mum. 'It's possible someone's been snooping.'

I frown, unsure if she's trying to appease Mum or deflect attention from me, putting off my statement. She thinks I'm hiding things.

She's not wrong. *Jay … the drugs, the party, the photograph.*

It was the photograph Ryan Campbell sent to half the kids on the island, as much as what happened in that cave, that prompted Holly's defection from the world.

Now Ryan's brother is in our house, snapping on plastic gloves with menace, not looking at me. Isherwood nods at Campbell, and he leaves the room. Ben already checked Jay's room, but he was looking for clues – a missing bag, clothes gone from the wardrobe, some indication of Jay's plan. He didn't find his hiding places, but these two look like they mean business.

I'm glad we smoked that last joint. I wish I knew if there was more to find …

It seems unlikely that Jay didn't have something incriminating here – money or product. If he had another hiding place at Haven, I hope it is a good one. It would suit *me* if the police looked in that direction, but I don't want Mum and Gina getting in trouble if anything is found beneath their roof.

Imogen offers condolences, then she's all business. She takes something from her pocket. 'I went to the cliff before coming here. I wanted to take a look at the spot where he—' She pauses, bites off her sentence in deference to Gina. 'Forensics were there last night, but the storm got ahead of us, curtailed the search … I had a look around, found this. I wondered if it might be Jay's.'

She holds up a clear evidence bag containing a phone in a grey case. My heart sinks. Gina steps forward to take a look, but Isherwood holds the bag out of reach. 'You can't touch, I'm afraid.'

'That's an iPhone. It's not Jay's; he had an Android. It's not been found – maybe it slipped out of his pocket and into the sea …'

'You're *sure* this isn't his?' Imogen frowns.

'Absolutely. He had one of those chunky cases that can be run over by a tank.'

'I see. Well, we can examine it and see who it belongs to … might be nothing to do with Jay—'

'It's mine,' I blurt. I knew the moment I saw it. 'That's my phone.'

Everyone looks at me, and I falter. But there's no point keeping quiet; like she said, they can unlock the phone and find out it's mine.

Isherwood's gaze makes me uncomfortable. 'Why would *your* phone be in the undergrowth at the edge of the woods by the cliff where your friend died?'

The way the question is phrased makes me uneasy. 'I suppose

I dropped it – on Friday night when I was looking for Jay. Or earlier, when I was running.'

'I see.' Toneless. *Deadly*.

'It's not like Finn to lose things,' Eve says in a voice that isn't quite her own. 'He was worried about his friend. And he was injured, so he wouldn't have been able to go back and look …'

Isherwood swivels. 'Don't answer for him.'

Eve looks cowed, which isn't something you often see.

'Can I … have it back?' I stutter.

Imogen's manicured nails close around the bag. She slides it into her pocket again. 'Not yet. This is … evidence.'

The interview takes place in the den. Not an official interview – I'm just giving a statement – but it feels official enough. She asks permission to record, and I nod. I don't think I have a choice.

That word rings in my ears: *evidence*.

Eve asks to sit in. The detective acquiesces, since I'm entitled to have an adult with me. Eve takes the armchair to my left, posture stiff.

Imogen sits across from me. Her hair is absurdly neat considering she was out on the cliff. Perhaps she's immune to weather. After the gentleness of PC Carmichael, who handled us with kid gloves, like victims, the detective's manner is disconcerting.

There's a hunger in her eyes that suggests she won't rest until she gets the truth.

I think about Harris Campbell, upstairs poking around Jay's room. Who likely – if he's spoken to his brother lately – hates me.

She asks everything, makes me take her through every move on Friday – how I drove us to school in Mum's car, how Holly went in for a meeting with her guidance teacher, how we came home without Jay – *easy to check*, no point lying.

I tell her I had a migraine and that's why I left early. Holly was waiting for me. It was the last day of term; it didn't seem like a big deal to skip last period.

'But Jay didn't go with you?'

I shake my head, don't offer any explanation. I tell her that I went for a run – again, easily checked; several artists saw me as they were heading to yoga in the summerhouse. I remember the chatter, the bright splash of their yoga leggings.

Imogen says, '*With a migraine*,' and raises an eyebrow, but it's not a question so I don't answer. I bite my lip: inventing the headache was a mistake.

I tell her that I spent the afternoon in my room, finishing homework, that Holly was with the artists, Mum prepping for a dinner party with the artists. I tell her that Jay didn't come home from school until late; even with the bus to contend with, he should have been earlier. When he did, he went straight back out in his car. I tell her I didn't speak to him that afternoon, then later spotted him from my bedroom window, tapping his smartwatch. I assumed he was going running. I tell her about slipping on the stairs, taking a tumble.

She takes me back, unscrambling my jumbled narrative. 'And you already ran … *alone*. Why did you go without him?'

I feel Eve's interest sharpen.

'I wanted to blow off steam after I got home, and I couldn't be bothered waiting.'

'With a migraine,' she says again, no inflection. 'Was it unusual for you to run alone?'

I catch Eve's eye. *Yes.*

'Not really,' I say. 'We didn't do everything together.'

She accepts this, but I'm not sure Eve does.

When we're done, Imogen Isherwood stalks from the den, tossing her perfect ponytail. She says she wants to talk to Gina.

Eve turns on me. 'Why didn't you mention the drugs … you should have *told her* that he was dealing.'

I glance at the door, still partially open.

Eve rolls her eyes. 'Yes, Finn, I *know*. Kirsty told me – Gav told *her*.'

Of course Eve knows. My heart thumps. 'Dealing is a stretch, Eve …'

'He was supplying drugs for money. That's the *definition* of dealing, Finn.' Her voice rises. 'Probably the *legal* one. You should have told the police. They'll find out anyway and it might be relevant. Jay might have been meeting someone on the cliff that night …'

'Ssh, Eve, please.' But she's right: the drugs do offer an alternative angle.

'I don't understand why you're protecting him.' Eve throws up her hands. 'I know you're loyal, but there's no point defending him now.'

She has the look in her eye that Cashew gets with a new bone. She's not going to give up. 'I'm not just protecting *him*,' I say. 'I don't even know everything Jay was into—' *True, sort of.* 'I wasn't involved, Eve, I swear … Jay was frightened. He wanted out, but he was working with scary people. He owed money. There was always one more deal …'

She looks sick, hands clasped between her knees.

I was scared for Jay, towards the end. I've hidden truths but that's no lie. I sigh, wilting beneath Eve's scrutiny. 'The only person I know *for sure* that was involved is one of Gav's mates. If I'm protecting anyone, it's Kirsty.' I don't think Gav was part of it, but I don't want to bring trouble to their door.

Eve sighs. 'This is a mess.'

She has no idea.

Chapter 16

Finn

In the kitchen, Isherwood is talking to Gina about the injuries Jay sustained before his fall. She asks Gina if she knows anything about Jay being in a fight before he died.

She asked me that too.

I debated the lie – I just don't know how long it can hold. I look around for Struan Fraser, who could shatter my untruth easily, but he's still out with the dog.

Good.

Gina frowns. 'I last saw him on Thursday before I left for my conference. He was fine. I don't remember him getting in *any* fights – the only person I know for sure hurt him is my brother, but that was months ago.' Her face clouds as she tells the story, Jay turning up at Haven that night covered in bruises, bleeding from a split lip. 'I know my brother, Inspector … I don't know what the argument was about, only Christian can tell us that now, but he wasn't fit to be a father. *Of course*, I took Jay in—'

'And you've still not heard from your brother?'

She shakes her head. 'Have the police had any luck finding him?'

'We're looking at CCTV from the ferry ports, checking car registrations against the manifest list. Christian's car left the island Friday lunchtime. After that … we're not sure, except that he travelled south.'

Gina presses a hand to her mouth. 'He left the morning of the day his son died! What horrible timing. I'm sure he and Cassie have taken the yacht somewhere—'

'Maybe. We need to find him. He may not have been on the island when Jay died, but we still want to talk to him. He needs to know what's happened.'

The door opens and Holly slips in from the artists' wing. She's keeping her distance from me. Footsteps sound in the hall, as Campbell returns. He doesn't give anything away in the look that passes between him and Isherwood. I have no way of knowing if they've found something in Jay's room.

Harris looks at me and I see that he knows what happened between me and Ryan. I doubt he knows *why* …

But he'll see me as the aggressor, a violent kid who can't hold his temper.

Uncomfortably, that temper starts to rise. I clench my fists, feel Holly's grip, her fingers pinching the tendons in my forearm.

'Ben may have explained he's going to be your liaison throughout the investigation,' Imogen Isherwood is saying, oblivious to the tension flexing between me and her officer.

Ben stands behind her, wide stance, arms crossed. His expression is serious – no longer the friendly, jovial guy who looked after us in the hours after Jay went missing.

'The post-mortem should be tomorrow or the day after. If you'd like to see Jay, it can be arranged, but you've identified him clearly from photos today, and we'll check records too. I'll be in touch, Ms Allardyce. Again, I'm so sorry for your loss.' Imogen glances at Campbell, jerks her head.

Harris Campbell eyeballs me as he passes. It was Struan who told me the police had decided to let the school handle things rather than pressing assault charges. The relief was immense. I thought I'd really messed up … *loss-of-freedom* messed up.

Campbell pauses on the threshold, almost out the door. He takes a ragged breath, turns to me. His jaw is tight, voice low as he says, 'I've no idea why they didn't throw the book at you. A few days' suspension wasn't sufficient punishment for what you did.'

My temper snaps, the fragile hold I've kept on myself through these days of ramped-up tension gone in a heartbeat, a moment of madness. Like before …

The words bubble up, unbidden, uncontrolled. 'And a broken nose wasn't sufficient punishment for what he did to my sister in that cave—'

I might as well have punched Campbell too. My words silence the kitchen, bringing all eyes to me.

Especially Holly's.

@QueenBee

GREAT article today – link in the comments. Turning the spotlight on Scotland's shocking record on rape convictions, especially so called 'date rape'. Time for change, let this be a call to arms! #dobetter #womensupportingwomen

Chapter 17

Last Summer

She lies supine on the verge, make-up smudged, wet hair knotted. She breathes steadily, ribs rising and falling beneath the oyster silk dress. Isla leans over her, checking for injuries while Jay slumps in the grass trying to get his breath back.

'I can't believe he'd do something like this,' Isla says. 'I can't believe *anyone* would.'

Holly smells of beer and the sea and something else … earthy. Her dress is ruined: stained, ripped at the thigh and chest, strap torn through, hemline split.

'I'm going to *fucking kill him*,' Finn says. 'I swear to God …'

Isla's eyes move over Holly, noting the blood smears on the girl's thigh, the fingertip bruises at her collarbones. She catches Jay's eye as he rolls to his knees, and understanding passes between them. He's seen the damage too, drawn the same conclusions. Probably best Finn doesn't see, the state he's in.

He's still pacing and ranting about Ryan Campbell. Jay takes off his sweatshirt and drapes it over Holly. Half-conscious, she whimpers.

Finn gazes at the house on the bluff, profile taut. 'I swear …' he repeats.

'Focus, Finn, Holly needs you.' Isla presses fingers to Holly's wrist, feeling the reassuring steady tick.

'Does she need to go to hospital?' Finn gets himself under control.

'Give her a minute.' Isla strokes the girl's hair. Holly starts to stir, eyelids fluttering, a low moan. When her eyes open, her pupils are blown, expression bewildered.

'We should take her home,' Jay says. 'She's drunk.'

'I don't know …' Isla begins, as Holly vomits in the grass. When she's done throwing up, Isla slides the girl's arms into the sleeves of Jay's hoodie. Holly whimpers again and tries to struggle free.

'I'm going up there …' Finn says.

Jay slaps him lightly on the cheek. 'Snap out of it. Ryan can wait. We need to take her home and sober her up.'

'Layla said she wasn't drinking …' Isla murmurs.

Finn's fists are clenched, and he gives no indication of hearing either of them. Jay grabs his shoulders. 'Leave it, Finn. Go get the car.' Finally Finn nods, fishing his keys from his pockets. His hands shake. 'Want me to drive?' Jay asks.

'No, I'm fine; you've been drinking.'

He jogs off to get the car, drives back to collect them. They get Holly into the car between them. 'It's all right,' Isla soothes, settling Holly's head in her lap. Jay leans in, supporting her legs. Holly groans and starts to thrash around, swatting at him. 'Best not touch her,' Isla tells Jay, frowning. 'She's so distressed—'

Finn drives like a man possessed, swinging into bends. Even Jay turns pale and grips the seat. At Haven, they slide to a halt on the gravel. 'We need Mum,' Finn says.

Holly groans, shakes her head. She begins to convulse again, and Isla only just gets the door open before she throws up on the gravel. Isla holds her hair. 'Best to get rid of whatever you've taken, sweetie.'

'What do you mean?' Finn gets out of the car and comes round to the passenger side, dodging vomit splatter.

'Layla said Holly wasn't drinking. Even if she had a couple of beers with Ryan there's no way she got this wasted so quickly. She's taken something … *or been given it.*'

Finn casts a look at Haven, anxious. No lights in the windows. Isla's warnings about drink spiking coming back to him. 'Holly hates drugs. She wouldn't take anything.' His sister has always been vocal about drugs … she'll barely take a paracetamol.

'Maybe not voluntarily.'

'You realise what you're saying?' Jay looks scared. 'You think Ryan's capable of that?'

Isla shrugs. 'Given the state of her, I'd say he's capable of anything.'

Finn shakes his head. 'We need to wake Mum … We need the police.'

Holly moans again.

'She doesn't want that,' Jay says. 'Let's take her inside and get her some water. Someone should stay to take care of her; we'll reassess in the morning.'

'I'll sleep in her room,' Isla offers. 'If she gets worse, we'll call for help.'

Finn carries Holly inside, arms limp around his neck. Isla bends to shush the excited Cashew as he rushes them in the hall and Jay brings water from the kitchen, taking care on the creaking stairs. 'I've got this, Finn,' Isla said, kissing him on the lips after he's set Holly on the bed. 'Get some sleep. We'll talk tomorrow.'

Finn doesn't go to bed. He drags his duvet into the hall and spends the night on the floor outside her room.

Date rape. Ryan Campbell drugged his sister and took advantage of her – Isla and Jay tried to cover the blood and bruises on Holly, but they weren't quick enough.

In her bedroom Holly insists on cleaning herself. Isla worries about destroying evidence, but Holly won't be dissuaded. She turns her back while Holly strips and wipes and changes clothes. She makes her drink a glass of water, tucks her in.

Holly falls fast asleep.

Isla plugs her phone into Holly's charger, changes into another pair of Holly's pyjamas and settles on the floor with her back against the bed. She opens her Kindle app on her phone. It's going to be a long night.

In the hall, Finn leans against the wall and tries to rid himself of his yen for violence. It's early when Jay appears with mugs of tea. 'You okay?'

'Not really.'

'What do you think Holly will do – go to the police?'

Finn shrugs. 'That's her decision.' He wants her to, but during the hours he's had to think, he's concluded that Holly must call the shots, dictate what happens.

'She's probably scared,' Jay says. 'Of telling the truth … the implications. Her reputation.'

Holly's door opens and she catches the end of Jay's sentence. She frowns, steps over their legs. She goes into the bathroom, slams the door and turns on the shower. She emerges, hair washed and brushed, her face scrubbed of make-up.

The damage is hidden.

A few days later the photograph appeared.

It wasn't sent to Finn – not even Ryan was that crass. Jay showed him: likely he didn't know what it was initially, thumbing the photo open assuming it was another drunken pic from the party which might distract Finn.

His face changed and he tried to swipe the image away. It was Monday lunchtime and they were in the canteen. Finn had skipped PE to avoid seeing Ryan.

Finn looked up as the noise of the younger year groups swelled around them. 'What is it?'

'Nothing.' Jay slid the phone into his pocket.

At a nearby table a group of girls smothered laughter, glancing at Finn. Holly appeared in the doorway, phone in hand. She stopped, frowning at her screen. The laughter rose and twisted about her. She spun and darted out of the room. All around, people were looking at their phones, nudging one another.

'*What is it?*' A chill crept over Finn even in the warmth of the refectory.

Jay sighed. 'Just Ryan … bragging.'

'*Show me.*'

'No, Finn.'

Finn gritted his teeth. '*Show. Me.*'

The photo showed Holly in the cave, beer in hand. Provocative: dress slipping off her shoulder, exposing most of one breast, eyes heavy-lidded, smile sexy. Ryan sent it to a couple of mates, and they did the rest, sharing the image that she never meant for anyone else to see.

'Shit!' Finn overturned his chair. People stared, anticipating a scene.

Jay tugged at his arm. 'Sit down, mate.'

Finn shook him off. The picture would destroy Holly – if she wasn't strong enough to speak against Ryan Campbell before, she surely wouldn't be now. 'You saw that. People will think …'

Jay dragged him into his seat. 'It doesn't mean he didn't force her.'

'She hasn't accused him … She hasn't said a word.'

There was a stirring as heads turned towards the door. Ryan Campbell parted the crowds like water, a knot of mates around him, trademark smirk and swagger.

Finn went for him.

From: @QueenBee
To: @MidsummersChick

Hey, just reaching out, from one survivor to another … one damaged Shakespeare groupie to another lol. I love your content and the fact that you're not afraid to say what you think. The video you shared the other day was so powerful. You're right, WE shouldn't feel THEIR shame. But I think you're hurting and maybe you need someone to talk to offline. DM me if you want to chat …

Chapter 18

Now

Eve

I'm in shock after the detectives leave – Finn's revelation has blown me apart. After he spoke, Holly made a horrible, inhuman sound and fled the room.

Isherwood hustled her junior officer out, looking pissed off, and Gina sat everyone down, made Finn tell all.

When he's done, I leave him to Mum and Gina, and go after Holly.

She's locked herself in her room.

As I stand in the hallway calling her name, Cate appears wearing yoga leggings and a cropped sweatshirt, her pink hair in fishtail braids, immaculate wings of black eyeliner drawn on. She leans on the wall and meets my eye, sympathy in her expression.

'You know,' I say softly. 'Don't you?'

Cate nods, places a finger on her lips. She doesn't want Holly to hear us talking about her.

'She *told* you,' I whisper. 'She … *talks* to you?' It hurts, though I try not to show it.

'She *talked*,' Cate corrects. 'She doesn't anymore. And actually, she didn't need to say the words. It was obvious.'

I frown. 'How long has it been?'

'When I first arrived, she spoke to me, but since Jay died, she hasn't said a word.' My stomach drops. Holly has been silent with her family far longer than with this stranger.

I knock again, beg Holly to open up. I can't imagine what she's going through. When she doesn't answer, I slide to the floor, knees bent.

Cate hesitates, sits beside me mirroring my pose. 'This isn't the holiday you planned,' I say. 'I'm sorry; we haven't been looking after you.'

She shrugs elegant shoulders. For all her slightness, she's strong, with well-defined muscles. She's pretty, with a gentle, melodic voice and huge, dark eyes. There's a serenity about her, which I suppose is the draw for Holls. 'That's okay … it's not a holiday exactly. More … an escape.'

'I haven't been shopping. You must be running out of food—'

'We're quite self-sufficient. I've been cooking for everyone, your family too. I like cooking … and Naomi gives me a discount on my room rate so … win-win. Fran's got a car, when she's sober enough to drive it.' Cate pulls a face. 'So we can pop into town for groceries any time we want. If we were dependent on your mother to feed us, she'd have to rebrand this place as a weight loss camp.'

I smirk. 'Accurate.'

She smiles. It's nice to talk about something other than the drama Haven has been steeped in since I arrived. 'Well, if you need anything, let me know.'

Cate waves a hand. 'You've got enough to deal with. We're fine.'

'I don't want the guests to leave,' I admit. 'Mum can't afford to lose business.'

'Fran, Leah and I are definitely not going anywhere. There's folk going tomorrow, but they were scheduled to leave anyway. I'm not sure if anyone's checking the website for new bookings …'

I didn't think of that. 'I'll have a look later.'

Cate nods and stands. Her smile falters. 'You need to give her time, Eve. It's not personal … it's just that some of the artists and I know what she's going through. You know that's what Haven's about – it's where we heal.' Sadness swims in her eyes, but it's quickly gone, her serenity returning. She taps her knuckles on Holly's door. 'Holls, it's me. Open up.'

There's a pause and the door opens a bit, just enough to admit her. Cate slips through, and gives me another apologetic look before closing the door.

The rejection stings.

Most of the women who come here have been through trauma, but it's sobering coming up close and personal with it. I think about Fran's tale, and wonder about Cate's and Leah's stories.

In the kitchen, Struan's returned from his dog-walk. I'd love to take a stroll with him now, or a drive. Maybe go to Liath Bay to sit beneath the stars, wipe the memory of that night away and start over.

What would happen this time if he tried to kiss me?

But from the sounds of it, the wind and rain have started again in earnest, and dinner preparations are in progress. Gina is setting the table, pausing by my mother to squeeze her shoulders. Finn is lying on the sofa.

Kirsty dishes up the stew. There's something cosy and domestic about the scene, but it's dispelled by a simmering pulse of grief and worry. My mother startles from a reverie when the plate lands in front of her. 'Struan,' she says. 'Be a love and pop down to the cellar for some wine.'

'Is that a good idea?' I pull out a chair, inhale the bittersweet scent curling from my plate.

Mum glares at me. 'I can't think of a single reason why not, Eve.'

'It's just a glass of wine,' Gina says. 'There's little enough joy at the moment.'

'I'll fetch a bottle,' Struan says, and heads for the cellar steps.

'Make it two,' my mother calls after him. 'And mind the door; the latch sticks. Don't close it all the way or you'll get stuck. I've been meaning to fix it.'

I roll my eyes: another thing broken and ignored. She's always *meaning to* fix something …

Kirsty sits beside me, glances at Holly's empty place. 'Holls not joining us?'

I shake my head. 'Cate's with her.' I'm desperate for my sister to talk to me, but I don't know where to start – what's happened to her is too huge, too catastrophic. It takes her farther from me to a realm I can't reach.

Struan emerges from the cellar, brushing cobwebs from his hair and brandishing two bottles of red. Gina likes her wine, and has built a decent collection, none of it so precious she doesn't want it to be enjoyed.

We eat and try to pretend things are normal, that my sister isn't upstairs coming apart at the seams, that we're not all reeling from the death of a boy who was nearly family, that there's no police officer lurking in the den – ostensibly here to support, but more like standing guard.

The food is good, the conversation stilted. In the middle of the meal, Gina puts her fork down and bursts into tears. 'My Jay,' she wails. 'My poor boy.' She wipes her eyes, but tears keep coming. 'And *Holly*, I can't believe all this is happening …'

Finn puts down his fork. 'I'm not hungry—'

Mum points at him with her wine goblet. She's had two large glasses, and her hand is unsteady. 'Don't move. You're not going upstairs. We should be together at a time like this.'

Finn ducks his head, hair falling forward. 'Holly gets to hide.'

I see a flush stain his cheekbones. Mum takes another gulp of wine. 'I won't dignify that with a response.'

Gina links her fingers through Mum's. 'Come, Nae, let's go and put a film on and distract ourselves. It might be a night to be together, but it's not a night to drink. Everyone's too fragile.'

She's right. There's a bit of me that feels the same tug towards oblivion my mother does ... the desire to drink until the pain fades, blast light and music and *life* defiantly into the darkness around Haven. To thoroughly drown our sorrows until they are obliterated.

I start to clear the table, but Struan stops me. 'I'll do the dishes; you go and sit with Kirsty and finish your wine.'

Kirsty and Finn have retreated to the sofa, Kirst on her phone, Finn lost in thoughts.

'You've already chauffeured my brother about, chopped the wood, walked the dog ... you don't need to clean up too.'

'I want to help,' Struan says evenly, a hint of hurt in his voice.

I lean against the counter. 'No one *can*.' We look at each other for a long moment and I wonder if he's remembering Liath Bay too.

Ben Carmichael comes in from the den and puts his coffee cup on the side. 'I'll be off now, Eve. I'll be back in the morning. I'll let you know as soon as we get word on the post-mortem.' He grabs his fluorescent jacket from the hook on the door.

'I thought he might move in,' I grumble, when he's gone. I wonder if Struan plans to stay. He's one of my best mates; the thought of him sleeping over has never felt awkward before ...

'I should head as well,' he says.

'I'll walk you out.' We stand on the steps, watching Ben's tail lights disappear down the track. I'm not sure what Struan's waiting for. We haven't had our moment yet, and I'm not sure when we will.

He fits our hands together, palm to palm.

My breath catches. 'Thanks for taking care of Finn today.'

'No problem. It was tough seeing the kids like that. The head is talking about a special assembly for Jay when school goes back. There's talk of a vigil in town tomorrow too – it's all over social media.'

'A vigil?'

He nods. 'I'll pick you up if you like.'

I nod. *I like.*

Struan's thumb brushes my palm, so barely I might have imagined it. I don't have a blueprint for us. I don't know what I want. 'Stru,' I whisper, catching at his hand, trying to preserve the moment.

He steps away, curt now. 'Tomorrow, we'll talk.'

I watch him walk into the wild dark, weather buffeting him as he jogs to the car. Back in the kitchen, Kirsty and Finn have cleared up, put the leftovers away and stacked the dishwasher. She pours three glasses of wine, and we pile back onto the sofa. Finn's head is on my shoulder and my feet are draped across Kirsty's lap. Finn's reading an old Stephen King novel of mine. 'You shouldn't ply a minor with drink,' I tell Kirsty, mock severe.

Finn shifts against me, and I wonder if he's tormenting himself for his outburst, for outing Holly.

What he did to Ryan Campbell makes sense now, but to have kept Holly's secret so long only to blurt it out … he must feel shit about that.

I want to talk to him about everything – the fight, the night Holly was hurt. I want to know how they could have kept something so major from me.

I feel sick. *Holly, drugged and raped …*

'It's only a glass,' Kirsty says, leaning past me to grin at my brother. I wonder what she'd say about him keeping Jay's drug dealing from the police in order to protect her boyfriend.

I pray Gav isn't involved.

But maybe there's a link between Jay's death and the drugs, the world he found himself in. The police obviously think there's more to what happened than mere accident, but we'll need the post-mortem to tell us more.

The prospect of someone out there on the cliff with Jay is scary.

Someone who meant him harm? I try to push the apprehension aside, sip my wine and draw the comfort of Haven around me.

We stay up later than we should, like we can't bear to break company and venture into the night alone. When tiredness overtakes us, we finally make a move. I'm drained from the day, exhausted by revelations, bad news, overthinking. I check the doors are locked – we rarely bother, but my mother's anxiety has rattled me.

Kirsty turns out the lights, disappears into the spare room with a yawn. When I come out of the bathroom, Finn has taken up residence on the floor outside Holly's bedroom. He has his pillow as if he means to sleep there.

'Finn,' I say, sliding down the wall next to him. 'She doesn't need you to keep watch over her ... She's safe.'

'She wasn't though,' he says, breath catching. 'I let her walk into the fucking *dragon's den* alone. It's my fault what happened to her.'

'Tell me,' I say, and draw the edge of his blanket over me to share warmth. There's a creeping draught, a chill in the midnight air.

Speaking in a murmur lest Holly wake and hear us, he describes the party, the fullness of the night, the velvet sky, the fresh breath of the sea.

Holly flirting with Ryan, the state of her when Jay brought her out of the cave.

'I don't understand why she went willingly with *Ryan Campbell*.'

Finn shrugs. 'Layla said she was acting weird. She thought Holly was trying to make Jay jealous. Things had changed between them, but I don't know why and now I can't ask him.'

I stare at the wall, the shifting shadows.

'It's my fault,' Finn repeats. 'I should have paid attention, stopped her going with Ryan.'

He tells me about the photograph Ryan took and sent to everyone in school – the reason Holly couldn't go back. I hate the idea of everyone gossiping over her, staring, the nasty messages, calling her a slag …

He tells me about the fight in the canteen, how he slipped into a space where he couldn't think, only act. It grows so late – *early* – that we're both nodding off, cramped on the floor. Eventually, I stumble to my feet. 'I need to sleep, Finn. It's almost morning. We should get the post-mortem results today.'

His eyes are closed, breathing even. I think he's asleep, so perhaps I imagine the fear that flickers across his features.

And perhaps I don't.

From: @QueenBee
To: @MidsummersChick

I'm so glad we connected on here. Thanks for sharing your story. Sadly, it's not unusual. So many women know their attackers, but to have to keep seeing him day after day … that must be TOUGH. Makes sense that you've stopped going to school. I don't know about you, but I get so angry when I think about all the women and girls (and boys too) falling victim to this culture of toxic masculinity, where these guys think they can just take what they want and get away with it. Help is out there, and I feel like reaching out to me was your first step. I'm going to send you some links to articles I found helpful when I was recovering.

Chapter 19

Eve

Tuesday dawns clear and bright, clouds sweeping away to reveal a duck-egg-blue sky. Behind Haven, the hills are bright with bracken, everything lush and damp from the rain.

Finn and I are like zombies when we make it downstairs. Kirsty looks like she slept badly too. She pulls on her coat after breakfast and says she has to get home to the baby. Mum, Gina and Holly haven't surfaced, and I send Finn back to bed after he picks at a piece of toast; he's pale this morning.

The post-mortem looms.

I try not to think of them cutting Jay open – of cold, metal tables and shiny implements, gowns and masks and blood washing down drains. I mooch about the house until Ben arrives, and we drink coffee in the kitchen. 'Bit of a scene yesterday,' Ben says, still rubbing his hands together from the autumn chill as I pass him a steaming mug.

'Yes,' I say. I don't want to get into Holly's business, or dwell on my brother's sins, but I'm not above taking advantage of Ben's propensity for a gossip. 'Any idea what DI Isherwood is thinking? Does she have a theory about Jay?'

He's cagier than I expect. 'The bruises have given her something to think about. His injuries too.' I nod, say nothing in the hope he will continue talking. 'She's new to these parts. Just moved to the Highlands from Glasgow, keen to prove herself.'

'Uh-huh.' My tone is mild interest. I'm intrigued by Isherwood, and I don't want to put Ben off.

'They don't understand island policing, these folks from the central belt. Different kettle of fish out here. She's been promoted young, but the word is she had to get out of Glasgow – bad business there; she blew the whistle on some corruption scandal … involving her man … who also happened to be her senior officer. She's hard as nails, apparently.

'On the way from the ferry she was telling me she's glad to be in the Highlands, though – nearer her mother and her disabled wee sister apparently.' He blows on his coffee. 'Waste of time bringing that big drink of water: Campbell; he's nae use to man nor beast that one.' He smirks. 'Mark you, his days on this case are over before they started, thanks to thon wee display yesterday.'

I struggle to feel sympathy for Harris Campbell.

Later, I arrange ferry passage for me and Gina to the mainland to view Jay's body. She doesn't need to, but says it's important to see him. Maybe, like me, she needs something to do, needs to get off the island for a bit.

There's still no word from Jay's dad when we depart. Mum watches us go from the steps of Haven. She's wearing flared jeans and an old sweatshirt of Gina's. She pretends she doesn't mind as she waves us down the drive, but I know she does. Her absence from my graduation was one thing, her inability to support Gina today quite another.

'You stay and keep an eye on Holly,' Gina said kindly, as they hugged goodbye. *Excuses, again.*

Mum shivered and looked around with that watchful, wary

stare I see whenever she's not inside Haven's walls. The police searched the outbuildings again at my request. They found those same signs of a fire in one of the rotten barns, scuff marks etched on the floor that gave them pause, nothing significant. They just think it was Jay or the twins mucking about, not a sign of an interloper. In my rational mind I agree, but Finn's denying ever going in there.

The crossing is smooth, the water flat and reflective. Calm falls over me as we stand on deck and watch the island recede.

We are shown into a viewing room. Gina holds my hand so tightly as we wait that my bones ache afterwards. Jay is covered in a sheet, only his face visible. I've never seen a dead body before but there's no mistaking it – the cold stillness, the pallor. I try not to think about what lies beneath that sheet, the scars and stitching from the ordeals he's been through.

The post-mortem was conducted before we arrived and we're still waiting for the results, the confirmation of exactly how he died.

I can't see the damage the rocks did to his skull, but I can see a dark cluster of bruising on his left cheekbone.

Gina clutches my hand tighter. We are out of the room in minutes, but that memory of it will cling to me forever. I wish I'd taken the time to get to know Jay better, taken the trouble to *like* him better.

We cross the sound again, silent. We drive in silence too, detouring past a supermarket to alleviate my guilt at not taking better care of the artists. Gina trails me round the store, as I mindlessly throw items into a trolley, fights me at the checkout over who's paying for the haul, wordlessly helps me to load the boot with bags.

Back on the road, the light has dulled, the sky turning a dimpled, dull colour. 'Are you coming to the vigil tonight?' I ask, as we make the final turn towards Haven.

'I suppose I ought to,' she says. She turns to me, blinking back tears. 'I'd only just started to get to know him, Eve. I wish we'd had longer. I could have been a better aunt.'

'We can always be better,' I say, thinking of my siblings and the times I wasn't there. 'But you're being too hard on yourself. You took him in when he had no one.' I hand Gina into my mother's care, and check on the twins – they're in Finn's room playing a video game, thumbs and eyes darting as they annihilate some nasty-looking creatures onscreen. Here they can banish the demons, get the bad guys.

Holly's ever-present green sketchbook is by her side, and she reaches for the book as I come in, concealing it with her hand. I lean down and kiss her cheek. It's nice to see the twins together.

I leave them to their killing spree and pad through the house. In the studio the artists are gathered at their easels. Leah is working on a canvas – a haunting self-portrait with eyes that draw me in. There's a sinister figure in the background of the painting, cast in shadow. Leah looks up and gives me a gentle smile as I gaze at the painting over her shoulder. There's a poignancy to her work that catches hold of me and won't let go.

In the guest wing I unpack shopping into the fridge, clear the living room of last night's glasses, turn on the dishwasher and leave fresh linen on the landing.

Then I set up my laptop at the kitchen table, make a pot of tea to keep me going and start work on an assignment due in a few days. I'm supposed to write a gothic-inspired ghost story. I'm not in the mood. With my mother's paranoia, a real mystery enfolding me and secrets and grief rippling through the house, truth is stranger than fiction now.

Haven feels *too remote* suddenly ...

Despite my conviction that there's nothing to be scared of, the walls close in, melancholy enveloping me as I stare at my screen and wait for news or inspiration.

There's still no word from DI Isherwood when we leave for the vigil. Ben went off duty at lunchtime, but said he'll see us in town later. He cautioned us against impatience: they rushed through the post-mortem, but the report could take a while …

Mum is morose when we leave, a mood not even Gina can cajole her out of. Leah, Fran and Cate are piling into Fran's battered blue car on the drive when Struan pulls up to give me, Gina and the twins a lift. I stand amid a swirl of fiery leaves, waiting. Sliding into the driver's seat, Cate smiles. 'Heading to the vigil?'

I nod.

'Us too.' She watches Gina, Finn and Holly struggle into the back of Struan's car. 'Would it help if Holly came with us? More room.'

I look at my sister. She's wearing a puffa coat, cropped Uggs, leggings – I'm cold just looking at her bare ankles. Her hair is braided in what I recognise as one of Cate's trademark styles, and she has on a blue wool headband I've never seen before, a cable pattern knitted into the neon band.

Holly stops shoving at Finn to make him move over. She springs out of the car and joins the artists almost joyfully, slipping into the back with Leah while Fran bustles importantly into the passenger seat having delegated the driving to Cate. 'Right,' I say to no one since Cate's already pulling away. 'I assume that's a yes.'

'Come on, Eve,' Finn says impatiently. 'Get in; we'll be late. Holls is fine with them—'

I look back towards the house. Purple dusk has fallen like a cloak, draped over the rooftops, and the wind is picking up again, stirring leaves and branches in a ghostly dance, shivering around the corners of the stone building. Two more artists left this morning, and the three who remain – in addition to Cate, Fran and Leah – went out for dinner and drinks. Too late, I realise that Mum is completely alone at Haven and will remain so until we return.

In her state of mind, that's not ideal.

She has Cashew, which is some comfort. He can protect her

from living and breathing dangers, but he'll be helpless against the demons in her head.

Finn

It's hard to find a parking space. It seems like half the island is here. Small bonfires burn on the headland as we ditch the car on the outskirts of town and walk back towards the harbour.

Ben is here – in an unofficial capacity by the looks of it. He's on the main street, leaning against an unmarked car, arms folded, watching the crowd that bunches along the harbour wall. When we reach the centre of town, the vigil is marked by banners and candles, a bunch of those lanterns that come with eco warnings and safety concerns. The Holly of old would have something to say about that.

One of the cafés has opened late and a queue snakes from the door into the street, people turning collars to the cold and stamping their feet as they wait for hot drinks. It's blustery. When we light candles and join the throng, I have to cup my hand around my flame to keep it glowing.

I see kids from school, some crying, huddled in groups, sharing heat and comfort. We're spotted and hustled towards the front of the crowd. Everyone wants to hug Gina, and she gets overwhelmed quickly. I suggest hot chocolate, put an arm around her shoulders and steer her away.

'Thanks, Finn,' she says, as we step into the warmth of the café. 'It's just a lot.'

Love for Gina squeezes my heart. She's been another mother to me more than half my life, loved me and Holls, as she might have loved Jay.

My throat aches. I've lost Jay; Holly's slipping away. I can't lose Gina too, but that's out of my hands now.

Chapter 20

Eve

While Finn and Gina head across the road for drinks, Struan and I find a spot at the back of the crowd. I wonder if we're about to have the conversation we've teetered on the brink of.

Not that the vigil for a dead teenager is the place, but I can't bear waiting any longer. As we pressed through the throng, I felt his hand on my back, warm through my coat. A protective gesture … or something more? His hand remained when we stopped.

I stretch on tiptoe, scan the harbour for sign of Holly.

Struan flashes me a smile that reminds me of him as a schoolboy passing me notes. Strange to think he's now the teacher.

Above the heads, I spot Gav: a glimpse of his vibrant red beard. He's carrying Mac, Kirsty snuggled close to his side. A proper little family.

I hope Gav doesn't prove to be mixed up in the drugs stuff. I see Gavin's mate, the one Finn says is caught up in it all. I only know him by a derivation of his surname; no one calls him anything else. *Ketty*. A bit of a lad, a wide boy. Someone I kept away from at school. I've socialised with him a few times since

Kirsty and Gav got serious, and he's nice enough. I never thought he'd be involved in anything as serious as dealing – though with a name like that perhaps I shouldn't be surprised.

Ketty and Gav greet one another with shoulder slaps and fist bumps, both grinning. Ketty tickles Mac's tummy, kisses Kirsty on the cheek.

Struan's hand shifts at my back. His lips are close to my ear as he whispers, 'You okay?'

'Not very,' I say, and he nods. Pulls me closer.

Someone starts singing and others join in. The voices soar, eerie and soulful, into the smoky night. The singing, the flying banners, the flames on the hillside lit in Jay's honour – it's so dreamlike. Struan's presence, solid at my back, anchors me to reality, and I lean close. I know I shouldn't ...

Perhaps he's the greatest dream of all ... the thing least likely to be real in all of this. Struan slides his arm more firmly around me as the singing lulls. 'How are the twins?'

I shrug. I could pretend we're huddling together against the low temperatures but it's not true. Butterflies skitter. 'There's stuff I should have known. They've kept so many secrets ...'

He accepts my unspoken rebuke – he's kept their secrets too. Surely he didn't know about Holly ...

'What is this?' I say softly, after a beat of supple silence.

'What do you want it to be?' His hand on my back stills and I'm scared he'll remove it.

'I don't know. That night ... on the beach, what did that mean?'

'Maybe it was just a kiss.'

I turn to face him, search his eyes. 'You don't believe that.'

'No,' he says softly. 'I don't. But you were clear—'

'That's not it. I wasn't ... I wasn't saying no, I was ...' I am flustered. Of course it felt like *no*. I fled the kiss, the beach, the island. I've barely been back, and we haven't talked about it. 'I was scared,' I say. 'Of ruining our friendship.'

A muscle tightens in his cheek. 'How's that worked out?'

'I know,' I say. 'And I'm sorry. I've wished so many times since …' I bury my face in his chest. The embrace is both friendly and … not. The silence between us is febrile.

After a moment, he presses his lips to my hairline. His arms around me tighten. My heart settles to a steady, contented thump. 'Will you come home with me tonight?' I blurt.

I'm certain he's going to say no, but he nods. I close my eyes with relief.

I open them quickly. *I still haven't found my sister.* 'Struan, can you see Holls anywhere?'

He cranes his neck. 'No, but she'll be with the artists. Look, that's Finn's girlfriend over there.' I follow his gaze to a tall, auburn-haired girl among a bunch of teens. She's looking around, biting her thumbnail.

Finn rejoins us with Gina, both carrying cardboard cups. Finn grins, and I realise how this must look: Struan and I entwined like a couple. Gina smiles too: she's eager for hope, for love to blunt the edges of grief.

I sip my hot chocolate, edge away from Struan. The red-haired girl catches sight of Finn. She detaches herself from the group, starts towards us. Finn slips out of our fold, muttering something I can't catch, heads in the opposite direction. The girl grimaces and returns to her friends who close ranks and console.

'Where are you going?' I call after Finn. He should be in one of those huddles – the boys in dark hoodies and girls in cropped jumpers. Young voices – no thought to censure or curtail themselves – slice the night, their hearts on their sleeves.

Holly should be there too.

Finn's tone is flint. 'I need to find her.'

Gina spots friends and goes to talk to them. Struan and I walk along the harbour wall, weaving between groups. The smell of fish and chips stings the air and for a moment the evening feels festive, before I catch myself. Struan excuses himself to the chip van, checking if I want anything.

Imogen Isherwood stalks towards me, a wool coat over her suit. Her hair is in its customary sleek ponytail, her lips chapped with cold. 'Eve,' she says when she accosts me, 'apologies for disturbing you.' She's trailed by Ben Carmichael, looking as if he'd rather be anywhere else. No sign of Harris after his unprofessional outburst.

I am weary of her, and being confronted *here* shortens my temper. 'What can I do for you, Inspector?'

Imogen looks tired. 'It's not about Jay,' she says. 'The pathologist is dragging his heels getting me that report … I won't share findings with Gina until I'm sure—'

Ominous. Or perhaps my imagination.

'What do you want?'

She clears her throat, scrapes the toe of her boot against the harbour. 'I wondered, does your sister need to speak to me – in a professional capacity?'

I'd love Holly to seek justice, bring the weight of the law crashing down on the boy who broke her. But I know she won't. Even if she did make a complaint, I don't think it'd go anywhere. I'm not even certain she's accused him of the offence aloud. Finn called it out, not her.

It seemed obvious, given the state they found her in; Layla's testimony that she went off with Ryan; the photograph he sent … But it's not evidence, it's not enough.

'She hasn't accused Ryan of anything,' I say. 'She hasn't spoken about what happened.'

'I understand. If she changes her mind …'

I nod, and Imogen turns away. She glances back at me. 'It shouldn't be as it is. It should be easier for victims like Holly. I know what it's like to be a woman in a man's world, and have your choices removed. I know what it is to be a sister too, to want to shield them at all costs.' She pauses like she's said too much, gives a quick nod. 'These are hard times for your family and with the post-mortem the ordeal isn't over yet. I'm sorry you're dealing with all this.'

I frown. Commiserating with me is not her role. I don't know if I like seeing this softer side. I'm conflicted. The tight-arse detective doesn't fit with this woman who empathises with what it means to be a victim like Holly, or a sister who can't erase their suffering.

'What was that about?' Struan asks, slipping his arm about me again – his touch is starting to feel normal. I relay our conversation. 'Weird that she'd approach you now about Holly …'

'I don't know. I think it was … kind.'

But there was something about her expression, her tone when she said the ordeal wasn't over … Does she know something? Should I be worried? Surely things can't get any worse for us.

From: @QueenBee
To: @MidsummersChick

You're so right, it's the predators who should be in therapy, not us. I understand your decision not to seek counselling at the moment. As long as you're talking to someone, that's okay. You have to keep talking, chick, especially since you don't talk in the real world (thanks for sharing btw; I'm honoured you felt able to tell me something so personal). Bottling up your emotions is dangerous. I'm scared for you, with your rapist still walking free, and still with easy access to you … That's a lot. Keep reaching out. We might not know each other IRL but I'm here for you all the same.

Chapter 21

Finn

The crowd at the vigil disperses after the songs are sung, prayers murmured that I doubt would have meant anything to Jay, but are oddly comforting.

As we head back to the car, I see Ryan Campbell with his brother and parents. He is relaxed, a confident smile flashing in the moonlight as he laughs at something his dad says. He rearranges his hair with his fingers, checks his reflection in his phone. He looks pleased with himself, untroubled.

I still hate him for the way he's treated my sister.

Along the harbour, the candle flames are snuffed, banners drooping. Gina catches up and links an arm through mine. She's been crying again, tears staining her cheeks pink. 'I just saw the detective. She said she'll be over in the morning to discuss the post-mortem.'

'We were supposed to get the results today.'

Gina shrugs. 'So it took longer than they expected; there was a backlog or something.'

'Did she give any indication of what they found?' Eve leans in to join our conversation. She and Struan have been cosy tonight, shooting lingering looks that anyone with half a brain can interpret. Good for them – Eve deserves happiness, and Struan makes her happy even if she won't admit it.

I tense at the question, and Gina pats my arm with mittened fingers. 'No. I suppose we will find out if the injuries he received before he died are significant.' Pain fogs her eyes. 'They *can't* think that someone would deliberately … I mean, *who*? *Why*?'

My heart thunders. I feel Gina's eyes on me. 'No one …' I mutter, wishing it were true.

Eve tucks a strand of hair behind her ear. 'Let's go. It's cold and I want to get back to Mum; she's been on her own too long. Where *is* Holly?'

'I found her, but she wouldn't come with me,' I say. She's with the artists. Suddenly, that bothers me more than it should. I break away from the others as I catch sight of Cate's pink hair, the brilliant blue of Holly's headband.

Holly doesn't get it – *we must stick together*.

'Finn …' Eve calls, but I ignore her. 'We need to *go*—'

'Come back with us, Holls,' I say, catching up and grabbing my sister's arm.

Holly tries to pull away. For a moment I hold on and see a flash of fear in her eyes. I drop her arm immediately, remorseful. 'Sorry …' I don't know what came over me, grabbing her like that.

Fran steps between us, furious. 'Leave her. She clearly doesn't want to go with you.'

I peer past Fran's bristling, imposing bulk. Holly is rubbing her arm – bit much; I didn't *hurt* her. I'd never hurt her. Leah hovers protectively at my sister's side and Cate twirls the car keys, frowning. Behind me, I hear Eve call my name again.

'Sorry, Holls,' I try again, ignoring the artists. 'It's just been a rough night—' To my horror, my voice cracks.

Cate's expression softens. 'Perhaps you should be with your family tonight,' she tells Holly, glancing between us.

Fran is still standing between me and my sister, glaring; I've gone down in her estimation tonight. I swipe a hand through my hair.

'Finn!' Eve's patience snaps; she shrieks my name this time.

Holly edges past Fran who looks like she might make another attempt to stop her. Cate puts a gentling hand on the older woman's arm. 'She's fine, Frannie.'

I'm pissed off – who is *she* to grant permission – but I bite my tongue. Cate and the others have been good friends to Holly these past weeks, I can't deny that. I'm on edge, and taking out my mood on the wrong people. Jay's death is a raw, gaping wound tonight.

Holly looks uncertain, but she comes with me, glancing back at her friends. Unconventional they may be but they're tight. If they're anything like my mother's usual guests, they've been through stuff – the kind of stuff that makes you wary ... protective.

It's an uncomfortable journey, a squash in the back. Eve is irritated as we drive out of town, following the artists' car. There's plenty of room in theirs. It was a stupid battle to pick when there are others I could choose to fight. Holly going back with the artists made more sense; but for some reason it seemed imperative that she come with us, so I might stand a chance of keeping her with us when we get back to Haven.

It was nice when she came to my room and played video games. It felt like old times. I want more of it.

I want her to *trust me* again.

And it feels safer, somehow, to keep her close.

The rain starts up on the way home. Twice the tyres slew on a corner. Each time Struan tightens his grip on the wheel and Eve tenses, but manages to keep her emotions in check.

It's a torrent by the time we get home. At Haven, we find Mum reading and dozing on the kitchen sofa. I immediately spot the knife on the table beside her – I'm the first to cross the room and lean down for a hug. The blade gives me a jolt of shock. Mum wakes, meets my eyes with a guilty grimace. She whispers, 'I got scared. Silly, I know, but I hate when the house is empty—'

I slide the knife into my sleeve and return it to the block. I don't want Eve seeing and having a go at her. Yes, Mum's paranoid. Yes, sitting in the dark with a knife in her hand seems deranged, but that's not an argument to have tonight and Eve won't be able to help herself.

Fran invites Gina and Mum to the guest wing for a nightcap and they accept. Eve makes tea and sits at the table texting Kirsty while Struan challenges me and Holly to a game of cards. I play with half a mind on my hand, and lose. Holly is eager to escape the game and get back on her phone. A smile touches her lips as she taps the screen.

I frown: she's always on it, but who is she talking to?

Gina and Mum return after an hour or so. 'We're off to bed,' Mum says. She seems calm again, no sign of the woman who needed a kitchen knife to feel safe in her own home.

I watch Gina swallow another sleeping pill at the sink. She and Mum hold hands as they climb the stairs.

I stand and stretch. 'I'm going up too. You coming, Holls?' I need to kill more zombies to numb my brain, and I hope Holly will join me.

She gets up, sketchbook in her hand – like her phone, the book is attached to her.

We leave Struan and Eve to it – I'm not getting in the midst of the debate that rages silently between them as they continue to make eyes at each other across the kitchen and try to pretend they don't want to race upstairs and rip each other's clothes off.

Gross.

Still, sex is supposed to be life-affirming. Makes sense – giving death the finger, taking back control ... Life is short, and all that, but it's also good.

I push the thought aside. It only makes me want Isla. I draw a sharp breath at a memory of her, start up the game and swiftly put a broadsword through the skull of the nearest zombie to quell my need. I can't have Isla now ...

She needs to think my interest has waned, because I can't share the reason we can't be together. I'm afraid if we spend time together she'll figure it out for herself.

What I've done.

Holly hesitates at my door. I look up from the game. She's holding her sketchbook and the look on her face is trusting again, like she expects me to have answers.

I sigh. She comes across the room to me. We hugged in the garden the other night when I was trying to bring her back to Haven, but that felt more like violence than comfort. Now she melts into me. A moment later, she's patting my back as if it's *me* who needs comforting. It takes me aback at first, but she's not wrong …

I sniff back tears. When we part, she looks at me, *really* looks at me. She's scared, and I pull myself together. Holly needs me strong. It's getting harder and harder to keep it together …

For a moment, the curtain lifts on her blankness and I see her as she was – not just a week ago, or six weeks, before the cave and the party and that strange simmering summer with Jay. *Years* melt away and she is sun and fire, all sassy brilliance. With Mum's artistic temperament, Eve's smarts, the snarky sense of humour that's all her own.

Before the bullies got in her head.

Before him.

She signs, struggling to spell the word, because why would she know the sign for that? *Post-mortem …*

I touch a finger to my lips. 'Holls. We can't talk about it …'

Irritation flares from her fingers. Only she could sign with a tone. It almost makes me smile.

Fine. Then the library, Finn … I think about all the times I've tried, begged, *bullied* her to talk. For ages, nothing. *Now* she's chatty. She's got my attention … *We should talk about it,* she signs.

Ironic, really – I'd laugh if I didn't feel so much like crying again. 'We can't.'

She makes an impatient sound. Any sound from her is a gift, even the scoff of a sister who wants to throttle me.

'I hit him,' I say, my voice so low it slides into the dark and disappears. 'I hit Jay in the library on Friday – how is that going to look?'

She doesn't have an answer, just looks at me steadily. I close my eyes. When I open them again, the curtain has fallen. Holly's mask is back in place. Her eyes slip away, and she drifts out of the door.

Chapter 22

Eve

Struan is in my bed and I'm not sure how he got here.

I mean, we've been heading here for weeks, months – maybe forever. But I don't know how we crossed that line *tonight*. We danced around it for hours after the vigil, drank wine and chatted, low and confidential. Let affection and comfort slide into something else. The emotions swirling around Haven intensify my desire: grief and regret, and the sense of time lost.

Once we hit the stairs, we're committed. 'We're acting like kids,' Struan whispers, smothering a laugh as we dart into my room, our hands everywhere.

We're kissing before the door closes and it's not like it was at Liath Bay – that awkward, tentative kiss I didn't see coming. It's so much more.

I need tonight before tomorrow comes and brings what it will. I need *him*.

I fall asleep in his arms with a smile, at peace for the first time since I got here.

We are rudely woken just after 2 a.m., jolted from sleep by hammering on the front door. I jerk upright; Struan is already scrambling from the bed, pulling on his jeans. As we run down the hall, Holly's pale face peers out from her bedroom. Thumping footsteps echo behind me, overtaking me as Finn takes the final three stairs in a leap, wincing when he lands on his bad knee. The knocking comes again. Cashew starts frenetic barking as Finn fumbles with the locks.

Holly creeps behind us. I can smell her coconut shampoo. The door to the artists' wing cracks open and Leah, Fran and Cate peer through. 'What's going on?' Fran demands, slurring – she must have kept on the gin after Mum and Gina left.

Where *are* Mum and Gina?

'We haven't opened it yet.' Fear and tiredness make me snappy. Why is that bloody door not locked? Not everything in this house is the artists' business.

Finn opens the door, a gust of cold wrapping my ankles. I feel underdressed in a T-shirt, and tug at the hem. At least Struan's clothed, but Finn and Holly must both have seen him emerging from my bedroom, still pulling on his top.

Ben Carmichael's face is lined with weariness. He's not in uniform, but his cruiser is in the drive, blue lights circling. The lights and the hour suggest urgency. 'Sorry,' he says. 'I know it's the middle of the night, but I need to come in.'

My heart races as Finn pulls the door wide to admit him.

'You need to get Gina,' Ben says as we pile into the kitchen, family and guests alike, but I can't bring myself to object.

'And Mum,' I say, as Finn makes a move for the stairs. Holly presses closer to my side, frightened.

Ben says gravely, 'She's not here. There's been an accident.'

That doesn't make sense. 'Of course Mum's here.' She probably took one of the sleeping pills too, slept through the commotion with Gina, cuddled up in their big bed. 'It's not possible,' I say stupidly. 'Mum's upstairs. Sleeping.'

Finn halts, his hand on the doorknob.

Ben shakes his head. 'No, she's not. She's in a helicopter on her way to hospital. She crashed her car into the bridge in the glen a couple of hours ago. She's in a bad way.'

Chapter 23

Eve

The hours before dawn are spent in jittery wakefulness. More tea, more questions we can't answer.

Gina's fingers twist in the roots of her hair. 'I don't *get* it. Where the hell was she going?' No one replies. 'I mean, was she *meeting someone*?' Gina persists, needing facts to cling to.

The twins are on the sofa, shivering with shock. The room is toasty, the Aga emitting reliable, reassuring heat. Struan is opposite me at the table, hair rumpled. Lying in his arms fades to a distant memory.

I feel a stab of guilt that I was with him while Mum's car was spinning into the river, as Jay lay dead on a gurney in the dark, and my sister cried herself to sleep.

'I didn't hear her go out,' Gina frets. 'I'm never taking those damn pills again.'

Fran, Leah and Cate leave us to it. Ben goes home to grab a couple of hours' sleep. He's told us all he can: Mum made it less than five miles from Haven when she lost control and hit the bridge. A young farmer on his way home from his girlfriend's place came round the corner as the crash occurred. He saw Mum hit the bridge, slide towards the river. He called the police, then called his dad and they got a tractor down with a hefty tow rope.

Along with Ben they they made sure the car wasn't submerged, swept away. Probably saved her life.

For now.

She has a head injury. It looks likely she'll need surgery, but we'll know more once her test results come back. Struan gets on his phone, checking the timings of the first crossing in the morning, booking tickets.

'I *hate* living on an island,' Finn says wrathfully. 'We should be with her.'

'They wouldn't let us see her anyway,' I say. But I know what he means. We are stranded, at the mercy of tides and timetables. 'She's being kept unconscious.' Gina called the hospital earlier and got only the briefest of updates. Mum's stable, but critical: her other injuries are superficial; the head trauma is serious.

I can picture the accident and its aftermath – helicopter blades scurrying through wet treetops, searchlights bleaching a scene of crushed metal, flattened grass and crumbled masonry. I can even see her pulling on her tall boots and ancient rain jacket as though nipping out to the field with Cashew or going to pick produce from her herb garden. But taking the car keys from the hook above the door? Opening the garage and sliding into the driver seat of the old car we've had forever?

No, I can't see that. Can't picture her driving down the track and onto the road.

The car's been Finn's since I left home, and he got his licence – what use is a car to someone who can't go more than a hundred metres from her front door? Suddenly I remember something. 'I thought the car wasn't working. Dodgy brakes, Mum said.' I turn my gaze on Finn. 'Was that it? If the brakes weren't working, maybe that's why she crashed.'

Doesn't explain why she was out there in the first place.

Finn shrugs. 'They were … grinding a bit, that's all.' He

drops his head, colour flaring in his cheeks – like it does when he's *lying*.

'She might have died,' Gina says, deathly pale. 'She still might. After everything we've been through with Jay … How could she be so stupid?'

'That's the ferry booked,' Struan says quietly. He gives my shoulder a squeeze. 'Shall I get out of your way?'

'No.' I don't even have to think about it. I don't care that Gina, Finn and Holly bear witness to my desperation. 'Stay …'

Finn

Fuck. Fuck. Fuck.

I pace, full of adrenaline. Gina eyes me like she wants to tell me to stop, but doesn't – each to our own way of coping. She's tearing at her hair so hard I think she might pull it out at the roots. I glance at Holly. She's on her phone, typing. It's been beeping constantly, and she snatches it up every time.

Eve is thinking, questioning, her brain firing a million miles an hour behind those clever eyes as she tries to piece things together. She wants a reasonable explanation for Mum to have left Haven. Gina does too.

I could give them one.

I need something else, something to throw Eve off the scent.

I wait until she goes to the bathroom, then follow her into the hall. She jumps when I step out of the shadows. 'What are you *doing*?'

'I need to talk to you. Alone.' I glance over my shoulder. Golden light from the kitchen spills around the door.

Eve switches on a lamp, sits wearily on the step. She's thrown on fleecy pyjama bottoms and a navy hoodie that must belong to Struan. 'When we got back from the vigil, Mum had a knife,' I tell my sister.

'*What?*'

'Keep your voice down, Eve.'

'Sorry, but … a knife?'

'It was on the table beside her. She laughed like she knew it was stupid, said she felt scared when she was on her own.'

'Okay, but … a *knife*? That's extreme.'

I nod. My face is hot. This is the closest I've come to outright lying to Eve. I've hidden truths, omitted plenty, tried to muddle along on my own, chart a path through this without her. But this is different … I'm deliberately trying to throw her, prevent her from figuring out things I can't have her knowing.

Bad things.

'She was scared. Not thinking straight.'

Eve's glare scours my face. I can't meet her eye. 'What are you saying, Finn?' Her voice is controlled, careful.

I shrug – let her figure out the rest. *Our mother is not of sound mind.*

She chews her lip. 'She wouldn't hurt herself, but nothing else makes sense …'

Job done.

Eve

We go to bed around 5 a.m. and grab a couple of hours – not sleep exactly. Struan lies beside me reading on his phone, his arm around me. I rise groggy with fatigue, and take a scalding shower, meet the others downstairs.

The sky is grey and watery when I emerge from Haven, my hands clasped around a travel mug of coffee. 'I'll drive,' Finn says, having already snagged Gina's keys.

Holly trails behind him, her hair in braids, another knitted headband, this time luminous green. I touch it affectionately, say, 'Where'd you get these, I like them?'

Holly shrugs, shrinks from my touch. Finn says, 'Leah made them. Holly has a set.'

I try not to resent the women who braid Holly's hair, give her gifts, and are allowed to comfort her in her darkest hours.

Cate runs out with packs of sandwiches, saying the hospital food will be lousy. It's a nice gesture and I feel guilty for my uncharitable thoughts. 'I'm so sorry about your mum,' Cate says, leaning into the car. 'Sending good vibes.'

She'll need more than that, but I manage a smile. Cate lingers with Holly for a moment, tucking a stray strand of Holly's hair beneath the knitted band, tweaking her top where it droops from her shoulder. Like Mum when she used to see the twins off to the school bus in matching uniforms. Fran and Leah appear on the steps behind. Leah has tears in her eyes as she watches us prepare to leave, and Fran wraps an arm around the older woman's shoulders.

Finn beeps the horn to hurry Gina, and she comes flying out of the door with scarves trailing. Struan is staying behind to mind Haven and look after the dog. He's on the steps too as we leave, hands in his pockets.

My brother is restless in the driver's seat, tapping his fingers against the wheel. 'Let's go,' he says, when Gina gets in.

I point down the drive. 'Not yet …'

Finn and Gina follow my gaze, spot Imogen Isherwood and Ben Carmichael swinging into the end of the track, moving towards us. 'The post-mortem—' breathes Gina.

'We need to get to the ferry,' Finn says.

'We've got time.' I get out of the car, and Gina joins me. On the steps, Struan and the artists look anxious.

Imogen's heels strike the gravel. She hasn't bothered with a coat, just her cropped, stylish suit jacket. 'Sorry to detain you at a time like this.'

'Is it the post-mortem report?' Gina asks. 'Do you have the results?'

'I do,' Imogen says. 'It's not the news you want to hear. I'd suggest we go inside and sit down, but I know you're in a rush.

I'm sorry to land this on you …'

There's a slam as the twins get out of the car and shut their doors in unison. Gina jerks her chin at the inspector. 'Go on …'

Imogen surprises me by stepping forward and clasping one of Gina's arms. 'Ms Allardyce, I'm very sorry to tell you that we have reason to believe Jay was … *killed*.'

Chapter 24

Eve

Gina's knees weaken and I understand why Imogen took hold of her. She's all that's keeping Gina from hitting the deck. I hurry over. 'I've got her,' I say.

Imogen steps back.

'Tell me,' Gina gasps. 'What exactly did the results show?'

'Jay died from injuries sustained before his fall,' Imogen says carefully; she's still not telling us everything.

'You said he was hit in the face, but that surely couldn't …'

'No, the bruises to his face are superficial, sustained some hours before death. These are internal injuries … *Catastrophic* internal injuries.'

Gina gasps and I tighten my arm about her. Finn looks distraught. He catches my eye and I nod. We need to go.

'The details can wait, Ms Allardyce,' Imogen says. 'I know you need to get your ferry. It's not nice to hear; I appreciate that. Obviously, the nature of our investigation has changed. Things are more serious now. You'll hear from us soon, I promise. Meantime, Ben is going to drop me off then follow you to the hospital.'

Gina presses a hand to her mouth. 'Okay, thank you.'

I help her into the car. The twins slide into their spaces. Somehow, Finn manages to start the engine, put the car into gear, move off down the track. Imogen and Ben's car slips in behind. We make a strange cortege. I feel the strain of their presence, and Finn – driving precisely with hands clenched on the wheel – must too.

Someone *hurt* Jay.

Killed him.

Someone knows what happened, how and why he died, and they're keeping it to themselves.

And all the while, my mother is fighting for her life in hospital. I didn't think things could get any worse. *Now I know they can.*

I take a breath, squeeze my palms, grit my teeth. We've got to get through the next few hours, then the ones after that …

And more beyond. I can't look too far ahead, lest the enormity of it all overwhelm me. Right now, we just need to get on that boat.

We are shown into a bland room to wait for the doctor. There's pastel-coloured art on the walls and scratchy, easy-clean upholstery. A box of tissues sits on the low table. It's a space in which to kill time, filled with silence that swings between comforting and acute.

We ate Cate's picnic on the crossing washed down with tepid ferry tea, so Finn goes off in search of the canteen, dragging Holly along. Once they're gone, Gina wants to talk. She speculates about her brother's whereabouts, says she just can't contemplate planning a funeral, can't believe that someone would wish Jay harm.

Imogen's theory that someone harmed him has upended her.

More than a theory; post-mortems don't lie. But it does seem impossible that someone would *want* to hurt him. And yet it chimes with my fears that he was involved in something he shouldn't have been, putting himself at risk.

'Have you noticed Finn acting strangely?' I ask Gina. My brother hasn't been himself. I'm scared he knows more about

Jay's dealings than he's letting on. What if he's involved in the drugs, and frightened to say?

Gina blinks. 'No more strangely than I'd expect. He's lost a friend …'

I'm dissatisfied with her answer. It's the one I've been giving myself too, but it feels like an excuse.

Gina looks earnest. 'Listen, Eve, I didn't know what had happened with Holly at that party … I promise I'd have told you if I did. I'd have called you to come home, made sure Holly got help. I didn't notice what was going on with her. I've been busy with work—'

'It's not your fault, Gee,' I say.

'Well, I blame myself. We'll have to sort out counselling for her when this …' She trails off, not wanting to say *over*, because neither of us knows what that looks like. 'Perhaps the school can help.'

'I'll talk to Struan.' I prop my feet on the table. I'm going to be climbing the walls, stuck here. 'Do you have any idea what Mum might have been planning … where she was going?'

Gina's face sags, lines deepening. 'No. I don't. I thought I knew your mother better than anyone. I thought I knew *everything* … But I can't get my head around this. I can't imagine what could send her out into the night like that. It's been so long since she's left Haven except to walk in the woods. Even then, she'd always rather be at home.'

'Kirsty and Finn think Mum's been strange lately too,' I say. 'Paranoid … manic. Finn caught her with a knife, when we came back from the vigil. She's not right.'

Gina looks at me blankly. 'What are you *saying*, Eve?'

I shrug. I don't really know.

When the twins return from their trip to the canteen, Gina is crying softly. Finn takes a wary look at her, drops the sandwiches and bolts. I go after him. It takes me a while to find him. I stumble upon him in a stairwell, leaning on a window ledge and looking at the lights of a city bigger than our island. 'Hey.'

He doesn't reply.

'Talk to me. Tell me what's going on, Finn.'

Nothing.

'I know it's a lot: Jay ... Holly ... now Mum. But there's something bothering you, isn't there?'

He folds his arms on the ledge. Holly's always resisted my mothering – *smothering* she calls it – but Finn has never minded. He's affectionate, easy-going. My open-book brother ...

Closed.

I've never had to worry about him like I do about Mum and Holly. Now I'm afraid. I touch his arm. 'Finn, *please*.'

He flinches, takes a couple of steps, stops with his back to me, hands covering his face. His shoulders shake. 'Eve, I've done something really fucking stupid ...' His voice cracks. 'Can you forgive me?'

'You're scaring me,' I whisper. 'What are you talking about? If it's school, I understand why you—'

He shakes his head. His blond hair is messy, dark from the rain that came on as we crossed the sound. Finn insisted on staying on deck and whenever I glimpsed him through the steamed windows of the cabin, he was staring into the distance, as bleak as the sea that swarmed around us.

'That's not it.' His head droops. 'I ... things have changed ... it's all wrong.' He brings a hand to his mouth, sniffs back tears, and when he turns and looks at me he is fierce, clear-eyed. 'It doesn't matter.'

'Finn—'

He shoots me a sorrowful look, shakes his head. 'I *can't*, Eve.' And he walks unsteadily towards the intensive care unit waiting room that contains the remains of our family.

@QueenBee

THIS! Check out this video, shared by my warrior queen @MidsummersChick. We will not be shamed into silence *#womensupportingwomen #thrivedontjustsurvive #dobetter*

Chapter 25

Finn

We sit in the room for hours with no news, no change. No reprieve from the monotony. Eve watches me closely after I nearly spilled my guts in the hall. Gina manages to sleep a little and Holly slouches in a chair, glued to her phone again, eyes bright and fierce as they track her screen. No one has been near us, except a harried nurse who promised a doctor would be in directly when they get the results from Mum's brain scans.

Ben waits on a hard plastic chair in the corridor. He looks up when I step out, needing to stretch my legs and get some air. 'Canteen,' I mutter, and ask if he wants anything. He holds up his cardboard cup, grimaces, shakes his head.

I head for the exit. I don't want a drink, I want peace, space to think. It's impossible that Mum is lying a few feet away, so damaged. The panic that overtook me the moment I heard she'd taken the car and crashed into the bridge, has barely ebbed. My pulse is too fast, and I feel sick.

What were you thinking, Mum?

But I know exactly what she was thinking …

I rush outside and gulp cold air. I settle myself, shove my

hands into my pockets. Anyone observing me would think I'm just another worried relative. I am, but I've got more to contend with than that.

Someone killed Jay; the post-mortem proved it.

We haven't heard the details yet or the detective's theories, but it's only a matter of time.

Back inside the cloying atmosphere of the hospital, I stop at a vending machine, buy a can of Coke and make my way back to the intensive care unit. I'm about to turn into our corridor when I hear a voice, gruff and carrying. Ben Carmichael, talking into his phone.

'I see. So you've sent the samples to the lab for testing? Uh-huh … That road doesn't lead anywhere but Haven, the cliffs. It's a turning point, if someone went the wrong way … aye, when I first examined the scene it was a mess of tyre marks; the ground was soft from all the rain … No, forensics didn't pick anything up except some tyre prints – too many to be useful – plus Finn McKinnon's phone.'

I press myself to the wall, wish I *had* my phone so I could pretend to be on it, and look less conspicuous.

'It would be easy to reverse into one of those boulders. Narrow road … veers close to the cliff edge. Not for the faint-hearted. Could be anyone, but if we have a car to test the paint samples against then it might give us something. The PM is definite … the injuries were caused by a car driving at speed into him?'

There's a long silence, punctuated by grunts of agreement from Ben and my own slamming heart.

'I think you're barking up the wrong tree. Finn's a good kid, and he and Jay were right pally.'

My head swims and I shrink against the wall. For a horrible moment I think I might pass out. A worried nurse passing by reroutes towards me, but I hold up a hand and give him an unconvincing smile. I draw myself straight, slow my breath and keep walking, round the corner and smack into Ben.

Finished with his phone call, he catches me by the shoulder. 'Woah there, you all right? You're a gey funny colour.'

I nod, unable to find words. The nurse backs up a step and peers at us. Ben gives him a nod as he claps a hand between my shoulder blades. 'The laddie's just worrying about his Mum,' he says. 'He's all right. I'll take him back to his folks.'

The urge to ask Ben about his phone call – I have no doubt who he was talking to – is so strong it drowns my thoughts. Somehow I keep walking, slip back into the family room. Everyone looks up when the door opens, wilting in disappointment when they see it's only me. 'Finn had a wee funny turn in the hall.' Ben jerks a thumb at me. 'Get that can of juice down you; the sugar will help.'

Gina and Eve fuss over me. Ben gives me a smile before he leaves, but I notice he can't quite meet my eyes.

Eve

Mum goes into surgery just after 4 p.m. The scans revealed a bleed on her brain, and they need to operate. The operation could last up to twelve hours, and Gina encourages me to take Finn and Holly home, come back in the morning once she's in recovery.

'I'll call you immediately if anything changes,' she says. 'The kids are better off in their own beds. You too.' I'm not happy with the arrangements, but it makes sense.

The surgeon who talked us through the operation was grave. It's a risky procedure. I get to see Mum before we go, look down on her in the huge bed with wires and machines surrounding her. 'It's going to be okay, honey,' Gina murmurs, stroking my hair as we say goodbye. 'Naomi will pull through. She's strong.'

I've never thought of her that way.

Finn insists on driving, even though he's knackered. 'I've had more sleep than you,' he retorts, when I object, which might be a dig at me for having Struan in my bed. Or maybe I'm overthinking.

I can't stop remembering Finn in the stairwell – *I've done something really fucking stupid …*

I text Struan on the drive, letting him know which ferry we'll be on. We cross the sea again. Some of my tension melts as we approach the island, and I think about getting home to Haven, and Struan. Unless he's had second thoughts after last night …

The sea is calm and pearl-smooth tonight, a gleam of late sunshine splitting heavy rain clouds.

Struan has cooked. I appreciate the effort, and my anxiety ebbs, although he doesn't attempt to kiss me. 'Kirsty's called a million times,' he says. He looks a little uneasy, but perhaps it's embarrassment after being caught in my room last night by two of his pupils.

'She's been blowing up my phone too.' I've sent Kirsty a couple of messages, promised to call this evening.

Neither Finn nor Holly eat dinner. Finn excuses himself to his room and Holly to the artists' wing.

Struan and I eat. I tell him about Mum's condition, the operation. 'They don't know if any damage has been done, and even if the operation is successful, we still won't know for a while.'

Struan's fingers brush my wrist. 'I'm sorry, Eve. That sucks.'

I nod. I can't believe this has happened, especially now, with Jay's death so raw. Struan toys with his food. His expression is troubled. He leans back, putting down his fork. 'Eve, there's something I have to tell you.'

I try a smile. 'No more bad news I hope; there's been enough of that—'

He pushes his hair out of his eyes, hesitates.

Now I'm worried. 'Struan, what is it?'

A pause. '… Nah, it can wait.'

'Stru—'

He swallows. 'I … just wanted to apologise, for not telling you about Finn's exclusion, or Holly not going to school.'

'It's okay, Stru. I understand.' It's *almost* true.

'I looked out for her, kept an eye for any repeat of the bullying that happened when she was younger. I promise I didn't know about ... *Ryan*.' He winces, and I wonder if he has some professional duty to take things further, even if Holly doesn't want to. It's a safeguarding nightmare, one student sexually assaulting another, distributing images all around school ...

Ben arrives before we can say more. I let him in, and Struan offers him leftovers, but Ben declines. 'I'm supposed to be taking care of you.'

I can't imagine it's much fun, the family liaison thing. Just a lot of hanging around watching us fall apart. 'So, what can we do for you?' I ask.

'I have news.' Ben is on edge.

'About Jay?'

'No, your mother's accident. This came in before I left the mainland, so I've already told Gina.'

'What is it?'

'The initial report on the crash.' Ben rubs at the stubble coating his jaw. 'It looks like your ma was driving at speed towards that bridge. Not just speeding for the conditions, *speeding up*. It appears that she ... crashed deliberately.'

Back when Mum drove, she did so like a little old lady. There's no way she'd drive recklessly.

I shake my head. 'You're suggesting she was trying to ... *kill herself*.' It's the news I've feared for years, the moment I've awaited with dread. Always wondering when my mother's demons might rise up and overtake her. Latterly, with Gina around, I grew less worried, but I've always known Mum wasn't entirely *safe*.

I think of Finn's fears expressed last night – her disordered thinking, the knife in her hand. Ben outlines evidence, but I barely listen. There's a buzzing in my ears I can't silence. After he's gone, I tell the twins. I expect abject denial from them, complete faith in our mother, but Finn drops into a seat, head in his hands, a resigned sigh shuddering through him. Holly blinks, eyes full of tears that never fall. When she tries to retreat, Finn grabs hold of her wrist and tells her she's not going anywhere.

Holly glares and struggles against him.

'Let her go, Finn,' I say, shocked, but it's Struan who steps in and parts them. I see the rage bubbling beneath Finn's skin, the fury in his eyes. I think of him beating Ryan Campbell, swearing at the artists, begging me to forgive him for some unspeakable sin.

I don't recognise my brother.

Chapter 26

Eve

I spend an hour on the phone to Kirsty in the den. The twins disappear to their various hideouts and Struan sits at the kitchen table with his laptop, grading essays he needs to hand back after the holidays. He grimaces. 'Adolescent Shakespeare analysis … my favourite.'

We exchange a wistful smile, and I think of Jay who will never turn in an essay again.

Kirsty and I talk about everything: the twins' secrecy, Holly's attack in the caves, the fact that Jay didn't just fall from the cliffs. And my mother driving at speed into the side of a bridge with only one outcome on the cards.

She's a good sounding board. When I get off the phone I feel calmer, though nothing has changed. It's only after I hang up that I realise *she* barely said anything, and I don't know what she was calling me about earlier.

I find Struan reading in the kitchen, lamps lit against the impenetrable island dark, the dog snoozing at his feet. I sit beside him. 'Earlier,' I say, unable to keep from returning to the subject. 'It seemed like there was something you wanted to say …'

He looks up from his screen. 'There are things we should talk about,' he says.

Self-preservation kicks in and I don't push. Later when I ask if he's coming to bed, he avoids my gaze and says he'll sleep on the sofa. I freeze, dread seeping in. *He thinks it was a mistake.* 'It's awkward,' he explains, 'with the twins in the house.'

Like my brother, Struan is a crap liar.

I call Gina first thing, before dawn breaks over the sea. 'She's out of theatre,' Gina confirms, exhaustion coating her words. 'The operation was a success, but she's still under. They're going to keep her sedated for a while.'

'Can we see her?'

'They'll let me in to see her in a couple of hours. You could come this afternoon. They won't wake her today, maybe not tomorrow either. I'm going to spend time with her this morning, and then head home as a foot passenger since you guys have the car. Do you think Finn could pick me up? This might be a long haul, Eve. We need to look after ourselves, and each other.'

'Struan could drop me off and pick you up,' I say. 'I can spend the evening with her. We can take it in turns.'

Gina agrees. I pause, remembering Ben Carmichael's revelations. 'Ben was here last night to talk about Mum's accident.'

'It's absolutely not true,' Gina says hotly. 'I told him as much.'

'That's what I said. But there was a witness ... the farmer who was first on the scene and brought his tractor down to help ... He said she was going too fast, driving straight at the river ...'

'She hasn't driven in years; she's out of practice.'

I head for the coffee pot to replenish my sanity. I envy Gina her certainty. 'Naomi wouldn't do that ...' she continues, with conviction. 'She wouldn't leave me.'

After breakfast, we walk on the beach with the dog. Not the cove, where memories of Jay abound, but a beach further along the coast. We stroll over piles of seaweed, watch Cash pelt across silver-slick sand at the water's edge, ears flapping as he chases his ball.

Holly meanders at the tideline. Finn throws the ball for Cashew, and Struan and I walk side by side, a little wary of each other. Our cheeks are bright with cold, the sun trying to shine. I start to relax.

But when we arrive back at Haven, Ben's police cruiser is on the drive again, Imogen Isherwood standing beside it.

'Does she have nothing better to do?' Finn growls. He ducks his head, but not before I see that he's scared.

'Crime rate's low,' I joke. 'We're it.'

My humour falls flat.

Ben rounds the back of the car and folds his arms, expression grim.

As we get closer, a hunted expression crosses Finn's face, and he turns to the woods we just exited. Then looks to the hill that reaches its stony peak behind the house, haloed in fog.

Like he's considering running.

'Finn …' I murmur. 'What's happening?'

Finn swallows hard, like he wants to say something. Imogen strides towards us.

'Eve,' Struan murmurs, strained. 'Finn … There's something I need to tell you both—'

My brother looks at him. 'You told the police, didn't you? About what happened in the library?'

Struan sighs. 'Had to, mate.'

My pulse pounds in my ears. The moment feels immense and inevitable. Imogen reaches us, Ben behind her looking like he'd rather be anywhere else.

'What's *happening*?' I murmur. 'Someone tell me what's going on?'

No one answers. Finn makes a low sound, somewhere between a moan and a growl.

'*Shit*,' Struan says, and I watch helplessly as Ben reaches for his cuffs.

Chapter 27

Eve

Finn McKinnon, I'm arresting you on suspicion …

I stare at Isherwood's shiny hair, her tailored suit. Too perfect to be the instrument of our destruction. My heart flaps like a bird in my chest. This can't be happening.

Of the murder …

I think I might faint, cold darkness sweeping up from my feet. Beside me, Finn shudders.

… of Jay Allardyce.

My brother goes stiff and straight. He pulls his shoulders back and says nothing as they cuff him. There are more words, but they blur in a soup of sound.

… say anything, but anything you do … in evidence … harm your defence … in court …

She's reading him his rights. There's white noise in my head, drowning her voice. I try to focus. Terror floods me, and it takes all my effort to remain upright.

Finn's gaze is steady, fixed ahead. He doesn't look at me. I wish he would, so I'd know – see the truth in his eyes: my open-book brother …

I shouldn't be questioning. *Of course* he didn't do it; he couldn't have. I don't need to ask – I *know* him, inside out. Except … these past few days I've wondered if I know him at all.

I've done something really fucking stupid …

The sound of the handcuffs is brutal, like the snap of bones. Behind me, Holly screams. I blink and they're taking him away, leading him towards the car, Imogen's palm flat and firm on Finn's back.

Leah and Cate stand in the open doorway, watching, open-mouthed. Fran's shocked face behind. Holly runs and falls into Cate's arms.

Hers. Not mine.

A curtain twitches and I see the last of the guests watching from the bay window of their sitting room, faces gaping, bleached by the circling police lights. If they didn't want to leave before, they will now: a mass exodus of paying customers.

Struan holds Cashew's collar to keep him from running after Finn, but there's no one holding me back; I dart across the drive as they're about to put him in the car. Mist hangs in low ropes over the trees. 'Wait!'

'Eve,' Imogen says. 'Let us do our jobs.'

I ignore her, try to make eye contact with my brother. I grab his sleeve. Finally he looks up and I wish he hadn't. His expression tears at me – raw, dark, wild. He swallows. 'I'm sorry, Eve.'

Why is he apologising? He's innocent; there's no need for sorry …

Imogen steps aside to give us a minute, motions Ben to do the same. She's impassive as she studies her phone. Whatever I've felt about her – those moments I've felt her warmth, I am reminded emphatically that she is not on our side.

I squeeze Finn's arm, wincing at the rattle of the cuffs. 'Tell them,' I say. 'Tell them you didn't do this.'

What I mean is, tell *me*.

'Eve,' Imogen warns, glancing at her watch.

'Just a minute. *Please.*'

'Eve—'

'You can't talk to him without me. He's seventeen.'

'You can follow us to the station. If Finn chooses to have you as his appropriate adult, then you'll be allowed to sit in on the interview. He has the right to legal advice.' There's a crack in her exterior, like she's speaking to me girl to girl again, a sister instead of a cop.

I'm about to argue – of course Finn will want me there, of course he doesn't need legal advice.

'Eve,' Finn murmurs, looking so helpless that a lump swells in my throat. 'Eve ... I think I need a lawyer.'

Before taking him away, Imogen searches Finn's room. She waves the warrant beneath my nose, but I barely read it. Ben sits in the cruiser with Finn, heads bowed, and I wonder if they exchange words while they wait, if Ben remembers seeing Finn in his first rugby game, aged twelve, alongside his own son.

I don't want to get in the car with Struan, but I don't trust myself to drive. Struan's betrayal bites deep, and I maintain frosty silence as we speed after the police car carrying my brother.

'There's legal aid, a duty solicitor,' Struan says, when I sigh in frustration at the expense of hiring a lawyer.

I want Finn to have the best, not whoever happens to be around, but the fact remains that we can't afford a private solicitor. Of course, I *want* him not to be headed to the police station in handcuffs at all, his rights read to him and a long night ahead.

'They're going to put him in a cell,' I say, my voice cold. 'He's just a kid.'

'They know that. They'll make allowances.'

I'm not so sure. He's above the age of criminal responsibility and he's been arrested for *murder*. 'What did Finn mean, about the library ... What did you tell them?'

Struan blows out a breath. 'I told the truth, Eve, but there's CCTV ... It's not like it wouldn't have come out.'

'Like *what* wouldn't have come out?'

He looks at me, green eyes dark with sympathy. 'That Finn was the one who hit Jay. They had a fight at school on Friday. I split them up.'

Town lights brighten below in the darkening sky long before I'm ready. Rain sweeps from leaden clouds as I fumble my phone with trembling fingers and wish I didn't have to make this call: it will tear this family apart. 'Do it, Eve,' Struan says softly, swinging into the final descent.

How do I tell Gina that Finn has been arrested for Jay's murder?

She calls me first, her picture flashing on my screen – maybe the police have told her they've made an arrest. Her photo is old-world glamour, a fifties movie star.

I swipe the screen and the image that replaces it is insipid and strained. Gina's voice is ragged. 'Eve … tell me it's not true. Not Finn. *My God!*'

'He didn't do it,' I croak. *He couldn't have done it.*

'Of course not,' Gina agrees, after a beat that breaks my heart.

'They took him to the station. I'm headed there now. They searched the house. I've had to leave Holly with the artists, but Cate and Leah are there so she'll be okay. We need to get this straightened out …'

Gina is quiet, a fissure of doubt in her silence. A fault line along which our family will split in two.

'They say Naomi was trying to protect him,' she says finally, her words blunt objects, landing with dull agony. 'The police. They think she drove off the bridge on purpose … not to harm herself but to wreck the car to hide damage that was already there. There's nothing wrong with the brakes. The car was involved in the crash that killed Jay, and they believe Finn was the one driving. Naomi crashed the car to destroy the evidence … She did it for him.'

Chapter 28

Eve

The interview room is colder than the waiting room where Struan and I sat while Finn was processed. I'm calm on the outside, but internally I'm reeling – Mum crashed the car to conceal a crime she believes Finn committed. She made excuses for not letting us drive it, insisting we use Gina's Jeep all week. Kept the car hidden while she worked out what to do.

The fact that Mum could plan this elaborate cover-up is beyond me.

And after my call with Gina, it feels like battle lines have been drawn – Gina on one side, Finn and Mum on the other. The division in our family tears me in two.

I text Kirsty from the waiting room to let her know what's happening, beg for information about the people Jay was involved with. We need *someone* in the frame for Jay's murder … someone who isn't Finn. Because he can't be guilty. If the police knew that Jay was dealing, surely they'd cast their net wider …

I'm not saying it *was* Ketty, but he might know who Jay was working for. And that's important. If Jay owed money, he would have been in hot water. Maybe someone arranged to meet him on the cliff and drove up there with the intention of sending him spinning over the edge …

He wanted out, Finn told me. *He was miserable, by the end.*

Jay was in over his head, in a world I can't begin to comprehend. And now he's dead.

That can't be coincidence.

I don't know if Kirsty responded – I was told to turn my phone off and it's now stowed in the depths of my bag.

They bring my brother in, and all other thoughts flee as I search his face for reassurance. He seems to have grown both younger and older in the short time he's been here. His hair hangs in his eyes, lank from running his hands through it. His eyes are haunted, circled in shadows. I know I'm not supposed to, but I hug him. He is stiff in my arms, already preparing himself for what comes next. I sigh and hold on, wishing I could refuse to let go, wishing I could spirit him far from here.

What would I be willing to do for him? *Would I break laws? Crash a car and risk my life?*

The duty solicitor saunters in, takes a seat. 'Oliver East,' he says smoothly, leaning past Finn to shake my hand. He's in his early thirties, hair shaved at the sides. Grey suit, waistcoat, nice shirt. He's done his best to achieve a look more befitting a high-end law firm than the guy folk call when they can't afford anyone else.

Someone passes me a paper cup of tea and I cling to it. Imogen prepares the table for interview, laying out water bottle, notebook, laptop, and turning on the recording equipment. Everything neat. She introduces herself, and the male officer beside her – no one I've met. We state our names for the tape. My voice shakes but my brother's is surprisingly steady.

Finn takes a breath and dashes the hair from his eyes. He's no longer cuffed, but he keeps rubbing his wrists as if he can still feel the shackles.

'Okay,' Imogen says smoothly. 'Finn, I'd like you to tell us about the nature of your relationship with Jay Allardyce.' Finn looks at Oliver, who gives him the briefest of nods.

'Finn—' Isherwood prompts.

My brother clears his throat. 'N-no comment.'

'Wait, *what*?' I lean forward. 'No, Finn. You have to tell the truth. You've done nothing wrong, answer the questions.'

Oliver, Finn and Imogen flash matching looks of irritation at me. My role is to be quiet, listen and not interfere. Oliver East – who met my brother less than an hour ago – is who we must pin our hopes on to get Finn out of here. It's his job to advise, decide how this plays out.

But what if he's advising badly?

I must sit here and keep quiet, watch my brother condemn himself. Everyone knows *no comment* means guilt, right?

And so it continues. Finn gives identical non-answers to every question, and Imogen keeps on calmly. Maybe she's used to this. She asks about Finn's friendship with Jay, his movements on Friday – from them driving to school together in the morning, to the fight that took place in the library.

A fight Struan broke up that I didn't know about …

She explores Finn's decision to drive home with Holly and leave Jay stranded in town, how he spent the afternoon, the run he took.

Was he so furious with Jay that he'd needed to work off his anger?

She probes Finn's lack of proper alibi for the time Jay died, his attempts to skew the investigation with false reports of Jay in running gear, going for a jog.

I can't believe we're talking about alibis, that we're in an interview room under caution, a solicitor making notes on his legal pad and shooting my brother side-eye when he hesitates over his no-comment.

My brother is under suspicion of driving a car at speed into his friend and killing him, and then … *What*? Heaving his body off the cliff; leaving him to die alone; lying to his family and friends and the police over and over again …?

No.

I'd be freaking out in his shoes, crumbling under the pressure, but no matter what they say, Finn doesn't flinch. He grows in confidence, calmly no-commenting every question.

Imogen narrows her eyes as she stares him down – no longer a grieving boy but her foe.

I glance at East to see if he's worried about the direction of travel, but he seems unruffled as Finn avoids another attempt to draw him in on the subject of the library. I don't ever remember Jay and Finn *arguing* …

'What did you and Jay fight about?' Imogen says. 'Was it a girl? Was it Isla Maxwell?'

A muscle ticks in Finn's jaw and something shifts in his eyes. 'No comment.'

'Come on, Finn. You can tell us what you argued about.' Imogen taps a burgundy fingernail and her tone softens as she tries to wheedle an answer.

My brother knots his fingers. I see the band of greenish bruising across the knuckles of his left hand. I noticed that before, meant to ask about it, but it slipped my mind with everything else going on. I assumed it was from his fall.

'How did you get that?' Imogen asks, pointing at his hand.

'No comment.' The muscle pulses in Finn's jaw again. Subtle, but I see it and I'm sure Imogen does too. He slides his hands beneath the table as if he can conceal the marks. Oliver gives a small sigh and I wonder if that was a bad move – does hiding his hands make him seem more guilty?

'Our duty doctor examined you when you arrived,' Imogen says, checking a page in her file – more for show than because she needs to. It's news to me that the doctor examined Finn. This seems like a violation. 'Are you left-handed, Finn?'

'No comment.'

She's annoyed. 'You can answer *that*.' Finn says nothing. 'The doctor thinks these marks are consistent with you having punched someone recently. Within the past week. And from the post-mortem we know Jay was hit in the face shortly before he died. It's not such a leap …'

My brother's chin drops. His composure is slipping. Imogen takes several items from the folder and arranges them on the tabletop in front of him – bright, high-definition portraits of Jay's dead face. Close-up images of the bruising. I saw him in the flesh, but these are shocking. Finn didn't see him in the morgue, and he recoils from the pictures. He starts to shake.

'May I remind you, Detective Isherwood,' snaps Oliver disdainfully, 'that my client is seventeen. A little warning, perhaps—'

'May I remind *you* that *my* client is dead,' Isherwood replies, tartly. She taps the close-up of Jay's face. 'And also seventeen. These injuries were fresh. They were sustained before death, but not long before. A few hours. Tell me what you know about that, Finn.'

'No comment.' Finn sounds like he is choking. Oliver and I both look at him in warning.

Perhaps sensing that she's on to something – or that Oliver will soon insist on a break – Imogen seizes the moment. 'Did you know that the high school had CCTV installed last summer? Communal areas – dinner hall, corridors … the *library*.'

My brother's head snaps up. 'No comment,' he stutters.

'Let's take a look at some footage from last Friday, shall we?' Imogen reaches for the laptop, taps her screen to life. The footage is pre-loaded. It's not a great angle and there's no sound, but my brother is recognisable, near a table in the corner. As is Jay, and a red-headed girl: Isla Maxwell. Imogen rewinds. *Finn scuttles backwards out of shot. So does Jay. Holly appears, then disappears. Imogen fast-forwards to the point that Jay joins the red-haired girl.* 'Let's watch.'

Finn stares at the screen as though he can't look away. It's hard to know what's happening, since we can't hear the conversation. *Jay moves towards Isla, drapes an arm around her.*

Finn's arrival is heralded by the opening door, but the pair don't seem to notice. I bite my lip, watching intently. Watching Isla's reaction.

Her hands flatten on Jay's chest, fingers splayed. She shoves. Her chair tips and she backs up as he recovers his balance and leans closer. She's trapped. Instead of pulling away, Jay moves closer still. Leering, predatory.

Finn comes into view. His movements are jerky in the poor-quality recording. He grabs Jay out of his seat, his arm swings and he lands a punch. Jay's head snaps back. I wince.

Imogen rewinds, plays it again. And again. The third time she lets it run. *Struan comes into shot from the opposite direction. He grabs Finn and pulls him away.*

This is what Struan told the police that led to Finn's arrest. Imogen had to have had reason to ask for these tapes. Had to have already suspected Finn.

'Do you have anything to say?' Imogen freezes the video on a still frame: Struan holding Finn back. Jay clutching his face.

'No comment,' Finn says tersely.

'Interesting. I thought you might want to comment on the fact that your best friend tried it on with your girlfriend less than twelve hours before someone crushed him with a car and ran him off a cliff …

'A car from which we have managed to collect paint samples that we believe will match fragments on a boulder at the edge of the cliff where Jay died. A car that you drove all the time. A car that your mother tried – and failed – to submerge in the river a few nights later. Lucky for us, that farmer hauled it out. Not only did he save your mum's life, but he might also have saved the evidence.'

Imogen leans back in her seat, hands folded. 'Strange, that almost all fingerprints had been recently wiped from the car's steering wheel, leaving only a few of Naomi's – presumably from the night she drove off the bridge. Who cleans their car *that* well? Not your mother, by the looks of the rest of the vehicle. Seems like she tried to cover your tracks.'

My brother covers his face with his hands. He heaves a breath through his fingers. 'I think,' Oliver says hastily, 'this would be a good time for a break.'

Chapter 29

Eve

I'm drained when we return to Haven. Struan waited hours for me at the police station, and we drove home in silence. He feels guilty, and so he should.

Not for telling the police – he had no choice about that – but for *not* telling me.

At least I'd have had warning of what was to come: Isherwood with her sights set on my brother, claws unleashed.

Things feel different between me and Struan, less hope and ease, more knots and thorns. We'll have to have it out at some point, decide what this is, what we want it to be.

I'm too tired to think about it.

It went against every instinct to walk away as they took Finn, but I had to. He looked over his shoulder as they escorted him down the hallway. He was scared. He looked too young to be flanked by burly police officers.

'They have twenty-four hours to hold him,' Oliver told me when I protested his incarceration. 'To look for evidence.'

'To *fabricate* evidence.'

Wisely, he ignored that. He shook my hand, gave me his number and said I should call if I had questions.

I have many questions, none he can answer.

We take the turn for Haven, through a looming landscape of pines, hills and mist. Haven without Finn, without Gina, without Mum ... no sanctuary at all.

'What are you thinking?' Struan asks, as he slows for the worst of the potholes. The artists' wing is lit, twinkling in the gloom. I wonder again how long the remaining guests will stay – this can't be much of a retreat now.

I'm thinking it's a plausible story ... Kid loses his head over a girl, takes revenge on the boy who tried to take her from him. A moment of madness – a car, a cliff, a dark night ...

A mother so desperate to protect him from the consequences of his actions she'd risk everything ... But it's only plausible if it's some other kid, not my brother. 'Anyone who knows Finn knows this isn't possible.'

Struan nods slowly.

I am running out of allies. Gina, for all that she loves my brother, has loyalty to her own. Ben Carmichael, for all his kindness, couldn't meet my eye as they took Finn away. Now Struan looks at me pityingly, like I'm blinkered.

I have another shot. 'You think Finn punched Ryan for raping his sister, but *killed* his best friend for trying it on with Isla. In what world does that make sense?'

Struan, to give him his due, considers this.

In a world where Finn hadn't dealt with his trauma from that night on the beach, from the photo, from what Ryan Campbell did. A world where he was so damaged by his sister's rape, he became dangerous, a time bomb.

That's what they'll make it out as ... that Finn lost it after trying too long to hold himself together.

Struan parks, turns off the engine, pockets the keys. I half expect him to drop me and turn tail, but he follows me to the house. At the door, he hesitates. 'Stay,' I say, curt and confused. 'This is all kinds of fucked up, but stay.'

He sighs, nods, and reaches past me to open the door.

Struan boils the kettle while I engage in a text exchange with Kirsty. She's horrified at Finn's arrest.

> Of course he didn't do it. That's ridiculous.

Her certainty is balm.

> I know, but they're going to make it look like he did. This has to be related to the drugs. Jay was in so deep that there's no way he didn't piss off the wrong person. It's a horrible coincidence that he fought with Finn, and it means the true culprit might get away with murder.

And then, because I want Kirsty to understand the extent of Finn's predicament, because I need her help:

> There's evidence she can use against him, Kirst: Finn's lied and kept secrets. And Mum crashing the car like that makes him look guilty.

Kirsty replies:

> Maybe she believed that Finn hit Jay with the car – an accident, but she knew he'd still go to prison …

Struan sets a cup of tea in front of me, and I manage a weak smile of thanks. I watch him snap on Cashew's lead and disappear out the back door.

Possibly. They took paint from the boulder at the top of the
cliff road. They're trying to match it to our car.

Kirsty responds:

I'm sure plenty of folk have got lost up that road, misjudged
the bend or tried to turn. Plenty of cars have likely scraped
those stones. There are lots of blue cars …

I sip my tea, remember the lack of fingerprints in the car, Finn
walking towards a cell with his head bowed, shoulders straight,
trying to gather strength to get through the night.
Kirsty insists:

They have nothing concrete, Eve.

They have a punch, a motive, an unexplained accident
involving a car he drives all the time and his mother, who can't
leave the house, going out in the middle of the night to protect
him. Confusion over a pair of running shoes, no proper alibi …

If we knew more about the folk Jay was involved with, we
could direct the police's attention to them … at least they'd
be investigating properly, not just pinning everything on
Finn.

Three dots hover, then disappear. *Come on, Kirsty,* I think.
I'm guilt-tripping her – if the police get wind of Jay's involvement in the distribution of drugs on the island, Ketty will be collateral damage. Throwing him under the bus might be for the greater good if there's someone higher up in the organisation Jay was involved in, who wanted him dead and doesn't care if my brother takes the blame, but I can't throw Kirsty under the bus with him.

If the police look at Ketty, they're going to look at Gav. Even suspicion would be damaging for him, for the farm, for Kirsty and Mac.

I push away my half-drunk tea.

The conversation is over. I tell myself Kirsty had to step away from her phone to deal with the baby, but I can't help but wonder if she's facing the intolerable choice: protect *her* family or mine?

I'm alone. Mum's not here to talk to, and Holly won't. Struan has a job and a position in the community to uphold; plus, he has his doubts. Kirsty has conflicting priorities. Gina is far away – a wedge and too much distance between us.

There's a sliver of doubt in *my* mind too. Maybe Isla made a show of pushing Jay away in the library, maybe she was betraying Finn with his best friend.

I picture Jay on the cliff edge, eyes wide in the moonlight as he searched for escape, seeing only the sharp drop, the rocks, an unforgiving sea. My brother behind the wheel hurling into the bend at the tip of the cliff, knuckles tight, eyes wild with a kind of madness. The forest dark and dense, the scattered rocks eerie in the mist. No sound, save the crashing waves below and the roar of Finn's engine.

It's a relief when Fran comes into the kitchen, distracting me from traitorous thoughts. 'Eve. Are you all right?'

There's no point trying to hide this from the artists. 'Finn won't be home tonight. They're holding him until they decide if there's enough evidence to charge him.'

'I'm sorry to hear that. He's a nice lad.' Fran's face is full of sympathy.

I swallow hard. 'Did you need something? Where's Holls? Is she okay?' I assumed she was with the artists, and start to panic that she isn't.

'She's fine. She's in the studio. Leah's giving her a tarot reading.' Fran rolls her eyes, and we exchange a smile. 'I just came to check on you, but I also need to tell you that more guests are leaving. I'm sorry; I know it's not a great time. With everything that's going on, it's not what they signed up for.'

I'm deflated. '*You?*' I can't bear for Holly to lose a friend right now.

She pauses. 'No, I'd like to stay ... Cate and Leah will be staying too – they have nowhere else to go – but the others are thinking of heading off tomorrow. It's no reflection on Haven ...'

I sigh. 'Hospitality isn't our priority right now.'

Fran nods. 'Some of them feel bad staying, like they're in the way. What you're all dealing with – Jay, now Naomi ...' She blows out a breath. 'We'll go if you want us to, but perhaps it would be helpful if we stay. We can keep an eye on Holly for you. Keep the place ticking over ...'

'Stay,' I agree. 'Holly will want you to. Mum too.'

She nods gratefully. 'Thanks, Eve. I'll let the others know.'

'No,' I say. 'Thank *you*.'

When she leaves, I'm too restless to stay in the kitchen alone, my thoughts too erratic.

It's cold out. There's no sign of Cash and Struan, and I don't venture far. I skirt the grounds, enjoying the brisk whip of wind, the icy chill in my lungs. I look back at the house, the studio lit up against the deepening dark, fairy lights and lamps gleaming. I glimpse Holly's silver flame hair. The artists are sitting on the floor, wine glasses in hands. A bottle is balanced on a nearby stool. They're not at work now, but deep in conversation, putting the world to rights.

My sister is right in the thick of things, sitting between Leah and Cate. Leah has an arm around Holly's shoulders. Her long, grey hair is loose, and her eyes crease with laughter. Mum left home when she was pregnant with me, so we've never known a grandmother's love. I envy again the closeness between my sister and the artists, the warmth and fellowship of the scene.

Cate reaches across the circle of cushions to retrieve the wine bottle. She tops Holly's glass and smiles at my sister in a way that makes my insides twist. Holly has found her place – and it's not with me.

Later … or soon … I will have to think deeply about my sister, how we pull her back from the brink. But for now, at least I know she's safe, cared for.

An island taxi is pulling up as I circle back to the front of the house. I can't hide my surprise seeing Gina. She gets out the car, her hair tied on top of her head, lippy on – glamour armour back in place.

I don't know what to say. In other circumstances I'd run to her, let myself be wrapped in her capable arms. I let Gina in when I was a teenager, despite my intention to need no one – to be the one *others* needed.

She was Mum's shelter in every storm, took the twins to her heart. I let her be my sanctuary too, let her love me.

A shadow has fallen between us – dark and cold, eclipsing what we had. But she hugs me, and I let her. She doesn't smell of her signature scent – she's wearing Mum's perfume, flowers instead of spice.

'You're not at the hospital,' I say.

She presses her lips, shakes her head. 'I had to come back. For Finn … for you.'

We go inside and she tells me there's no change in Mum's condition, which is not necessarily a bad thing. She pours a glass of wine from the stoppered bottle by the Aga, offers me one.

I hesitate. 'I might have to drive.' I'm thinking of Mum in the hospital and Finn at the police station. Never mind that I can't *get* to the hospital once the ferries stop running for the night. Mum's an ocean away and Finn's equally inaccessible to me.

'Drink with me,' Gina says, and I'm tempted.

'I'll be the designated driver,' Struan offers, coming in behind us with the dog. 'Is it okay for me to crash in the den again, Eve?'

Our eyes meet. The night we spent together seems like a dream. Gina tilts her head and studies us like she's trying to figure out our deal. *I'm* trying to figure it out too.

We sit in the kitchen drinking wine, while Struan works in the den. Perhaps he's doing the honourable thing not putting me in the position to choose tonight. There's too much going on for my choice to be about us, for it to be a real decision and not a reaction to circumstance. That's not how Struan wants it, not – if I'm honest – how I want it.

Gina and I share our hurt, our gaping, aching hearts. Gina keeps the wine glasses topped. We talk about everything: Mum's accident and the controlled coma they're keeping her in until they decide it's time to bring her round; the first brain scans, which are cautiously positive. We talk about Finn, how impossible it is that he'd hurt Jay on purpose. I tell her about the arrest, the handcuffs, the intensity of the interview room. She shudders. I'm relieved she's still thinking of Finn as her boy, not a killer.

We talk about Holly's lost voice, and Gina swears again she and Mum didn't know about the rape. 'She'd have done something, Eve. She'd have helped. She counsels strangers through this very thing …'

'She never told me about Finn … the fight with Ryan.'

'Because she knew how you would react.'

'Someone has to react to *something* around here.'

Gina winces, and I know I've hit the bone. My frustration mounts – Gina never taking Jay to task, never pushing Mum to change. Mum not paying proper attention to my sister's fragile mental state. 'Didn't Mum punish him at all?'

Gina says that, for once, Mum did. She lost her shit at Finn. When she'd finished yelling, she took his phone, grounded him. Finn didn't complain. 'You know Finn; he hates getting in trouble, but he took it. I think he knew he'd gone too far. He could have been *charged* …'

Now he might – not with assault but murder.

Finally, we talk about Struan. 'He's hardly left your side this week,' Gina murmurs. 'He's been a real trouper.'

'He's a good friend,' I say, and she gives me a shrewd look.

She might be conflicted ... but she's here and I'm grateful. I curl against her like I'm twelve again, like Mum's having one of her bad days and the pressure of looking after the twins is too much. 'Finn didn't do this,' I say, breathing in my mother's wild-meadow scent from Gina. 'Even if Jay did try something with Isla ...'

She strokes my hair. 'I know, Evie. But we're in some mess, and I'm not sure how we get out.'

Chapter 30

Finn

They put me back in my cell and I nearly come apart. It's the tiny cell with its cold walls and solitary blanket, the grim, stainless steel toilet.

It's the camera mounted in the corner, the bolts on the door that clang into place.

It's the hopelessness in the air, thicker than the stench of chemical air freshener. It's the fear that swarms up my spine when I imagine spending another minute here, let alone the night – *or longer*.

It's the shameful snap of the handcuffs I'll feel the ghost of forever.

It's the shoes they took from me, along with my belt in case I choose to harm myself – my socked feet on the dirty floor, jeans riding low on my hips. It's no phone, no friends, no choice, no access to the world. It's my voice in my head on repeat: *no comment, no comment, no comment*.

It's Inspector Isherwood with her cold, eager eyes, and perfect hair, the hard lift and fall of her Glasgow accent.

All of it a toxic cocktail that eats at me. I lean against the wall, let my body sag into the cement and stare at the stained ceiling. I don't let myself cry. I want to, but I don't.

Above all, it's Eve's face. Her disappointment. Her words haunt me: *Tell the truth, Finn. You've done nothing wrong, tell them.*

But I couldn't. I couldn't tell some parts and not others. I couldn't work out what to say, what not to. So I followed the advice of the guy in the suit: *no comment, no comment, no comment.*

I held on to the words like they were a lifeline keeping me from drowning. Except now they feel like a hook, reeling me in.

The cell closes in on me, blackness creeping. I imagine I'm back in one of the yoga classes Mum made us do when we were younger – *lion's breath*, and *Ujjayi*, me and Holly choking on laughter, dodging Mum's death stares.

I push off the wall and lie on the hard single bunk, wrap myself in the blanket and try not to think about who else it has covered. I keep breathing to keep myself tethered.

Somehow, I keep myself together.

Chapter 31

Eve

I wash the wine glasses in water so hot it scalds, scrubbing smears of wine and lipstick as if it is the only thing that matters. I go upstairs, contemplate the emptiness of Finn's bedroom, wonder if he's sleeping in his cell. I resolve to stay awake, in case. It might be some company for him, if I'm awake, even if he doesn't know it.

On the landing, Holly's door is closed, a thin seam of light beneath. The faded sign she made years ago hangs askew: *Don't disturb, I'm disturbed enough.* The letters curl in childish calligraphy. I trace a hand over them, as the door opens, and Cate and Leah slip out.

Leah puts a hand to her chest. 'You gave me a fright.'

'What were you doing in there?'

Cate closes Holly's door gently behind her. 'Holly didn't want to be alone. She was upset about Finn ... We stayed until she fell asleep.'

I nod, humbled. I've dropped far down my sister's list. Before I can help her, I must find a way to get close to her.

Cate says, 'She's sleeping now ... maybe don't wake her.' She and Leah are between me and the door. It's a narrow landing, and there's nowhere to go, so I back off towards the stairs and leave them to it.

In the kitchen I make coffee, stake out the sofa with a book and a blanket in silent solidarity with my brother.

I plan a solo vigil, but fate has other ideas.

Struan comes in as I'm making my nest. He stands in the doorway, hair mussed, his T-shirt stretched across broad shoulders. 'I thought you'd gone to bed.' He holds up a glass. 'I came for water.'

Cashew follows him. Struan grins. 'Sorry. He seems to have adopted me. I think he's missing Finn.'

Me too, I think. *But you don't see me curling up in your bed for comfort.*

Except, of course, that's exactly what I want to do. 'Do you want to have coffee with me? I've made a pot.'

'You'll never sleep.'

'That's the point.'

He joins me on the sofa, but draws the line at caffeine. In the lamplight, I see traces of old hopes and fears in Struan's eyes, the ghost of the boy I knew superimposed over the sharper angles of the man. I remember his angst over the decision to go to university – the first boy in his family not to be a trawlerman. I remember how brave he was, standing up to the pressure. I remember him following me into scrapes and risking trouble: sneaking booze beneath his mother's nose and sleeping under the stars when we were fifteen ... taking the blame for our note-passing in class when I started it every time ... skipping school to spend the day with me when I was sad that Mum hadn't come to the prize-giving where I won a creative writing award.

'Do you want to talk about it?' he says when I'm on my second cup, the silence taut between us, humming with possibility. 'Finn ... the investigation ... *us.*'

I'm all talked out when it comes to Jay. I say, 'If you regret it ... if you'd rather go back to the way things were ...'

He grabs my hand. 'I don't regret *anything*. I thought *you* regretted it. I thought you were mad at me, for keeping secrets.'

'I am mad,' I say. 'But … not really.'

He tilts his head, eyes serious. I smile, self-conscious. 'What?'

'You're beautiful,' he says. 'And you're an idiot.'

'*Excuse me*?'

'Don't you know by now that I love you, Evie? I don't care if you knock me back; I need to say it.' He looks up, jaw set, like when he pleaded his case for uni to his family. His bloom of confidence fades and he's back to himself: reserved, unpresumptuous. 'Shit, have I messed things up? My timing …'

'I'm scared,' I blurt.

'You're worried about ruining our friendship again?'

'No, I … it's stupid.'

'Tell me.' He takes my hand again.

'Everyone *expects* it.'

'So what? Why do we care what people think?'

I study our joined hands, turn them over in wonder, something new and familiar at the same time. 'Because I don't want to live on the island, and you don't want to leave.'

He starts to laugh, sees my expression. 'You're serious. Tonight's not the time to make life decisions, but we can figure this out. It starts with talking, with being honest.'

Tonight, for the first time, I have. The relief only goes so far.

Struan doesn't relent on our sleeping arrangements, though I grumble and tease. He kisses me gently on the lips, then again with hunger, leaving me breathless. He cups my face, stares into my eyes and I feel *seen*. Despite everything, hope is a dazzling flare.

'Goodnight,' I murmur. He's almost at the door when I say, 'The car …'

He turns, tired but curious.

'It's kept in a garage that isn't locked – you know no one locks their doors around here. Anyone could have taken it, worn gloves, used it to kill Jay and returned it afterwards, knowing suspicion would fall on Finn since he's the only person who ever drives it.'

'Not impossible,' Struan says, surprising me. 'Anyone from around here would know that the chances of the garage being locked were slim. The island is safe.'

Was safe. Until now.

'So someone with a grudge against Jay could have stolen the car, used it to kill Jay, then returned it. Whether the true perpetrator knew Finn and Jay had fought or not, he made a good scapegoat.'

I can't tell if Struan is considering this theory or if he's humouring me. Either way, hope flames brighter.

He crosses the room, cups my face in his hands again, presses his forehead against mine. I close my eyes. 'I know you want Finn to be innocent.'

I swallow past the lump in my throat, the sensation of being let down gently.

'I do too,' he says. 'But it's not looking good for him, Eve …'

Chapter 32

Eve

The sky is a marble of grey and blue, like one of Mum's palette-knife paintings. I sip tea on the deck, aching with tiredness. My eyes are gritty, and I rub at them and wait for the frigid air to clear my head.

I snuck into the den this morning and into bed with Struan, revelling in the fledgling state between us. He drew me sleepily into his arms, and I snuggled in, sinking into his sleep-heat, running my fingers over the twined muscles and bones of his forearm, my stomach fluttering at the brush of his fingers on my hips.

My thoughts were in overdrive, so I left him sleeping and wriggled free, came out here to think.

Fran, Leah and Cate emerge from the guest wing. They're kitted out in hiking boots, with rucksacks and walking poles. Fran seems to be doing an inventory, checking everyone's equipment. Satisfied, she nods, raises a hand to me, and leads the way through the garden towards the brackeny track that snakes into the hills.

After today, they'll be the only guests left. Last night, Gina put a temporary freeze on new reservations, reimbursed the bookings already in place for the next month.

I hear sounds in the kitchen and go in. Gina is making one of her famous tagines. Country music seeps from the speakers and the air is heady with garlic. I kiss her, then go to take a shower. In the bathroom, I lather up, wash my hair, let the hot water beat down on me and try not to dwell on Finn, what he's doing right now, the uncertainty of the coming days. Back in my bedroom, blasting my hair dry, I check my phone and see a text from Kirsty asking me to call.

I will, but I want to call the hospital first. I pull on jeans and an olive sweater and head back downstairs. Struan is up, sitting at the table with his laptop. He looks up when I come in, blushes. I smile.

Gina serves croissants fresh from the oven. She's wearing my mother's *Chicks* T-shirt, and her lips are a darker shade than usual. 'We need to keep our strength up,' she says, proffering the tray.

Cashew tussles with a rope toy on the mat. The coffee pot hums and pale light spills through salt-caked windows.

A domestic, ordinary scene, but the kitchen is empty. Mum should be here, in her tatty robe, sketchbook on the table before her. Finn should be playing tug of war on the mat with Cash, laughing in that loud, careless way of teenagers, elated at some idiotic video on his phone – *Holls look at this … Eve, Eve, here, watch all the way to the end …*

Gina should be scolding him for the carnage of clothing, mud and charging cables in his wake, and he should be grinning at her, unabashed. Holly – *old Holly*, not the zombie girl who inhabits my sister – should be drinking cold brew and lecturing us on the carbon footprint of carnivores. Dainty, loud-mouthed, funny girl, bent over her sketchpad with a felt pen, mingling lines of poetry with motifs and illustrations, chattering about the latest *BookTok* sensation.

The absence of them hollows me out. I can't magic Finn and Mum back where they belong, but I can make Holly join us for breakfast.

'I'm taking Holls a cup of coffee,' I say, reaching for the oat milk.

'I called the hospital,' Gina says. 'Nae had a comfortable night. They're doing another scan this morning. I'm going over. I'll stay in a hotel on the mainland tonight.'

I wonder what they'll say to each other when Mum wakes – I can't even contemplate it as an *if* now. It'll be quite the conversation. *I thought my son killed your nephew, so I covered his tracks by driving my car off a bridge. Sorry if I scared you …*

'I need to stay here,' I say. 'For Finn.'

She nods, and I think again of battle lines being drawn.

My phone vibrates and I head out onto the deck for privacy. 'Eve, Oliver East here. I'm calling about your brother. He's being released this morning.'

'Oh, thank goodness! They're not charging him?'

'Not at the moment. They're … exploring other avenues. Some new evidence.'

'Can I pick him up?'

'It'll be about an hour. There's paperwork to do. They called me in earlier – they wanted to reinterview Finn.'

'Why wasn't I contacted?'

'He just asked for me. They weren't interested in him this time. They wanted to know about Jay's relationship with his dad. And they had questions about Jay dealing drugs.'

'Then these new lines of enquiry point towards his dad … and the drugs?'

Oliver sounds distracted. 'I assume so. Anyway, Finn's free to go for now.'

'Thank you.'

'He's still a person of interest,' Oliver warns me, but I don't care. I want my brother back. 'The paint samples remain crucial. If they turn out to be a match for your mother's car—'

'Yes,' I say tersely. 'I know. Thank you.'

I head inside to tell Gina and Struan the news. Gina's on the phone too, crying, with Struan standing beside her with a hand on her shoulder. 'Thank you,' she says. 'See you soon.' She looks at me, watery-eyed. 'That was Christian. *Finally*. They berthed in Marbella and local police caught up with him. He already knew that Jay was dead, so I didn't have to tell him.' She shudders and Struan guides her to a chair.

'Oh, Gee,' I say.

'His phone was stolen, during one of their stops along the way. Worst timing. He and Cass have been cruising the Med, as I thought. He's flying back later today.' Gina clenches her fists. 'I'm furious with him … for not telling us he was leaving the country, for the way he treated Jay … But I'm glad he's coming home.'

Christian ignored Jay most of the time – lavished gifts on him when it suited him, used his fists to ensure compliance. I can't get on board with him as a doting dad, but he's Gina's family.

'He's my brother,' Gina says, echoing my thoughts. 'He's all I have left.'

'You have *us*,' I remind her, before remembering that our family is broken too.

Gina is quiet, and my heart stutters. The prospect of losing her makes me giddy. 'Finn is being released,' I say. 'They've realised they were looking in the wrong direction …' I'm not sure if this is strictly true.

'That's good.' But she can't hide her confusion – if Finn didn't do it, why did Mum crash the car?

Maybe Mum got it wrong. Or maybe she was in a bad way, and tried to end it all. 'The police are pursuing the drugs angle. Someone must have tipped them off.'

Gina shudders. 'I can't imagine Jay in that world … So dangerous.'

I can, but it won't help to say so.

Struan interrupts. 'Are we picking Finn up?'

We. 'You must have better things to do than drive me around,' I say, remembering that I'm out of transport options. Mum's car is a write-off and Gina is taking her Jeep to the mainland.

'I'm not overloaded with better things to do.' He reaches for his body warmer. 'Let's go.'

'Let me tell Holly the news about Finn … Oh, her coffee. I'll take it with me. She'll have to come with us since there's no one here to keep an eye on her. The artists have gone hiking.'

I'm back in the kitchen in less than a minute, coffee slopping down the sides of Holly's llama mug from sprinting down the stairs. 'She's not there,' I say, breathless, when Struan and Gina stare at me, halted in their preparations to leave. 'She's not in her room and her bed doesn't look like it was slept in.'

Chapter 33

Finn

Even after they let me out of the cell, I can't stop shaking. My hand trembles so I can barely sign the release forms. The old sergeant on the desk looks sorrowful as he hands me back my stuff. I don't belong here.

Except ... maybe I do.

The voice is my head is vicious, insistent. It's been tormenting me all night, with thoughts of court cases and handcuffs and locked doors, years of my life trickling away. A hand claps my shoulder. Ben Carmichael looks better rested than me, and he's shaved since I last saw him. 'Finn, I'll walk you out.'

I'm full of shame when I step into the light of an ordinary island morning. Does everyone in the street know what's happened to me? There's a stiff breeze, clouds scudding off the sea. I sigh, take a deep breath of salt air. In the deepest, darkest miseries of last night, I wondered if I'd taste this air again, feel the sun. I started to imagine forever behind bars ...

I glance at Ben. He's been with us from the start. Through the days of searching, the discovery of the body, the transition from tragedy to *murder*.

'Bad business,' he says, as we stand facing the harbour, our backs to the utilitarian slab of police station. I look down at my shoes, badly laced in my haste. 'How's your mum doing?'

I shrug. 'The last I heard she was still unconscious.' Pain stabs. I take a shallow breath. Mum did such a stupid thing … and a brave one.

He nods. 'I hope she gets well. Is someone coming to get you?'

'My sister.' Without a phone, I had to rely on the solicitor to call Eve while I was being processed. 'Can I ask you something?'

Ben looks wary. 'Not about the case.'

I chance it anyway. 'I wondered if you knew that Jay was into drugs?'

He pulls a face. 'I'd heard rumours. Place like this—'

'He didn't mean to get into dealing. It was supposed to be a one-time thing.'

I remember him that first night, high on success, flashing the cash he'd made – his own money for the first time, not an allowance from his rich daddy. It all went wrong. He showed off to the wrong folk, believed his hype, got made a fool of. Some lads stole a package off him; he owed money and had no way of repaying it. He was under pressure.

'I don't think anyone really means to get into that life,' Ben says. 'Maybe some, not kids like Jay. They're easy targets, easy scapegoats.'

'It was simple money at first, then he hated it. Hated not being in control.'

Ben nods. 'You did the right thing, telling the detective what you know about that. It's possible Jay pissed off the wrong people, and that's what got him killed.'

I see in his face that he wants it to be true; he doesn't want *me* to be responsible.

I frown. 'It wasn't much. I couldn't give names.' Well, I *could* … but I didn't. 'I'm surprised they let me go.'

Ben claps me on the back again. 'It wasn't on the strength of what you said; someone else gave the names they needed.'

'Who?'

Ben nods across the street. I follow his line of sight and see her standing by the railings, jiggling the pram: *Kirsty*. The street is a bustle of normality, and I am dizzy, disorientated. I bid goodbye to Ben and cross the street. 'Kirst.' I rub the back of my neck.

'Not here.' She takes my arm.

'I'm waiting for Eve.'

Kirsty pushes the pram handle into my hands. 'I'll text her, tell her to meet us at the park.' We follow the curve of the harbour. Gulls swoop and wheel overhead, and cars crawl along the narrow street. Shops are opening their doors – breakfast smells emanate from a nearby café, and my stomach growls.

Kirsty grins. 'Maybe the coffee shop instead of the park …'

'Sounds good.'

We choose a table in a corner. Kirsty puts Mac in a high chair. He starts to giggle and bang his fists. 'You spoke to the police,' I say. 'What did you tell them?'

'I gave them what they needed – a name.' She lowers her voice. '*Ketty*.'

'Kirsty …' I'm overwhelmed.

'Gav will be fine. We had it out last night, I made damn sure he wasn't involved before I went to the police. He might be cross with me for giving Ketty up, but he'll get over it. Gav was already distancing himself – he's a dad now, has to put family first. Ketty and Jay knew each other, worked closely. He's small fry, like Jay, but he's a link in the chain. He might be able to give them the information they need.'

'This could be dangerous, Kirst.' I worry she's embroiled herself for my sake.

She scowls. 'I'll be fine.' She goes quiet while a waitress brings our coffee, and a bacon roll I want to devour in one bite. 'I couldn't see you blamed for something you didn't do, Finn. It wasn't right. Of course you didn't kill Jay; it's ridiculous.'

Her faith is overpowering. I focus on my breakfast.

'The police should look elsewhere. Drugs are what got Jay killed, not some stupid fight over a girl.'

I blush: she knows about the fight in the library. I say softly, 'He was in deep with people who don't take shit, and probably don't like it when folk talk.'

If the police don't close in on whoever was behind the island drug ring soon, there will be dangerous people looking for leaks in their organisation. If Ketty talks, he's at risk; if he doesn't – and there's enough evidence against him – he's going to prison.

'It'll be okay,' Kirsty insists, stubborn in her conviction that good will triumph. That's Kirsty all over – like Eve. 'It was the right thing.'

I squeeze her hand, mine greasy from my bacon roll. 'It was a brave thing. Thank you.'

She shrugs. 'The police needed a push. As if anyone could believe *you* capable of murder.'

I'm uncomfortable with her brimming confidence in me. 'Did the police ask anything else?'

'About Jay's dad. I said he was a brutal piece of shit who liked to beat up his son. I hope that was okay.'

'Fine by me.' Impulsively, I hug her, reaching over the table and squealing baby.

She pats my back, says, 'Look, it's your sister.'

Eve is blazing through the door. 'Finn.' She swoops down on me.

She looks me over, checking I'm in one piece. I hold my breath, wait for the questions, the lectures. I don't expect what she says next. 'Finn, we can't find Holly anywhere.'

Chapter 34

Eve

Finn is free. He's exhausted, shredded, but whole. I want to cling to him, never let him out of my sight again. He endures my attention briefly, shrugs me off. 'I need to breathe, Eve.' *That's more like it.* He's himself again, not the sullen, scared kid in the police station, but the brother I know and love.

And trust.

He sobers when I tell him about Holly. He's more worried than me. I'm inclined to view her disappearance as a stunt, a cry for attention perhaps.

At the alarm in his face, mine rises to match. What if something *has* happened to her?

'It's a pain you don't have your phone,' I tell Finn. 'We could get a message out among your friends, see if anyone has seen her. Could your girlfriend do it?'

If Isla puts the word out, someone's bound to spot her. She can't have gone far. She doesn't drive, doesn't have a car. We live in the back of beyond …

'I don't know—'

'What's her number?'

'I *don't know*. It's saved in my phone.'

'For God's sake! Your bloody generation and your phones … You can't survive without them.'

Finn smirks. 'Same generation, remember. You're not *that* ancient—'

'I can help,' Kirsty says, plucking Mac out of his high chair and cuddling him in one arm while she thumbs her phone. 'Gav's sister works in the Co-op with Isla's auntie. She types furiously. A few minutes later, she has the number. I compose a message for Isla to distribute among the island's young folk and she replies once she's forwarded it to everyone she knows. *Let me know if there's anything else I can do to help.*

Struan joins us, having parked his car and had a scout around town for Holly, to no avail. He orders us drinks to go, and buys Finn another bacon roll in a grease-spotted bag.

'Thanks … *sir*.' Finn gives him an impish smile, and I am cheered by his resilience.

'Right,' I say, when we hit the street. '*Think*, Finn, where would Holly go?'

'She's only ever with the artists.'

'Well, not now. I saw them leave and she wasn't with them.' I wonder if Holly hiked a different route and joined them on the way up the hill. I don't have a phone number for them, so I message Gina. She'll have their contact details and be able to find out if Holly went with them this morning or not.

'Holly's turned off location on all her apps,' I say. 'So I can't track her, before you ask.'

Finn looks at me askance, around another mouthful of bacon roll. 'I wasn't going to … *stalker*.'

Emotion wells in me and I don't trust myself to speak. It's a thing between me and Holls. Though we don't talk or text much, she'll sporadically drop a pin so I can see where she is: just random places like school, the beach, the pier in town. I'll do the same, show the distance between us – miles of moorland and water, mountains and motorways. We *always* do it when I'm coming home, watch the gap of land and sea between us shrinking.

Struan sees my consternation, slips an arm around me. 'I'm sure Holly will turn up soon.'

'That's what we said about Jay.'

Finn finishes his roll and tosses the wrapping in a bin. My phone beeps with another message from Isla Maxwell.

> Are you with Finn? Sorry to ask but there's a rumour going around that he was arrested. I know he doesn't want to talk to me, but I just need to know he's okay.

I thrust the phone at my brother. 'Call your girlfriend.'

He recoils. 'She's not my girlfriend …'

I don't know what went wrong between them, but I don't have time for their angst. 'Because Jay tried it on with her? She pushed him away, Finn; I've seen the tape. She wasn't interested, and she keeps trying to contact you. *Talk to her.*'

Do I imagine the look that passes between Kirsty and Struan? A hint of smirk, a knowing eye-roll. *Took you long enough to take your own advice, Eve.*

I dial the number. When Isla answers I push the phone at Finn, so emphatically he has no choice but to take it. He walks off, phone reluctantly at his ear. 'Hey … Yeah, it's me.'

Kirsty, Struan and I run through options while we wait. Kirsty suggests splitting up – decides a couple of us should go and search the coast around Haven. 'I'll text Gav's mum, ask her to take Mac for a couple of hours …'

Finn jogs back, hands me my phone with a scowl. 'You're welcome,' I say tartly.

He ignores me. 'Isla's going to meet us. She's got an idea where Holly might be.'

'*Where?*'

'It's easier to show you. We'll need a car, though.'

'Take mine.' Struan tosses me his keys. 'You're still on my insurance from the summer. I'll go with Kirsty and check the beach.'

'We're going to a beach too,' Finn says.

'How would Holly get to a beach a car ride away?'

'Bus? Maybe she hitched.'

An island this size, most folk are known, and tourists stand out a mile. Holly could easily have been picked up and given a lift. Hitchhiking is less dangerous here than on the mainland, but I don't like it. Would Holly have the confidence to get in a car with a stranger? The old Holly, absolutely … but the girl who's lost her tongue and lost her way? I'm not sure.

Struan lingers with a hand on my arm, reluctant to leave. I want to kiss him, but Kirsty and Finn are watching with interest. 'We're only giving it an hour or so before we tell the police,' Struan says. 'Agreed?'

The last time the police were at Haven they took my brother away in handcuffs. They failed to look for Jay, left him lying on a lonely ledge for a night and a day. But my sister is vulnerable; she's had too much to deal with lately for her disappearance to be anything other than concerning. I nod, still hoping she'll be with the artists, come wandering down from the hill for dinner with no care for the fuss she's caused.

Struan and Kirsty go one way, Finn and I another. I adjust the seat and mirrors and drive faster than I should. We've only gone a mile out of town when a message pings from Gina:

> She's not up the hill with the artists. Cate and Leah are worried. They're coming back to help look. Call me as soon as you hear anything, Eve.

Chapter 35

Eve

I know these roads, but my mother's accident is in my mind as I hurtle out of one bend and steady the car for the next. Finn is silent beside me. He hasn't slept and his past twenty-four hours have been hell. I glance over. He is changed: tense and watchful. Not a child any longer.

'Should we be worried?' I ask. I'm thinking of cliffs and heights and cruel seas and broken girls with no one to talk to … who choose not to talk, *or can't*.

It doesn't make sense – Finn and I should be her safe harbour. Her silence should not extend to us.

'I don't know,' Finn says, hollowly. I hug another curve, slam my hand on the wheel in frustration.

'Pull over, Eve.' His instruction is last minute. I hit the brakes, pull onto the verge. I swipe the wipers to clear a fine mist of rain. We're parked on high ground looking over a sweep of champagne-coloured sand.

We get out. Wind tears at me. It's exposed up here. 'That's the Campbell place,' Finn says, pointing out a huge sandstone house set back from the road, with a long drive lined with bay trees and a lush expanse of lawns.

I shudder. 'What are we doing here?'

'We're not going near the house,' Finn says. He nods towards the cove that opens up before us.

It's one of the prettiest beaches on the island. A party beach by night, a tourist hotspot in summer. I remember it from my youth, sand rippling with the light of illicit bonfires, elongated shadows of drunken teens against the glow.

The dunes are vast and grassy – protected, but that didn't stop us from sliding down them as kids. At the far end of the bay, steep cliffs climb upwards, their surfaces scarred and jagged. The caves are labyrinthine, spreading through the rock, wending deep inside the cliff. Kirsty didn't like it, and I was scared too, torch beam trembling. There were boys involved, I recall, and strong cider.

This place will forever be tainted by what happened to my sister a decade after my own innocent forays into those caves.

This is where Ryan Campbell brought her, where he drugged her – and *raped her*.

My eyes follow a path that snakes along the clifftop. Those hulking brutes make the cliffs at Haven seem insignificant. I blanch, picturing Holly at the top, leaning above the drop. My daredevil sister. As a child she was always the first to scale a tree, or attempt to make her way up a seemingly impassable cleft in the rocks. She was never scared of anything … *until she became scared of everything*.

Would she deliberately hurt herself?

Finn follows my line of sight and shakes his head as though he follows my line of thought as easily. 'We're not going up there, Eve.'

He points to the beach. It's empty, so unless Holly is inside the labyrinth … 'The *caves*? Why would she go there?' Foreboding swells inside me.

The red-haired girl from the vigil gets out of a mud-splattered Mini. 'I'm trying to get in her head,' she says. 'If she isn't thinking straight, those caves make sense.' She's wearing sports leggings, a loopy scarf. Her hair is pulled into a long, curling ponytail. 'Nice to meet you, Eve,' she adds.

It's awkward watching her and Finn try to figure out how to greet each other.

I tire of their dithering. 'Nice to *finally* meet you, Isla.'

Finn groans. I suspect he'd be embarrassed by anything I said to her.

Just like that, he's my kid brother again.

Isla smiles faintly. 'I haven't been down yet. I think the tide is coming in.'

We climb down sandy steps cut into the side of the dune. Silver tidelines still mark the sand, but the sea is slowly reclaiming the beach. I watch the water for a few seconds, determine that the tide is indeed on its way in.

'There's time,' Finn says. He grabs Isla's hand, and they sprint across the beach. I struggle to keep up. When we reach the towering rocks, he has second thoughts. 'You should both stay out here. I'm a strong swimmer.'

'*Swimmer*?' I echo. I have no intention of any of us swimming any time soon. I throw an anxious glance over my shoulder at the tide. The waves swell and pulse, creeping towards us.

'I'll just have a quick look,' Finn says. 'If she's in there and she's lost track of time … Can I get your phone, Isla? I need a light.'

'You're not going in, I am,' I argue, following him to the narrow entrance.

Finn faces me. 'Eve. Let me do this.'

We're wasting time. I have no great desire to go into the cave, beyond my usual compulsion to protect him. Water pools around the entrance. A channel of cold froth claims my foot and I jump back. 'Be quick and be careful.' Isla hands him her phone.

Finn flashes a grin, disappears inside the rock.

We wait.

Isla shifts, hugs herself as the seconds tick past. 'Did Finn tell you what happened to Holly?'

'*Ryan?*' I nod. I don't know Isla well enough to discuss this with her, even if she was here the night it happened. She gives me an odd look. She's pretty: creamy skin dotted with freckles, navy eyes, hair that shimmers like flame.

The swell keeps coming. My boots sink into the sand. Waves, each bigger than the last, spread across the beach. 'Come on, Finn,' Isla mutters. We step up onto the rocks to avoid the encroaching tide.

'That's it,' I say, as the waves start to lap at the cave mouth. 'I'm going in.' I jump down, alarmed to plunge into ankle-deep water. 'Stay there,' I call to Isla.

The caves are cold, dark. Water drips in a steady percussion and the floor is waterlogged, sucking at my boots. The walls close in on me, rock brushing my shoulders as I edge sideways through a gap, trying not to give way to panic. Inside, the cave opens, light filtering from above.

This is where Holly came to harm, this unprepossessing space filled with boat debris and the stink of seaweed. An image of her lying here, waiting for the sea to claim her, fills my head. The cave is empty.

No sign of my brother. I plough on, squeezing through another gap. I have to rely on my phone torch, and the light bobs at my erratic scrambling. I bump into Finn coming the other way. 'What are you doing, Eve? She's not here. I've gone as deep as I can …'

Behind him, darkness yawns. I have no desire to go further.

When we clamber into the main chamber, my heart sinks. Water covers the cave floor, laps at the walls. Ahead, the aperture has shrunk, a thin slice of light between sea and rock. How did the water move that fast?

I'm frozen, clinging to the rock wall.

'Eve, let's go!' Finn's tone is urgent. He tucks Isla's phone into the neck of his hoodie, secures it with the ties, and steps down into the water. It tugs at him, thigh-deep.

I can't move.

Finn wades a few steps, straining against the current, before he realises I'm not with him. He comes back, holds out a hand. 'Eve, it's okay.'

'I'm scared of small spaces,' I gasp, my voice weirdly high, my lungs constricted.

'And yet you still thought you'd come in here and rescue me,' Finn says, shaking his head. But there's warmth in his tone. He reaches his hand towards me again, struggling to stand still against the weight of seawater. 'Maybe let me have this one.'

I grip his hand, let him guide me. The current grips like a vice around my thighs. The shock of cold steals what little breath I have left. It's only thanks to Finn that I make it to the shrinking cave mouth. He half drags me along.

The beach is transformed: angry waves lashing the rocks, beach dwindling. Sensibly, Isla has sought higher ground, but there's no way back around the rocks – they're too steep. She has to step into the sea with us. She flings her arms around Finn and almost knocks him off his feet. 'I saved your phone,' Finn says with a grin. 'Come on, or we'll have to swim for it.' His voice is almost drowned by the whoosh and crash of the sea as it slaps at the cliffs at our backs. The current sucks at us as we try to outrun the tide.

It's hard going, and every so often one of us stumbles. Finn keeps hold of us both. Finally we make it to softer sand, which gives way to needles of grass. We sprawl on our backs, safe. 'That was scary,' Isla says. I look back: the swell has risen above the gap in the rock, submerging the cave, its vennels and passageways.

'It was *stupid*,' I gasp. We've lived on an island long enough not to take chances with the sea.

My boots are full of water and wet jeans cling to my legs. I'm light-headed from the near miss, from the fear that paralysed me in that cave. I look at my brother. 'Thanks.'

Finn is prone in the grass. 'No problem.' I appreciate that he doesn't say anything more. My decision to go into that cave when Finn's a strong swimmer and I'm crippled by claustrophobia was foolhardy. 'Let's go get the heater turned on in the car and get warmed up.'

Isla scrambles to her feet. 'I've got some towels in the car,' she says. 'They're for the dog, but they'll do.' She glances between me and Finn. 'Then you can tell your sister the truth about what really happened here that night.'

From: @QueenBee
To: @MidsummersChick

OMG, I can't believe it! Now I understand why you couldn't say anything, with the position it would put your family in. If your brother finds out I wouldn't want to be in that monster's shoes. Some guys really are allies … I wish I was there to give you a hug, chick.

Chapter 36

Finn

Heat blasts my face. The windows are steaming up. Five minutes longer and we wouldn't have got out of that cave alive; I shudder, and Eve mistakes it for cold, tossing another of Isla's towels at me. I'm in the passenger seat beside her, with Isla in the back. She's barefoot, cross-legged, drying her long hair.

I've never seen Eve scared like that, and it alarmed me as much as the rising tide. I think of the night of the party, Holly passed out in the cavern, how easily she might have drowned.

I tilt towards the heater blast, try to quell my shivering. Isla leans between the seats. 'So …'

I knew this was a risk – it's why I've been avoiding Isla these past days. It's a double risk bringing her together with Eve, but there's something inevitable about this moment. Drained from my sleepless night, I can hardly think, and my façade is crumbling. I can't maintain my shield of lies.

I tell Eve about Jay carrying Holly up the steps from the beach in his arms, saving her.

Holly bloodstained, bruised, lifeless.

'I *know* this,' Eve says, distressed. She gazes at the Campbell mansion on the headland. 'I'd like to punch him myself, smash every beautiful bone in his face – the worst predators are the pretty ones.' Her fists clench.

I stare at my sister, usually so controlled. 'Eve,' I murmur. I need her to let me finish, or I'll lose my nerve.

Isla touches my shoulder, takes up the story. Her faith in me, like Kirsty's earlier, is overwhelming. She has more reason than anyone to doubt.

'I knew right away she'd been spiked,' Isla says. 'She doesn't like beer; Layla said she only had one before they started dancing. Jay said he got her one later. She was in a proper state – it made sense that someone had put something in her drink. I thought Ryan …'

'Of course,' Eve says. '*Bastard*.'

I stare at my hands, grazes on my knuckles from the rocks layered on top of the old bruises I got from punching Jay in the library, in the final moments of our friendship. Outside the sea surges, waves slamming the shore. Rain streaks the glass and obscures everything, increasing the sense that I'm trapped in a bubble …

'She was flirting with Ryan. According to Layla, she went down to the beach with him.'

Eve is impatient. 'I *know* this. Finn told me.'

'Just listen,' I say softly, and Isla continues.

'There was no reason to question what happened. It was obvious when Jay brought her out of the cave that she was hurt. Her dress was torn; there was blood on her. Jay told us he saw Ryan leaving the caves, swaggering across the sand. We filled in the rest. She's never accused Ryan. In her bedroom that night, I asked her the question, but I phrased it wrong.'

Eve twists round in her seat, very still, eyes locked on Isla. I tip my head against the seat back and close mine.

'I asked: "Did he rape you?" She nodded, just once, then she clammed up, wouldn't speak to me, even look at me.'

'I don't understand …'

'I asked: "Did he rape you?"... Not "Who raped you?"'

The energy in the car shifts. I open my eyes and see realisation dawn on Eve's face. 'No,' she whispers.

'*Jay* told us he saw them going to the caves together, and Ryan leaving alone. *Jay* told us Holly was hurt when he found her, that she was already unconscious. *Jay* told Finn that Ryan was bragging about getting with her. *Jay* showed Finn the photo Ryan sent to everyone.'

I hear the soft susurrations of Eve's breath, can almost hear the tick of her thoughts. She looks at me. Reluctantly, I meet her eyes. 'Finn—'

'Yes, Finn,' Isla says, her voice stinging me. 'Do you still think I'm wrong? It took me too long to work out, but once I did, it was obvious – the way Holly acted around Jay – even that night she shrank from him. The fact that she wouldn't speak, even at home ... Then there was the way he was with me in the library – predatory, entitled – it made it hit home. I saw a ... darkness in him and it all just fell into place. I texted Finn on Friday night to tell him my suspicions and ask him to keep Holly away from Jay, but he didn't reply. When he did, next morning, he said I was mistaken, that I'd got it all wrong ... Do you still think that, Finn?'

I breathe out slowly, surprised to feel as calm as I do. I'm detached, listening while the layers are peeled away, my motive exposed. Jay being Holly's rapist is a far more believable reason for me to hurt him than what he did to Isla in the library.

How can Isla – knowing this – *not* think me guilty? I turn to her and see in her eyes that she believes in me ... *really believes* in me. It's humbling. I take a ragged breath. 'You're not wrong,' I say.

I asked Holly outright on Friday night, and she confirmed it. I should have noticed sooner. The signs were there – Holly avoiding being alone with him, retreating into herself if he was in the room. It shouldn't have taken me so long to see what was going on under my nose.

Jay brought the roofies to the party and put them in her drink.

Jay found her in the caves after an argument with Ryan. *Jay* waited until she was out of it.

And *Jay* raped her.

Now he is dead and I'm firmly in the frame for his murder.

Chapter 37

Eve

I drive back to Haven slowly, my hands trembling on the wheel, the wipers in overdrive. Isla sticks close behind in her Mini. She was fierce in her defence of Finn, and I love her for that.

It makes me feel bad, too. I can't deny that when I heard what Jay did, I doubted Finn. The rage that flared in me must surely be matched or exceeded by the rage Finn felt when he learned the truth. What might *I* have done, on a dark, wet night, knowing that about my best friend and my sister …?

I'm scared for my siblings, more scared than before. 'Inspector Isherwood can't know this,' I say, looking at Finn.

'You're the only one who knows … besides Isla. And Holly.'

'Will she say anything … Isla, I mean?'

'I don't know. She could have said something before now. She respects Holly's privacy; it's her secret to tell … I don't want her to lie for me, if she's asked.'

'It's unlikely that Isherwood will ask directly; she'd have no reason.' I tap my fingers on the wheel. Finding Holly feels more imperative than ever. With everything she's dealing with, she isn't safe … 'She had no choice; she couldn't accuse him, could she?' I say quietly, my heart aching for her.

Holly had to keep quiet or risk tearing her family apart, setting Mum and Gina on opposing sides, making them choose … How lonely it must have been for her. How terrifying, living under the same roof as her rapist.

Finn sighs deeply and I know he's already gone there, more than once. Tormented himself with the ways he *didn't* protect her, the way he laughed and joked with her abuser all those weeks.

'You told us about Holly being raped right after you revealed to Ryan Campbell's brother that Ryan took her into the caves. You let us think it was *him*.'

'I'm not proud of that,' Finn says. 'I believed it was Ryan for so long, it was hard to let go of hating him. He still treated her like crap, Eve. He took her to the caves, put pressure on her, left her there when she wouldn't have sex with him, then sent that photo to everyone to shame her—'

'Still,' I say. 'You practically accused him of *rape*. To *his brother*.'

'I know.' Finn looks away.

I chew my lip. There's no way for him to make amends without revealing the true face of Holly's monster, and no way to do that without making Finn look even more guilty.

I slow for the Haven turning, hoping fervently that when we arrive, Holly will be there. 'This will destroy Mum and Gina,' I say, half to myself.

'Mum knows,' Finn whispers.

'*What?*'

'She knows. Not the whole time. It's true she thinks I was driving the car that killed him, Eve. That's why she crashed it – Isherwood wasn't wrong about that part. *Mum thinks I'm guilty*. She nearly *died* believing I killed someone.'

I think of my mother these past days, grieving for Jay and comforting Gina. Her show of sorrow a lie. Finn is silent, burrowed in his seat. He shakes his head, refuses to say more.

Did Mum find out about Jay before or after Friday night ... and what makes her think Finn's guilty?

At Haven, the police car is back on the drive. I feel Finn tense beside me, and I give his arm a squeeze. In the kitchen, everyone is gathered: Ben, Struan, Kirsty, Cate, Leah.

No Holly.

'You didn't find her?' I say, bursting into the room. Isla and Finn are behind me, holding hands.

'Find who?' Ben says, as the others shake their heads. 'I just got here. I wanted to speak to Gina, but she's back at the hospital, I believe.'

'Holly's missing,' I blurt.

'Missing?' Ben's gaze sharpens. A second missing teenager on his watch is concerning, given what happened to the first.

'She hasn't been seen all day ... maybe since last night.'

'Who saw her last?' Ben looks between us.

'Cate,' I say, turning to look at the girl. 'Didn't you say you were with her right up until she went to bed?'

'Yes,' Cate says. 'She went to sleep around midnight. We watched a movie together. Leah was there too.' She appeals to the older woman, who nods in agreement. 'That's the last time we saw her.' She takes out her phone and taps the screen. 'I've called and texted, but ... nothing. I'm sure she'd answer me.' Her certainty stings. I used to be sure my sister would always answer *my* calls.

Ben says, 'Eve, a word in private?'

I force myself not to look at my brother as I follow the police officer to the den. 'What is it?'

'In Gina's absence, with your mother incapacitated, I thought you'd want the update.'

My heart beats faster. 'What update?'

'There's a warrant out for Christian Allardyce's arrest.'

'*What*? Why – does Gina know?'

'I've asked an officer from the mainland to go to the hospital and tell her. He'll be helping with our enquiries – *once we find him*. Evidence has come to light that he didn't leave the island when he said he did. An islander came forward with dashcam footage showing Christian driving his fancy sports car near the Allardyce estate on Saturday morning.'

'But I thought there was CCTV footage of him boarding a ferry on Friday.'

'His licence plate was picked up boarding on Friday, aye. And his car was on the manifest for the Friday morning crossing, but Christian wasn't in the car. The dashcam footage clearly shows him on the island on Saturday. It's him. Looks like Cassie left the island on Friday, and Christian joined her later.'

'That means …'

'He was on the island at the time of Jay's death, with an alibi that placed him elsewhere. And by all accounts he wasn't up for any father-of-the-year awards …'

'Still,' I say, 'it's hard to imagine a father killing his son.'

'It happens. Maybe they got into an argument and Christian tried to drive off. Maybe Jay stepped in front of his car to stop him and—'

'The police are *seriously* looking at him for Jay's death?'

'We're asking questions. Pursuing the drugs angle too, but I can't say too much about that at the moment.'

'Wait, did you say "When you find him?"'

Ben is impassive. 'He's disappeared since landing in the country.'

I'm reeling from all this. 'Thanks for telling me, Ben.' Gina will be devastated; she's gone from the boy she thinks of a son being implicated in her nephew's death, to her own brother. And Christian's missing, *again*.

We return to the kitchen where Ben takes details of Holly's disappearance. Cate has checked Holly's room, says her phone and sketchbook are missing but nothing else as far as she can tell.

I don't know if that's better or worse.

Worse – I'd prefer my sister to have had the strength to pack a bag and run away with a plan in mind than just flee in a panic.

A plan that doesn't wind up with her beneath the waves. I'm scared of what she might do.

'She's not been doing so well,' Cate says, chewing on a nail. I can see she's upset and feel guilty for my uncharitable thoughts about her – she really cares about my sister. It's not her fault Holly finds her company preferable to mine.

Leah squeezes Cate's arm comfortingly. 'Maybe Fran will find her; she's gone for a walk about.'

'We checked the cove thoroughly, and the woods,' Kirsty tells Ben.

'And I've called the parents of loads of her …' Struan stumbles over the word *friends*, corrects it to *peers*. 'The only ones I can't get in touch with are Layla Mason's, but I think they were going away for the October break. I teach her brother, and he said something about Portugal.'

'Okay.' Ben nods. 'I'll get the word out, and we'll start searching.'

'We'll keep looking as well,' I say, and Finn heaves himself off the sofa where he collapsed when we came in. 'Not you,' I say firmly. 'You're going to sleep.'

Finn gives me a look that says I'm going to have a fight on my hands, and Isla tilts her head, looking between us like she's not sure which side to weigh in on.

Before an argument can commence, the door opens and Fran bursts in. She looks a little wild – but like she's been at the gin again, rather than out on the hill looking for Holly. Cate and Leah exchange glances.

'I can't do this anymore,' Fran says, looking at her fellow artists.

'Fran …' Cate's tone is firm. 'I thought we agreed.'

Leah edges closer to Cate, blinking rapidly.

'I'm sorry, Leah, but I can't keep quiet any longer,' Fran says.

Her gaze rests on Finn. 'I can't let that poor laddie get in trouble and not say anything …'

Ben Carmichael puts his hands on his hips and blows out a breath like he wishes he'd left to start the search for Holly five minutes ago. 'What is it you have to tell us, Miss …'

'Meikle,' Fran says firmly. 'And it's *Ms*. Not married. I have to report a car accident.'

Cate closes her eyes, and Leah drops into a chair, covering her face with her hands.

Fran continues. 'On Thursday – the day before young Jay died – I was a passenger in a car driven by my good friend Leah—' She breaks off to nod towards the older woman, who shrinks in her seat. 'We were driving back from the pub around 10 p.m., and I was a *teensy bit* worse for wear so Leah drove. She overshot the drive and as it's such a narrow road had no choice but to continue until it widens. Up at the lookout point, where the woods open out onto the cliff, there's room to turn.' She blinks. 'I think that's the same spot where Jay died the next day.'

Ben can't feign patience. 'I'm not sure I understand the point …'

'She hit the boulder,' Cate says quickly. 'She's not used to driving, and she hit one of the boulders at the top of the cliff. They're there to stop cars plummeting over the drop I suppose, and they did their job …'

Ben growls. 'This was *before* Jay died, so why—'

'The point is there are a few nasty scrapes on Fran's car now. Of course, it's an old car and it's had no shortage of dings, but these scrapes in particular might be important.' Cate rests a hand on Leah's shoulder. The older woman looks upset.

'My car is blue,' Fran adds.

I finally get the point of all this. 'The paint they took from the boulder might be from *Fran's car*, not Mum's.'

My knees turn weak: Christian Allardyce is a person of interest, the police are looking into Jay's criminal associates and there's a plausible explanation for the forensic evidence that places a blue car at the scene of Jay's death …

Finn might have a motive, and Mum might have doubted his innocence sufficiently to risk her life on that bridge, but it really does seem like my brother is off the hook.

From: @MidsummersChick
To: @QueenBee

Thanks for your support. I don't have anyone else I can talk to. I wish you were here and we could talk in person. He's always there, always watching me, touching me. It's draining, always having to be on my guard, keeping out of his way. I don't know how much longer I can go on. I'll be honest, I've thought about ending it all; sometimes I can't see another way out. You're right: if my brother got wind of it he'd kill him. But I'd hate for it to come to that, which is why I'm not telling him.

Chapter 38

Eve

My phone vibrates on the table. I set down my mug to answer it – Kirsty insisted on tea and biscuits to replenish our energy before we head out.

Ben is on his phone outside, and Kirsty is packing a rucksack for a foray into the forest, this time the dense, spooky woods to the south of Haven. Fran announces her intention of joining our search. Cate takes an emotional Leah back to the guest wing – whether anything will come of Fran's revelation about Leah's driving mishap remains to be seen. Isla taps away on her phone, messaging half the kids on the island. When Struan points out that he already did that, she suppresses a smirk, says no, he called *the parents*, not the same thing.

Gina's name on my screen makes my stomach twist with apprehension.

'Eve.' She sounds weary. 'Brain scans are looking reasonable. They're going to try bringing her round.'

'Ok-ay.' It sounds positive, but Gina's tone is less than reassuring.

'There are no guarantees, Eve. We'll have to see how she is when she wakes. She's had a traumatic brain injury; there's a long road ahead.' I am quiet, watching Kirsty and Struan get organised for the search: provisions, first-aid kit, map and compass, silver foil blanket in case of casualties. Through the window I see cars piling into the drive – the word is out that another search is underway at Haven.

No one wants it to end the way of the last.

'Any word on Holly?' Gina asks.

'No. We're just about to head out again to look.' Panic flickers in my chest; every minute that my sister is missing the stakes increase.

'Okay, keep me posted.'

'You, too … and Gee?'

'Yes, Eve?'

'Ben Carmichael told me about Christian.'

There's a long silence. I hear Gina take a breath as though steadying herself. 'The investigation needs to run its course. I have no idea what to think, so I'm just focusing on Naomi. I'll deal with the rest later.'

'Okay.' We are part of that '*rest*', the life she's built here interleaved with ours. My mother's accident – if accident it was – has pulled the rug from beneath Gina and no matter the outcome of the investigation at this point, she loses *something*.

I end the call and hurry upstairs to change into fleece-lined leggings. When I return to the kitchen, Finn is fighting a losing battle against a united front. Kirsty, Isla and Struan are all adamant he's not coming with us.

'Stay with me,' Isla cajoles. 'We'll keep sending messages. We're more likely to find her this way.'

'You need to sleep, and you've done quite enough tramping around on that knee,' says Kirsty severely.

Struan employs his teacher voice. 'You're staying put. Frankly, you'd only slow us down.'

Finn scowls. He looks hopefully at me, and I grin and ruffle his hair. 'You think *I'm* the most likely to give in? No chance.'

Finn huffs, but accepts the verdict. 'Fine, we'll stay here in case she comes back on her own.' He moves to sit beside Isla at the table and I see the extempore way she tilts towards him, bumping his knee beneath the table with hers. *She loves him*, I realise. I'm glad.

'Gina will call when Mum comes round,' I tell him. 'If she does, ring me right away.'

Finn nods.

Outside, the volunteer search party has gathered in outdoor gear: a serious-looking, heartening assembly. Isla's dad, Ian, is heading operations – he's a tree surgeon, used to navigating the forest. Gav's here too, and he and Kirsty share a brief moment, foreheads touching. I hear her say, 'I'm sorry about Ketty; it was the right thing to do.'

'It was a *risky* thing to do,' Gav says.

Kirsty tosses her head. 'I'm not scared of Ketty.'

'I don't mean him. I mean the people they were both working for …'

Kirsty is solemn when she falls into step with me as we head for the trail Struan mapped out. Ian Maxwell assents after *brief* disagreement with Struan about the route. 'We're fine,' Kirsty says in answer to my unspoken question. 'Gav knows he can't make Ketty's choices for him. It's hard, because they're friends, but …' She gives a shrug, focuses on the ground beneath our feet: broken branches, slimy roots, hillocks of moss. The air alters as we step between the trees, temperature dropping, the scents of pine and loam scouring my nostrils. The sounds are familiar: the scritch and shuffle of invisible creatures, the rattle of branches in the wind, the crunch of our footsteps. An occasional rook call and flurry of movement high above in this vast cathedral.

For hours we walk, the rhythm of our steps hypnotic. Occasionally we pause, consult maps, study the topography of the forest, debate the way. I keep my eyes peeled for sign of Holly. It would be easy to get lost in this place, with the crowns of the trees towering above, the shadows long, and paths abrupted at every turn by fallen logs, dips and rocks and underbrush.

An ominous rumble alerts us to the incoming storm. Ian Maxwell stops us, and we gather in a tired huddle, gulping from water bottles and wiping sweat from our brows. 'The weather isn't great,' Ian says. 'Thunder, getting closer, and it'll be dark within the hour. We should head back. There's been no sign of anyone in these woods.' He's been keeping a keen eye out for a trail.

'But Holly is still out here,' I object hotly, aware of Struan's hand on my arm. 'If it's dangerous for us to be out in this weather, it's worse for her.'

'We don't know she came this way,' Fran says reasonably. 'Like Ian said, there's no sign of her at all. No footprints but our own.'

The consensus is clear, and I have no choice but to fall in with the rest when they make the turn for home. I could stay out here searching, but I'd be alone, and Ian's right – thunderstorms and forests are not a harmonious combination. Plus, it's already darker between the trees, the light fading fast. My phone reception is poor; for all I know Holly could have been found by now.

Mum might have come round.

Christian Allardyce might have been located and charged with his son's murder.

'Eve.' Struan tugs gently on my arm. 'The police are looking too, maybe there'll be news when we get back—'

Our walk has taken us in a loop and when we emerge from the forest I see that we're near the cliffs. A sad strip of police tape flaps in the wind and slabs of ancient rock hunker beneath storm clouds. Out of the cover of trees, the rain is relentless, freezing.

I'll be glad of a change of clothes, and the warmth of the Aga. I pray Holly's home when we get there, not out in this.

The searchers pile into cars, defeated. Struan thanks everyone for coming. Fran heads through to the artists' wing for a shower. In the kitchen, Finn has fallen asleep on the sofa covered in a blanket, feet hanging over the edge. Isla sinks into an armchair by the window, her expression serious as she checks her phone.

Cate, her pink hair twisted into a ballerina bun, takes the tagine Gina made – *was that only this morning?* – out of the Aga while Leah sets the table. I study Leah's face, but she seems recovered from her earlier upset. 'No news,' Cate says quickly, before I can ask. 'I take it you didn't find anything either?'

I kick off my boots, reply with a swift shake of my head. I help Leah with the cutlery, pausing to give her arm a quick squeeze, check she's okay. Her bones are frail as a bird's. She looks up with a shy smile. 'I'm all right,' she says. 'I just feel like a fool. I've never been the best driver; my husband did all the driving when he was alive …'

I smile reassuringly. 'No harm done.'

I wake Finn and we wash up and eat. We have just sat down to eat when Ben arrives. He doesn't knock now, just lets himself in the back door like one of the family.

'No news,' Ben says – both question and answer.

'Do you want something to eat?' I rise to fetch a plate.

Finn is tetchy, picking at his tagine. 'Holly's out there somewhere and we're just sitting having a *dinner* party.'

Isla leans over and squeezes his knee.

Ben ignores him, accepting the plate I pass him. 'Patrol cars are keeping an eye out in all the larger towns and villages; we've put out an appeal on local radio and via our usual communication channels – social media and whatnot.' He turns his attention to Cate who is in Gina's seat at the head of the table, Fran fresh from the shower on one side of her and Leah, trying to put a brave face on for us, on the other.

'You lot seem to spend a lot of time with her,' Ben says. 'Any clues as to her whereabouts?'

Cate's eyes shimmer. 'I wish I did. She seemed okay – I mean, not *okay*, but … I just hope she's with someone, warm and dry and not out there in the storm.' She appeals to the others; Fran sighs and Leah bites her lip. 'I'm sure someone's taken her in,' she says hopefully, but her voice lacks conviction.

There's a ribbon of doubt woven through all our conversations: none of us trust Holly's state of mind.

'The outbuildings,' I say suddenly, clattering my fork onto my plate. 'Please tell me someone has checked the outbuildings.'

Ben frowns. 'I assumed you'd already done that.'

I spring from my seat. The artists jump up too. Fran is the first out the door, with her capable, determined stride and Finn, Cate and I are close behind. The rain is torrential; we make a mad dash across the yard.

Haven has a network of outbuildings in various states of disrepair. Mum is always talking about converting them to expand the scope of the retreat – a spa, or some little log cabins perhaps – but she hasn't done it yet.

Several of the buildings are filled to the brim with junk and rubble, detritus from the last renovation when the studio was added to the footprint of the building. There's a barn that still has a roof and it's here that the remnants of a fire were found in the initial search for Jay. We stand and contemplate the scorched ring of earth. Nearby, two logs are laid out like seats.

Ben walks the perimeter while Finn goes deeper inside, disappearing into the shadows. Cate shivers and wraps her arms around herself. 'This is creepy,' she mutters. Even girl-guide Fran seems to baulk at venturing into the spidery depths of the barn, and contents herself with bouncing her torch beam around the rafters and walls.

I cast about, helpless; I don't know what I'm looking for, but I am disappointed, nonetheless. No Holly, no sign she was here except the strange firepit in the doorway – *who lights a fire in a barn with a wooden roof?*

I sit on one of the upturned logs. From here, you can see to the south of Haven, to the clustered pines of the vast forest we searched earlier, and beyond that, the hills. It's not a bad spot to come for someone seeking solitude. 'Anything?' I yell to Finn.

His voice comes from deep in the building, strained from the exertion of climbing over mounds of builder's rubbish and broken gates. 'Nope.'

I don't know what I expected – Holly curled up in a nest she'd made for herself, asleep like a little babe in the woods?

I'm about to give up, suggest we return to the warmth of the kitchen and our dinner, when something catches my eye. Scratch marks in the dirt and dust of the floor. I lean closer to examine them, shining my phone torch over the area to better see the scuffs. They are not random, I realise. They're symbols.

'There's something here,' I say.

Finn scrambles back into the space, hair dusted with cobwebs. Cate, still lingering by the door, barely inside, comes tentatively forward. Fran almost knocks her over in her eagerness to get in on the action. She shines her torch on the section of floor I'm indicating.

'It's some sort of marks, almost like … *runes*,' Fran says. Whatever they are, I have no idea what they mean. Most of them have been scuffed out, and there are only a few lines and loops remaining. I snap a picture, zoom in on it. Turning the screen, I realise that I've been looking at them upside down. The right way up, the marks are distinguishable as letters.

'It's writing,' I say, showing the others. Cate, Fran and Finn crowd in to look. '*Super* creepy,' Cate says. 'Let's get out of here.' She shivers again.

There are too few letters remaining for me to begin to make sense of the message someone has carved in the dirt of the barn floor. Even if the marks have anything to do with Holly, I have no idea what they mean or how they might help to find her now.

Disappointed, we turn to head back to Haven. Fran lingers, still trying to decipher the message in the dust.

We've just left the barn when the back door to Haven opens, the security light illuminating the yard. Isla stands in the doorway. 'Guys! Come back.'

We run, tumbling into the kitchen. We cluster round Isla, expectant. She waves her phone. 'Layla Mason just posted on Instagram. Her parents and brother might be in Portugal, but *she isn't*.'

Chapter 39

Finn

Ben and Struan head to the Mason's house. Eve wants to go of course, but it makes more sense for it to be them – Ben in his official capacity and Struan as a known adult. He might not teach Layla, but she knows him from school, and the police turning up on her doorstep when her parents are out of the country might spook her.

'Now I think about it,' I say, 'I *might* have seen her at the school the other day …'

'You didn't,' Isla says with authority. 'Nor was she at the vigil. And her social media's been quiet for a few days. This is why – look.' She holds out her phone. I read her post from Saturday – the last until the one a few minutes ago, which snagged Isla's attention.

Typical! Sick for the school holidays. Feeling sorry for myself with movies and soup! #fightingthiscoldlikeawarrior #bringmevitamins #snifflesandselfies

This beneath a heavily filtered selfie of Layla lying among a heap of pillows with a box of tissues, a teddy bear and a glossy novel.

I look at the post from earlier this evening. The image shows two pairs of feet, toes pointing, nails painted – one set neon pink, the other deep green. Beneath the feet, an expensive-looking blanket that reminds me of the ones Mum buys for the guest sofas.

#girlsnightin #bestfriendfeels #shushdonttell!

'Are those *Holly's* feet?' Isla asks.

'I mean, I can't be certain,' I reply. I never thought I'd be trying to identify my sister from her toenails. 'But Layla's in the country and she's not been answering messages asking if anyone's seen Holly, and she's clearly with someone, so …'

'I think it's her,' Fran says. 'Green is her favourite colour.'

It's enough to send Struan and Ben out into the downpour to check.

'I didn't think they were friends any longer,' Cate muses, glancing over Isla's shoulder to look at the picture again.

'She told you that?' I look at her.

Cate goes pink. 'She signed it.'

Eve looks wounded. '*You* know sign language?' It's a source of guilt to Eve that *she* never learned it.

'Well, I wanted to be able to communicate with her after she stopped talking, so, yes, I learned.' Cate rubs at her forehead. 'If no one minds I think I'll go and lie down for a bit. All the drama has given me a headache, not to mention the worry.' She smiles, gives us a quick, awkward salute and slips out. Leah follows, offering a cup of tea, medicine, a cold compress. She and Fran mother Cate, but in different ways – Leah gentle and affectionate, Fran no-nonsense and robust.

Like they mother Holly.

Gina phones again after Cate and Leah go upstairs, while we're all still waiting to hear from Ben and Struan if Holly's at Layla's place. I watch Eve's face shift from hope to fear as she listens to Gina's voice and leans forward. 'What is she saying?'

Eve puts her on speakerphone and Fran, Kirsty and Isla diplomatically excuse themselves to afford us a bit of privacy.

'It didn't go so well ...' Gina says. My heart sinks. 'Don't panic – she's okay. But when they tried to bring her round, she was distressed. Her stats went crazy, and they decided to sedate her again. They'll try again tomorrow.'

Eve exhales slowly. 'Well, we knew it might not be straightforward. Like you say, there's still tomorrow. Any sign of Christian yet?'

'No,' Gina tells us. 'No one knows where he is. The police are looking. He was supposed to go in for an interview, but he never showed. I've seen Cassie and she's *losing it*. Talking about police brutality, for fuck's sake ...' She pauses. 'Sorry, Finn.'

I smother a laugh. Gina swears like a trooper, but gets mad at herself if she does it in front of us – like we don't say worse.

'Apparently the police are searching their house ... *houses*. They seem to be looking into his business dealings. Cassie's staying in a hotel for now ... in the lap of luxury of course.'

'Of course,' Eve murmurs. She tells Gina about Leah's car accident, leaves it hanging like she wants to add: *so you see, more evidence that Finn didn't hurt Jay*.

Awkward, I fiddle with the cuffs of my sweatshirt.

'I spoke to another officer today too, about Naomi's crash. They definitely think it was deliberate. They were asking questions about ... her mental health.' Eve sucks in a breath. I catch her eye and we both still. 'I told her Naomi's state of mind was ... patchy. I can't rule out that she was out of her mind with worry about Finn, thinking that he was responsible for Jay's death. It's *possible* that she wanted to do herself harm.' Her voice shakes as she says it, and I know how hard it is for her to admit that. She never talks about Mum's agoraphobia, won't let anyone else acknowledge it either.

'Gina ...' I begin, with no idea what I'm going to say.

'Don't worry, Finn; I *know* you didn't do it. You're not capable of hurting Jay, and if you had you'd have taken responsibility for it. I *know* you. Plus, your motive is pretty weak – if he got handsy with your girl a punch would have been reasonable.'

Eve's eyes widen and I wonder if she can hear the thudding of my heart.

I open my mouth, but I don't know how to tell her that my motive isn't so weak since her beloved – *dead* – nephew raped my sister.

Eve

I feel for Gina, I really do. I know how it feels to have a brother accused. And I can't imagine what she's been going through all alone at the hospital waiting for Mum to wake up so she can ask the questions she needs answered.

No matter what she says, there's still a cloud hanging over Finn. I *shouldn't* want my mother to wake up and confirm that she drove her car off a bridge because of a mental breakdown, that she was trying to hurt herself … but it's the lesser of two evils.

It's really not such a stretch to think that Mum could take her life. I've been there before, sat with the fear. With Gina living half the time on the mainland for work, she only sees the best of Mum. The mask she wears, the *life-and-soul* vibe she cultivates, the manic edges of her mood. She's at her best when Gina's home weekends and extended breaks. The rest of the time, she's … different. I've seen how low she can sink.

Mad theories invade my tired brain – could *Mum* have somehow been involved in the drugs with Jay?

Ridiculous – you can't be a stay-at-home drug dealer.

Could she have killed Jay herself?

She knows what he did to Holly. Hell hath no fury like a … *mother lion defending her cub*. Or something like that.

I still don't know when she found out – *before* or *after* Jay died – however, Mum was in the midst of one of her loose-vibe dinner parties with the artists when he went missing (dinner is a misnomer; it was all about the gin).

But she was in the artists' wing all evening, as far as I know. That's what she told Ben Carmichael when he asked where everyone was that night – before the thought entered my head that they were being asked for *alibis*.

Holly was in and out of the artists' wing too, glued to Cate and Leah's side. Everyone said so.

Only Finn was alone in his room, un-alibied.

Before finishing the call with Gina, I steer the conversation back to Mum and the doctor's attempt at waking her. 'Did she say anything?' I ask. 'When she first came around?'

'She just kept calling for Holly, saying her name over and over.'

We end the call after Gina tells us they will run more scans and tests tomorrow before trying again to bring her round.

Kirsty and Isla have made more tea while we were talking. I am awash with tea, but I accept a cup. I wonder aloud about sleeping arrangements, since Isla has confirmed that she's checked with her dad and he's happy for her to stay tonight – *no way is she sleeping in Finn's room* – and it makes sense for Kirsty to stay too, avoid driving again on what's shaping up to be another stormy night. If I sleep in the den with Struan, Kirsty and Isla can have my room, one of them on a blow-up on the floor.

Maybe I'm being prudish, probably Mum would let Finn and Isla share … But I don't think Ian Maxwell would. Still, I don't think anyone will feel like sleeping unless Holly is found safe and well.

We sit drinking tea and glancing at our phones, willing them to illuminate with good news. Finn stays by the window, staring out into the dark.

Waiting.

Chapter 40

Last Summer

The night felt precarious. So much hanging in the balance, so many parts of Jay's world unstable. He hated the rollercoaster life had become, the constant adrenaline, the fear.

He drank to drown his thoughts, to distract himself from doom impending. He'd been stupid, cocky. He'd lost the package, been made a fool of – had it taken from right beneath his nose. He didn't know what to do.

He hung out with Holly and Layla for a while, wanting to see how the land lay with Holls now – whether or not he'd burned that bridge.

Things had been good with Holly at first. They kept it secret, and he liked the romance of it, sneaking around. She looked at him like he was her *everything*. It was powerful, being adored, being someone's hero.

But she wouldn't take it to the next level. She wouldn't have sex. Jay had slept with girls before – he could sleep with someone tonight if he wanted – but it was Holly he craved. Holly who captivated him. She was ethereal, other-worldly, nothing like the other girls here.

He knew she was a virgin. He wanted to be patient, but he wanted her more.

He'd pushed too hard before, got carried away. In the woods, beneath a canopy of sun-filtered green. She'd shoved him off, run away.

Now she was all aloof, avoiding him, shearing away when he approached. Finally he'd cornered her last night and they'd rowed. Well, not rowed exactly. He'd pitched a fit, threatened to dump her. She'd shrugged, said: *fine, I don't want to be with you anyway. You're not the boy I thought you were.*

What the hell did that mean?

Like he even wanted to be some fucking knight in armour, some old-fashioned hero like her brother who handled Isla like she was made of both glass and steel, wouldn't allow even a bit of light-hearted ribbing about her.

Jay had responded with the disdain Holly deserved, ignoring her last night and today. *Let her see how it felt.*

He'd wanted her paranoid, desperate, realising what she was missing.

Tonight, she played him at his own game and it *fucking hurt.*

Watching her flirt with *Ryan-fucking-Campbell*. No way she'd rather have that prick than him. He watched them go down to the beach and wanted to hit something.

Maybe if it was just Holly, if he wasn't dealing with all the other shit, it would have been okay. But he was so scared to face his dad. After their last big fight, Jay knew what Christian was capable of. Standing on the bluff, drinking a beer, eyes narrowed on the caves below the cliff, he remembered his father's unrivalled rage, his words like blades, the fist in his face.

He'd cowered like a little kid, hating himself. He wanted to be strong, face up to his dad – *square* up to him. He wanted to shout back, hit back.

He'd deserved it, though: that punch. It had been a moment of madness, a rush of blood to the ... well, not to the head exactly. He hadn't meant to touch Cassie. It had just happened, one of those moments where Jay felt like he was standing outside of himself, watching.

He'd been walking past their bedroom, caught a shadow of movement. Stepped closer, looked round the door. Cassie was naked, her back to him, brushing her hair. He'd stepped closer, holding his breath. She hadn't looked up. He took another step. Her skin was golden, soft as peach flesh.

She screamed bloody murder when he touched her. Grabbed a robe, backed away from him screaming some more and calling him all the names under the sun.

Yeah, he'd deserved his father's anger, deserved the hit. He'd been terrified, hiding in his room waiting for his dad to come home that night, knowing it was going to kick off.

Now he had to face his dad again, tell him he'd lost him money. Christian Allardyce was going to *lose his shit*. Nothing and no one came between him and profit. Jay had only got into dealing for his dad in a vain attempt to get back in his good books – pathetic. Living with Gina was fine, but he couldn't handle being ostracised by his dad, not being part of the Allardyce brand anymore. Christian was untouchable, the Allardyces unimpeachable. No one would suspect him of heading up the biggest drugs operation in island history.

The rush had been enough, for a while. Now, he wanted to tell his dad he was done; *he wanted out.*

Jay had crossed him enough times to be truly scared. He'd seen the dark side – not just that night, after Cassie, but again the first time he said he wanted out. Christian had picked him up in his gleaming fourbie, driven to a remote spot – no shortage of them – and punishment had been served. No hits to his face this time – bruises would attract Gina's attention. His ribs ached at the memory.

Even at Haven he was never beyond his father's reach. The messages were constant, threatening. *You're nothing without me,*

Jay. Less than nothing. I own you. Promises of further penalties: of being disowned, even jail.

Yes, he was very, *very* scared of telling his dad what had happened. Christian would deliver swift retribution on the neds that stole his drugs, even swifter to his son who'd let him down, *again*.

Coming to the party was supposed to take his mind off it. It wasn't working. Holly wasn't playing ball. He'd slipped a little something in the beer he'd given her, like a peace offering. Next thing he knew she was skipping down the beach steps with *him*.

It wasn't fair.

Jay started down the steps, headed in the direction of the caves. He hugged the coastline, keeping to the rocks, thought Ryan Campbell didn't see him when he came out, rearranging his clothing – *bastard*.

He didn't mean Holly harm, not really. He was just wound too tight, the good guy in him buried beneath layers of coercion, obligation, violence.

When he'd slipped the tablet into her drink he'd imagined being the one to look after her when she was wasted. Putting his arm around her, bringing her water and telling her it would all be okay. Tucking her in …

Being her hero.

And yeah, he imagined other stuff too. The line between hero and villain was irrevocably blurred for Jay now.

@QueenBee

OMG are you guys seeing this??? Why do these monsters get away with it? Another queen lost. Controversial opinion alert (no change there, you know me!) – this isn't suicide, this is MURDER. Everyone who turns a blind eye has blood on their hands. Our *government* has blood on their hands. If the authorities won't protect us, maybe it's time we started protecting ourselves … #dobetter #thrivedontjustsurvive #womensupportingwomen #nojustice #someguysareallies

Chapter 41

Now

Eve

I can't sit still, and I definitely can't drink any more tea. I leave the others in the kitchen. The artists' studio is empty, in darkness. The silence in there is strange, with ghostly echoes of industry and creativity.

I turn on a lamp and make a circuit. The place is messy, piles on every surface, paint everywhere. Mum's seascape is nearly done. I admire Leah's screenprint, Fran's epic vase awaiting the kiln. Cate's current piece is strange but beautiful. I look at it for the longest time, trying to make sense of the angel shapes crafted in shimmering paint and delicate material.

The other easels stand empty – abandoned. Mum's absence is most tangible here.

I am about to leave the studio, restored by a moment of peace, when I bump a low table by Mum's easel and send a tower of sketchbooks skittering to the floor. I stoop to retrieve them. As I'm restacking, I come across a book that gives me pause. It's squat with an emerald cover. Etched into the cover, a dragonfly insignia.

This is my sister's. The sketchbook she's been guarding since I got home. The one that Cate found missing from her room, which we all presumed she'd taken with her wherever she's gone.

I shouldn't look – a sketchbook is private, like a diary. But art is a language; and Holly and I have scant means of communication left.

I flip the cover open, guilty. She'd hate me doing this. On the first page is a dramatic charcoal portrait of Jay, beautifully drawn. I don't make it further, nearly jump out of my skin when the overhead lights flick on. I don't know why, but I stuff the sketchbook beneath the hem of my jumper, thankful for the bulky knit. Cate and Leah stand in the doorway when I spin round.

I shriek in surprise. Then start to laugh. 'You guys scared me. I thought you were sleeping,' I say to Cate.

'My head's better, and we wanted to do some work.' Leah is pulling the sheet off her current work, picking up a stick of charcoal. I remember that life is ticking along for them, though for me it feels as if it's come crashing to a halt. 'We fancied an evening sesh. Distraction, maybe.' She glances past me, her gaze flitting over the piles of paints and books that scatter the studio.

Leah pauses the examination of her portrait to glance over her shoulder at me. 'I suppose there's no word of Holly?'

'No, but Ben and Struan should be arriving at Layla's any minute now.' I hold up crossed fingers.

Leah nods and Cate sighs as she toys with a paintbrush at her desk. Her work is unusual, combining fabric and thread with acrylic, the stitching woven through the paint.

I wonder how much Holly has confided in the artists. Of course, if she'd confided anything that hinted at her current whereabouts, they'd have said. But do they know the real identity of Holly's attacker?

If so, they're a danger to Finn, could turn him in to the police at any moment. It still feels like Isherwood would jump at the chance to pin Jay's death on my brother.

I hover between Leah's and Cate's easels. 'Did Holly ever talk about her relationship with Jay?'

Cate's eyes widen, beneath stripes of black liner. 'I know she liked him, but that was before I came. It was just a crush, I think.'

She doesn't know. I breathe easier.

Fran comes in, carrying a huge pot fresh from the kiln. The glaze is beautiful, recreating the stormy landscape of Haven perfectly. She catches my question and chimes in. 'I got the feeling she'd sworn off boys ... even before Ryan Campbell.'

The artists settle to their work. Music fills the studio. Cate starts to mix pigment on her palette, Fran walks a circle around her pot examining it for imperfections, and Leah gets lost in her work, the eyes of that self-portrait burning through me. There is something disturbing about her work – her art is definitely an outlet for her trauma.

'I'll leave you to it.' I edge towards the door, the guilty weight of Holly's sketchbook against my ribs.

Cate's voice halts me. 'We want her found.'

'I know. Thank you.'

Fran looks up from her pot. 'What Ryan did to her ... There's no punishment severe enough, is there?'

Not Ryan, *Jay*.

Okay, so Fran has no idea that the boy who hurt Holly has paid the ultimate price. I need to keep it that way. If the police find out about Holly's attacker, it might be enough for them to put Finn back in an interview room under caution.

We can't risk that.

I bite my lip, wondering if I can let everyone go on thinking that Ryan Campbell is a rapist. *To save my brother, absolutely.*

'No,' I say. 'None. I ... I'm glad Holly's had you all, this past while. I should have been here ...'

Fran shakes her head at my self-reproach. 'You'll tell us as soon as Holly's found?'

'I will … we'll get her through this,' I promise.

I slip out with Holly's sketchbook close to my heart.

I want to take the book to my bedroom for privacy, but I've been gone long enough. I return to the kitchen cradling Holly's secrets to my heart. Kirsty, Isla and Finn are at the table where I left them, talking quietly. Cash whines when he sees me and sniffs the back door. I slip the sketchbook between a stack of cookery books on the counter, not wanting to leave it lying out, and pull on boots.

Outside, the air is cold, rich with rain. Cash sniffs, the wind scuffling his fur. He ventures cautiously beyond the circle of the security light.

I'm listening for cars on the track, for Ben and Struan's return, but all I can hear is the wind, the sea's mournful melody. I'm too aware of our isolation, my silhouette backlit by the glow of the house, clearly visible to any watcher in the dark …

A shift in the air raises goose bumps, but it's only Finn, coming up behind me. 'No sign yet?' he says, hopeful.

'No.' I check my phone, but the reception is bad – must be the weather.

'I might take a walk,' Finn says. 'Check the cliff one more time …'

I want to stop him, but like at the caves, he's resolute. He *needs* to do this. 'She won't be there,' I say, and a vision of Holly, tossed onto the rocks far below the cliff edge, slices through my thoughts. Once there, it won't be dislodged.

Finn

I went back to the cliff that night too.

It was early, dawn not yet breaking over the cove. The wind was dying. The rain had turned the grass at the top of the cliff to a quagmire.

I can't tell Eve that I was on the cliff in the first place … *or that I went back.*

I texted Isla from the clifftop that morning. Sitting on one of those huge stones that preside over the bay. Her message went unanswered the evening before – suspicions undenied. In the morning, I said it was fine, *Holly* was fine. I told her she was wrong about Jay.

I needed her to believe me, stop asking questions, but it didn't work.

I went as close as I dared to the edge, looked over, head spinning. That's when I saw the flash of orange, far below. I jumped to the conclusion that it was Jay's trainer. No one could survive a fall into the jaws of those rocks – easily forty metres. The tide was sweeping in; soon it would carry him away. *He was already dead when he fell. There was nothing I could do.*

Back there now, pelted with rain that feels like punishment, the wind trying to rip me off the land, I wonder how I got it so wrong. *What did I see if not Jay's running shoes?* He was on the ledge, invisible, twenty feet below me, not caught in the teeth of the rocks waiting for the tide. But *something* down there caught my eye.

It was a mistake, like forgetting the ledge.

Texting Isla was another one. The police think I lost my phone Friday night when I was looking for Jay, but I had it Saturday on the cliff. If the loose threads are tied together, they won't match. *The police will know I lied.*

Isla will doubt me.

In my panicked, sleep-deprived state I must have dropped it after I sent that message, when I was limping home. I realised only later that it was gone, and by then it was too risky to go back.

I lean again, fighting the vertigo that almost sends me over the edge. I am convinced I will see Holly this time, with her limbs twisted, her hair draping the rocks like pale weed.

There's nothing there. I retreat from the edge. I should have called the police, told them I'd found Jay, but I hoped he'd be carried off by the sea, problem solved. If I'd remembered about the ledge … if I hadn't been convinced I'd glimpsed him in the sea, maybe I'd have made another choice.

Climbed down to the ledge, checked for a pulse, called for help – *or helped him on his way over*.

There's no way to know whether I'd have chosen right over wrong, morality over justice. My morals are skewed now, and I no longer know what *right* is.

I leave the cliff with one last shuddering look and head home.

Chapter 42

Finn

Ben's car is back on the drive when I return. I start to run, grimacing as my knee protests. In the kitchen, she's there, flanked by Ben and Struan. I sag against the doorframe. Holly looks okay: no blood, no visible injuries.

'We found her at Layla's,' Struan says. I want to rage at my sister, pepper her with questions – what prompted her to run from Haven *now*, when the danger of Jay has passed and I've shown her my fealty, my commitment to her protection at any cost.

Ben takes up the story. 'Her parents *are* out of the country. Layla and Holly were holed up in her bedroom eating ice cream. Layla felt bad, texted Finn to say Holly was okay, but she didn't know he'd lost his phone. She didn't want you to be worried, Finn.' Ben meets my eye, his kind face weary.

I look at my sister and see no such compassion. I'm furious with her, but also I want to pull her into my arms, keep her safe as I've been trying – and failing – to do for so long.

I'm here, I try to convey my support silently. *You don't need to run.*

Holly's eyes drift to me. She blinks to dispel the fear that remains.

'We were so worried,' Eve says, giving Holly a hug. Holly hangs, limp, in her embrace. Her eyes dart around the kitchen – like feeling unsafe is a habit she can't break.

'I'll take my leave,' Ben says, squaring his shoulders to brave the weather again. 'I'm glad this had a happy outcome.'

Unlike the other times he's been called to Haven.

'I'll see you out,' Eve says. 'And let Cate and the others know Holly is back. They've been worried.' Kirsty goes for more towels – Struan and Holly are damp with rain, and I'm drenched too. The artists scurry into the kitchen and surround Holly. Isla and I take a step back as they fuss over her.

'You're freezing,' Fran says, squeezing both of Holly's hands.

'I'll run you a bath.' Leah puts an arm around her shoulder and leads her towards the stairs. Cate follows behind them. I sense their mistrust.

Their reluctance to leave Holly with *me*. My arrest has left its mark.

We need to talk, me and Holls, about how we're going to ride this out. If we can hold our nerve a little longer, things might be all right. The police are looking elsewhere now – by absconding, Christian Allardyce hasn't done himself any favours; he's played into my hands.

If Holly can just keep it together …

I feel bereft, when Holly is gone. I take a towel from Kirsty, shrug when she asks if I want more tea. Looking up, I catch Isla watching me, speculative.

Eve

We should be overcome with relief that Holly is found, but we're all a little flat. Holly is upstairs, being coddled by the artists, and I try not to be jealous. Finn is restive. He paces, looks like he wants to talk but doesn't know where to start.

Kirsty pulls me aside. 'Gav's going to pick me up. I know I

said I'd stay but …'

'It's fine,' I say quickly. 'You should get back to Mac.'

She nods. 'Gav wants me at home, safe.'

I look at her. '*Safe?*'

'He's probably overreacting, but … after I told the police about Ketty, and with Christian Allardyce missing …'

'He thinks you're in *danger*?'

'No, no.' She tries a smile. 'Just …' She trails off, shrugs.

I frown, my earlier unease swimming to the surface. I think of the fire pit in the barn, the garage unlocked, the car, my mother's conviction that there's been someone out there, *watching*.

'I understand,' I say. 'It's fine.'

She smiles briefly. 'Thanks, Eve. And … keep the doors locked, won't you?'

Fifteen minutes later, Gav's headlamps sweep the kitchen. Kirsty says a hasty goodbye and runs out to meet him.

Finn and Isla curl up in the den watching Netflix, and Struan gets his laptop out again. I remember Holly's sketchbook and decide it's time to take a look.

It's harder to justify, with Holly no longer missing. I slip the volume from between the cookbooks and carry it upstairs to my room. On my bed, I flip the pages.

I gaze at the first portrait of Jay, Holly's limerence shining through every pencil stroke. I turn the page …

And freeze.

Every page is Jay. Portrait after portrait. Scratchy pencil sketches and soft, smudgy charcoal. I follow the story of their summer, turning from longing to love, to … something else.

Obsession.

Jay silhouetted on the beach against a sparkle of sea; Jay in a baseball cap, bare-chested, tossing a frisbee; Jay grinning; Jay looking moody. Jay on the cliff, in the garden, the woods, the cove.

Happy, infatuated images, documenting nearly every move.

As I turn the pages, anger consumes her drawings: lines sharp, anguished, deliberate. The work changes, subtly. Like a flip book, each alteration moves me forward in their story. The images are Jay … but not.

It's his face still, but darker. Indifferent, aloof. Holly's realism slips and soon Jay's superimposed onto every dark and demonic creature she could conjure.

The lines press so deep they score the paper and threaten to tear through. I am shocked and impressed in equal parts. They are brilliant … *and terrifying*.

I reach the final page.

It's Holly. Rendered like a bad-ass angel with hair flying and sword in hand. Her face is a mask of fury and there's blood on the blade … Jay crouches at her feet, a pathetic, wizened creature.

I close the book abruptly, open it again, and force myself to examine every detail. Angel-Holly has tears on her cheeks and scars on her arms. A black lettered tattoo wraps her neck like vines, or gripping fingers.

I read the words. *You cannot have me.*

I'm trembling violently. I lean against my headboard and work back through the images, returning to the flowering innocence of early summer, moving through the story again until I am faced with loathing and vengeance.

Holly hated Jay, and her hatred is plain to see in these pages.

I wonder who else has seen this – hopefully no one.

You cannot have me.

The sword … the blood … her fury.

Maybe this was her fantasy: revenge. Holly taking back control, claiming power over him when she had none.

The idea when it comes is like a firework exploding. My heart thrums. Was this a prophecy, a plan?

Could *Holly* have hurt Jay?

From: @QueenBee
To: @MidsummersChick

I'm angry today, chick. Angry for you. Angry for me, and for all the hurting queens out there. The online stuff is an outlet, but there's so much I can't say on there. So much I WANT to say. Like, why are we sitting back and taking this? The law won't protect us, so why don't more of us take the law into our own hands and make this right? Know what I mean?

Chapter 43

Finn

Isla is looking at me, her hand hot on my chest. Her eyes the dark blue of summer seas. It's just the two of us and peace spreads through me. 'I'm glad you're here,' I say, gruff, not trusting my voice. I want to preserve the moment even as it's poised to slip away.

She smiles. 'Me too.'

If the tables were turned, and it was Isla under suspicion of murder, evidence mounted against her … if she had so strong a motive, and I knew she'd lied … would I be so trusting?

Easy. Of course I would. Because there's no way Isla would do something like that.

No way I would either.

But I'll let the police think I did – *to save my sister.*

Eve comes into the den with a book in her hand, as a gust of wind howls down the chimney, drowning the dialogue on the show we're watching. I look up. Isla's fingers are splayed across my ribs, her body curled into mine.

I see in Eve's face that she knows. Her face is paper-white, and I feel mine drain of colour to match. Her lips compress to a narrow line as our eyes meet.

I stand too quickly, forcing my weight onto my bad knee. The swelling has worsened, pulsing beneath the bandage Kirsty replaced earlier. I wince and sway. Isla looks up in alarm and Eve rushes to catch my arm. 'Sit down,' she says. 'Sit down and tell me what's going on, what *this* means.'

She shows me the book and I stare at the cover, the dragonfly, the ornate *H* inscribed in gold. Eve looks at Isla. 'Would you give us a minute, please?'

Isla pauses the TV show and gets up, giving me a worried look. I don't want her to go, but she can't be part of this. I don't want her to be another accomplice, forced to lie too.

'I'll go if you want,' Isla says haltingly. 'But I think I've worked it out.'

Of course she has.

I close my eyes. I'm relying on everyone believing that Jay died because of his choices, the dangerous game he was playing. Or his dad's predilection for violence. I need enough smoke and suspicion to occlude the truth, to keep them from asking questions. I can't have Holly fall under suspicion – she'd never stand it.

But both these women are too perceptive, too clever. I feel the house of cards, formed of my lies, teeter.

Eve swithers, looking from me to Isla. Finally, she cracks the spine of the book and displays a page before us.

I stare at the image and understand. I had no idea Holly had drawn this, but it makes sense how Eve made the leap – the drawing leaves little room for doubt: Holly depicted as an avenging angel holding a sword dripping blood, a cowering and diminished Jay at her feet.

Isla gasps, leans for a closer look.

Holly, what have you done?

I suppose she needed an outlet. Some way of processing it since she couldn't talk to anyone. I can't blame her, but this book will have to go. 'We need to burn that,' I say.

'So, it's true?'

I don't reply. I glance at Isla, and she takes my hand. 'I *knew* you didn't do it,' she says with such conviction that I could cry.

Eve closes the sketchbook, fingers shaking. 'Mum *did* crash into the bridge because there was damage to the car that could be traced back to Jay's death. She was doing what any mother would, protecting her child. But it wasn't you she was protecting, was it, Finn?'

'Because *Holly* was driving the car that killed him,' Isla finishes.

I don't know exactly what I'm feeling: some potent mix of despair and relief. It's over. *They know.*

Weakly, I nod.

Chapter 44

Eve

I stare at my brother. *For once I did not want to be right.* 'Tell me everything,' I say sternly. 'But first, I need a drink.'

'We all do,' Isla chimes. Her voice is soft, but there's a steeliness about her that says I'd better not try to send her away again. She's part of things.

I wish she wasn't, wish she wasn't snared in our family mess. But she knows and there's nothing we can do about that. Back in the kitchen I pretend nothing is wrong, drop a kiss on Struan's cheek as he glances up from his screen – oh, what I'd give to be spirited away to his cosy cottage by the river right now, to watch a movie, burrowed in his big bed beside him.

'You okay?' he says, rubbing tired eyes. I offer him wine, but he declines, says he needs to finish his marking.

I nod, grab an open bottle and three glasses. 'Don't judge; they're seventeen and it's just one drink …'

Struan shrugs, and mimes zipping his lips. 'Finn may as well enjoy the evening before he gets this essay back …' He returns his attention to the laptop.

Somehow, I think a failing English grade is about to be the least of Finn's worries.

In the den, Isla takes a sip of wine. She's calm, which is more than can be said for Finn, who looks like he might pass out. 'Right,' I demand. 'Start talking.'

Finn doesn't seem capable of speaking. Isla puts her glass down. 'I'll start. I've put it together. Some of it I've known a while – like the fact that *Jay* hurt Holly, not Ryan. I worked it out that day in the library; I saw how scared she was of him, and it reminded me of that night when we got her out of the cave, how distressed she was when he went near her. After Finn and I had our text argument, he ghosted me, and each time I saw him – at the school, at the vigil – he avoided me. He might just have lost interest, but I didn't think so …'

I envy her confidence.

'Holly messaged over the weekend, let me know Finn had lost his phone, but she said he lost it *Friday* which I knew wasn't true – he'd texted me on Saturday morning. When I heard about Jay dying I was upset for Finn … not because I thought Finn had hurt him, but because his last interaction with Jay was a fight, and I knew that would stay with him forever. And because, no matter what Jay had done, it was a horrible way to die.'

She reaches out, takes Finn's hand. He closes his eyes.

'Then they arrested Finn, and Naomi drove her car into the bridge, and it didn't look great. But I still wanted to prove he hadn't done it. Finn's not a liar, so I asked myself what *would* motivate him to lie. Not protecting himself, but protecting someone else – *Holly*. I've been watching her; her fear doesn't make sense – Jay's gone, but she's still scared, *still* not talking. *Because she's hiding something*.'

I look to my brother. 'Finn,' I say gently. 'Tell me everything. Now.'

He looks at us and, somehow, he finds his voice. 'I had such a bad feeling that day, knowing Holly was in school unprotected.

She was in the library – what if Ryan found her, or some of those bitches who were so brutal to her, making TikToks about her, calling her names? I told my teacher I had a migraine and skipped. When I got to the library I didn't find Holly, I found Isla. Jay had his hands on her and I just lost it. I only hit him once, but I'd have kept going if Struan – Mr Fraser – hadn't stopped me. I saw a totally different side to Jay in that moment.

'Later, Isla messaged me and told me what she suspected. I didn't want to believe it. I asked Holly outright, and I could see the truth in her eyes. She ran from me, and I didn't know where she was. I didn't know where Jay was either and I got scared. I'd seen him heading out, that was true, and he definitely checked his watch – but maybe he was reading a message. If he was going to meet someone … going to meet Holly … I didn't trust him with her. I don't know what I was planning when I went after them. I'd have confronted him, fought him. But I wouldn't have *killed him*.'

I swallow. 'Go on.'

He drags in a breath. 'Jay was my best friend.' His voice cracks. 'He'd been unravelling for weeks. I felt sorry for him until I saw him with Isla, until I contemplated that *he* might be Holly's monster. I was scared and angry. Holly was nowhere to be found, and Mum and the artists were already halfway to being drunk. So, I wrapped my knee and went looking. I went into the woods. Suddenly my phone buzzed, and it was her. She'd turned on her location like she wanted me to find her. She was *at the cliff*.

'The weather was awful, so much rain. When I got to the clifftop, I saw the car in the gloom and Holly on the ground beside it. She'd taken it out of the garage, I guess, driven up there to meet him. She can drive, though she hasn't taken her test – I taught her on the track last summer. At first I thought it was an accident, that she'd lost control. But the look in her eyes … and when I asked her what had happened, she said *I just needed it to be over*. I started to wonder if she'd arranged to meet him knowing what she was going to do …'

I swallow bile; I feel sick at the thought of our sister plotting murder. 'I got there too late,' Finn continues. 'Holly pointed at the cliff edge. She was shaking, out of control. I tried to calm her down. Jay was in the sea, gone. My priority was getting Holly home, keeping her safe. She was covered in mud, soaked through – and she had *blood* on her forehead for some reason. She threw herself into my arms when she saw me. The driver's door was open, the keys in the ignition, engine running. I asked her again what happened, but all she could say was that Jay was dead, that the car had hit him, that she *needed it to be over*.'

Isla and I are barely breathing, our eyes narrowed on Finn. My fingers clench around the stem of my wine glass so tightly I'm afraid it might snap.

Finn takes a deep, shuddering breath. 'I asked her about Jay again while we sat on the cliff, asked her if he'd hurt her again or if it was just that one time. She went silent again, started signing. She told me it had happened again, *many times*. He was always there, and she couldn't get away from him. I asked her why she hadn't told me, or Mum … or anyone. She just looked at me. Of course she couldn't tell us. Jay was Gina's nephew. He was *family*. I felt so bad, I didn't know what to say. I told her to check her phone, get rid of any messages that might be incriminating, and get in the car. I think I knew, even then, that we weren't going to tell the truth.

'After I drove Holly home, Mum sent me back to drive over our footprints and tyre tracks to make it look like the ground was churned up from cars going back and forth. There were scrapes on the car from where it hit Jay and the stones, but there wasn't much we could do about that. We assumed he'd been swept away … Mum said the body was unlikely to be found, and by the time it was, there would be little evidence left of how he died so the dings on the car wouldn't matter, or we'd have time to get them repaired. Back at the cliff, the rain was worse than ever, and the wind was wild.' Pain swells in his voice. 'I tried to lean out, to look for his body below, but the swell was massive, and my head spun when I got too close to the edge. I was scared.'

I am stunned, imagining these moments unfolding – the frantic hours before Mum called me and made me complicit in their lies, part of the story, an elaborate alibi. And after, while I sat in my kitchen drinking tea and worrying, while I booked my ferry crossing and drove across the country.

She called the police and reported him missing, knowing her daughter had killed him.

Finn looks broken. 'I went back again on my own next morning when Mum and Holly were still sleeping. I sat on the cliff as the dawn broke and the weather cleared. It took me ages to steel myself to look, and when I did, I saw what looked like one of his trainers on the rocks below, but that was all. The cove is so remote … I thought any evidence would be long gone before anyone started looking.' He sucks in air and his voice cracks, tears coursing down his cheeks. 'We all forgot about the ledge.'

From: @QueenBee
To: @MidsummersChick

YOU NEED TO GET THIS SORTED! Seriously, chick, this guy is so dangerous, and he's living in your HOUSE!!! He's charmed everyone around you so that he can keep preying on you, keep you silent. He's not going to stop. If not you, then someone else. The guy's a predator. He has a disease that can't be cured. You're going to have to do something about him … You owe it to all of us. You owe it to yourself.

Chapter 45

Eve

'We can't involve Struan, Kirsty or the artists in this,' I say. 'Nobody who doesn't already know.' If we do, we'll be expecting them to lie, and I won't ask that.

I'm an accomplice – from this moment onwards, I'm going to lie to defend my sister. I'm going to help her cover up a murder, just like Finn and my mother have been doing for days. I look at Isla, wishing to God she was anywhere but here. 'It's okay,' Isla says, fierce. 'I'm in this with you. I saw her that night, when Jay brought her out of the cave. Holly's the victim in this.'

I think of my sister, pale and fragmented as she was led upstairs by the artists. I recalibrate my view – she's not fragile, no helpless victim, but a warrior, capable of saving herself in the worst way imaginable.

I wonder if she's told any of this to the artists, as they're so close. Surely they would have *said* something. Isla might feel part of some righteous collusion, but she saw Holly broken by Jay, and she loves Finn – she's got good reason to stand with my sister. I won't put anyone else in that position. We can't afford for Cate, Leah and Fran to know the truth. I won't let Struan lie for us either, even if it means pushing him away again.

I have more questions. I want to know exactly what went down on that cliff. She had his blood on her – did the force of the car hitting him push him over the edge, or did she help him on his way? The thought makes me shiver.

I'm astonished that Finn and Mum have managed to lie with such conviction. They pretended Jay was a missing person. Reported it to the police, to me, to Gina, as if they believed he might walk through the door at any minute. They feigned shock when his body was found, when the post-mortem report revealed its truths … Astounding.

If he hadn't landed on that ledge, they might have got away with it being a freak accident.

Finn ducks his head. 'I'm sorry. I couldn't tell you the truth. Mum and I did what we did to protect Holly. I burned the clothes in the barn because the weather was so bad, I couldn't get a flame to light outdoors. Mum put Holly in the bath and washed her hair …'

'I wish you had told me. I wish you hadn't gone through this alone.'

Finn bites his lip.

'Is there anything else I don't know?'

He shakes his head. 'That's all. Holly went to meet Jay that night because she was sick of being scared. Tired of hiding, watching, pretending. He was there every day – at the dinner table, sleeping down the corridor from her.' Finn's trembling, and I wonder how many times he's been over this in his mind. 'I suppose she took the car because it made her feel safer … an easy getaway.'

It could also be classed as premeditation. A weapon.

'She must have been close to going over the drop herself,' I say.

Finn rubs his hands over his face. Maybe I don't *need* to know if my sister got out the car, crept over to where Jay lay, shattered and bleeding, and rolled him off the edge, thinking he'd be lost to the waves …

I take my brother's hand and reflect on everything he's been through these past days. The weight of Holly's crime on his shoulders, trying to keep our mother steady. 'I didn't know Mum was going to do that with the car,' he mutters.

'She'd have been better setting fire to it,' Isla says, matter-of-fact, and we both stare at her. 'I'm just saying, if she was going to destroy evidence …'

Finn looks at me. 'What do we do, Eve?'

I don't know, and his trust weighs heavy on me. Supposing I can get past the truth that my sister killed a boy, that my mum and brother have lied to conceal it, there remains the irrefutable fact that Imogen Isherwood *knows* Jay's killer is close to home. She suspected Finn, but it doesn't matter – one thread will unravel all. He won't betray Holly, but she might come forward to save him. Either way, *we're fucked*.

Imogen can investigate Leah's collision with that same boulder, and Christian's dodgy business dealings all she likes. She can probe Jay's involvement in dealing drugs, but nothing will tie up the case like one more scrap of evidence against my siblings.

Finn will lie to defend Holly; my mother will lie to protect them both. Either Finn or Mum will take the fall for her.

One of them will answer for this.

I can't save them all.

We have an early morning visit from Ben Carmichael. Unsurprisingly, I didn't sleep. I pour Ben a mug of coffee as he rubs his hands to warm them. My thoughts are more disordered than ever, and his uniformed presence isn't helping.

'Anything?' I say, trying to keep my tone casual, wondering if I sound jumpy.

He slurps his coffee. 'We're still looking for Christian, but we have CCTV footage of him and Jay arguing in town on Friday afternoon.'

'Really?' I try not to sound too hopeful.

Ben nods. 'Shouldn't be telling you this, but the guy's up to his neck in the distribution of drugs. *He* was using Jay as a runner. Between his financials and a witness who's prepared to sell him down the river ...' Ben grins uneasily.

A witness.

Ketty?

Thank you, Kirsty.

I hide my hands beneath the table to conceal their tremble, remembering Finn doing the same thing in the interview room in the police station. Will I find myself in such a place? Or in a courtroom, with my only choice to condemn one of my siblings or perjure myself?

'You must be relieved that Holly's home, Finn out of custody,' Ben says. I nod absently. 'Layla Mason told me that Holly was on her phone the whole time she was with her but wouldn't tell Layla who she was messaging. Layla assumed it was you. That's why she didn't feel too bad about hiding Holly's whereabouts, or posting that picture on *Insta-thingy*.'

I shake my head. 'Holly wasn't messaging me.'

'She must have other friends – online maybe. Kids are different these days. All the stranger-danger stuff we used to teach, but it's online that they meet dodgy folk, isn't it?'

I nod again, my fingers drumming. I think of Holly's deleted accounts. A year ago, I wouldn't have batted an eyelid at the prospect of Holly talking to unknown friends online, scrolling for hours. But now, it seems less plausible. Since he mentions it, I've noticed Holly on her phone *a lot* lately ...

We pass long minutes in silence, Ben drinking his coffee and me glancing at my phone – stubbornly silent. I am waiting for a call from Gina.

'I hope you don't think I'm overstepping, Eve,' Ben says. 'But I don't want you to hear this from someone else. You know what the rumour mill is ...'

My gaze snaps to him. 'What?'

'Ryan Campbell is telling anyone who'll listen that he's been falsely accused of raping Holly. He's saying it wisnae him, that she was fine when he left her, that they had a kiss but that was as far as it went.' There's a buzzing in my ears as I stare at Ben. The officer heaves a sigh. 'He's saying that Jay Allardyce was on the beach when he left the caves. His theory is that if anyone raped Holly, it was Jay. I don't like to speak ill of the dead, but like I say, I cannae have Gina hearing this on the grapevine.'

My whole body turns cold. *We can't have her hearing it at all.* Isherwood either.

'Ryan Campbell has a vested interest in shifting the blame.'

'True. And even if he didn't do … *that*, he still took that picture, sent it to everyone. Wee shit that he is.'

I reach for my coffee cup, as Ben says, 'Holly mebbe needs a wee bit of help, Eve.'

'I'm aware of that, thank you,' I snap, then think better of my anger. 'Sorry. I'm wound a bit tight this morning, waiting to hear from the hospital …'

Ben nods. 'It's fine. Oh, that's something …' He reaches into his inside pocket, pulls out an evidence bag. 'Inspector Isherwood asked me to find out if anyone here recognises this before it goes to the lab.' He unfolds the bag. It contains a strip of fabric, a dirty, sea-stained scrap of bright orange wool. I slide the bag closer, study the garment through the plastic. My heart patters painfully when I recognise the diamond patterns stitched into the wool. It's identical to the headbands I've seen Holly wearing – neon blue and green. This looks like the third in a set.

'No,' I whisper. 'I've never seen it before. Where did you find it?'

'Isherwood saw it, at the cove. Caught on some rocks.'

Evidence found on a beach could come from anywhere, swept in on the tide.

I think of Finn, looking over the edge on Saturday morning, seeing something he thought was one of Jay's trainers. *Something bright orange …*

Ben turns the bag over. A rust-coloured stain catches my eye. *Blood.* DNA evidence. 'Aye, as you say …'

Holly had Jay's blood on her forehead that night.

I catch a glint in the light and see, as Ben picks the bag up to pocket it, several long, pale hairs snagged in the wool.

From: @QueenBee
To: @MidsummersChick

You can do this. I believe in you. You HAVE to do this. Don't trust anyone. They can't help you now. Not even your brother has the balls for what needs to be done. I'm the only one you can trust. I wish I was there with you.

Chapter 46

Eve

I gaze out of the window at a mounting weather front while I talk to Gina on the phone – it's blowing a hoolie out there. 'That's brilliant, Gee,' I say, a rush of relief crashing over me. *Good news finally.* 'Yes, of course, I'll tell them right away.'

I shout for the twins who appear from different ends of the house – Finn from the den where he's been holed up with Isla watching TV since they came back from a brisk, wild walk up the hill, and Holly from her bedroom. I want to scoop my sister up in a hug, but I know she wouldn't let me. 'Mum's awake,' I tell them. 'She's doing okay. She's talking.'

'No brain damage?' Finn's face lights up as he smiles for the first time in days. I hug my brother, enjoying the clean blast of relief from the incredible stress we've all been under. Like the cool sweep of sea air on a hot day.

I was *certain* my mother was going to be okay … and yet, I couldn't shake the fear that if she woke, she wouldn't be the same. Mind, she's got her troubles to face.

I haven't told the twins about the headband; I can't even *think* about it …

I haven't managed to talk to Holly either. She's closed down again. Although she does seem to be spending less time in the artists' wing today. The artists are keeping a low profile. Cate, Leah and Fran are giving us space.

I accept a mug from Isla and curl up in Holly's favourite window seat. I watch the wind shaking the trees in the forest so violently I'm sure there will be more down by morning. I pull up the forecast on my phone. Storm *Evlyn* is predicted to sweep the north and west of the country from mid-afternoon onwards, likely to last most of the night. It's never a good sign when they name a storm, even less so when they call it something pretty.

Struan comes in from outside, where he's been checking the house and outbuildings. He whistles through his teeth, shakes rain from his hair. 'It's rough out already.'

He hangs his jacket on the back of a chair, kicks off his boots and comes to kiss me. Finn snorts from the table where he and Isla are drinking mugs of tea; she's got her feet up on his lap and they're watching videos on Isla's phone. Struan looks over at him. 'Maybe it would be better use of your time getting a redraft of that Macbeth essay you submitted last week.'

Finn's head snaps up. 'I don't have a resubmission to do …'

'Not yet.' Struan smirks. 'But I was doing some marking last night. You could wait for me to hand it back … or you could rewrite it now. Resubmit by Monday and we'll pretend the first version didn't exist – probably best for all concerned if it never sees the light of day.'

Isla laughs and pokes Finn in the ribs.

'Nasty,' Finn mutters.

'*Fair*,' says Struan, still smiling. 'If you want any help …'

I don't know if he's trying to distract my brother as a favour, or if Finn's essay sucks, but either way I'm grateful. Finn needs something else to focus on.

My brother gets up with a weary sigh and retrieves his laptop.

I envy Struan his ignorance, envy Finn and Isla the way they're in this together – wrapped around the same secret, whereas Struan and I are on opposite sides of the truth.

They're teenagers, with a less well-developed sense of consequence. I know Finn's worried, but he can push his fear aside in a way I can't.

The storm is a brief reprieve – Imogen Isherwood is trapped on the mainland with the ferries cancelled while we're holed up here. On the other side of things, I'll have to find a way to navigate this, deal with the fact that Holly killed Jay. Our family won't survive unscathed.

I think of Gina, happily ignorant at the hospital. Will Mum tell her? Speak the words that bring everything crashing down? I gaze out of the window again, glad of the Aga's rumbling warmth, my woolly socks, the thickness of Haven's walls. It's only mid-afternoon, but the sky is darkening at an alarming rate.

'Crap,' Isla says, looking at her phone. 'Looks like you're going to get peace to do that coursework, Finn. My dad wants me back home before the weather gets worse.'

Struan glances out the window. 'Not a bad call. The roads aren't going to be great later on.'

I look up. 'You should go too, Stru. While you can.' I want him, but I can't cope with this unwieldy secret between us. Struan looks hurt but quickly masks his disappointment.

'Isla, do you need a lift home? Finn can drive your car over tomorrow or bring it to school Monday when the weather's cleared. I don't like the idea of you driving in this—'

His easy assumption that Finn will be at school on Monday both reassures and chills me: it reminds me how far apart we are in this.

Too far to go back.

Isla accepts. There will be flash floods all over the island tonight. She runs upstairs to gather her things and Finn drifts behind to help – or snatch a final few minutes together. Struan leans over to kiss me again, and I tilt my face so that his lips land on my cheek.

He stills. 'I could come back after dropping Isla off ...'

I can't look at him, can't face the hurt I know I'll see in his face. 'No, that's okay.'

He draws back like I've slapped him. His tone is casual on the surface, steely beneath. 'I don't like the thought of you here alone,' he says.

I don't let my shield drop. 'I'm not alone. I have the twins ... and the artists.'

Christian Allardyce has given police the slip. No one knows where he is, but he's resourceful enough to get back here ... Still, I know I don't have to worry about him. Christian Allardyce is not the murderer Struan believes he is.

Though he might be a vengeful father ...

I shake off the worry. 'We'll be fine.' I reach for Cashew, curled across my feet with his long, spanielly ears folded over his face and paws outstretched. 'We've got this fearsome beast to protect us.'

Struan doesn't smile. 'You really want me to go?'

I nod, not trusting my voice.

'Okay.'

Five minutes later Haven is deserted. It's just me and Finn in the kitchen, my brother sighing over his essay. Holly lurks upstairs, unreachable. The artists are in the studio – I make a mental note to check on them, but the thought quickly goes out of my mind. They've been fending for themselves this long.

The kitchen is quiet. Just the ticking clock, the tap of Finn's laptop keys, his fidgeting as he tries to get his brain in gear. I get up and turn on the radio, but the storm is messing with reception. Instead, I flip on the kitchen speaker and connect my phone, put on a smooth playlist of songs that Gina and my mother love to dance to. I hope the Wi-Fi won't be the next casualty. We often lose electricity in storms like this.

I sink back into my seat and close my eyes, try to conjure the ghosts of good times spent in this kitchen.

We'll be fine with the Aga, and there are camping lanterns

and candles. In other circumstances, it might be fun, romantic. We'd gather in the kitchen, make a meal, drink wine, play cards by candlelight.

I take advantage of the quiet to work. I've hardly touched my laptop since I got here, but I can't put it off forever. I check my email, reply to a message from my tutor, log on to the course page where our student updates are posted. I am out of the loop. Whilst I'm online, I email my boss at The Bookish Beat, apologising for my ongoing absence, letting her know about my mum's accident and the fact that she's in hospital. She's understanding to a point, but I have no idea when I'll be back.

We pass an hour in silence. Finn makes a pot of coffee, and I go to the pantry for biscuits.

My phone startles me sometime later and I snatch it up from the window ledge. *Struan*.

'Eve, I just wanted to let you know there's been a landslip on the road, about a mile from the turn-off for Haven. A couple of trees down. Must have just happened after I drove through. I … won't be able to get back. I know you said you didn't want me to, but—'

God, he's a glutton for punishment. I pinch the bridge of my nose and fight not to beg him to battle his way back to me.

'They won't be able to get anyone out to deal with it until the storm clears.'

'Shit.' I slide my laptop off my knees and pace the kitchen, feeling caged. There's only one road to Haven, and if it's impassable, then we're cut off for the duration of the storm. Perhaps I should be pleased – the police won't be able to get here either, which means no more questions or accusations.

I feel oddly claustrophobic, even with so much space around me.

Gina is stranded on the mainland, and Kirsty and Struan are the wrong side of fallen trees and slipped earth. I rub my arms as I listen to Struan apologising, promising he'll be back as soon as the road is cleared. *Like he doesn't believe that I don't want him here.*

Goose bumps prickle my skin. 'Stay indoors,' Struan tells me. 'The worst of the weather is forecast from 8 p.m. onwards, but Haven is solid; you'll be all right even if the power goes out.'

His urgency chills me. Struan isn't prone to melodrama. I think again of Christian, the tumble of outbuildings with their nooks and crannies, my mother's paranoia, the fact that she needed a knife at her side to feel safe the one time we left her alone …

'Sure,' I say with a sigh, pushing the thoughts away: normally I don't scare easily. We say our goodbyes.

Finn looks up. 'What's going on?'

I tell him about the landslip, and he pushes away his laptop. His forehead creases. 'What's going to happen, Eve?'

'We'll be okay. There's plenty of food in the house. The storm will blow itself out by morning. These storms never last—'

'No,' he says. 'I mean *everything*.'

He gets up, follows me back to my window nook where I attempt to recreate my bubble of peace. He leans against the wall, arms folded. After a moment I realise he's silently crying. I get up, grip him by the shoulders. 'Finn …' He's so much taller than me, but he looks like a child as he breaks down in my arms.

'One of us is going to prison,' Finn sniffs. 'Me or Holly. *Or both*.'

Or Mum, I think. More likely – she'll go full mama bear to protect the twins. If the crash has shown us anything, it's that.

'I won't let that happen,' I say, soothing Finn. I have no idea how I will keep this promise, but I must. *Somehow*.

He straightens up. 'I'm scared, Evie.'

'I know.' A sound attracts my attention and I look up to see Holly frozen in the doorway, eyes huge. She must have overheard everything Finn said about prison … 'Holls—' I say. 'Wait.'

She flees in a swirl of hair, up the stairs.

Another door opens, and Cate comes in. She looks awkward. 'Sorry,' she says as she slips past. 'Just need to borrow some oat milk …'

'That's fine.' I sigh. We've been neglecting their needs again. 'I'm sorry about all this.'

She waves a hand. 'The weather's not your fault.' She stops, looks at me, past me. Sees Finn trying to stem his tears, both of us with our emotions pulsing close to the surface. 'Not more bad news?'

'No, no. Good news, actually. My mother woke up from her coma. It's just ... a lot,' I finish lamely. Finn buries himself behind his laptop again, embarrassed to be caught crying. 'Oh, also, I've just heard that there's some trees down on the coastal road, between here and the main road. Haven is ... cut off. For the duration of the storm.'

Cate shivers theatrically. 'Eek, how creepy.' But she's smiling. 'I'm sure we'll be fine. I'll probably just work on my painting. Storms always inspire me. Is there anything I can do to help? I could make dinner ...'

I nod slowly. There's something comforting about the idea of being looked after, particularly tonight. 'That would be amazing. Thank you. Of course, we won't be charging you guys for this week.'

Cate smiles. 'It's not a bother. We like helping.'

'You ... you couldn't check on Holly for me could you? She's ... weird today. She could do with a friendly face.'

Cate nods. 'She's not really connecting with any of us today either ... but I'll try. I'll go do that first, then I'll make a start on dinner. With so few of us left, we should stick together.'

I agree, try to get back to work after she leaves. Finn abandons his essay and slumps on the sofa. He pats the cushions for Cash to join him and cuddles up with the dog. When I glance over in a few minutes, he's fallen asleep.

My muse deserts me. I can't concentrate. I keep running over things in my mind, trying to work out a solution – one that doesn't involve me losing one or both of my siblings, or letting my mother sacrifice herself.

The police don't have any real evidence, I remind myself.

Except that headband, if forensic tests reveal Jay's blood and Holly's hair …

Rain batters the windows and the wind blows so fiercely the glass shudders beside me, making me flinch.

Holly has an alibi. She was with Cate and Leah all evening. They must have been mistaken, thinking of another night, but it was a lucky mistake. It will be a disaster if one of them remembers at some point that it's not true.

Finn has no alibi. My mother was partying with the guests too, but she'd have been flitting in and out of rooms, as is her wont. I'm sure the time-of-death window must be wide enough to include the early hours when she could have sneaked out and committed the atrocity. If the police are convinced one of them did it, will they care which?

Will they let my mother take the rap for my sister or keep probing until they break her, free the truth?

I can't take the idea of Mum in a police cell. A hospital is bad enough. She won't survive, away from Haven. *Home might be a prison, but it's of her own making.*

But Holly in a cell – or a psych ward, medicated and trapped – is worse.

My heart accelerates. As long as we choose a story and stick to it, we'll be fine. I deliberately slow my breath, try to calm myself. We've got all night to work out what we're going to say. The storm has bought me that time.

My breathing is almost back to normal when I remember the sketchbook. Evidence of premeditation, of Holly's state of mind. It was enough to plant the seed of doubt about her for me; it will be enough to plant a similar seed in Isherwood's mind.

I jump up, head over to the counter. The last time I saw the sketchbook was when I slipped it back into the stack of cookbooks and mess. I scrabble about, displacing junk mail and bills, scattering postcards, random recipes, ferry timetables, invoices …

I'll have to burn it. Holly will be furious with me for destroying her art, but it's for the best. In the long run she'll understand.

I put my hands on my hips, survey the mess I've made. Finn moved everything around when he dug out the cafetiere earlier. Maybe he moved it somewhere safe, *like I should have done the moment I found it*.

Ben was here this morning. If the police get an inkling about Holly it will be over … She won't withstand the pressure like Finn did. What will happen when she proves not unwilling but unable to speak? Will they judge her incapable, insane …?

I can't shake my worry that maybe *Ben* found the sketchbook and has taken it to Isherwood. Did I leave him alone? No, but my back was turned when I made the coffee and when I fetched milk from the fridge. Maybe I didn't put it back among the cookbooks, but left it lying out.

I wake Finn, rousing him ungently. He rises to meet my fear when I tell him what I'm looking for. We search high and low, but we can't find it.

The sketchbook is gone, and I have no way of knowing in whose hands it might be.

Chapter 47

Finn

Eve's in a panic about the missing sketchbook, but there's no opportunity to keep looking because Cate and Leah are back, rummaging through the cupboards for ingredients to make dinner. Cate tells us Holly wouldn't open the door when she tried to check on her earlier.

Eve's scared Holly's drawings will be enough to condemn her. I should be scared of that too, but honestly, I'm kind of numb. Shock, long delayed, is catching up with me. 'The sketchbook has to be in the house,' I murmur when Cate goes into the pantry and Leah leans into the fridge. Eve wants to burn the book, but I imagine hurling it over the cliff instead, to be taken by the tide, and become swollen with salt and water, images slipping loose.

Eve turns to me, bleak. 'Did you and Mum discuss this? Did you talk about which of you would take the blame if it all came out? Did you have a *plan*?'

'*What*? No—' I grimace. 'Eve, it wasn't like that.' I glance towards the pantry. Cate is still in there, and Leah is singing to herself, as the playlist croons in the background, drowning our voices.

Eve frowns, looks away – is she imagining the three of us plotting, ghastly whispers in the dark? It wasn't so calculated; it was desperation and disarray, that night. Disbelief and blind panic.

'We need to talk to Holly,' Eve says. 'Now we're here alone, it's a good time. We need to agree on a story. Stick as close to the facts as possible. We *must* stick together.' She reaches out her hand to grip mine, squeezes urgently.

We're not alone, though.

Cate emerges from the pantry, arms full of tins, tatty onions, bunches of Mum's herbs. She smiles at me as she dumps everything on the table, comparing notes with Leah's findings from the fridge. 'Won't be long, I'll rustle something up.'

I return to the sofa, dig up the dog-eared copy of the Stephen King I was reading the other night. Eve picks her laptop back up, and I can tell her mind is still going a million miles an hour.

Something snags my attention on the window ledge. A flash of light. I lift a splayed magazine, find Holly's phone beneath it, lighting with a notification.

I pick it up. I know I shouldn't, but I'm compelled to look. A fear that she's not been careful, that there might be something incriminating on her phone. She was careless enough to leave her sketchbook lying around, her intentions bare for all to see. What if she messaged Jay, threatened him, set up a meeting that night on the cliff? She was barely in her right mind when I found her, and she's hardly been rational since.

We thought Jay's death would be ruled a careless, calamitous accident, thought his body would be too battered to betray its secrets when – *if* – he washed up.

We covered our tracks, created a narrative of a missing boy: frightened family phoning round, search parties like we believed he had wandered off and got lost in the hills.

But we didn't go far enough.

I didn't think about phone records, the secrets they might hold. If the police get hold of them, which they surely will …

I don't know where Jay's phone is. I assumed it tumbled into the sea when Holly pushed him over the lip of the cliff. Now I hold *Holly's* phone in my hand. What if this is a missing link?

I weigh it in my hand, considering her privacy. We're far beyond normal rules. I jerk my head at Eve, and we slip out of the kitchen into the den, where piled blankets remind me that my sister has been spending her nights in here with my English teacher.

Eve blushes as she tidies up the bedding.

'It's Holls' phone,' I tell Eve. 'Should we?'

She bites her lip. 'We don't know her password.'

'I could have a stab at it—'

'*Should* we, though?'

'Probably not. But what if there's evidence on here that we don't know about? I don't know what Holly's going to do or say. She's as much of a risk as Mum.'

She nods. 'Do it.'

I try a few things – Mum's birthdate, mine and Holly's, Eve's. Nothing. Then I get a flash of inspiration. I type 185202 and the phone unlocks.

Eve looks at me in awe. 'How did you do that?'

'Easy. Holly's always going on about how I'm two minutes older—'

'Only because you rub it in all the time.'

'So, her password is the time she was born. 18:52. Two minutes after me, so 02.'

'That's … *weird* that you'd know that.'

I shrug. Maybe I've seen her tap the numbers without even realising. Maybe I've buried a memory of the digits, or she's *that* predictable, or I'm *that* perceptive when it comes to my twin.

We huddle over the phone. 'So, what are we looking for?'

Now the phone is unlocked in my hand it feels wrong. But my curiosity won't be curtailed. 'Messages between her and Jay. Photos of them together. Her socials.' I shrug. Who knows what the device might be hiding.

'She doesn't have any social media accounts anymore,' Eve says quickly; then reddens. 'I used to follow her, read her posts as a way to stay … connected.' It's her turn to shrug and be embarrassed.

I shake my head, but I'm smiling. 'Proper stalker – you know that?'

Eve slaps my arm. 'I am not!'

I smile to soothe her outrage. It feels good, bickering with Eve. Like old times.

'It's not stalking when you do it in plain sight. She accepted me as a friend on all her platforms; she knew I was able to see what she posted. You and Mum followed her too.'

But it's not the same: Eve read Holly's social media to understand her better, to stay in touch without actually interacting. It makes me sad that their relationship was reduced to that. God knows, Holly has kept us all at arm's length at times, but Eve more than most. Their sisterly bond has long been strained by unspoken comparisons, by the way Eve mothered her – not so different from the way she tries to mother me, but perceived differently for sure.

'Do you stalk me too?' I ask, and Eve gives me another admonishing tap. 'It took me a while to realise that Holly had deleted her socials.'

'I guess it was around the time of the *rape*.' She flinches. 'When that picture was doing the rounds at school. Maybe she was getting hassle online, cyberbullying or something.'

I swipe the screen, studying the collection of apps. Eve's right; there's not much left. The X icon catches my eye and I click on it; maybe she kept one account. I'd rather check something public than delve into her private WhatsApp conversations just yet – that seems more of a violation, though it might be necessary if I'm going to understand what secrets her phone might offer to prying eyes.

'She definitely deleted that account,' says Eve, looking over my shoulder. Her tone turns wistful. 'I loved her posts: so feisty, so innocent.'

The app loads. 'Well, looks like she set up another one.' I show her the screen. The app is logged into an account called … *@MidsummersChick*. There's no profile photograph, nothing to identify the account as belonging to Holly.

'Wait, what?' Eve leans across to look. 'What – who is Midsummers Chick?'

'Maybe something to do with *A Midsummer Night's Dream*? But I don't know what the significance of it is.' It's a weird play. We studied it last year, and I remember Holly was into it. 'Holly is one of the few people I know who actually *likes* Shakespeare,' I add.

'*I* like Shakespeare,' Eve says.

I give her a look. 'Why doesn't that surprise me?'

I tap on the profile icon, zoom in on the pencil sketch she's used instead of a selfie. Then I gasp. 'Oh, shit—'

It's the image from her sketchbook: the avenging angel with the bloody sword. Thankfully, she's cut out the cringing boy at her feet.

'Jesus,' says Eve. She peers at the screen as I scroll down, studying the posts and comments and retweets. 'It's all—'

'Yeah.' I don't know what to say. There are links here to articles, victims' accounts of domestic violence, rape, sexual assault, gaslighting … Women committing suicide after suffering attacks, women murdered by boyfriends, serial killers, police officers … Women who kill their abusers when they just can't take it anymore.

'Fucking hell!' Eve says. Our eyes meet over Holly's phone. Along with the drawings, this could be construed as evidence that Holly was considering doing Jay harm. *Planning*.

She was obsessed with stories of women who are victims of men, particularly those who seek revenge.

'We need to delete this right now,' Eve says, her voice shaking. 'We can't let the police find it.'

I try to think clearly. It might just be an area of interest, a craving for the world to be a different – *better* – place. Not so dissimilar to Mum's desire to save, protect and nurture women who have been forced down dark, difficult paths in life …

'Finn.' Eve reaches for the phone, but I pull it out of her reach. 'Wait, I want to check her DMs.'

This feels like a definite breach, but I do it anyway. There's only one main account @*MidsummersChick* was interacting with via private message. @*Queen Bee* is the handle.

The display name on the account: *Queen of the Witches*.

My blood runs cold as I read through the stream of messages that flow between them.

Chapter 48

Finn

We finish reading and look at each other. Eve is pale with a hectic look in her eyes. 'The Queen of the Witches appears in *Macbeth* – that's another Shakespeare play.'

I give her a look. 'I know *Macbeth*, thank you. That's the play I'm writing about for English … *rewriting* about.'

'The Scottish Play.' Eve shivers ostentatiously. 'Supposed to be bad luck.'

Holly's *@MidsummersChick* account and the anonymous *Queen of the Witches* have Shakespeare-inspired X accounts and an obsession with violence against women in common. Though they're careful enough in their posts and DMs – there are no explicit threats to meet violence with violence, evil with evil – there's enough here for me and Eve to realise that Holly has been talking to someone genuinely unhinged in the weeks leading up to Jay's death.

Someone who made her better, stronger, louder – more the avenging angel she depicted. Someone who could take matters into her own hands. The anonymous friend speaks in loose terms of vengeance, taking back control.

I can see how intoxicating that must have been, how enticing to Holly, isolated and imprisoned in her own home.

It's all talk, nothing specific. Unless they moved their conversation onto WhatsApp or similar. If she's deleted everything, we'll have no way of knowing what else this person might have said to twist Holly's thoughts, turn her fear against her and make her act.

'What if someone told her to do it?' *Like grooming, but … for murder.*

Eve's sigh is sceptical. I don't blame her – it sounds far-fetched. 'I'm going to get a drink.'

I sit scrolling through the *@QueenBee* messages.

Back in the kitchen, Eve pours herself a glass of wine. She doesn't offer me one – back to responsible big sister.

I sit at the table, Holly's phone beside me, watching as Eve sinks a glass faster than she usually would. The wind howls and the windows shudder, but the kitchen is cosy. The pan on the Aga bubbles, filling the room with the scent of onions and garlic, balsamic, oregano. Cate and Leah are in good spirits as they cook, chatting away, oblivious to our turmoil.

Eventually they leave the sauce simmering. Leah joins Eve in the window nook, and Cate pulls out the chair opposite me. 'Oh!' she cries, reaching across the table. 'Is that Holly's phone? She was looking for it earlier.'

I hesitate. I can't pretend it's mine; everyone knows that mine was lost and is still with the police. I glance at the screen of Holly's phone. It's dark again, so she can't see I've been snooping. I don't want her to see that account, or the messages between her and *@QueenBee*.

We don't need anyone else learning of Holly's part in Jay's death.

There isn't time for me to delete anything, which means I'm going to have to find a way to nick my sister's phone again later. I curse myself for wasting the opportunity. 'Yeah,' I say slowly. 'It's hers. I was … checking a message from Isla.'

'Right.' Cate's fingers close around the phone. 'Well, I told Holls I'd take it up to her if I found it.'

I let it go reluctantly.

She pockets the phone with a smile. 'Thanks, Finn. I won't be a minute …'

Eve

The storm rampages along the coast as afternoon slams into evening, the weather wrapping around the house, trapping us inside. I turn up the volume on the speaker to drown out the wailing wind, sit at the table with my phone in one hand, a hefty glass of red in the other. I'm lurking on *Queen of the Witches*' X feed, following threads and leaping down rabbit holes, trying to uncover the human behind the handle.

It could be anyone, anywhere. I hate that some stranger has taken advantage of Holly at her most vulnerable, twisted her thinking, led her not to redemption and survival, but revenge.

The tone is vitriolic. It makes a mockery of the survival stories, the MeToo hashtags, the endurance of the women *Queen of the Witches* purports to champion.

This sort of chat turns victims not into victors, but villains.

I consider the possibility that there was no ill intent behind *Queen of the Witches*' rants and rhetoric – that the danger was all in Holly's reading between the lines, her interpretation of what was said. *Who knows?*

I wish I could go back in time, intervene at the right moment, tell my sister that revenge is not the road to healing.

Cate is back, with Fran in tow – apparently neither of them had any luck drawing Holly out. Cate tries to get the others to dance along to the music. Leah indulges her, but Fran's having none of it. 'Give over,' she says, and begins briskly grating cheese.

Finn lays the table with a good grace. He's trying to be nicer to the artists, after his outburst the day Jay's body was found.

Traces of his old self, those good manners, please me.

He's being *particularly* nice to Cate. With her youthful features and dark eyes, she's pretty, though she is a good bit older than the twins. She's cool, with her pink hair, those twining tattoos.

Finn stops by my chair, leans over to place my knife and fork. 'Will you read my essay later, Eve?'

It's such a normal request that I am transported to a different world: simmering chilli, the smoky bite of wine on my tongue, the words dancing on the page as I read over my story; Finn laying the table, talking about his homework. For a moment it might be any trip home. If only Gina and Mum were here, bickering and laughing.

The signs of normality are as incongruous as they are welcome. And fleeting. Upstairs, refusing to engage with the world, my little sister nurses her pain, tries to drown it in silence. I'm not doing enough for her.

Does she think of herself as a killer, or has she managed to block that out too?

'You've finished it already?' I'm surprised by Finn's diligence.

'Nah, just … made a start. You could read it and see if I'm on the right track.'

'Sure.' With the rain battering Haven and the wind shrieking, the fate of my family hanging in the balance, I doubt I'll be getting much sleep again tonight. I might as well help my brother write the best goddamn Shakespeare essay of his life.

Finn drops into a chair. He might be fighting for his freedom come morning, and homework will be the last thing on our minds.

He gestures at my phone. 'Find anything?' He keeps his voice low, and with the music and clattering pots, I know we won't be overheard. All the same, it feels reckless to speak openly.

I shake my head, lift my wine glass to my lips. 'Nothing helpful. This person could be anyone, anywhere. Plus … it doesn't change anything, does it?'

The deed is done.

Cate decants a second, very nice bottle of Burgundy liberated from the cellar earlier. Nicer than the stuff I'm drinking. I switch without complaint, clink glasses with Leah. Fran joins us in a glass too, but Cate isn't drinking.

She calls for Holly before dishing out bowlfuls of chilli. To my surprise, Holly comes but looks guarded. The six of us dig into the meal, mindful of so many empty seats at the table. 'Holly, I thought we might do some yoga after tea,' Cate says, with a sweet smile at my sister who picks at her food.

Holly gives the barest of nods, but it still cheers me to see any reaction at all from her. 'If anyone wants to join us …?' Cate looks at each of us in turn. I shake my head, Leah says something about old bones, and Finn snorts.

'Don't knock it, Finn. Some of the best athletes practise yoga alongside other training.'

'Mum's been trying to make me and Holly do it for years,' Finn says. 'She got Eve sucked in, but Holly and I just used to take the piss—'

He smiles as he looks fondly at our sister, remembering better days. Cate turns her attention to me. 'Eve! You must join us, then, if you're already a convert.'

I tap my wine glass. 'I'm two glasses in and pretty tired.' Surprisingly, this is true. I've no sooner pushed my plate aside than I'm yawning, feeling spaced and sleepy. It must be the wine, and the tossing and turning I've been doing these past few nights.

'Your loss, all of you.' Cate grins, and rises to clear the table.

'I'll wash up,' Finn says gallantly. 'You already did all the cooking.'

She beams at him. 'Thanks, sweetie.'

The tips of Finn's ears go red as he turns away to start the dishes. The wind howls again. 'Isn't it eerie,' begins Leah, her grey eyes glowing purple in the light of the fat church candles. 'Being completely cut off up here in this storm?'

As if to mark her words, there comes another violent gust, and the old house shifts on its foundations.

Chapter 49

Finn

The music seems to mellow us – I'm not sure if Eve changed the playlist before falling asleep on the kitchen sofa, or if Cate did. The unfamiliar track has a low, thready beat that catches and clings. A cool-café vibe. The mood shifts, as if the music cradles us, smoothing rough edges. My fear seems far away, rounded, softened.

Leah and Fran excuse themselves after dinner, to catch up on a TV show, and Holly disappears to her room, presumably to get ready for yoga. She didn't eat much, but she sat at the table. She even drank the glass of wine Cate poured for her, which Eve pretended not to notice. Cate poured me one too, handed it over with a conspiratorial smile. I only had a few sips. I didn't feel like drinking. Fran was getting stuck in as usual.

Cate thanks me for doing the dishes like *I'm* the guest. She ties her hair back and goes off to do yoga. When she returns – without my sister – she makes a cup of herbal tea and says she's going to paint.

'I do love painting in a storm.' She flashes me an unholy grin. 'Snow or thunder would be better, but I'll take a good old rainstorm.'

As if on cue, thunder splits the sky, and we all jump as lightning flashes across the windows. Cate grins again like she conjured it.

With the barrage outside, rainstorm seems too clean a description. I let Cash out to pee, hoping he won't go far. I call him back and he returns promptly, sodden, to settle himself on the rug in front of the Aga, starts to dream, paws scrabbling. Eve is sleeping peacefully, her snores soporific. I pull a plaid blanket off the sofa and tuck it around her, take my laptop and head upstairs.

I plan to do more work on my essay, but I'll probably switch on the Xbox first, lose myself in battle for a bit, distance myself from reality. So much for taking the opportunity for me, Holly and Eve to talk. It can't be put off forever.

My foreboding returns – the storm has put space between us and tomorrow … but tomorrow still looms: the detective with her questions, the spotlight on us …

We'll talk later, when Eve wakes from her nap. It seems ridiculous that Holly's been doing *Warrior* and *Goddess* when we ought to be devising a plan for keeping her from facing a murder charge.

Keeping *me* from one too – I'm the one whose card is marked by Isherwood, and I won't sacrifice my sister to save my skin. I think about justice and consequences, paying dues; but nothing righteous or rhetorical fits. I pick up the Xbox controller, click to start the game and start shooting things. I instantly feel better.

As usual when I'm gaming, time loosens. I have no idea how long has passed when I am disturbed by knocking. The staccato beat repeats until I tug off my headphones and pull open the door.

Cate looks anxious, phone in hand. 'Sorry to interrupt,' she says. 'I need your help; it's Holly.'

'*What*? What's happened?'

'She sent me a message a few minutes ago,' Cate says. A pulse of alarm. 'We went our separate ways after yoga. I was painting. She … she sounds … *oh*, just read it.' She swipes her phone, shoves it in front of me. I am looking at a message sent from Holly to Cate eighteen minutes ago, an innocuous little speech bubble …

I've made a mistake that can't be fixed. I can't put my
family through this any longer. Tell Finn I'm sorry. Eve too.
They won't forgive me and that's okay. Mum will – she
understands.

Then there's a gap of seconds, a follow up bubble.

Thank you for your friendship; it's meant a lot. By the time
you get this, you will be too late to stop me. I beg you not
to try. I don't want anyone else to get hurt.

'What the fuck?' I look from the message to Cate's white face. 'Is this what I think it is?'

'We have to hurry,' Cate says. 'I know she says not to—'

I'm already reaching for my trainers. We head along the corridor, take the steps two at a time. 'She'll go to the cliff, right?' Cate says. 'I checked and she's not in her room. I searched the house, but there's no sign.'

'She'll go to the cliff,' I agree. It's always been her place. Still is, but it means something different now. 'We need Eve.' I head for the kitchen. The house is strangely quiet, with the crescendo of the storm outside. Some people find a storm soothing from inside, safe and cocooned. I am the opposite – the swelling of sound spikes anxiety.

Cate tugs on my arm. 'She's not there. I couldn't find her either.'

I stare at her. That makes no sense. 'She was here,' I say, staring at the empty sofa where the blanket I used to cover Eve lies puddled on the cushions.

'She might have been, but she's not now. Maybe Holly messaged her too and she went off to look.'

I frown, at a loss. 'She wouldn't do that without telling me.'

'Eve always wants to protect you and Holly. She might think she can bring Holly back without worrying you—'

It makes sense, but I'll be angry if it's true. Going off on her own in a storm is bad enough – she'd give me hell for doing that – but sailing in single-handedly to save the day too … *typical* Eve.

'We need to call her,' I say, as we pull on waterproofs. Cate doesn't bother whose coat she pulls on, *and we need to get out there*.

But I don't have a phone, and Cate doesn't have Eve's number. I stand in the utility room, my head birling trying to work out what to do, trying to bring my sister's phone number to mind.

'I'll call Holly again,' Cate says, and holds the phone to her ear. She waits a minute, drops it again with a quick headshake. No luck. She scrapes her pink hair back and tucks it into the hood of her borrowed coat. 'We need to go now.'

I need no second bidding. 'With the flooding, going through the forest on foot will be quicker than driving.'

I don't have a car at my disposal anyway, though I suppose Cate could take Fran's. I pause on the threshold, pushing the door against the heave of wind. 'Wait … What about Leah, and Fran?'

'You're joking? Fran's *drunk* and Leah's over seventy years old. It's just us, Finn. We're it.'

I want to call Struan, Isla. Gina, Kirsty, Mum.

I want my familiar pillars of strength around me. I know how lucky I am to have each and every one of them. If Holly survives this, I bargain with myself, I will appreciate them so much more. I'll tell them what they mean to me. I'll do better …

The back door is open, though I *know* I locked it after letting Cash out.

Oh, Holls … where are you?

The weather is ferocious. We jog through grass that snags our boots, onto the muddy hill track towards the forest. Among the trees we will be sheltered. The storm rises around us: seeming to come from all directions, rain cold and needle-sharp. The woods are a relief after the exposed slope of the hill, where the wind hurls straight off the sea with nothing to slow its fury. It's dark and hard to see where we're going as we batter through branches that claw at us. The trees crowd close, a canopy that shields us from the worst of it. It's dark: a soft, loamy gloom that usually comforts me, but now feels sinister.

My boots squash through a mulch of mud and fallen needles. The trees shudder and creak, and when I crane my neck, some are swaying alarmingly, fragile peaks dancing in the wind. 'The wind will bring trees down,' I call to Cate, practically shouting to be heard above the storm. The forest may not be the safest place to be …

Cate's face – the disc of it visible within the pucker of her hood – is fearful: I can tell it's for my sister's safety, rather than the danger of falling timber. Probably the chances of being caught beneath a tree as it falls are slim, but the way the wind seeks to tear holes in the fabric of the forest is unsettling. The trees are tough, enduring, but the storm is stronger.

'What if we're wrong?' I call. 'Maybe she isn't at the cliff.'

'Got any better ideas?'

I don't. And with Eve gone too, I don't know what's going on.

We keep on – the cliff is the only possibility. I remember the night Jay died, Holly turning on live location because she wanted to be found. Maybe she'll do it again. Between breaths, I tell Cate about it, and we stop, our backs pressed against a thick trunk, to check WhatsApp on Cate's phone.

'Nothing. Damn it!' *She doesn't want to be found.*

'It was a good shout,' Cate soothes.

'What if we're too late? She's a danger to herself.' I struggle to keep the panic from my voice. I don't want to be out here again rescuing Holly from herself. I didn't do a great job last time. I found her at the scene of a murder, blood on her hands and a body beneath the cliff.

What will I find this time?

'Ssh, Finn.' Cate's musical voice is low, gentle. She grabs my wrist with her bare hand, her skin scouring me with cold. 'Don't even think it. Come on!'

We break into a run. Cate's fast – with all that yoga and hiking, she's fit. The forest track has never seemed so long, nor so winding. It's less than a mile through the woods to the cliff, but it feels longer tonight, stumbling in the dark.

My thoughts won't stop; they run in looping circles like one of those maze puzzles you have to unravel. There's something I haven't worked out – it nags at me, just beyond the flare of conscious awareness.

Holly ... distracted these past weeks, always staring at her phone, tapping away; *Queen of the Witches* in her ear whispering hate from a distance, and the night on the cliffs hysterical, and ... *confused*.

Like she didn't know what was going on.

Understandable, since she'd killed a boy. I'd assumed some sort of fugue state – that she didn't know what she was doing. Her words come back to me with crystal clarity.

I didn't want this.

A thought occurs: the police were suspicious about the car because there were so few prints on it: just Mum's the night she crashed. It makes sense Mum would have wiped it clean. But another odd memory about the car come back to me.

When I picked Holly up the night Jay died, I remember sliding into the driver seat on the cliff, readjusting the seat position. I'd barely been able to fit my legs in before I slid the seat back – Holly is nearly as tall as me; she'd never have the seat so close to the wheel ...

Queen of the Witches has been spilling poison into her ear, taking her trauma and twisting it into something deadly. Eve and I assumed @Queen Bee was some online troll getting off on controlling vulnerable girls like Holly from a distance ... maybe they didn't think Holly would do it, maybe they didn't care one way or another; it was just a game.

And maybe it was more than that. Maybe it was personal.

Maybe *Queen of the Witches* was not just an encourager, but an accomplice. Or ... the perpetrator. Dragging Holly along for the ride and abandoning her when I showed up.

It's never made sense that Holly would kill Jay. I remember sitting in the wet grass on the cliff edge, holding her in my arms and not recognising the face she was showing me. *Because it wasn't her face.* She was telling me a story, wearing a mask. Protecting someone.

My heart beats so hard, Cate *must* hear it above the storm.

Who had motive for killing Jay and access to Holly?

Christian?

Ryan Campbell?

There's nothing to say *Queen of the Witches* is female. Ryan is as tall as me and in my panicked state I can call to mind only a vague impression of Christian's height – like his son, he's not particularly tall for a guy.

Wishful thinking – I don't want to think Holly capable of murder. I seek another villain, one I can get behind hating. Most likely, this is the rambling of an overwrought, stressed mind. I'm so scared for Holly I'm creating stories and conspiracies. Out here, in the dark and storm, it's easy for my thoughts to play tricks ...

I need to find my sister.

Cate stops, turns to look at me, impatient. 'What are you waiting for, Finn?'

'Nothing.' I catch up, take the lead. We're coming to the last bit of the track, the final bend before the trees thin where a peeling barrier stops cars driving into the forest.

Glancing into the trees, I shiver at the depth and darkness of the forest on all sides. I stumble on a slick root and almost fall, catch myself. My knee is throbbing – I'm going to pay for this later. I think I hear something and spin around, but there's only Cate, pressing in my wake. Her eyes widen as she catches my panic. 'What is it?'

I shake my head, turn back to the path, the smudgy strip of

sky ahead – we're coming to the road.

We're almost at the barrier when I hear a blood-curdling scream from Cate. Before I can turn towards the sound, something smashes into the side of my head, and everything goes black. I slide to the ground.

From: @MidsummersChick
To: @QueenBee

I wish you were here with me too. It sometimes feels like you are …

Chapter 50

Eve

I wake in darkness and have no idea where I am. My head aches and my tongue is sour. My mind fuzzes as I swim back to consciousness. I'm slumped on a bowed stone step, knees bent, back jammed against another step – equally cold, the sharp seam of concrete pressing into my spine. Wherever I am smells musty – dust with a peal of damp. There's a faint light. I stand, curious, crack my head on a low stone slope – the underside of stairs – and curse as I fall to my knees.

Christ, that hurt.

I peer at the milky blue light, crawl towards it on my hands and knees. I know where I am: the wine cellar beneath the kitchen. The glow is the light from the drinks fridge Gina installed a few months ago. Somewhere to keep the Prosecco bottles chilling without taking up space in the kitchen fridge.

How did I get here? And why was I *sleeping*?

My location would suggest I came looking for another bottle of wine. That's conceivable; I was drinking earlier, but I also remember thinking that I needed to stop. I'd already had two large glasses with dinner.

I feel as hungover as if I'd drunk a whole bottle.

Once I get my bearings, my eyes adjusted to the gloom, I reach for the door. I have a horrible feeling …

Yep, I'm locked in. I rattle the handle. That damn faulty latch. Usually I'm so careful not to close the door behind me – we've all got ourselves stuck in here a time or two, and had to bang on the door, laughing and shouting for help. Half drunk, I might have been careless …

I don't remember getting drunk and coming down here, or realising I was locked in, or sitting down on the chilly stone of the steps and falling asleep.

'Fuck!' I lean against the door and groan. Finn is three floors above, no doubt with his headphones on and a soundtrack of shooting and angry music in his ears. He'll never hear me, even if I scream myself hoarse.

I don't know where Holly is, but if she's back in the artists' wing then they won't hear me either.

I pat the pocket of my jeans for my phone – surely Holly will hear hers ringing and either come to my rescue or send one of the artists. I feel ridiculous to have to call for help, but—

My phone isn't there.

Great.

I have no idea what I've done with it. I definitely had it with me in the kitchen earlier – I was googling *Queen of the Witches* and *@QueenBee* and trying to figure out what, if anything, this persona had to do with Holly's descent into violence.

Fear for my sister swims in my gut – not just the distaste of her crime, but the worry that she is *past* damaged, that she has become susceptible, suggestible, no longer capable of discerning right from wrong. Tipped off her moral compass by someone compelling and complacently violent.

I don't know how to pull her back on track.

I sit on the step again, rub my aching head. Without my phone, and with my thoughts so disordered, I've no idea how I'm going to get out of here. Except wait for someone to come into the kitchen and hammer on the door to attract their attention.

I eye the door speculatively, wondering if I can force it, batter it down. Thirty seconds and a bruised shoulder later, I conclude that I cannot. I sigh. Nothing for it but to wait.

As I sit there with nothing to do, nothing to think about but my sister's folly, the messages come into my mind again. I need a puzzle to serve as distraction. The queen of witches …

The Goddess of witches from Greek mythology … the queen of the crones in *Macbeth*.

Hecate.

Something slots into place. A half memory of a guiding hand on my elbow, an encouraging voice. Plying me with more wine.

Finn

I come to in a car. I am lying across the back seat, legs folded awkwardly and my head on the armrest, neck cricked. Rain trickles down the cold glass and I can hear the moan of the wind, feel it rock the metal box around me. Whose car am I in, and how did I get here?

My head aches abominably – a thrumming lurch that feels like someone is stabbing me repeatedly in the temple.

I remember the crack, the dull weight of something smashing me in the head before I lost consciousness. Did a tree branch fall on me?

But that wouldn't explain the car unless someone has come to my rescue, put me in here to drive me home.

I remember Cate's scream before I fell, and try to sit up – is she hurt?

I struggle to move, the questions making my head throb harder. But as I try to pull myself upright, get my hands beneath me for leverage, I realise I can't move them. My arms are trapped, somehow.

'Cate—' I blurt, fearful that I've led her into danger. It was stupid to come out in the middle of the storm – a felled tree could crush a person in an instant, no time to run. A nightmarish image of her, trapped beneath the knotted trunk and tangled branches of a pine ripped up by its roots by the wind …

She might be dead.

'Yes, Finn,' comes a musical voice, cutting through my thoughts, anything but soothing.

Chapter 51

The Night on the Cliff

The library had been quiet, which was how Holly liked it. A bookish hum filling the room: the whisper of pages, the reassuring murmur of Ms Fairlie on the phone, the soothing clack of the librarian's nails on her keyboard. It felt – *almost* – safe.

When the door squeaked, Holly's eyes snapped up, her book trembling in her hand.

She relaxed when she realised who it was: Mr Fraser with his laptop under his arm, coffee cup in hand, disappearing into the meeting room at the back of the library and ignoring Ms Fairlie's glower – *no food and drink in the library*.

Holly turned a page, tried to concentrate. She was aware of every minute passing.

She felt okay, with Ms Fairlie surveying things – like some custodian of ancient knowledge instead of a high school librarian.

As okay as Holly had felt anywhere since the cave …

She hadn't wanted to come today. She couldn't face the stares, raised eyebrows, jeering smiles. She was defined by that photograph. In the car she shrank inside her clothes, avoided Jay's eye, his lupine smile.

Just pop in, collect your assignments, speak to your guidance teacher and leave, Mum had said, the irony of being forced out of the house by her agoraphobic mother not lost on Holly.

She endured Jay's presence in the car, the monologue from her teacher who spoke about stuff like *art therapy* and *academic adjustments*.

Now she sat in plain sight, waiting for her brother.

The photograph hovered, as always, in her thoughts. It had been forwarded to her, and for days people smothered laughs behind their hands, judgement in every glance. It was shocking: her peely-wally limbs and mermaid hair, her hiked-up skirt and come-hither eyes.

Holly hunched her shoulders, stared at the pages of her book. The library was quiet, but anyone could come in, so she was vigilant.

Jay could come in. At Haven, he was always there, looking, trying to touch, wanting them to be alone. She had taken to hiding in the artists' studio or trailing after her mother; until Naomi grew exasperated.

Finn was mostly with Jay, so she couldn't hang out with her brother. The artists were a godsend – especially Cate. She seemed to know what Holly needed without her having to say.

There was a look in Cate's eyes sometimes that spoke volumes. Holly felt … seen. They all had a story and they were pretty open about sharing them – Fran's army career ending when she was attacked by a group of fellow soldiers on a night out … Leah surviving domestic violence, which only ended with her controlling husband's death. But it was Cate, who was date-raped in her first (and only) year of college, who seemed to really understand.

The door opened again. Holly flinched, risked a look. *Please, not him.*

It was Isla. She breathed out. That was okay – Isla had looked after her the night of the party.

Isla tossed her tumbling ponytail. She wore her school tie in a fat, loose knot, and her Dr. Martens bore turquoise laces. Isla smiled, came over.

Holly steeled herself. Awkward conversations were *more* awkward now she didn't talk.

Isla sat down, hands on the table. She had oval nails painted glossy mint, with neat cuticles. 'Hey,' she said. 'What's up?' Her smile was warm.

Isla didn't judge her like the girls Holly feared: the ones who looked at her like she was a one-woman freak show. *Who even are you to get Ryan Campbell?* the looks said.

They condemned her for falling under his spell; like they wouldn't give their eye teeth for a chance with him.

Holly shrugged, added Isla to the list of people she'd like to talk to but couldn't.

'Free period,' Isla said. 'Mind if I sit here and study?'

Holly shook her head.

Isla opened her notebook. 'Honestly, Mr Cooper is the worst. You should see the amount of maths homework he's given us. Who thought Advanced Higher Maths was a good idea?'

Holly's lips twitched.

'Fair point,' Isla answered as if she'd spoken. 'Idiots who apply to study it at uni, that's who.'

She reached across and thumbed through the pile of assignments in front of Holly, keeping up a running commentary. She didn't seem to mind that the conversation was one-sided. Suddenly, she stopped and grabbed Holly's hand, held her eye firmly. 'You know, you can talk to me if you want. Or …' She slid her notebook towards Holly. 'You could write it down, if there was something you needed to say.'

Holly imagined the words spewing out like a burst sewer. She's been through this a million times; it's not worth it. *Keep quiet or risk destroying everything.*

She had her *@MidsummersChick* account as an outlet, a virtual headspace. Online she had a confidante … And she had the artists too, though she couldn't talk to them about anything *real*.

'I think,' Isla continued. 'Maybe there was more to it that night in the caves. What happened was bad enough, but you're *still* not talking, and—'

Holly blinked, looking at the paper, the uncapped pen.

'I think we should have told someone, so you got help. I'm not sure we did the right thing keeping quiet.'

Holly started to tremble. If Isla spilled her secrets it would be a disaster, especially when the secret Isla *thought* she was keeping wasn't the real one at all. Bad enough that Finn had gone for Ryan that day – *what would he do to Jay if he knew the truth?*

Isla slid the pen closer, and Holly imagined taking it, writing a name. Once it was out, that would be it. She wondered what would come next – the denials, Gina and Finn forced to choose sides, the bloody battle for the truth at the heart of her family tearing them to pieces.

The door opened again. All the oxygen left Holly's body in a rush when she saw him loping across the library.

Third time unlucky.

She sent the pen skittering to the floor in panic. Isla gave her a strange look and retrieved it.

Jay closed the distance, his cheeky-chappie smile pasted on. Holly could see through it, the predator beneath a convincing skin.

She stood up, swept her stuff into her bag. She tried to pass him without touching, but he was too close, one of her legs bumping the table painfully as he caught her shoulder, his fingers pressing deep.

No doubt it looked like affection to Isla. Holly felt the bruise of his touch.

'Where are you off to in such a hurry?' Jay's pleasant tone was wrapped around an iron core. His smile was megawatt; trying to charm Isla and frighten Holly with one face, and it was weird. Would Isla notice?

Holly said nothing. She let herself go limp in. His eyes softened.

Isla could be forgiven for thinking they were having a romantic moment, that it was attraction holding her there, spellbound.

Instead it was terror.

'Aren't you waiting for your brother to give us a ride home? Don't tell me you're risking the bus.'

Isla was looking at them, a curious line between her brows.

Holly said nothing, but she didn't sit back down like Jay expected. His fingers gave a final pinch of frustration, but he let her go. 'Whatever. I'll be seeing you later, Holls.'

It was a threat, of course. Another weekend, forty-eight hours of avoidance, trying not to be caught alone with him. Trying to pretend she was not revolted, fearful. He had infiltrated her home. Her abuser with his handsome face and dark heart was everywhere.

Holly lifted her backpack, shot Isla a last look – had Isla had seen something else in their exchange? She thought about what Isla said: *something more to that night in the cave ...*

Holly prayed Isla hadn't guessed. She couldn't risk being believed ... or disbelieved. *Lose-lose.*

Jay settled himself in the seat beside Isla. He was smiling, his hair swept artfully across his forehead, his uniform dishevelled. Warm toffee eyes, that big smile ...

She felt a sudden glimmer of fear for Isla, for all the girls that Jay might one day meet. Did she owe them? Was this *bigger* than her?

But Isla was Finn's girl. Jay wouldn't be that stupid ...

Holly fled the library, palms sweating; she slipped out, headed to the bus stop in town, texting Finn as she went telling him not to wait for her.

Finn ditched school and came to find her at the bus stop, leaning to open the passenger door with a terse: 'Get in.' On the road home, he told her about Jay and Isla. The skin on the back of his hand was raw from the punch.

At Haven, Naomi was in the studio – smells of freshly brewed coffee and linseed drifted through the lower floor. Holly stayed close to Finn, trailed him to the bathroom and took care of his hand. Fresh fear curdled in Holly's belly, and she had the sense they were hurtling towards some conclusion, some cataclysm.

Jay was escalating.

She found Naomi's half-empty tube of arnica, the metal creases folded sharp. Finn sat on the side of the tub, an air of defeat about him. He ran his uninjured hand through his hair while she dabbed cream on the damson bruise that stained his knuckles. 'I don't understand; why would Jay do that?' he said.

Holly's heart stuttered. *Because he wanted to*, she thought. *Because he can*.

Jay always did exactly what he pleased.

She DM'd @QueenBee freaking out about Jay's parting threat. @QueenBee replied instantly:

You must do what needs to be done to stay safe.

She knew what *Queen of the Witches* wanted, but Holly didn't have it in her. Her plan was to spend the evening in the artists' studio. With a bit of luck, Cate would slip her a glass of wine when her mother wasn't looking. She'd read or draw while Cate painted. The studio was her refuge. But the artists would often down tools early at the weekend and eat, drink and make merry and an empty studio was prime preying ground; Holly would stick close to Cate either way.

On Friday nights, Jay would usually run, then hunker down with Finn for an Xbox battle, but Holly doubted that would happen now. Jay would be a loose cannon after the fight. He came home long enough to get his car and blasted off down the drive in a shower of gravel.

Finn wanted to be left alone, so Holly shut herself in her bedroom, switched to WhatsApp to continue her conversation:

@MidsummersChick: *He tried it on with my friend today, touched her in plain sight. She's my brother's girlfriend.*

@QueenBee: *He's growing bolder, more reckless; he's going to strike again.*

@MidsummersChick: *Don't, that's scary ...*

@QueenBee: *Don't be scared, be angry. It's time to do something about him.*

@MidsummersChick: *You know I can't tell the police. If I do, my family falls apart. Whether they believe me or not, I lose everything.*

@QueenBee: *Who said anything about the police? It's time to take him down.*

@MidsummersChick: *I'm worried about Isla. She's on his radar now.*

@QueenBee: *She's not in his reach, you are. I'm more worried about you. It's time to take back your home, your family. It's time to ACT!*

Holly tossed her phone aside. She didn't know what to say. Her anonymous friend was braver than she. Queen of the Witches was no one's victim. Holly wished she was a warrior like her.

She was more on edge than ever. Jay, humiliated, was dangerous. He would seek her out, for sure. The artists, and Mum, would be drinking, oblivious. Gina wasn't here. Finn was nursing his misery in his bedroom.

It was up to Holly to keep herself safe. She had to stay out of his way. The walls of Haven were thick, and she wasn't convinced she'd be capable of screaming when no sound had passed her lips in so long.

Trapped and claustrophobic, she went to the garden; it was relatively safe with Jay gone. She would see him turn into the track and have time to disappear somewhere. Again, she imagined telling someone, *anyone*, what had happened to her. There were people under this roof who would help in a heartbeat. People who would tell her that rape is rape – that it doesn't matter what she was wearing, that she was flirting with him for months, that she'd kissed him on the beach all those times like she was starving and he was food.

She couldn't get past how this would impact Gina and Mum. She wouldn't put Gina in the position of having to choose.

The only person she could confide in was @QueenBee

Her phone beeped and Holly reached for it, expecting more from her anonymous, online friend. *It was Jay.*

> Tonight, baby. You and me at the cove. Meet me at the cliff?

She trembled, stared at the screen as he typed again.

> That was a misunderstanding with Isla. You know it's only you. I'm sick of waiting. It's time to make the magic happen again, Holls. Meet me 9 p.m. on the cliff path, by the clearing.

Her heart was beating out of her chest. Holly reread the messages. Was he deluded enough to think she still wanted him, that she was just playing hard to get? Did he not understand … or did he just not care?

She opened her WhatsApp conversation and explained what had happened.

> @QueenBee: *Shit! No way. What did you tell him?*
> @MidsummersChick: *Nothing. Obviously I'm not going to meet him.*
> @QueenBee: *This is your chance …*
> @MidsummersChick: *Chance for what?*
> @QueenBee: *To get him out of your life. For good.*
> @MidsummersChick: *???*

> @QueenBee: *Think about it. A stormy night ... a treacherous cliff path ... an arsehole who thinks he can rape and threaten you and still you'll come back for more ... I've got your back, Holly. I'll help ...*

This time when Holly threw the phone it bounced onto the deck, nearly slipped through a gap. She had a horrible feeling about @QueenBee now ...

Jittery with adrenaline, she retrieved her phone. The rain was starting in earnest, and she pulled up her hood. No sign of Jay, but she could see Finn disappearing down the track, setting out on his lonely run. Rain landed in heavy spots and overhead the clouds massed, ominous.

A stormy night ...

Something nagged at her, as she walked towards the outbuildings for shelter, her battered Uggs skiffing the gravel.

A treacherous cliff path ...

Halfway to the barn that used to be a hiding place of choice when she was little and escaping only the mundane irritations of family life, she paused. She could hear the hiss and boom of the sea at the foot of the cliffs. It wasn't yet high tide, but the waves were ferocious.

Something wasn't right ...

She and *Queen of the Witches* had found each other online. Holly had been aware of the Queen's presence for a while, but it was *Queen of the Witches* who reached out to her, after reading one of Holly's posts. The Queen's opening gambit: *from one damaged Shakespeare groupie to another ...*

They'd been talking for weeks, and the Queen knew it all – Holly's perfectly imperfect family, her safety in silence ... *She knew about the night in the cave. About Jay.*

What the Queen didn't know was Holly's name, and where she lived.

So, how did she know about the storm, the cliff path? She'd

told the Queen that Jay wanted to meet her, but not where. *And how had she known to call her Holly?*

She had found in the Queen a sounding board, a mirror to reflect her pain. They hash-tagged and shared and validated and supported. Holly had always supposed that the Queen was a survivor too, though it occurred to her now that she didn't know anything about them.

Their friendship wasn't real – on some level Holly had always understood that. But at times it has been her lifeline. At times, it had *literally* saved her.

From loneliness and despair, from the danger of her own thoughts.

Tonight, @QueenBee seemed to be advocating something else – revenge in real life? Not just talking about it, but doing it.

There was something compelling about the notion.

Holly slipped inside the dusty interior of the barn, breathing hard, wondering who this online presence actually was. The barn was where they stored firewood, a few poorly cared for tools. It had become a dumping ground, and every so often Gina would feel impelled to sort it out.

She towed a log near the entrance and sat, keeping a weather eye on the track.

She wanted to ask *Queen of the Witches* what they meant, but she was afraid of the answer. She wanted to ask how they knew about the storm, the cliff, her name – but she was *very* afraid of those answers.

A thought, hot and excruciating, cometlike, shot through her brain now, leaving a blazing trail. Could *Queen of the Witches* be someone she knew?

Someone from school?

One of the bitches who revelled in her downfall perhaps …

Please, not that!

She whimpered, the sound mingling with the whine of the wind as she typed. *Who are you?*

Footsteps crunched gravel outside. Holly held still, barely breathing. She would have heard Jay's car on the drive if he'd come back – she always heard him: engine revving, braking hard with a slew of stones, door slamming.

'Hey, Midsummer,' came a musical voice. A shadow filled the doorway, and Holly looked up at the familiar outline. 'It's me. Hecate. Get it – hey *Cate*!'

Chapter 52

Now

Finn

Why can't I move my arms? My brain is clouded, stupid. It takes me longer than it should to turn my gaze and take in the strange, navy fabric that covers me – canvas pulled taut. A blanket … no, not that. A sweatshirt … not that either; my arms are trapped to my sides beneath the heavy fabric. I am swaddled like a baby. I can't move.

Like … some sort of straitjacket.

I start to panic at my confinement, looking around. The car's upholstery is old and faded, and the front windscreen has dirt gathered in the corners of the glass. There are nicks and chips in the pleather dashboard. The percussion of rain on the roof is deafening. Somehow I pull myself into a sitting position, wedging an elbow against the doorframe.

I slump, exhausted from the effort and the blinding pain in my temple.

Cate is looking at me, leaning around the driver seat. She seems to be in one piece, and she is smiling. 'Ahh, the prince awakes.'

I stare at her. 'Are you okay? Were we hit by a tree or something? What happened?' I look down at my bound torso, still trying to comprehend what's going on, to get my thoughts in gear. My brain is a bike chain that keeps slipping off track.

'No.' She laughs. She is unharmed. 'No tree.'

'I don't understand.'

'I must have clonked you on the head harder than I realised—' She laughs again, and the sound seems to bounce around the confines of the car. Her eyes gleam like ink, and her teeth are white and sharp, apple-red lips peeling back.

'I don't understand,' I repeat, stunned and still stupid, unable to make my brain work. I try to move my feet this time, try to kick out; but they, too, are bound. I can move them together like one, awkward club; but they've been wrapped in rope and towels that make them useless. 'Did … *you* do this to me?'

Cate frowns. 'You wouldn't understand, you're not that clever. No imagination. Plenty of loyalty – but loyalty like that can be a liability. Can't it, Holly?'

My sister is in the passenger seat. '*Holly!*' I scan her for signs of shackles, or damage. She has the charcoal hood of my sweatshirt pulled up, damp hanks of hair hanging on either side of her face. She's so pale she seems almost transparent. Her eyes can't meet mine; they flit away like nervous moths.

A further scan of my sister suggests that she is not restrained. I can see the narrow bones of her wrists poking out of her sleeves, and she has one leg folded beneath her. My blood goes cold. Cate might be fit and flexible, and stronger than she looks, but she could never get me from the woods into this car by herself. She had to have had help.

Holly.

I turn back to Cate. She is gruesomely calm.

'Did *you* do this?' I repeat, kicking my useless feet and pulling with all my strength against my bonds.

'Loyalty,' she repeats, musing on the word as it rolls over her tongue. 'Holly knows all about loyalty, don't you, sweetie?'

'Holls,' I say urgently, trying to keep fear from my voice but failing. 'You have to untie me; we need to get out of here—'

Holly stares ahead.

'You don't own Holly's loyalty, for all that she has yours – I've been impressed with your devotion to her. Willing to be taken away in handcuffs, locked in a cell … But you're also curious, Finn, and curiosity is a failing. The combination of loyal and curious … it adds up to a blind spot and that's what got you here …'

I lick dry lips, trying to understand. My brain is blurry from the blow that knocked me out.

She leans forward, taps the canvas that binds me. 'This was meant for Jay, you know. But he very helpfully took himself to the *exact place* I wanted him to be. I didn't need this in the end, after I'd gone to all the trouble of making it too … all those weeks of preparation. Jay was short-sighted, thought *he* had Holly's heart. But he didn't. And neither do you.'

I frown. 'I don't know what you're talking about, Cate. Of course Holly and I are loyal. We're twins. Jay was a piece of shit, he did a terrible thing, but that doesn't mean he deserved to die for it.'

She giggles, a dark, terrifying sound. 'I love your morality, sweetie; it's cute … but boys with morals have never been my bag. Ironically, I prefer the depraved ones. And yet, there's a certain type of depravity that must be punished—'

Her face changes. Anger consumes her features, twisting them into something alien and unsightly. I recoil from the force of her fury as she leans towards me, eyes searing like hot coals. 'You don't have her loyalty, *Finn*, because you don't deserve it!' Every word is enunciated carefully, and tiny flecks of spit land on my cheek. There's rage in those eyes. 'I have her loyalty because *I do* deserve it. I'm the one who saw her … who *heard* her … who *helped* her.'

I see Holly shudder from the force of Cate's anger, but she

doesn't say anything, doesn't make any move to help me.

'I admit, I've not been the best brother.' I'm talking to Holly now, not *her*. Pleading with my sister. Cate doesn't like that. She reaches out, grips my chin hard between finger and thumb, wrenches my head around until I look at her.

I drop my gaze, refuse to look her in the eye. A small rebellion.

She draws her arm back and there's nothing I can do to defend myself. Her hand streaks across my face, tearing my skin. I wince, and can't help crying out as the force rocks my head to the side.

Slowly I meet Cate's gaze; it's what she requires of me, the reason she hit me. She is triumphant, jubilant. She puts out a hand, traces my cheek with her fingertips. 'I wish you hadn't made me do that.'

I swallow, saying nothing. My skin burns where she slapped me. Holly doesn't react to the blow, or Cate's words. She picks at her nails, bites her lip, catching at strips of loose skin.

'*Not the best brother*?' Cate sneers. 'Bit worse than that. You took her to the party where she was raped. You were with your girlfriend while Holly was drugged and dragged into those caves below.' Her voice rises, catching with a spark of anger, flaming righteously. 'And afterwards, you laughed and talked with her rapist day after day; you gave him unfettered access to her. You ignored her pain, her silence, because it was easier to look away. You didn't even *try* to hear.'

Holly makes a small sound, and one quick, terrible glance from Cate silences her.

'I didn't *know*,' I say desperately. 'I beat up the boy I thought did it.' Arguing with her is pointless. Guilt swells within me at her words. She might be insane, but there's a truth there that sickens me.

'The *wrong boy*. All the while, the monster was under her bed. Waiting.'

I look at Holly, horrified. 'Did it happen again?'

'Many times,' Cate answers for her, enjoying my flinch. 'There was no one to stop him. No one except me.'

'*You* killed Jay?'

Cate is tiny … The seat was too far forward.

She holds out her arms, bobs as much of a bow as the space will allow. 'Someone had to put an end to him.'

'But you left Holly to take the blame. You left her on the cliff.'

She scowls. 'That was your fault. You weren't supposed to follow us. Your fall was meant to incapacitate you.'

Holly leans against the headrest, staring straight ahead, still ignoring my predicament, but listening. I wonder if she knows how much danger we – *I* – am in.

Alone in a car on a cliff with a murderer.

Holly starts humming, and the sound chills me more than the frenzy in the eyes of the woman smiling at me. 'Have you worked it out, Finn? With that smart brain of yours. I contrived your fall, to keep you out of the way that night. I needed Holly to meet Jay on the cliff alone. Well, *almost alone*. He wasn't expecting *me*. Your appearance wasn't part of the plan, and I had to think fast. I knew you'd do anything to protect your sister, even cover up her crime; but you wouldn't have any loyalty to *me*. So I made myself scarce.' She giggles again. 'I hid in the boot of the car, didn't quite close the lid.'

She was in the car the whole time.

I drove us back to Haven with Cate in the boot.

'You did almost everything perfectly, Finn. All the hard work. Burned Holly's clothes, took her home, hid the car. But you told your mother, which wasn't the best move—'

'Leaving damage on the car wasn't the best move,' I retort, a flash of temper rising through my fear.

I think she's going to hit me again. Her eyes blaze and her hands clench. But she stays in control, scoops one pretty eyebrow upwards. 'A bit of spirit. I appreciate that. Yes, there were several things that didn't go to plan that night. Holly grabbing the wheel to save him at the last minute, meaning I hit the boulder more squarely than I hit *him*; you showing up. And that damn ledge of course—'

'What are you going to do?' I say. How does this end? 'You don't need to do this, Cate – it's *me* the police have their eyes on. Me and Holly, and our mum.'

'You found my messages. I saw you with Holly's phone. And she's been weird with me these past few days – locking her room, running off to stay with that crappy friend of hers. I'm not sure I trust her anymore.' She shoots Holly a venomous glare, contradicts it with an affectionate pat on the knee.

She's freaking me out. She's unhinged, unpredictable, untethered.

'You're Queen of the Witches?' I say. '*You* planned this?'

She nods, a hint of pride in her face, throws wide. 'I am queen of *all* witches,' she says, grandiose, calamitous. 'And I will wreak havoc on all who deserve it.'

Her expression sobers. 'Now, there is much to be done. You'd have worked it out by morning; don't pretend you hadn't considered that someone else might have been involved that night … And I *know* someone snooped in my room. I know what you took.' She gives me a glittering look that makes me cringe.

'I considered someone being there, but I didn't think it was *you*. And I haven't been in your room.'

'Liar!' she screams at me. 'You suspected me. You'd have told the police. Might have been tough, getting them to listen, but you had nothing to lose, considering one of you was going to go to prison for Jay's murder. Plus, you had my messages on Holly's phone – she *promised* me she'd deleted everything – and the evidence you found in my room—'

'I don't know what you're talking about. I didn't take anything from your room—' I recoil as soon as the words slip past my lips, convinced she's going to slap me again.

'Enough,' Cate says curtly. 'Let's get this done. Holly will grieve, but she'll get over your death. The police will find your suicide note at Haven, which will clearly outline your guilt. You couldn't live with what you had done, *blah blah* ... so you took the final step in the same place you killed Jay. Only, you'll remember about the ledge, this time ... You'll jump cleanly, let the sea wash you away. It's a shame; you're one of the good ones ... sweet manners, cute, and that loyalty ... but it can't be helped. You know too much.'

'Holly,' I beg, my voice shaking with fear now. 'You can't let her do this. You can't *help* her do this.'

Nothing. My sister sits, turned to stone, while this witch talks openly about killing me, staging my suicide.

Cate laughs. '*She's mine now* ... And before you start imagining anyone coming to your aid, I can assure you that it's not going to happen. Leah and Fran are both ... incapacitated – last of Jay's *roofies*.' She giggles. 'Although later, Leah will swear blind that Holly and I were with her all night – she's good like that: knows what side her bread is buttered on. Fran won't remember anything, the lush, and come morning, the keys to her car will be back in her bag where she left them.' She waves a gloved hand at me. 'No prints, see?'

'Eve,' I whisper. My stomach is clenching, and fear is threatening to get on top of me. I know I have to remain calm, level-headed. I have to be strong if I'm to have any chance of getting out of here. *Think*. Cate has made mistakes before; she might again ...

'Eve mixed sleeping pills with too much wine, how silly—'

'*Eve* wouldn't take pills—'

'Not intentionally, no. And then, she accidentally locked herself in the wine cellar. Your mum's been meaning to get that latch fixed for months, but she's not the most proactive person, your mum, is she?'

Fuck! The gravity of my situation dawns. With the storm and the landslip, we're alone. Cate has taken perfect advantage of her opportunity; she's probably been waiting for a chance to end me since that night when I interrupted her plan ...

'Right,' Cate says briskly. 'You're nicely immobilised – there will be no evidence of that, no messy handcuffs or zip ties for you to strain against and leave marks – but I think we need a little help ... I can't imagine you'll go quietly, and I don't want to sustain any injuries in the process.' She reaches into a bag at Holly's feet, takes out a plastic water bottle.

A bubble of hysteria rises in my chest – for a minute I actually expect Holly to express concern about single-use plastic though she shows no concern for *me*. She's going to let Cate kill me. Somehow this woman has got inside her head, taken up residence there, taken advantage of the suffering that tore through Holly's psyche.

'Holly won't help you,' I say, more to reassure myself than to convince Cate. Or perhaps it's one last-ditch attempt at reaching my sister.

Cate looks at Holly speculatively. 'No-o,' she says. 'I don't think she will. That might be too much to ask. She'll wait in the car.' She draws the keys from the ignition and waves them at me, and I understand. The knowledge lands with a sickly thump in my gut.

I'm fucked.

Holly will be locked in the car, unable to help me. I imagine her coming to her senses at the last moment, slamming her hands on the window as she tries to break free, watching Cate heave me over the edge into the sea.

No one knows we're here.

But to make it look like suicide, she'll have to untie me – how's that going to work?

She unscrews the lid of the water bottle and holds it to her lips but doesn't drink. She looks speculatively at Holly, whose eyes are sliding closed. I see the whisper of silvery lashes against her cheek as her eyes dart behind the lids. 'How are you feeling, sweetie?' she whispers. 'Sleepy?'

I see a matching water bottle in the cupholder. Empty. *Shit*! She's drugged Holly as an extra insurance policy. All the time we've been talking, the drugs have been seeping into Holly's bloodstream and now she's out. She can't help me, even if she wanted to.

Cate looks at me, eyes speculative. She holds the water bottle out. 'Drink.'

'Fuck off.'

She hits me again, another resounding slap. She's obviously not bothered about leaving *some* evidence if my body is recovered – the rocks will do damage, a few marks on my face will be nothing compared to how cliff and sea will disfigure me. Who knows when I will be found, and in what state.

If not for the ledge, she'd have got it right first time, with Jay.

I am her do-over.

There's no way I'm drinking that water. Once the drugs hit my system, I won't be able to fight; I'll be helpless. A dead weight for her to drag from the car and tip over the cliff. It will be hard going – she'll struggle with my bodyweight – but she's strong; it's possible. I glance from the window and realise how close to the drop we are.

Cate climbs into the back seat, straddles me. Her knees pin my hips, and she pushes her weight on my chest, forcing me against the door. She tries to pry my mouth open, and I fight her, clench my jaw so hard I think my teeth might snap, then try to bite her fingers when she hooks them into my mouth. She grabs the bottle and aims it at my face. There must be a *fuck-lot* of pills crushed in it because she doesn't seem too worried about spillage. Without the use of my arms and legs, still woozy from the blow to the head, it's becoming hard to fight. I wrench my head to the side, trying to avoid the water, but I can feel her overpowering me.

She drives her thumb against the wound on my temple and I scream. She takes advantage of the moment to pour water into my mouth.

Some of it goes down. She holds my mouth open with all her might and I can't fight her. This is happening. I'm going to die here.

Suddenly the water bottle goes spinning out of her hand,

showering the upholstery, the floor, her precious liquid spilling out to soak the carpet and my joggers. '*Bitch!!!*' Cate screams.

I look past her, see Holly, awake and staring at me. She's twisted round in her seat, her arm still raised from knocking the water bottle out of Cate's hand.

She's saved me … temporarily.

But, *Jesus*, what's Cate going to do to us now?

Chapter 53

The Night on the Cliff

'Cate?' Shock forced the word from Holly's throat, her voice a stifled yelp.

'I prefer *Hecate*, but you'd be surprised how many people baulk at the name of the queen of witches—'

Holly stared, not sure if she was joking, trying to put the two personas together: the gentle artist who looked out for her, and the online warrior she'd spilled secrets to. Her face heated at the duplicity of it, the shame at not having figured it out.

'Sorry, I should have come clean before now. It was disingenuous of me.'

Holly said nothing and Cate continued. 'I came here for *you*. To watch over you. I could tell from your posts you were in a bad way.'

Holly did the maths in her head. Cate and Leah showed up around a fortnight after the rape, a week after Holly's first @MidsummersChick post.

'I knew you needed me,' Cate said simply, her eyes shining in a way that was suddenly creepy. 'You're in an impossible situation, Holly, but I can help.'

'How?' Holly whispered.

Cate smiled approvingly. 'Good girl ... good question.' She took a step forwards. She was all in black – dungarees, a long-sleeved T-shirt, hoodie. She'd tucked her pink hair back, removed the rings and bangles she usually wore. Gone were the paint-scattered jeans and brightly patterned yoga leggings. Her eyeliner was thick and black, her eyes glittering black too. The only splash of colour the gleam of an orange headband beneath the shade of her hood. 'The answer is … *vengeance*. We're going to teach Jay Allardyce the lesson of a lifetime.'

Holly thought of all the times she'd hung out with this woman – laughing over TikTok, chatting about trending books, working on their art in companionable silence, drinking illicit glasses of wine, braiding each other's hair … And all the while, the real conversation was hiding beneath the surface of their interactions. Messages flying back and forth between Midsummer and Hecate, the fae and the witch, the victim and the avenger.

Cate paced, turned and circled back to Holly. She knelt before her, smiled a wide, wicked smile. 'This place is perfect for plotting dark deeds, don't you think? This is where I come to think … *to plan*.'

Holly shivered. 'In thunder, lightning or in rain,' Cate mused, and her face split in another indecent grin. 'Seriously, this is perfect.' She slid into a cross-legged position, beckoned to Holly. 'Come, join me.'

Holly slipped off the log and sat opposite her, mirroring. 'So, yeah, I basically cyber-stalked you, hunted you down and befriended you – that all sounds a bit creepy, I know; but I meant – *mean* – you no harm. I make it my mission in life to punish men who abuse women. We just can't trust the law to do it for us—' She was sincere, secure in her convictions, disconcertingly calm.

Holly stared at her, mouth hanging open.

'I'm on your side,' Cate said. 'Jay is dangerous. Tonight's the night, Holly. Time to seize the moment and act. If we can't take him down by fair means, then foul is our only option.'

Holly wanted to speak, but her voice was shrivelled. She took out her phone, opened the WhatsApp conversation between her and @QueenBee, and typed:

What do you have in mind?

Cate shook her head. 'I don't want a digital trail. And you need to promise me that you're in before I tell you the plan.'

Holly typed, then deleted:

I need to know what I'm promising first.

Cate held her gaze. 'You're promising fealty, Holly. Promising that everything that occurs tonight will stay between us.' She lowered her voice. 'We're going to take him down. Together.'

'I've considered a few options,' Cate continued when a minute had passed. 'I thought about setting it up to catch him in a compromising position, getting a picture like the one Ryan circulated of you. That would be quite satisfying – *very karmic*, given how Jay treated you. But I think Jay might take revenge porn as a compliment. I'm not convinced it would be sufficient punishment. Plus he's too dangerous; I think it might backfire on you.' She rubbed her nose with the back of her hand. 'Then I thought about trying to capture a confession. If you could get him talking, record him, maybe we could get him to admit what he did. With proof, we could blackmail him into leaving and going somewhere far from here.'

I like that, typed Holly frantically. She was scared of the lengths to which she now believed Cate might go.

'Bit of an issue considering you don't talk, though.'

Holly took a deep breath. She opened her mouth but only a squeak emerged. She swallowed, tried again. 'I … could try …' Her voice was hoarse, rusted. She had a sick feeling that if she didn't agree to this, Cate would suggest something infinitely worse.

Cate nodded thoughtfully. 'Maybe it could work. Let's set up a meeting.' She took Holly's phone from her, held it out to be unlocked and navigated to Holly's thread with Jay. Holly had deleted every message he'd sent her since the party, and until their earlier exchange the last message was an incongruous request from weeks ago sent on behalf of Gina asking him to pick up milk on his way home.

Holly peered over Cate's shoulder as she typed. *Okay, I'll meet you.*

The reply comes almost immediately. *Nice one, Holly. Thought you were mad at me ... playing hard to get. So, the cliff at 9 p.m.?*

That's what you get for flirting with Isla, Cate typed, and winked at Holly as if they were co-conspirators in an elaborate practical joke.

A longer pause this time as if Jay wasn't sure what to make of that. *Jealously doesn't suit you. I already told you that was a misunderstanding.*

Cate put down the phone in triumph. 'Rattled him. He doesn't like girls with a voice, does he?'

Holly shrivelled, and Cate grimaced. 'Sorry, that was insensitive. You'd have stood up to him if you could. He took advantage when you were at your weakest, and he's kept you weak. He's using your family against you. He knows you'd never risk your relationship with Finn, or put your mother in the position of having to choose between you and Gina. It was almost perfect, on his part.'

Holly picked up a stick and carved her next question in the dirt of the floor. *Almost ...?*

Cate's grin was ungodly again, light dancing in her eyes. 'He didn't count on me showing up, did he?'

Anxious about her meeting with Jay, time passed slowly. Finn came back from his run, and took a shower. Cate made dinner for the artists, and decanted the wine. Jay returned around 5 p.m., having obviously had a few beers. He filled up Haven's spaces with heavy presence, and the stink of his aftershave. He winked at Holly, but she ignored him.

The artists and Mum piled into the dining room. Cate kept

Holly close – perhaps afraid that Holly would change her mind if left alone. Cate drank and danced and laughed, totally at ease. 'Don't worry,' she whispered to Holly. 'Leah will swear you and I were with her all night. We stand by each other. She owes me.'

It was later that Holly thought of the word *alibi* and wondered why they'd need one, if all they were doing was trapping Jay into a confession. If they got Jay on tape, that was their leverage; he wouldn't tell anyone he'd been duped by them and risk exposure ...

She hid in the bathroom for a while, sitting with her head in her hands as fear of the impending ordeal raced through her. It wasn't long after that she heard the shout and went to investigate, finding Finn on the landing, holding his knee and cursing.

Cate was there, feigning concern.

Around 8 p.m. she dressed as Cate had told her to – leggings and an off-the-shoulder sweater, hair pulled back into a long braid, mascara, lip gloss.

Bait.

Holly didn't like this. She crept outside and stared into the dark mouth of the forest, afraid.

The cliff was her sanctuary. Plus Cate would be there. She checked her pocket several times to make sure that her phone was there. Checked the recording app was working, checked her battery.

Jay messaged again:

Can't wait to see you.

Holly deleted the message like all the others. She was heading for the trail when she felt a hand on her shoulder. She jumped a mile, but it wasn't Jay; it was Cate.

The darkness was profound, the moon obscured. 'Sorry, didn't mean to startle you.' She was still dressed in black, her hood pulled up over the distinctive baby-pink hair. She held out another big, dark hoodie and made Holly put it on over her sweater. 'Come on, this way.'

Holly frowned as Cate tried to lead her in the opposite direction. She pointed to the trail with a trembling finger.

Cate's teeth flashed in the dark. 'Yeah, no, we're going to intercept him. Much more fun.' She waved something and Holly saw that it was the key to Naomi's car.

The car was parked where Finn left it earlier, easy to slip it out without being noticed. Cate kept the headlights off. 'They're all hammered,' Cate said with a melodic laugh. 'I put a little something in the wine to make sure they have an extra-good time. Courtesy of Jay, of course. I felt he owed us that much ...'

She grinned again, and Holly shuddered. Something about this felt very wrong.

'I wanted privacy for us,' Cate said. 'Plus, it's ... fun. So sue me! Don't look like that; they'll be okay when it wears off. Best thing is, their memories will be vague so when I tell them stories about the evening and weave us into them, they'll believe we were there.'

Fear like a drip of cold seawater down her spine. She felt her hands start to shake and clamped them in her lap as Cate started the engine and pulled slowly out of the drive.

Cate sped up once the lights of Haven had faded behind them. She was driving too fast, and the fog was reaching off the hills like ghostly fingers. 'You're clear on the plan, yes?'

Holly was shaking so much she could hear her teeth clattering together. She knew the plan, but she had no confidence in her ability to carry it out. She was supposed to meet Jay, flirt, tell him that she wanted to be with him, but she couldn't until she got what happened in the cave off her chest; she had to trap him into confessing it all, fool him into thinking that she could forgive him, but only if he'd admit to being in the wrong. They'd use the taped confession to blackmail Jay into going far from here, leaving her alone. He could take off on his dad's yacht, use his ill-gotten gains to start over.

Morally, it repulsed her, but the prospect of freedom was too enticing to refuse. This way, she could live without his shadow over her all the time, without having to risk her family's happiness by revealing his crime. If he just left the house, the island, she would be able to breathe again.

She was terrified, had no idea if she could act well enough to pull off a manipulation so intricate. Especially when it had been so long since she had spoken. What if her voice let her down when she most needed it?

'This is important,' Cate said. 'I know it's hard, but if you can just put everything aside for a few minutes and get this done, it'll be over; we'll have Jay where we want him.'

Holly nodded. She didn't want to let Cate down when she'd come all this way for her. But how was she supposed to put everything aside and just chat to Jay like nothing had happened?

It didn't work like that.

'If you really can't speak, then I suppose you could put it all down in your notes app. I mean, I think it'll be less powerful that way—'

'I can do it,' Holly whispered, scared of complying, terrified of not. They were still driving too fast up the coast road and she gripped her seat.

Grass and bushes flew past her eyes, flashes of black water between tussocks of heather, the faint glow through the sea fog from a distant lighthouse. Cate continued to accelerate. 'We're nearly there,' she said, exhilarated, like they were on a great adventure. 'Hopefully I've timed it just right.' Her smile was disturbing, off-kilter.

Holly felt a twang of alarm.

'I've timed this drive several times. I've timed the walk through the woods too. I know to the second when he is likely to emerge onto the road—'

Holly didn't understand what this had to do with the plan. She chewed her lip, stared ahead as the road looped, as the car lurched, as the back slewed beneath them, as Cate corrected and somehow managed to hold the curve.

The darkness of the forest rose to Holly's left as they hurtled between cliff and trees.

They were almost at the place where the forest trail opened into the road. The lookout, with its stones placed at the highest point before the vista. Tonight, in the dark and mist, Jay would not be stopping to admire the view. He would come out of the woods, cross the road and wait for her, eager to pick their way down the cliff path to the shelter of the cove.

The tide was in. There would be only the smallest spit of sand in the nearby inlet, no beach at all beneath the cliff. There were gaps in the rock, places to shelter, spots where they could be alone. Behind them, the rough-hewn slope, to one side cold black sea, and the other, a deadly stretch of the cliff face.

Holly didn't want to go down there alone with him. It was wet and inhospitable, and she didn't trust him.

As Cate continued to speed towards the lookout her words replayed. *I've timed this.* When Jay emerged from the trees, the car would be there: headlights blinding.

Trapped in the passenger seat as they jerked round the final corner, glancing sideways at the determined, calm profile of the woman she'd believed a friend, Holly had a dreadful premonition of what was to come, what Cate had planned all along.

There would be no confession, no recording, no tears. There would be no blackmail.

They had come here to end him.

'CATE!' she shouted as something loomed before them. Not a deer scrabbling out of the forest, or a rabbit seized with fear.

A boy.

Jay.

He stood, immobilised in a blaze of light, tried to dive to the side when he realised the car was heading straight for him. There was nowhere to go but over the cliff and he was on the wrong side of the gap to reach the soft slope to the inlet, where heather might break his fall. He was poised over the steepest part, the direct drop to the sea.

Holly heard her screams fill the car. Cate pulled the wheel, tyres sinking into mud as they left the road. The car lurched towards the boy, and she slammed on the brakes. Holly couldn't help it; she reached out and jerked the wheel left, dragging them away from the figure in their lights and towards the drop.

But it was not enough. She felt her organs move before the rest of her caught up as her chest slammed the dashboard when the car collided with something hard and soft at the same time. Something no match for metal. There was a screech and thump as bone and flesh and stone gave and the body slipped beneath their wheels. The car glided to a halt a metre from the drop.

Cate panted and leaned over the wheel, laughing. The clashing notes of her hilarity reached horrible heights. Then she stopped abruptly, glared at Holly. 'What did you do that for? We hit the boulder. We've damaged the car.'

She got out to check, and Holly tried to remember how to breathe. *Damaged the car* – they'd hit someone, who cared about the car?

Willing her legs to work, she got out. Walked around to the prone body. Maybe he'd be okay, just winded, a few bumps and bruises, but alive. She wanted a way out – wanted this fucked-up night to end with everyone tucked up in their beds safe and sound. Maybe he'd need a trip to the hospital, but he'd be okay.

They would buy Jay's silence with her own.

Cate pressed her hand to her mouth like a child caught out. 'Oops,' she said, grinning.

Oops?

Fear crawled through Holly's veins. She sucked air in. The rain was brutal, stabbing diagonal slices into her skin. Wind tore at her hair and hood, and the boom of the sea below was deafening. She could hardly think, and she needed to.

The headlights illuminated the carnage. Floodlit peaty mud and tangled seagrass, the face of the boy – one arm flung out, a leg bent, bones snapped, ribs crushed and leaking blood.

She leaned over, saw the mess of his head – a sticky, crimson soup.

She immediately tore off her hoodie to try to soak up the blood. Cat stopped her, wrenching her back. 'Oh, no you don't. You're not going to save him now, Florence Nightingale. *Don't touch.*'

Holly was already stained with Jay's blood. She was bending over him, checking for a pulse, unable to hear a heartbeat over the sound of her own, which pulsed in every cell and fibre of her.

'Quite the dilemma, isn't it?' said Cate. She was between Holly and the car, between Holly and safety. Holly felt the softening of the ground beneath her feet, the slide towards the drop. Her calves burned as she balanced herself – it would take so little effort to tip her over, send her hurtling down to be torn apart by the rocks.

Her breath caught in her throat. She was terrified of Cate then. She looked from Jay to the woman with the demonic grin. A soft sound escaped her, but she couldn't find her voice.

Perhaps she'd never speak again, after this.

If she lived ...

Cate's voice was eerie – dead calm. 'Does the monster deserve to be saved? What do you think, Holly? Is he breathing? Alive? Or is the decision already out of your hands?'

Holly looked at her hands. She recoiled from the smears of scarlet. She held both up before her as though she held his life in them, weighing his soul.

'Clock is ticking,' Cate said. 'If you're phoning for help, you'd better do it quick.'

Holly gazed up at her. Her body was leaden with shock. Cate crouched, stared into her eyes, her voice a wisp. 'I did it for you, Holly; this was *all* for you.'

Then, she pressed her fingers to the soft give of Jay's windpipe. She was wearing gloves. 'He's gone.'

Holly braced again on the slope of the cliff edge, feeling the earth slip beneath her. She clawed towards flatter ground and at the last second Cate reached out to help her.

'Tragic,' Cate said. 'Went for a run on the cliff in the storm and fell to his death.'

Holly frowned. *He'd been hit by a car – it didn't look anything like a fall.*

She turned, glanced over the dizzying drop, saw the sea heaving and rolling beneath her, a long way down. At the bottom of the cliff jutted perilous shards of stone. The bay was lethal. They were poised over the steepest part, and Jay was close to the edge …

And he was already dead.

Cate dipped one gloved finger into the blood pooling around Jay's temple. She swiped it down the centre of Holly's forehead. 'There … first kill.' Holly scrambled from the precipice, watched helplessly as Cate, grunting with effort, rolled Jay's body from the clifftop.

Chapter 54

Now

Finn

Holly shrinks in her seat as Cate leans towards her. Eyes dark with menace, teeth bared. 'What the *fuck* was that, Holls?' Holly cringes, brings her hands up to shield herself but the blow doesn't come.

Cate breathes hard; I can almost see the thoughts forming and floating, bursting like bubbles as she tries to figure what to do next. Without the drugs to make me compliant, without Holly helping, how is she supposed to get me out of the car and across to the cliff?

I take a deep gulp of air and try to concentrate. My thoughts are spiky and unfinished, my brain short-circuiting with fear. I won't go quietly. I will fight, bruise and bloody her in the process. That will be a problem in the wake of my disappearance, when she has marks to explain away, but it will be a bigger problem for me, if I'm *dead*.

I stare at the sliver of Holly's face I can see. Her head is turned away, and I try to gauge if she has another battle in her. Cate is stronger than her, more muscled, but Holly is taller. If she has some fight left, we could overpower Cate together.

I'll have to time it just right, and I can't rely on Holly now. Our twin bond is silent. 'Holls …' I say softly. 'Look at me.'

'Shut up!' Cate screams at me and slaps me hard. She reaches into her pocket and lunges between the seats again, sitting on me hard, winding me. She clamps something over my mouth, and I taste something musty and unclean. I spit, twist my head, but she manages to bind the cloth about my face, fastening it behind my head. The gag pulls tight. It tastes of turpentine from the studio.

Breathing is harder, with my mouth covered and her weight on me. I concentrate on drawing in air, so I don't pass out.

Cate returns to her seat with a grunt of effort, leans across Holly and reaches into the glovebox. She takes something out, something she holds up to the weak gleam of the interior light.

Light shines on the blade of the craft knife. I forget how to breathe again.

'Right. We'll do this the hard way then. Please don't make the mistake of thinking that I don't have a plan B. I didn't have one before, with Jay, I admit. Didn't think I needed it. A stupid girl and her boy scout of a brother got in the way and messed everything up.' She flicks a dispassionate glance at Holly. 'I've learned my lesson. Now, let's put that twin loyalty to the test, shall we?'

My eyes widen. Fear writhes in my gut. Holly is curled in a ball against the door, whimpering softly. I make a noise through the gag, trying to tell her to run. *She* could get free, save herself.

She doesn't, though.

Cate grabs her like a rag doll, pulls her towards her across the centre console. She gets an arm around Holly's neck, presses the point of her blade beneath Holly's chin.

Holly freezes and her eyes fly wide to match mine. I protest, but only noise escapes the gag – furious, vengeful sound. *Murderous* noise.

I will kill her, if I get free.

Cate smiles, smug now that she's regained the upper hand. 'Okay, this is what's happening. Holly and I are getting out of the car now.'

She reaches behind herself and thrusts her door open. Then she tugs at Holly, dragging, careless of how Holly's knees bash the gearstick. Both Holly's hands grip Cate's forearm as it tightens on her neck, squeezing her windpipe thin, and she quivers at the touch of cold steel pressing the delicate flesh below her ear. One thrust and she'll bleed, the blade slipping into her jugular, draining her in seconds.

Without hands, she's awkward, limbs flailing as she's dragged from the car. Cate manoeuvres them both out, showing no concern for Holly's joints rattling off the doorframe. She sidesteps, opens my door too. 'Get out.'

I flop like a landed fish trying to get myself out of the car with my arms and legs bound. I exit the car head first, land with a thump at Cate's feet. I'm immediately encompassed by the storm. The noise of it is incredible, the rain soaking me in seconds. 'Stand up!'

I glare at her. *I'm trying.*

Holly whines as Cate gives me an incentive to try harder, sliding the blade up and down Holly's neck like she's about to peel an apple. I gasp and fight to my feet.

I use the car to help stagger upright, wedging my shoulder into the wheel arch. When I'm standing, unsteady, my head swims with our proximity to the edge. I can see the churning chaos of the sea below.

'You're a risk to me,' Cate says softly – her softness more menacing than anger. 'Holly will fall into line. She's like Leah – pliable, easy to bend to my will. But *you*?' She shakes her head. 'I gave you a chance by setting that tripwire, placing your trainers so you'd think you'd fallen over them. I wanted you to stay home, Finn – for *her* sake. I didn't want you to be part of things. But you ruined everything, and now you've got to go. I'm not going to prison because of *you*.' She gives the blade a twist.

It doesn't cut, but the movement makes Holly and me flinch. Holly goes limp in Cate's arms, and I know I've lost her. Maybe I lost her a long time ago.

When I failed to see her monster, failed to protect her.

'None of this has worked out the way it was supposed to, but I need someone to take the blame. The police are already looking at you, so … Your suicide note was eloquent, by the way. I think you'd like it. Your English teacher certainly will. Perhaps a tad poetical, but I couldn't help myself. I've a flair for the dramatic.' Cate waves an elegant hand, smile amused.

My body is trembling all over. My knees weaken, a chill permeating my bones. This is it; I'm going to die out here. I'm so close to the drop, one push could tip me over …

'You're going to do this for me, Finn,' she says, and there's a moment where I see the appeal – her ability to draw people in and make them do what she wants. A strange kind of magic.

'I know you're scared, but just think about the fact that you're doing a good thing. For your sister. No one will know, but *she* will.' She jerks her head at my twin, and I look at Holly and see tears spilling down her cheeks as she shakes her head at me. 'You're a hero. Saving your sister. Making amends for letting her down—'

'Not him,' Holly croaks and it's so long since I've heard her voice, the sound sparks a light inside of me. A last gasp of brightness like a flame guttering before it goes out. '*Me*,' Holly says. 'Please.'

Cate ignores her. 'I'm going to have to untie your arms for it to look like suicide. This is going to be risky, but I want you to remember that one misstep and Holly dies. Understand?'

She's desperate, and desperate is dangerous. But she's also far from the original plan, in which Holly was a willing accomplice. She didn't expect to have to deal with both of us at once. There's still a flicker of hope in me, despite the fear. *I'm not dead yet.*

I *am* perilously close to the edge, however, with Cate advancing. The ground is slick and unsound beneath my feet. She brings Holly with her, keeps an arm around her, knife at her neck – one slice and she'll be gone. If I make the wrong move, my sister will die before I can get us to safety.

I need to find a way to save us *both*. I'd jump off this cliff to save Holly, I would, but I don't want it to come to that. 'Turn around,' Cate orders, and I comply.

She is behind me. I am centimetres … seconds, from *gone*.

Wind scours my face. Rain slides down my skin. I close my eyes as the vertigo rises up and over me, clawing at my lungs, my throat. I feel the sharp tug of the blade as it rips through the canvas bindings. While the knife is cutting through my bonds, it is not pointed at Holly. *This is the moment.*

But Cate is close enough that she could push me over with barely a flick of her hand. I am running out of time, out of options.

She slices the gag too. Any moment now I will feel the flat of her hand between my shoulder blades send me soaring. If I survive the drop – doubtful since Cate has me poised by a narrow ravine that cuts into the cliff – I won't be able to swim with my feet bound. She won't risk untying my legs: I might conceivably have bound them myself to prevent a change of heart, a last-gasp flailing attempt at survival in the water.

My window is closing, my moment passing. I spin, arms raised to knock the knife from her hand. Our forearms clash, a shudder of bone that makes Cate grit her teeth and shriek wildly at me. Without Holly as hostage, she knows I can overpower her. She pushes her weight towards me, and my feet slide on the slick edge.

I need to get away from the drop.

My attack gives Holly a chance – a small one, but a chance. I hope by some miracle she takes it.

Holly drops to the ground and Cate lunges for her, startled by the movement. I surge towards Cate, away from the drop, fear fizzing in my blood with how close I am to the cliff, how easy it still would be to give one good push. Cate's footing is destabilised by my strike, and it takes her a precious second to regain her balance. She gets hold of Holly's top, tries to drag her back by her hood, knife quivering, pointed at my chest.

I freeze as the blade sweeps towards me, block the swipe with my arm and feel the blade tear through fabric and flesh.

We're out of time again.

Holly slips out of her hoodie leaving Cate with a fistful of material. There's nowhere for her to go, and she crab-crawls across the cliff. 'Holly, the edge!' I cry; she's heading right for it. She must be disorientated in the dark.

Holly looks back at me. She smiles briefly, and slips. Over the drop and down.

Cate screams, falling to her knees on the wet rock. The bottom falls out of my world, life draining from me as I stare at the grey space where Holly disappeared.

My sister is gone.

Chapter 55

Isla

The cottage by the sea is warm; the wood burner has been on all day. It should be a perfect place to read and wait out the storm. Isla is curled up on the sofa in hiking socks and jammies, a book in her hand and the cat drowsing on her lap. Her father is dozing in his armchair and the combined effect of her sleeping companions is soporific. There are mugs scattered and a half-eaten packet of biscuits spilling on the coffee table.

Her mum is at work – she's a nurse at the community hospital, with Kirsty's mother. Given the severity of the weather, she'll stay over with a friend in town to save her travelling home on treacherous roads after her shift.

Isla checks her phone, but she has no messages. Of course, Finn doesn't have his phone, but she half hoped he might borrow Holly's and send her something. A goofy smile lights her face at the thought of him, and she bites her lip and schools her expression lest her dad wake and wonder what she's grinning about.

Her dad is a big softy, surprisingly okay about the idea of Isla having a boyfriend; but she's not keen to introduce Finn to him as such, with everything hanging over him.

Meet my boyfriend – straight-A student, great rugby player, likes sea swimming, Stephen King books and horror. One small thing, he's currently under suspicion of murder. He didn't do it – it was actually his sister and he covered it up – I'm sure it will all blow over …

Isla picks up her book, sighs as she tries to refocus. Outside a voracious wind whips up: trees, grass, the tarpaulin covering her dad's dinghy, all caught in the teeth of the gale. Their house sits on a wee rise, so she's not worried about flooding from an errant wave, but still, she flinches from the incredible noise of the sea – a howling war cry that distracts her from her page.

Or maybe it's her thoughts that keep disconnecting her. They've been in overdrive since she left Haven – since she sat with Finn and Eve, and heard Finn's story haltingly, hauntingly told.

It still seems fantastical to her: Holly, a girl she has known most of her life, killing Jay.

Still, it's hard to condemn her – the rape has mushroomed in Isla's mind since she came to understand the extent of Jay's perfidy. She was there that night, accepted Jay in his role as hero – lugging Holls up from the cave like her saviour. Holly was not just drugged and assaulted; but prepped for it, set up, tormented, made to live in fear for weeks and months to follow. She must have felt like she was losing her mind all that time, under the same roof as him. Her attacker was charming, credible, and cruel. The extent of his evil astounds her; she wonders how no one saw the truth.

She got a glimpse of it that day in the library, when Jay looked at her like prey. She saw the rage in his eyes when she pushed him off with a snapped, 'Away you go, Jay Allardyce, who do you think I am?'

Isla doesn't blame Holly. Doesn't blame Finn for helping to cover it up.

Maybe Jay met justice on that cliffside – unconventional, immoral, but justice all the same. But still … there's a sense of waste and distaste about the whole affair.

Melancholy hangs about Isla like an island fog – she'd be in danger of settling in for a good wallow, save for one thing …

Something no one but Isla knows. Not even Finn.

A secret she didn't want to reveal until she'd got her head around what it meant. She would have said something by now, talked it out with Finn and Eve, maybe even gone to the police.

Except the storm overtook them, and the message came from her dad to get home quick, and momentum swept her up; before she knew it, she was in Mr Fraser's car heading back home.

Carefully, Isla displaces the displeased cat and straightens. She watches her dad, mindful of every movement as she slips quietly out of the room, stepping lightly on the stairs to minimise creaks. In her bedroom, she opens her bag, slides out the item she took from Haven – recovered on a secret snoop about the artists' quarters earlier.

That was another reason she didn't say something: she was ashamed of sneaking about, delving into the artists' privacy.

She found it in Cate's room – the one she searched first, for reasons she can't quite put her finger on. A sixth sense perhaps, a flicker of something she couldn't quite capture or put into words – *like that day in the library, when she just knew there was something off about Jay …*

For the past few days she's been watching Cate: a stranger who seems to Isla to be overdoing the friending. She's been watching the dynamic between Cate and Holly. Wondering …

Cate took Holly over so completely. At first glance it seemed like it was Holly seeking out the older girl, tagging along, tolerated. Harmless hero worship, perhaps. But on closer inspection, Isla's fairly sure the overtures were coming from Cate.

Not just overtures – insistence. *Smothering*. Why would that be? A mute, fragile teenager didn't have much to offer a confident, twenty-something woman like Cate.

Compassion would take you so far, but this was something else, intimate – almost *obsessed*.

Isla observed Cate when Holly was missing – everyone else

was focused on Holly, but Isla found Cate's reactions interesting: she was angry, beginning to panic; not in the same way everyone else was panicking – it seemed personal. When Holly was found, Cate was most at pains to be the one to fuss over her and lead her away.

Because she wanted to control the girl's story, get inside her head? Maybe Holly left Haven to get space from *Cate*.

Isla is interested in the relationship between Cate and Leah too. Apparent strangers prior to their arrival at Haven, yet there's a symbiosis between them that seems too ingrained to be new. Most often, it was Leah deferring to Cate, watching, checking everything with her, letting Cate speak for her.

Enough to trigger curiosity, nothing more. Nothing so concrete as a suspicion.

Not then.

But she took advantage of the opportunity while Cate was engrossed in the studio to sneak upstairs in the artists' wing and have a look in her room. She had no idea what she was looking for …

Until she found it.

The phone: a slim, black Android in a heavy-duty case. Cate had always had hers on her – Isla had noticed its distinctive purple case.

This phone was in a drawer, wrapped in a piece of canvas that seemed to have once held paintbrushes or pencils, shoved beneath a pile of frothy underwear and smelling of linseed oil from the brushes. Isla was hot with shame at searching someone's underwear drawer, but it didn't stop her.

She unwrapped the phone, careful not to touch it.

When she turned it over, she saw the screen was cracked with a jagged spider web of fissures. And there was a smear of something on the shattered screen: something that looked like rusty paint until Isla looked closer and decided it was blood.

The phone battery was dead – with her sleeve pulled down

over her hand, she tried to turn it on – but there was a sticker on the back that Isla recognised. It was a drawing Holly had done in the summer when Jay was toying with the idea of getting a tattoo and asked her to sketch out a biomechanical eye.

It had given Isla the creeps the first time she'd seen it, and Finn had urged Jay to think about it some more before committing. Since there were no proper tattoo shops on the island – even Jay wasn't reckless enough to let some enthusiast with a tattoo machine set up in his front room loose on him – he'd consented to wait. He stuck the image on the back of his phone so he could decide if he liked it enough to get it scribed into his skin.

Now the picture was dirty, curled at the corners. There was a smear of blood across the eye too, which made it even creepier.

It was Jay's phone.

In Cate's bedside drawer.

There hasn't been much time for Isla to think about that, try to figure out what it means. Now, sitting in her bedroom, waiting out the storm, she has nothing *but* time. She rewraps the phone again, cursing herself for bringing it into her house.

This is evidence. In a murder enquiry.

She should have given it to Ben Carmichael straight away. Or asked to see Inspector Isherwood, handed it over and let them figure it out. She would have done, but it might put Finn and Holly further into the shadow of suspicion.

The whole story might have come out, then they'd be back to the problem of who was going to take the blame: Finn, Holly, Naomi …

Isla tried to fathom Cate's involvement. Finn didn't mention anything about her knowing or being part of things. It would be too risky for Finn or Holly to have hidden the phone in Cate's room – she'd have found it and asked questions.

The phone surfacing is an issue for Holly – if there are messages on it confirming that Holly was to meet Jay on the cliff the night he died, then the last thing either twin would want is for it to fall into the wrong hands. They'd have got rid of it. Which means Cate took the phone of her own accord.

So … was Cate there when Jay died, or did she come by this afterwards?

Perhaps *she* suspects Holly too, is trying to cover for her. But it'd make more sense to get rid of the phone. She's had ample time to throw it into the sea where it can cause no further trouble.

Outside Isla's window, darkness sweeps up the inlet with the tide. Her windowpane is splattered with rain, and she hasn't closed her curtains on the storm. She shivers, pulls the comforter around her and starts googling. **Cate+Duncan+artist**

No results. Nothing on LinkedIn either.

Isla's seen some of Cate's work and it's good – strange and haunting but good. She must sell or exhibit if painting is her livelihood. She tries a few more things, looks up Cate on Facebook. There are plenty of Cate Duncans, but most of them seem to be in the States or Australia. There's no sign – personal or professional – of the Cate Duncan who resides at Haven.

Eve has always complained that her mother is too trusting, never properly checks her guests' credentials. Haven would be a great place for someone escaping not just personal troubles, but legal ones too.

It would be easy for Cate to reinvent herself here – maybe she's hiding from an abusive ex – but if that's the case, wouldn't she *tell* Naomi, and Holly? Putting women back together is what Naomi is all about.

Women helping women is Haven's way.

Isla has a bad feeling in the pit of her stomach. She can't explain it, thinks she's possibly overreacting. Her imagination forced into hyperdrive by the seclusion of the storm. She tries Eve's phone, and Holly's. Both go to voicemail. She tries again, leaves them messages, sends a WhatsApp apiece, and chews her thumbnail while the ticks fail to turn blue.

She debates what to do. The road back to Haven is closed,

so she can't go up there to check on them. Nor can anyone, by road at least. She peers out of the window. Hardly a night to be hiking across the moor to Haven from the main road. Positively dangerous in fact. But less dangerous than the coastal path, with unpredictable storm waves that might sweep her from the cliffs …

If she had Mr Fraser's number, she would call him. But that would be weird – she'd feel stupid trying to explain that she has a *feeling*. A suspicion that the sweet, pink-haired artist who's been cooking everyone dinner and comforting Holly this whole time might not be who she claims to be.

The nagging unease tugs at her – if Finn, Holly and Eve are stuck there with a woman who isn't who she says she is, Isla thinks they should at least know it.

As she's trying to fathom what to do, a message appears on her phone screen. It's from Holly: one of those one-time opening photographs on WhatsApp. Frowning, Isla taps it. It's a screenshot of a conversation:

@QueenBee: *Shit! No way. What did you tell him?*
@MidsummersChick: *Nothing. Obviously I'm not going to meet him.*
@QueenBee: *This is your chance …*
@MidsummersChick: *Chance for what?*
@QueenBee: *To get him out of your life. For good.*
@MidsummersChick: *???*
@QueenBee: *Think about it. A stormy night … a treacherous cliff path … an arsehole who thinks he can rape you and threaten you and still come back for more … I've got your back, Holly. I'll help …*

Then a pin drops, a dot at the edge of the world. *The cliff.*
A moment later, Holly's offline, and when Isla calls her, it goes to voicemail. No location, no more messages.

Isla catapults off her bed, searches her bag for the business card Imogen Isherwood gave everyone peripherally involved in the investigation. She doesn't want to call the police, but she also can't go trekking out to Haven alone, and she has a *very* bad feeling now.

Imogen answers on the second ring. 'DI Isherwood.'

'It's Isla Maxwell. The thing is … Oh, it's too hard to explain. I don't have time. Can you please give me Ben Carmichael's number?'

'Is this to do with the investigation?'

'Yes! Please, I need his number. I'm in a hurry.' Isla is shaky with adrenaline now, her unease morphing into full-blown panic. Holly wouldn't have sent her location unless something was wrong. She wouldn't be on the cliff, sending Isla screenshots of strange messages …

Unless she was in danger and needed someone to know.

So if something happens to her, Isla will be able to unravel the truth …

'How's the storm out there?'

'Bad. *Please*, DI Isherwood …'

'If it's to do with the investigation you should be telling me what you know—'

'I don't have time. You're not on the island. Ben *is*.' Isla doesn't have the patience for politeness.

Finally, Imogen must hear something in Isla's voice that galvanises her. 'I'm not handing out his number, but give me yours and I'll get him to ring you. I want to know what this is about.'

Chapter 56

Finn

'No!' Cate screams. She catches herself before she too plummets off the edge. She stares, then turns to me with her knife hand outstretched, eyes dark and ... dead.

I am hollow. With Holly gone, I feel nothing, barely even concern for my own life.

Only rage.

It doesn't matter what happens to me, I *will* avenge Holly. I stare at the point of the blade, into the cauldron of Cate's gaze. She advances slowly. I have my arms free, but my legs are still bound. She circles me, backing me up. I feel the surge of the wind at my back, the gusts that might be enough to topple me, the madness of the storm. I brace myself, legs aching from the effort. Vertigo from the drop makes my head swim.

'A twin suicide pact,' Cate muses. 'How sweet.'

'You're fucking insane,' I tell her. I don't care what she does now. I don't care about anything. If the knife was in my hand instead of hers, I'd drive it between her ribs without hesitation. I'd spill her blood here.

I owe it to Holly to *fight*.

I bend my knees, bounce on my feet, trying to learn my new centre of gravity with my legs bound like this. Cate is agile; I know that. And she's fast. But I can hit harder.

If I go down swinging, however, there's a good chance she'll slip beneath my blows and stick her knife in me.

Maybe I don't care: I *want* this fight, for the satisfaction, the soothing violence. *For retribution. For Holly.*

Tears press against my eyes, but I can't let them fall. I can't break.

For her, I must survive a little longer.

A movement catches my eye, and I am momentarily distracted. I glance for less than a second, seeing nothing, and when I look back Cate has moved disconcertingly closer. I can smell her, the sweaty fear that coats her skin. She's scared too. And she's tiring. There might just be a chance for me …

The movement again. This time I don't avert my eyes, but stare past her ear, letting her slide out of focus. A face, wet with rain. A hand outstretched in warning. Telling me not to move, not to act. Not to speak.

A green-clad figure moving slowly. Another behind that. Two men, both of whom I recognise.

Ben Carmichael. Ian Maxwell.

Relief floods me, quickly replaced with despair: they are too late – *Holly is dead*.

I don't think I can survive long with my legs bound and Cate's knife towards my throat; I don't know if I have it in me.

Fight. Holly urges me through our twin bond, even though that can't be. She's gone but there's an echo of her in my mind.

Ben creeps closer, baton outstretched. Ian is close behind him. They must be making noise, boots whispering through undergrowth, but the sea is so loud it drowns everything else. If I close my eyes and listen to the sea, I can already feel how, after the initial fear of the fall, the chaos of the water, calmness will come over me beneath the surface.

Even in a storm, I *love* the water, the power of the waves. Mum has a hard time keeping me from going surfing when a storm front comes in. The bigger the waves, the better. Dangerous – but it's when you're close to death that you feel most alive.

Fight.

A surge of adrenaline shoots through me. I'm fuelled by a fury that transcends everything. The people who destroyed my sister deserve to be destroyed in return.

For her, I think. I imagine throwing my weight forwards, imagine how Cate will stumble, predict how long it will take her to react.

I have one chance – if I miss, she'll knife me. She'll be caught since there's a police officer right behind her but that will be cold comfort to me. She won't have time to push my body over the edge, and maybe I'd rather she did – if I'm to die, the sea is how I want to go.

I push aside the grim thought. Arms swinging, with a roar that comes from the pit of my soul, I go for her.

Isla

She doesn't stay back like her dad told her to. As soon as she sees Finn on the cliff, she comes out of the shadows and starts forwards with Eve, following Ben and her dad as they creep forwards.

Things moved fast after Ben called her. He listened, accepted without question what she had to say, agreed to meet her on the main road as close to Haven as he could get. Isla tried to sneak out, but her dad woke up as she was at the door in her hiking boots. She wasted precious minutes trying to explain, talking too fast, trying to make him understand. Luckily, he trusted her enough to try. She's glad he's here.

Isla is usually calm, ill-disposed to drama – her father knows that. Like Ben, he caught the urgency of the situation without having the faintest idea what she was on about. He believed her.

He threw on his outdoor gear, a lightweight coat that dispels the rain, heavy boots, and grabbed the keys to his truck.

In the car, Isla looked up @QueenBee. What she saw helped the pieces to fall into place. And brought a fresh wave of fear.

It was a couple of miles from the tree blockade on the main road to Haven, cross-country. An arduous trek in the storm, over rough ground. Isla gritted her teeth, kept her head down and pushed on. She kept up with the men, desperate to reach Haven and be proven wrong – but she knew, somehow, that she would not be.

She tried to explain at points as they walked, but she was rambling, throwing out snippets of a story Ben and her dad had a hard time assembling. Ben understood more, better versed in all things Haven. Her poor dad had no clue what was going on, but he ploughed gamely on without complaint.

'The artist with the pink hair?' Ben checked, as Isla rattled on about a phone, anonymous messages, and something about a witch online.

'Yes!' Isla agreed. 'It was her all along.'

At Haven, they found the house eerily quiet, doors unlocked. Cashew was the only occupant awake and he barked frantically when they entered, then immediately ran to the door that led down to the cellar. The banging started up almost as soon as the barking did, and they were quickly able to free Eve from her makeshift prison.

Eve was confused by the party that greeted her, and Isla grabbed her hands and said, 'It wasn't Holly.'

Eve darted an anxious glance at Ben, confused as to why Isla was speaking openly before the police. Of course she didn't want Holly to be a killer either … Isla realised in that instant that Eve hadn't fully figured things out yet. 'The person in her DMs … feeding her all this stuff about revenge …' she said. 'I think Queen of the Witches is Cate.' She didn't have time for Eve to catch up. '*And I'm sure she killed Jay.*'

Eve had questions, but the most pressing prompted her to look around and say frantically, 'Where are the twins?'

A speedy search of the house revealed no sign of either twin, and no sign of Cate either. The discovery of Finn's suicide note in the den – scrawled on a torn-out page of a sketchbook – was chilling.

'Absolutely not!' Eve expostulated, as Isla said swiftly, 'Finn didn't write that.'

Leah and Fran were asleep in their rooms – sleeping so deeply Ben suspected it was unnatural. Combined with Eve's reports of feeling groggy and passing out in the cellar, and a dreamy memory of Cate helping her down the steps, he opined that they had all been drugged. He rang an ambulance, though both women had strong pulses and were breathing evenly. There was no likelihood of an ambulance, air or otherwise, making it through soon, but he had no idea what dosage they'd been given. Better safe than sorry.

This added substantially to everyone's worry for the twins. If Cate felt it necessary to get everyone else out of the way, what did she have in mind for them?

The cliff was the logical place to look – after that brief flash of Holly's location on WhatsApp. The scene of the crime …

Ben put in a further call for backup – again, futile – forbade the others from coming with him, and set out. Isla's dad followed at his heels. When Ben tried to instruct him to go back – he was a civilian and would be putting himself in danger – he gave Ben a stubborn look and continued. Isla and Eve followed at a wary distance, and when her dad caught them tailing them through the woods, he was firm. 'No matter what we find, you stay back. Understand?'

Eve is still feeling the effects of the drug, stumbling and slow. Isla keeps hold of her, pulling her along. There was no way either of them was willing to stay home, and it was unlikely they would stay back when they reached the cliff.

However, they are sensible enough to see that Ben is right to go quietly. The only advantage they have on Cate is the element of surprise. Eve's nails dig Isla's palm as she grips her hand at the sight of Finn so close to the edge, his legs bound, the blade pointed towards him.

When Finn leaps at Cate, Eve screams his name. Ben and Isla's dad rush forward, breaking cover and closing on the pair quickly.

It is over in seconds. There are shouts, arms flailing, a flash of metal, a clash of bodies. Finn and Cate are both on the ground, her dad and Ben blocking Isla's view. No sign of Holly.

She and Eve drop hands and run.

Chapter 57

Finn

There's blood; I feel it seeping from me as I lie on the clifftop, roll awkwardly onto my back, stare up at the angry sky and feel removed from it all.

I'm alive. For the moment, that's all I'm capable of understanding.

There's a scuffle nearby, and when I turn my head, I see the art knife lying in the grass. Ben has control of Cate, flipping her onto her front and snapping handcuffs on her wrists. She screeches, screams obscenities at him, but he is unfazed. A man crouches beside me, says something incomprehensible. I frown, try to focus through a blur of white noise and storm. He's asking if I'm hurt.

Blood seeps down my arm. I don't know where it's coming from. There's no pain. And then there is. It floods in after a long beat of nothing. My arm hurts. I lift it, feel the pull and scrape of a long cut that traverses my forearm. It's deep-ish, and the blood leaks freely.

I let my head fall back. That can't be all. With my good arm, I search for injuries, prodding my torso, the precious areas where organs lurk beneath the skin, where real damage might be done.

And then I remember: Holly, the cliff. My twin – *dead*. I twist frantically, inhibited by my bonds. 'My sister—'

The man looks alarmed, tick-tocks his gaze between me and the sea. 'She fell.'

Jumped to save me.

He gives me a once-over, reassures himself that I am unharmed beyond the superficial. Mind you, superficial fucking *hurts*. Now that I'm feeling again, it's agony.

Numb was better.

The man goes cautiously to the edge. He gets down on his knees, not risking a slip of earth or a virulent gust. I look away; I dread what he might see: my sister's slender limbs and silver hair splayed on rocks far below … or *nothing*. Holly could have been lost to the current already.

Ben has secured a spitting, swearing Cate, and returned her to the car, which I can't imagine is an ideal solution but what else is he supposed to do with her up here? He gets on the radio, but I am too far away to hear what he says. A moment later, Eve and Isla hurl themselves to the ground at my side. They are both talking at once, but I can't concentrate on their words; I'm trying to work out how to tell Eve that Holly is gone.

I look back at Isla's dad, still peering over the edge.

'Isla saved your life,' Eve says. 'She figured out there was more to Cate than meets the eye and she made us listen even though it sounded crazy.' She smiles at Isla. 'Sorry, but it did—' She frowns as it dawns on her that we are not all present and correct. 'Finn … where's Holls?'

I clench my teeth and avert my gaze again, unable to hide the truth, unable to tell her. Mr Maxwell is leaning out over the drop. 'Oh, no!' Eve springs up; Isla and I grab an arm each and pull her back. The last thing we need is Eve coming to harm too.

Mr Maxwell laughs, which is not what I expect. He leans back on his heels, shouts down: 'Don't move. I'll find something to pull you up.'

Isla, Eve and I sit stupefied and stare at him. He grins at us. 'She's fine.'

The ledge.

Holly didn't go off the cliff where Cate wanted me to jump; she went to the left, rolled over the edge, not above a roiling sea, but over the ledge she has climbed to many times before – once with a book between her teeth. My sister is fearless, and heights have never bothered her.

She's on the ledge that caught Jay's body and prevented the execution of what might have been a perfect crime. The ledge that very nearly got me condemned as a murderer.

The ledge that has now saved her.

I'm a daredevil in water, but she's the one with the head for heights. I laugh too – my clever, brave sister. Mr Maxwell returns from the woods with a sturdy branch, tells Eve and Isla what to do. As the rescue mission commences, I think that it is probably unnecessary; Holly can climb up as easily as she climbed down, like a mountain goat.

Except ... perhaps not with the rocks so wet, *Rohypnol* swirling in her system and shock turning her limbs to spaghetti.

A few moments later, with Eve and Isla holding his feet, Mr Maxwell pulls my sister up and over the lip of the cliff. She's lost a shoe, torn the knees of her leggings, grazed her cheek.

But she's alive, and smiling at me, our twin bond pulsing with relief.

Chapter 58

Eve

Imogen Isherwood sits in our kitchen drinking herbal tea to warm her bones after the chill of the crossing. The ferries resumed at lunchtime, and she was on the first one, accompanied by a forensic team of scurrying white suits who have sealed off the artists' wing and are painstakingly going over Cate's room, Fran's car, the cliff …

Leah and Fran were taken to hospital to be checked, but seem none the worse from the drugged wine. Once they're discharged, they'll need alternative accommodation since the guest wing is out of bounds. The police will need to talk to them too, but for now that will have to wait. We are allowed to stay at Haven since the family wing was searched when Finn was a suspect, on the condition that the connecting door remains locked and guarded by Ben Carmichael.

A message my mother should heed – time she imposed some boundaries, kept strangers from infiltrating our lives.

Except she won't. I know. Mum will never stop trusting, and I wouldn't want her to. I just want her to pay a bit more attention to who has her daughter's ear. Holly's tale, poured out last night, of how Cate came to manipulate and control her was terrifying, and I'm already thinking about the years of therapy she's going to need to put right the many wrongs that have been wrought on her.

Cate kept a close eye on her since Jay's death, guarding her, managing her every move. *Swapping one monster for another.* When Holly started to peel away from her, she kept her compliant by threatening Finn.

Last night, after yoga, when I was locked in the cellar, and Finn was battling zombies, she coaxed Holly into Fran's car and drove up to the cliff. There was enough sedative in Holly's blood from the wine at dinner to make her sluggish, biddable. But Holly still had the wherewithal to send Isla that screenshot as they wound up the cliff road. She didn't know what Cate had planned, and she'd grown afraid of her.

She managed to send the message with her phone tucked down between the car seat and the door, send her location with barely a glance at the screen. *Skills.*

She sent the message and location to me too, but I was unconscious in the cellar. Entirely useless. Thank God she had a backup.

Cate was wise enough to take Holly's phone when they reached their destination, turn it off and toss it in the sea. Arrogant enough not to check her messages – she still thought Holly was *hers*.

First, she used Holly's phone to send the message to herself that would lure Finn out of the house. Then she pocketed it, locked a sleeping Holly in the car with a bottle of water that contained more of the drug, and jogged back to Haven.

She underestimated my siblings, undervalued their bond.

Ian Maxwell and Struan – he came haring over as soon as he heard what happened – spent most of the night out on the road with chainsaw, axe and flashlights, chopping up and removing the fallen tree that blocked our road. It's still raining, and the sky is dull, but the winds dwindled overnight.

The normalcy that resumed is far from the reality we're used to: vehicles clog our drive, strangers flit through our home, blue tape criss-crossing doorways to keep us out. Police, forensics, and medics swarm Haven.

I'm not unaffected by the hours I spent in that cold cellar, but I managed to convince everyone that a trip to hospital was unnecessary. I had a bump to the head, and it's taken an age to get warm, but I quashed suggestions of hypothermia and concussion, iced my head and let Struan wrap me in blankets.

Ben wanted Holly to go to hospital, but Isla's mum – the nurse – arrived in the early hours. She stitched up Finn's arm, checked Holly over. Finn is resting now, sore, but mostly fine. Holly is snoozing on the opposite end of the sofa, and they are like bookends, long limbs tangled.

Cate was transferred to the police station as soon as they could navigate the gap Struan and Ian created in the tree blockade. It was a rough night; no one got much sleep.

Imogen Isherwood sips her tea, and looks at me consideringly. 'I think you have a story to tell.'

I stare at her, defiant. She's already talked to Isla, who was the first to work it all out – *smart girl*. Even Finn didn't realise what was going on until it was too late, when Cate spelt it out for him on the cliff. And I … well I was too quick to believe the worst of Holly. My suspicions of Cate came much too late.

Mum, Finn and I will spend a long while atoning for doubting Holly.

Her continued silence makes sense now I know she was protecting Finn: Cate was becoming unpredictable, kept Holly compliant by threatening what she loves most. Holly ran away to Layla's not to get away from us, but to escape Cate's control and scrutiny.

Cate mistrusted Finn from the moment he appeared on the cliff the night Jay died, but he became a significant risk to her once she knew he'd discovered the existence of @MidsummersChick and @QueenBee – which she realised when she saw him with Holly's phone. If Finn stopped thinking *Holly* was the culprit, he'd stop keeping the secrets that kept Cate safe.

When she believed Finn had raided her room and found her souvenir, *he had to go* – she had no idea that had been Isla.

The mistake Cate made was thinking that her forged connection with Holly could be stronger than blood, closer than the twin bond that's fused my siblings to each other since they shared a womb.

'So, let's go through it one more time,' Imogen says, her face wreathed in steam.

I'm tired; I'd rather not. There will be interviews – interminable conversations on tape where we are asked questions, and our answers compared and scrutinised. A whisper of unease stirs – does Imogen *believe* Holly's story about Cate using her to lure Jay to the cliff, driving the car into him, tossing his body over the edge …?

As if she's read my fear, she says softly, 'No one was there that night.' Only Holly and Cate. And Finn, later, but he didn't see Cate. 'It will be one girl's word against another.'

My heart sinks. This nightmare continues. 'You can't think—'

'It doesn't matter what I think; it's what a jury thinks.' She is unblinking. 'We have three witnesses to Cate's attempted murder of Finn, none when Jay was killed.'

'Holly and Finn are witnesses.'

'So they say.'

I am weary, sick of suspicion. 'She had Jay's phone, with his blood on it.'

'Which Isla Maxwell saw fit to remove from his room, compromising the evidence.'

Crap.

'And then there's the headband we found snagged on the rocks.'

I remember the orange knit band, bloodstained, with that long, pale hair.

Imogen takes a long, slow breath, exhales steadily, sips her tea again. The moment stretches, expectant. She meets my eyes, hers bright and intense. 'I rushed through the results on the initial analysis.'

I hold my breath. Even after everything my siblings went through last night, they're still not safe. We've circled back here, to analysis and doubt. Cate drugged me, drugged my sister and tried to make her complicit in her brother's murder … She took a knife from the studio, tried to make one twin commit suicide to save the other and cover her crimes … Yet still my siblings are under this cloud of distrust.

I hold my breath.

Imogen looks at me, blinks. 'We'll need DNA samples for comparison, but … under a microscope, the hair isn't blonde. It's pink.'

I breath out.

Isherwood tells me that she's been up all night since Ben's call to tell her he had Cate in custody. She's found out everything she can about the woman we knew as Cate Duncan. And the first person she wanted to talk to this morning, at the hospital, was *Leah*.

'It seems Cate's done this before … many times. Leah's been under Cate's protection, under her spell, a lot longer than Holly. She's kept her secrets, given her alibis. She'll stand as a witness against Cate, now she knows what Cate tried to do to the twins.' Isherwood tells me about the pseudonyms, the men she's targeted; all abusers, whose victims are women Cate – and Leah – have been close to. Whilst there's nothing concrete yet, she is confident she'll be able to link Cate to a number of deaths. Her first kill was her own abuser, when she was still a teenager. Her second, Leah's husband. Since then, Leah's been her co-conspirator in a brutal vigilante campaign bringing justice to the silenced.

'She's been … chatty since she was arrested,' Imogen tells me. 'She's *proud* of what she did. Sees herself as an avenger, a righter of wrongs.'

I think about Haven and my mother's quest to heal those who

find their way to her door. Cate took Mum's mission several giant leaps further.

Isherwood's brow creases. 'Taking the law into one's own hands is never right.'

I don't condone what Cate did, but I know if I'd come face to face with Jay, in the certain knowledge of what he'd done to my sister, I would have felt like killing him too.

'So, what will happen to Finn and Holly now?' I ask, fearful. They don't seem to be off her hook yet.

'I don't know, Eve. We have to consider whether to charge them. Perverting the course of justice … accessory to murder. Manslaughter, in Holly's case.'

I close my eyes.

'It depends what they tell me in interview, how *much* they tell me they … helped, or concealed.' She lowers her voice to a wisp. 'You understand what I'm saying, Eve, yes?'

My eyes fly open. Maybe she's not so far removed from us after all. I don't trust myself to speak, and Imogen fills the silence. 'I have a sister. I told you that before. We were raised by a single mother. We've always had to fight for my sister to be treated as a person, not an affliction. A few months ago I left a man who, while he wasn't abusive, wasn't the man I thought he was, or the man my future kids – if I have any – deserve to be raised by. I'm no misandrist, you understand; I like men. I've met some fine ones right here on this island – Ben Carmichael, your brother, that boyfriend of yours …'

I smile, despite my tiredness. *Boyfriend.* The word makes me grin like a love-soaked teen. 'I'm sorry for your struggles,' I say. Imogen shrugs. 'But what does this have to do with my siblings?'

She looks at me shrewdly. 'Don't be dense, Eve.' She glances at my sleeping sister; Holly's socked feet look so innocent – how can a girl in fluffy cat socks be a criminal? 'We have nothing concrete on your brother and sister. I suggest they keep it that way. Let the guilty be guilty.'

She glances around the empty kitchen. 'Of course, I will deny ever saying that.' She takes a deep breath, hiding the grim glimmer of her smile. 'If anyone *ever* hurt my sister …' She doesn't finish her sentence. She doesn't need to.

'When will you interview them?'

'Probably tomorrow. We need to sort out a sign language interpreter for Holly …'

I nod. Now that Jay and Cate are out of her life, their hold broken, Holly is beginning to find her voice. I have time to talk to the twins, make sure that they say enough, but not too much. Isherwood has thrown me a lifeline – gossamer fine, but maybe strong enough to pull us out of this mess.

Let the guilty be guilty.

Epilogue

Eve

'I'm panicking, sweet girl …' My mother's voice, frail and strained, brings a waft of familiarity. *Relief*. I close my eyes and tilt my face to taste the tang of the sea. There was a time when I didn't know if I'd hear her voice again.

Hair blows across my face; salt stings my lips. The graveyard behind me is a beautiful resting spot, as graveyards go, hunkered on the headland with a spectacular view, the scourge of sea wind on the stones, the whisper of it through the grass.

I don't think I'll visit again.

The funeral party is dispersing, bleak in black as they're blown down the hill towards their cars. I stand alone on the verge, open my eyes and stare at a heaving sea, ribbons of colour woven through the grey. The sweep of the tide is merciless, relentless, comforting. White breakers foaming on rocks that I know are slowly dissolving, but seem so stoic. My black jacket flaps and my feet feel strange in heels.

'What's wrong, Mum?' I've spoken to her several times from her hospital bed since she woke from her long sleep, but I can't offer the reassurance she seeks. She wants me to tell her everything will be all right, but I won't lie to her ... *or to myself.*

We're a long way from all right, but we're on the right road at least.

'You *know* what.' There's a hint of reproach in her voice. She expects me to have all the answers, but I don't, and maybe that's okay.

'She still hasn't been to visit,' I say, not really a question since I know how much Gina is hurting from all this, from the lies as well as the loss. She hasn't seen Mum since it all came out. She was with Mum when she woke, but since then, she's been keeping her distance. There's a lot to unravel between them, trust to rebuild.

Mum sighs. 'No. She hasn't. And she's not taking my calls.'

Mum is weak, but doing well. The doctors expect her to make a good recovery. She's talking about getting an undercut to disguise the shaven hair, the jagged scar that zips across her skull – more pragmatic than I'd expect from her. We haven't talked yet about her agoraphobia, whether that's something she's ready to get help with. The anxiety that led her to spin a narrative of prowlers and watching eyes, which made her focus on the wrong dangers, has taken over and needs addressing.

One thing we *have* talked about sits with me now, unaddressed: the reason Mum needs to help those women, the reason she understands what Holly went through. She's walked in their footsteps, tasted their fear. Her own rape was so long ago – twenty-six years, forty weeks almost to the day before she brought me into the world ...

That's something I'm going to have to deal with at some point.

I don't answer. I'm not meddling in Gina and Mum's relationship. I glance back to where Gina is thanking the minister. Her scarlet hair stands out against the monochrome of headstones and mourners – if they can be called that. Like me, it is obligation that brought them here; not mourning, not love.

The funeral of a teenage boy should be brimming with love, an outpouring of it comforting those who knew and cared for him. But Jay is notorious, rumours of what happened seeping out despite our best efforts to protect our privacy as our family tries to heal.

I'm sure there are some who came for the spectacle, but Gina was careful not to provide one. She was amazing throughout the service, a total queen: face serene, chin high. She didn't look at her shamed brother – head bowed, cuffed to police – let alone talk to him.

Christian Allardyce may have been exonerated in the death of his son, but he's on remand for his part in the island's biggest drugs ring in years, the financial impropriety in his business that led the police to uncover what he was up to. Gina's forgiven Christian a great deal over the years, but she can't forgive him for dragging Jay into that world to be used and abused, a world that might have killed him if Cate hadn't got there first. She can't forgive him for not being a better father to his son, for not teaching him to love and respect and cherish.

'I don't know what to tell you, Mum.' I watch my brother detach from Gina's side and amble towards me, one hand in the pocket of his suit trousers, the other tugging at his uncomfortable tie. I see Isla Maxwell watching him from the roadside – he looks good in a suit. He and I had a heart-to-heart last night, and he apologised for everything, the lies and collusion, for keeping me out. I don't judge him for what he did – who's to say how I would have acted in his shoes, coming across Holly on the clifftop like that, at the scene of a crime, Jay's body at her feet and her silence speaking volumes?

Holly didn't come to the funeral. She didn't want to, and no one expected it. Struan offered to stay home with her – we're wary of leaving her alone at the moment, but when I think about it, there've been times in the past weeks where she's been the strongest of us all.

She had to go through the worst of this alone. She's a survivor, and she'll go on surviving one day at a time. We'll help. We'll take the fragile threads of her trauma and weave them into something better, something robust and capable of holding her weight.

'But she has to forgive me,' Mum wails, as if I'm being stubborn by failing to make it happen for her. 'She *has* to.'

I'm not sure that's true.

There is a limit to the amount of pressure you can put on love before it breaks. Mum and Gina are there, meeting their edge. Who knows if they'll come back from this …

The low point was when Mum came round and after the initial blur of confusion, confessed to a crime we all knew by then she didn't commit. She was willing to sacrifice Gina's love to save her daughter. She was willing to go to prison, let Gina believe she'd killed Jay.

That's a whole other level of love, right there. Another level of betrayal too.

I saw that love in Finn, when he explained how he'd helped cover up what he believed Holly had done, without care for his own freedom, and when he was willing to die for her or kill for her on that cliff.

I see it in Kirsty and Gav when they gaze at the squalling bundle of Mac, and I glimpsed it in Imogen Isherwood when she spoke of her sister.

Family: love greater than the sum of its parts.

Imogen hasn't pushed for charges to be brought against my siblings for the steps they took to cover Cate's crime. For someone so by-the-book, she's remarkably susceptible to nuance. I've concluded there is no justification for murder, but the social media jury is still out on whether Cate will be lauded as hero or condemned a villain.

Is she the monster, or the monster-battling vigilante bringing justice to those without voice or hope?

Imogen is building a case against her, nonetheless. Forensics have shown both Jay's blood and Cate's hair on the headband I feared was Holly's. Cate's fingerprints on Jay's phone. She's got

Leah and Fran ready to give testimony against her now, and evidence of Rohypnol in the wine, plus the remains of the drugs in Cate's paint box.

The messages Holly saved from @QueenBee were damning, but they've mysteriously *disappeared* from all our phones.

Besides, Imogen thinks she'll get a confession – Cate is too egotistical for anything else. She wants the world to know what she did. Her backstory is depressing – a flower trying to bloom in poor soil: a climate of violence, fear, control. It might have had a different outcome, if someone had offered her the help she needed.

I'm going to make sure Holly gets that help.

Cate has done this *many* times before: befriended women online or through support groups for the battered and abused, sought vengeance in the most biblical and final way.

Gina steps away from the well-wishers at the graveside and turns to the sea. I see her settle the new weight of her world on her shoulders. What happens to love that is no longer acceptable to feel? I've seen her struggle with that in recent days – remembering Jay as a baby no bigger than Mac, a toddler so innocent. A boy, dependent on the adults around him to build his world, shape his soul.

And then, something else: an entitled young man who took what he wanted. A product of a mother's abandonment, a father who cared more for money and status. Gina could have loved him as he needed but he came to her too late. I watched her heart break when I told her what Jay did to Holly in that cave, what he'd been doing to her every day since.

'Eve,' Mum says, startling me from the reverie I've been slipping into so easily these days. 'Are you there?'

Finn reaches me. My phone beeps with a call waiting. The scrapes and bruises my brother sustained on the cliff are beginning to fade but Finn wears them like a badge of honour, a reminder of the fortune, courage, wit that saved him and Holly that night. He gives me a half smile. It's his first funeral: he was too young to remember Aunt Maisie's death, and in spite of – or *because of* – the complicated circumstances of this memorial, it's touched him deeply.

I'm proud of how he carried himself throughout, his composure. I'm proud of how he and Holly worked together to stay alive.

The loss of a friend will leave a scar even if the injuries don't. Like Gina, he's struggling to align the memories of the boy he knew with the reality of who Jay became.

Isherwood and I stood side by side at the fence line at Haven last night, watching a gold moon rise in the dusky sky. Talking about the case is against the rules, but she's broken them many times in the past days. She told me my siblings were safe from prosecution, but I must ensure they get help for everything they've suffered – *so no more monsters are made.*

'Eve!' Mum's querulous voice comes as another beep sounds. I glance at my phone, and Struan's handsome face lights my screen. 'Mum,' I say gently. 'You and Gina are going to have to figure this out yourselves. You need to be patient, and you need to accept her choice to forgive you or not … I have to go. I'll see you soon.'

Mum goes quiet. I picture her biting her lips, pale and chapped, her IV-laden arm wrapped around her knees beneath the hospital blanket. *Confused* – this might be the first time I haven't offered her empty promises, hefted her problems on my own shoulders.

She's stronger than she thinks; it's time we stopped letting her hide it.

Though she's been burned by life's flames, though she might have to go it alone without Gina at her side, at least for a time, she won't stop helping women, won't stop providing a haven for those who need it. I can't let Cate's actions detract from the importance of Mum's work.

Beside me, Finn shivers and squares his shoulders against a gust that whips off the sea. He turns his back on the view and looks up the hill, where Isla Maxwell perches on a drystone wall. She waves, long red hair flying on the breeze. He dips his head, smiles shyly.

'Struan,' I say softly.

'Eve.' His voice is gravel, honey, warmth. He sounds … *like home.*

There's so much I want to say. I want to thank him for looking after my sister, for sticking around as we've weathered the worst storm to hit us. I want to tell him I love him and I'm sorry for taking so long to realise it. Last night I lay in his arms and told him I was giving up my course to come home. Leaving the flatshare, The Bookish Beat. Not giving up my dream for him, but pursuing a new one. He was silent for a long moment, then he said, '*No.*'

He wants me to stay and stick it out, get yet another degree to add to my collection. He smiled, said: *Then come back on your own terms if you want, if you choose.*

In the meantime, he says we'll take it in turns to catch a ferry, alternate our weekends between island and city.

I had another motive for quitting my life overseas – to be here for Mum and the twins through the gruelling weeks and months. Struan said practically, 'You'll be home every other weekend anyway, and they'll have Kirst and me to keep an eye on them too.'

Kirsty was firm. 'Leave them *be*, Eve.'

It's the twins' final year of school. Holly needs to recover, and Mum isn't at her strongest. I want to guide Finn through his exams and Holly her therapy. Not because they can't do it without me – they've shown me that they can – but because I don't want to miss out.

'How was the service?' Struan asks.

'Sad,' I say. Finn tires of waiting for me to finish and strolls over to Isla. I watch them flirt, subtly because … it's a funeral after all.

Struan says it's my choice to make: long distance, or short. Kirsty says I've been anchored to this island all along; it's high time I accepted that.

She says it's not always a backward step … *to go back.*

**Gripped by *The Silent Twin*?
Don't miss *The Psychologist*, Jen L.
Crow's next unputdownable thriller.
Available to order now!**

Acknowledgements

Writing stories is a solitary occupation which involves inhabiting a world in your head for inordinately long stretches of time, conversing more frequently with fictional characters than real people. For this reason, my first and foremost thank-yous go to my real people, for letting me live in the depths of my imagination and pulling me out from time to time, forcing me to step, blinking, into the real world. Firstly my husband Chris, for bringing me cups of tea, saving my back from ruin by insisting I stop writing hunched over on the sofa and setting up a proper writing desk for me, and quite simply for always being there waiting for me to step out from between the pages. Thanks also to Brittany, who always says yes to a 'research trip' especially when I say I need to visit a Scottish island (which shall remain nameless since I messed with it so thoroughly). It wasn't an excuse to eat nice food, potter about on beaches and drink Prosecco at all! Thanks to Mum for reading the (very) unedited version, and for her strong opinions on how much profanity is acceptable – you'll see that I listened when you read the final version.

However, it's only once you're brave enough to pull it out into the light that a manuscript becomes a book. This novel owes a huge debt of gratitude to my agent, Jenny Brown, who asked me all sorts of interesting questions over coffee and helped me to steer a near sinking ship into publishable waters. I love that right away you saw potential in this project and spoke about my characters as if they were real people. And a massive thank you to Sophia Allistone, whose editorial insights have helped me to shape my story into the novel that exists today. I loved our little comment conversations in the sidebar of the manuscript and your enthusiasm for the book has made the editing process a pleasure. I'd like to sincerely apologise to both Sophia and to copy-editor Helena Newton for my quite unacceptably liberal use of dashes and hyphens! Thanks to Helena for her rigour and insight, which helped to put the finishing editorial touches to the manuscript.

Thank you to Georgina Green and everyone at HQ Digital who has helped to bring *The Silent Twin* to readers. Being published is a great joy and privilege and I can't wait to do it all again!

Dear Reader,

We hope you enjoyed reading this book. If you did, we'd be so appreciative if you left a review. It really helps us and the author to bring more books like this to you.

Here at HQ Digital we are dedicated to publishing fiction that will keep you turning the pages into the early hours. Don't want to miss a thing? To find out more about our books, promotions, discover exclusive content and enter competitions you can keep in touch in the following ways:

JOIN OUR COMMUNITY:

Sign up to our new email newsletter:
http://smarturl.it/SignUpHQ

Read our new blog www.hqstories.co.uk

𝕏 https://twitter.com/HQStories

www.facebook.com/HQStories

BUDDING WRITER?

We're also looking for authors to join the HQ Digital family!
Find out more here:

https://www.hqstories.co.uk/want-to-write-for-us/

Thanks for reading, from the HQ Digital team